Dr Dan Moves On

Laurie Graham

First published in 2020 by Laurie Graham
Copyright ©2020 Laurie Graham
Cover design by Jane Eldershaw

ISBN: 9798689034782

In memory of Howard, fairest of critics and
staunchest of fans

Chapter 1

It was my final day at Tipton Road West and as if to mark it, our mystery sign vandal had been at work. He'd gone quiet recently. The sign hadn't been tampered with for weeks and I'd wondered if he'd grown bored with us. Or had he died, or been taken away for a while, at Her Majesty's pleasure? Then, on Wednesday morning, there it was: WEIRDO PANTS MEDICAL CENTRE.

Was it a salute to me on the day I was leaving, or just a coincidence? The thought crossed my mind, and not for the first time, that the culprit might be Trevor Buxton himself. He'd handed over the senior partner role to Helen Vincent and one of her first, inexplicable decisions had been to change the name of the practice. It had been The Lindens forever, since Trevor's father's time, but Helen wanted to put her stamp on things, I suppose. We became the Tipton Road West Medical Centre and for a while the pace of sign-tampering had quickened. More letters to play with. We'd had RAT POND and TIT DROOP and SNOT DRIP.

As Trevor's working life wound down and he saw fewer and fewer patients, was this his little way of having some fun?

Did he sit at home, planning them in the margin of his *Racing Post*, then sneak out after dark to rearrange the letters?

He was in Reception, helping Mary to open the post or hindering her, depending on your point of view.

'Dan Talbot,' he said. 'You look like a man who's going places.'

I said, 'Trevor, I have to ask. The sign? Did you do it?'

'What a suggestion!' he said. Which was no answer at all. 'Why, has it been nobbled again? What does it say?'

'Weirdo Pants.'

'Far too clever for me. Now Mary, who have you got lined up for Dr Dan before he leaves us? A nice selection, I hope. A cracking morning surgery for him to remember us by.'

'I don't know about that,' says Mary. 'All I know is, I need you to keep him out on house calls while we get his surprise party ready.'

Trevor clicked his heels, or at least tried to. 'Can do, will do,' he said. He looked at my pile of patient files.

'Elsie Turney,' he said. 'What a lovely way to start the day.'

Mrs Turney was one of the first patients I saw when I started working at Weirdo Pants. Only sixteen months ago but so much had changed. I was still a trainee then, finding my feet, sitting beside Trevor Buxton and hoping to benefit from his forty odd years of experience. Strictly speaking Helen was my supervisor, but it was Trevor I'd really learned from. I felt lucky to have known him before he was forced into full retirement, incapacitated by his own illness. 'Smokers' emphysema' he calls it. We refer to it as COPD nowadays. Chronic Obstructive Pulmonary Disease.

Elsie Turney is one of our older patients and one of the fittest. She walks everywhere and she always seems to be carrying a loaded shopping bag. Tins of cat food for one neighbour, tinned fruit for another, and occasionally a bottle of rum, for her own bedtime cocoa. For 86 Elsie is a low maintenance patient and apart from an acute glaucoma scare last year, all she comes in for is a blood pressure check and a chat.

She said, 'They've took your name off the door. Have they sacked you?'

I explained that I was leaving.

'Well,' she said, 'they could have waited till you'd gone. Where are you off to, then?'

'Colwyn Bay. It's in North Wales.'

'Oh, I know Colwyn Bay. When our boys were nippers we used to have a week in a caravan in Prestatyn. August, when they were off school. There was an amusement arcade they liked in Colwyn Bay. Why are you leaving us? Was it something we said?'

'I'm fully qualified now. It's time to broaden my experience.'

'I suppose it is. People move around so much these days, don't they? I've lived all my life in Tipton.'

'How's your eye?'

'Champion. They drilled a hole in it, you know? In the coloured bit. It sounds horrible, but I never felt a thing. You can see where they did it.'

There was a tiny black triangle on her right iris. I checked her blood pressure. 150/80. Brilliant for her age.

She said, 'I saw Dr Buxton on my way in. I'm glad he's still around. They haven't got shot of him yet. Next time I come, will I be able to see him, or will it be another new face?'

'It can be Trevor, if you ask for him.'

'Good. I will. I shall miss you, though. Get to my time of life, you don't have many handsome young men holding your hand. Now seeing as you're leaving, I shall give you a hug. Only don't read anything into it!'

I felt quite tearful when she left. But as people kept reminding me, every practice has an Elsie. Every practice has its treasures and its timewasters. Tegan Strange and Dawn Beamish were two names I preferred not to see on my list, and that morning I got both of them.

Tegan was only nineteen and she'd already had her money's worth out of the NHS. The first time I saw her she wanted to be referred for removal of a tattoo because it featured the name of a boyfriend who'd become an ex. The next time I saw her she was gravely ill, in septic shock from an infected wound where she'd tried to remove the tattoo herself. She'd been nursed in the ICU and needed dialysis for a while too, but she seemed to have no sense of how lucky she was to have survived, no sense of gratitude. Now she was back with a new demand. She wasn't happy with her neck.

She said, 'I need lipo.'

'Liposuction?'

'Yes.'

'I don't think they do that on necks. What's the problem exactly?'

'It looks fat when I take a selfie.'

'That's because of the camera angle.'

'How'd you mean?'

'If you hold your phone down here, your neck's bound to look fat. Anybody's would. But if you hold your phone up here, you'll look completely different.'

'What if I don't?'

4

I said, 'Tegan, we all have days when we don't like what we see in the mirror. You could always stop taking selfies.'

She looked at me as though I was completely mad. She said her neck was affecting her quality of life. Tegan knows all the buzz words.

Dawn Beamish was next up. Dawn was an interesting patient. A woman in her mid-forties who showed no sign of growing in wisdom. The first time I saw her, she'd presented with 'flu symptoms and an enlarged spleen. She'd been in Nigeria, visiting a young guy she'd met online, intending to marry him, and she'd brought home a bout of malaria as a souvenir. Fortunately for her, it was a falciform infection and so not likely to recur, but, a bit like Tegan, I had the feeling Dawn didn't understand how reckless she'd been, travelling to Nigeria without taking any anti-malarials or having any vaccinations.

I hadn't seen her since her malaria episode, but I knew from Pam Parker that it hadn't been the end of Dawn's Nigerian saga. Pam was our go-to for ladybits and Dawn had consulted her about getting pregnant using donated sperm. She seemed to think a baby would improve her boyfriend's chances of getting a visa to live in England. Specifically, she wanted to know, if he jerked off and sent her his semen in a jar, would it survive the journey from Nigeria? Pam hadn't completely crushed her hopes. As she said, why waste your breath? Failure to conceive could always be put down to Dawn's ageing ovaries.

Now I had Dawn sitting in front of me. How was she?

'Not great,' she said. 'It's me hair.'

'What's wrong with your hair, Dawn?'

'It's gone dead thin.'

Her hair was a bit wispy. Was it wispier than usual? I had no idea. Chloe complains I don't notice things like enviably lustrous hair or skin newly brightened by some expensive serum. Maybe she's right.

Dawn didn't seem to have any bald patches. Was her hair falling out? No, she said it was just dead thin. We'd treated her with oral Riamet when she had malaria. I checked online for possible side-effects. Nothing about hair loss. What to say to her? What did she expect me to do about her damned hair? I was feeling irritated. I wanted my mid-morning coffee.

Then she said, 'Only I'm wondering if it's because I'm a crispolic.'

For a moment I didn't catch what she meant. Crispolic?

She said, 'I can't stop eating crisps.'

I said, 'Dawn, everyone finds crisps moreish. They're manufactured that way.'

'Only I was reading …'

Words I was growing to hate. Every week I seemed to see more patients who told me what was wrong with them, based on something they'd read in a magazine or on the Internet.

Dawn said, 'I was reading how you have to listen to your body.'

I said, 'There's truth in that, Dawn. Your body is telling you to stop buying crisps. And your hair looks fine to me.'

'I don't know,' she said, on her way out. 'I reckon I might have a deficiency.'

She was right, of course.

Ron Jarrold was the final patient on my morning list. There was a time when I'd dreaded Ron. He'd been an officious, opinionated little rooster, as classic a presentation of Short Man Syndrome as you would ever meet. His wife was Freda. Freda Jarrold, BOG. BOG was a Buxtonism. It stood

6

for Been on Google, an aide-memoire Trevor had written on her file. Then I'd added SMS to Ron's, something I'd come to regret doing because illness had taken the wind completely out of his sails.

Ron had a Stage IV prostate tumour with metastases in the bones of his pelvis. He'd had hormone therapy to slow the growth of the tumour, but it appeared the tumour was winning. He walked in very slowly, leaning on a stick. He'd lost more weight, his face and neck were haggard, but his legs were swollen.

Freda usually insisted on sitting in on Ron's consultations, but not that morning. Maybe he'd thrown her off his trail. 'Just popping out for a paper, dear.' Ron and Freda had different agendas. Freda wanted to keep Ron fighting and trying new treatments she read about. Ron just wanted relief from pain. I was glad he'd come in alone.

He was scheduled to have radiotherapy the following week, to help control his bone pain.

He said, 'It's an injection. Strontium 89. I shall be radioactive. They told me it'll be in my urine.'

'But only for a few days.'

'Yes. They said I should be careful, you know, to mop up after myself but the thing is, I've been having some little accidents. I don't care to trouble Freda about it, so I got myself some of those lady pads they advertise on the telly. Only, I'm wondering, if I spring a leak in the night, will she get radiation poisoning?'

I said, 'How long have you and Freda been married?'

'Thirty-six years. Why?'

'Then I don't think Freda would feel you were troubling her, if you discussed all this with her. In fact, if I know Freda, she'll come up with a plan.'

7

It was a stupid thing to say. Freda's plans were the very thing he was tired of. He gave me a weak smile.

He said, 'I'll just carry on with these pads, then. I'm keeping them in my filing cabinet, so I don't think she's noticed.'

I said, 'Internal radiation therapy is very effective at controlling bone pain. I hope it helps you, Ron.'

I told him it was my last day.

'Is it?' he said. 'Well, all the best then. Can I see Buxton next time I come in?'

'You can.'

He struggled to his feet, shook my hand.

He said, 'They say they can repeat this strontium business every 90 days.'

'Yes.'

'I can't see that happening. That's three months. I reckon I'll be gone before that comes around.'

I thought he was probably right.

'Ah well,' he said. 'We never know what's around the corner, do we? Cheery-bye.'

And that was that. My final Weirdo Pants surgery had ended on a very poignant note. Or so I thought. I was collecting up my bits and pieces when Mary looked in.

'Dr Talbot,' she said, 'would you mind squeezing in one more? I've told him he can only have five minutes.'

'Sure. Who is it?'

'Mr Bibby,' she said. 'He's been very insistent.'

Kyle Bibby. Now *that* was the kind of patient I needed as a send-off.

He came loping in.

He said, 'You're leaving.'

'I am.'

'I just heard. What you want to go and do a thing like that for?'

'I was offered a nice job.'

'Promotion, like?'

'Yes, I suppose it is.'

'They'll miss you here.'

'I hope so. Are you ill, Kyle?'

'I've got a terrible sore mouth.'

Kyle opened wide and I examined the Bibby cakehole. My father-in-law must do a lot of that. Laurence is in ENT. Private practice, but nevertheless, open mouths are part of his domain. Peering around the debris of meals, shining a light up crusty nostrils and into waxy ears. There was a tag of loose skin hanging from the roof of Kyle's mouth.

I said, 'It looks like you've burned your mouth on something.'

'Pizza,' he said. 'They should put a warning on the box.'

'You need to brush your teeth, Kyle.'

'Yeah?'

'Do you own a toothbrush?'

'I might do.'

'If you don't brush every day, you'll get gum disease and lose all your teeth.'

'Yeah?'

'Still,' he said, 'more trouble than they're worth, aren't they, teeth? Proberly better off without them.'

Kyle was very sad to see me go. He told me so. He said in future he'd ask to see Trevor or maybe Jean Boddy because he'd heard she was nice, but he wouldn't go to Helen Vincent, not even if he was at death's door. Dr Chilly Drawers, he called her. Helen had collected a lot of nicknames, none of them complimentary. People saw the brisk, buttoned-up side of her. The Ice Maiden, Bitch Face.

If they only knew.

Chapter 2

Trevor had his coat on, ready to leave.

He said, 'Come on, lad. Don't linger.'

I thought he must have a lot of house calls to make.

'Your car or mine?'

'Neither. We're going to the pub. House calls can wait till this afternoon.'

'What's the hurry, then?'

'We have to vacate the premises so the women folk can blow up a load of daft balloons and shout "surprise" when you walk back in.'

We walked round to the Black Bear.

He said, 'I see Kyle Bibby dropped by to say adieu.'

'He did. I wonder who'd told him I was leaving.'

'Yes, I wonder. You all packed up at home?'

We were. Home didn't feel like home anymore. We'd bought a house in Rhos but it needed work, rewiring and a new heating system, so we wouldn't be moving in for a few weeks. Plan A was for us to stay in a hotel until the house was habitable, but everyone said that was a bad idea. They said Colwyn Bay was a small town. Word would get around and I'd have addicts knocking on my door at all hours, demanding drugs. I was still thinking about plan B when we heard that

Chloe didn't get the job she'd applied for at the Glan Clwyd hospital.

There were plenty of other places for a cardiologist to work, but she'd taken the rejection badly. So far, she hadn't applied for anything else. Chloe had always been a bit of a golden girl. Things had always gone her way. But in the space of a year, she'd had a series of setbacks: not getting the registrar's job she'd been so confident of; her brother, Charlie, going to prison when she'd been assured he'd get away with a rap over the knuckles; and then, the worst of all. Her mother's completely preventable death.

Two doctors in the family and still Vinnie had slipped through the cracks. It had been a perfect storm of soldiering on, putting social commitments before medical advice and downplaying the possibility of a ruptured spleen.

The final blow for Chloe was the discovery that her adored and sainted father had a girlfriend, his long-time secretary, Jen. Instead of being felled by grief at the death of his wife, Laurence had openly shacked up with Jen almost immediately. Even I thought it was a bit hasty. To Chloe it was unforgivable.

People said I must be patient with her. Well, *some* people said that. Her sister, Flo, thought she should just buck up and said so at every opportunity.

'All very well for her to say,' was always Chloe's reply. 'She's known about Daddy and that schemer for years. Well, how would she feel if Henry had a bit on the side?'

The very idea of Flo's husband taking a lover was comical. His life revolved around his pigs and his family, possibly in that order.

Flo also irritated Chloe by being very enthusiastic about our move to North Wales, especially about the house we were buying.

'Five bedrooms,' she said. 'And right by the sea. How thrilling. We'll be able to have free holidays.'

Chloe said we'd see about that.

So, our new house was uninhabitable, and Chloe didn't have a job, but I'd signed a contract and they needed me at Meddygfa Parry & Hughes. Iestyn Hughes's wife was pregnant and coping with three-year-old twins, so she was only doing one surgery a week, and the 'flu season was upon us. I had to go.

It was arranged that we'd lodge temporarily with the practice nurse, Bethan and her husband, Merv. They had a granny annexe they'd built for Merv's mother, but she'd died before they could move her in. It seemed like a great solution. Chloe begged to differ.

'Lodge?' she said. 'What do you mean, 'lodge'?'

'It's just for a few weeks. We'll have our own bathroom.'

'No, we won't,' she said. 'Because I'm not going. We don't even know these people. I'll stay at Dee's and carry on working at the Arden until we can move into our own place.'

I wasn't happy with the idea of Chloe living with her friend, Dee. They'd drink too much and sleep too little and Dee would never miss an opportunity to tell Chloe that marriage was an outdated institution designed to control women.

I said, 'Will you at least come to Wales for weekends?'

'You mean like conjugal visits?'

'Wouldn't that be nice?'

'I suppose. What if they listen to us?'

'Listen to what?'

'Us having conjugals. Merv the Perv and Betsy Boop.'

13

'We can have silent sex. I can't not see you for weeks.'

She said I should have thought of that before I decided to drag her to the ends of the earth, away from everything she knew. She did agree to visit me though.

Trevor got the drinks in.

He said, 'I don't envy you, moving house. All that crap you didn't realise you had. I've told our James, when I drop off the twig, he'll have to take charge. Mrs Buxton won't be able to stay in the house on her own. She hasn't got her licence back for one thing, and she's too nervy. She's always hearing things that go bump in the night. He'll have to get her into one of those nice residential units. Not like the Sorrento. I mean one of those places where they have bridge parties and the ladies get their hair done once a week.'

'Chloe's grandparents are in somewhere like that. God knows what it costs. What about your daughter? Have you talked her about, you know? The future?'

He groaned. His daughter Alice was a sore point.

He said, 'It's not that Alice wouldn't care about her mum. I'm sure she would. It's the Micky factor.'

Trevor's daughter, Alice, lives with a woman called Micky. I'd met them at Mrs Buxton's birthday lunch and Micky's appearance belied her reputation. She was short and skinny but, by all accounts, she packed quite a punch. Micky ruled and Alice obeyed.

I said, 'you never know, it might be the push Alice needs. It might give her the courage to leave Micky. Why are we talking about this? You're a long way from dying.'

'Yes,' he said, 'on a good day. Sometimes, on a bad day, I hear the crunch of the Grim Reaper's loafers on the gravel outside our front door. And there's no harm in planning ahead. Now tell me about these Welsh quacks you're joining.'

14

'Parry and Hughes. David Parry's 56. He trained at Liverpool, wife's a GP in Llandudno, two kids. He's reserved, pleasant, a very smart dresser. Conservative but stylish. Iestyn Hughes is in his thirties, married to Polish Aggie who covers the ladybits medicine when she's not pregnant. Ginger, scruffy, speaks Welsh. Iestyn, that is, not Aggie. I haven't met her yet.'

'And what's the demographic?'

'A lot of hostels, quite a few retired Brummies and a sprinkling of locals.'

'Drugs?'

'Heroin mainly. Pills, but not so much.'

'We're going to miss you, lad. What was ailing our Kyle this morning?'

'Burned the roof of his mouth on a slice of pizza.'

'It can happen.'

When we got back to Weirdo Pants the scene was set. Balloons, Asti Spumanti served in specimen cups, little cakes decorated with what looked like pus. Pam Parker had made them.

She said, 'Lime jelly made with milk. Realistic, isn't it? I think I may be wasted in medicine.'

I was presented with an IKEA voucher and a photo album. It had pictures of every variation on the signs for The Lindens and Tipton Road West, and a group photo of everyone. Mary had slipped in an old photo of Moira.

'So you don't forget her,' she said.

As if.

Moira and Mary weren't identical twins, but they could have been. It had taken me a while to tell one from the other and just as long to win them over. Moira, in particular, had been quite a challenge but once I'd gained her approval, she couldn't

15

have been more helpful. She had total recall of patients past and present, where they lived, who they were related to, and which ones a trainee might need warning about. She'd been like a fierce but kindly aunty, until she got sick. Then she'd softened and accepted her fate with good grace. Acute myeloid leukaemia, and as galloping a case as I'd ever seen. Ten weeks and she was gone. Chloe and I had been on our honeymoon when she died, so I didn't even get to attend her funeral.

Trevor gave a little speech, not long, but Helen Vincent kept looking at her watch. She'd hardly spoken to me since I told her I was leaving. She thought she'd made me an offer I wouldn't refuse - a full-time salaried position - and Helen doesn't like to be thwarted.

Pam Parker gave me a farewell hug, said she was going to miss me. She said it had been a relief to work with someone who had a sense of humour. We'd had some laughs. Amber Evans with a mobile phone jammed in her vagina. Dawn Beamish and her clueless quest for a Nigerian baby.

'And not forgetting,' she whispered, 'the time we cornered young Miles Vincent and gave his crown jewels a warning squeeze. That took teamwork, Dan.'

She was right. Helen's son, Miles, had had it coming. He was a bully, an aggressive pill addict who thought the surgery was his mother's little kingdom and he had prince's privileges. It was Pam who'd seen an opportunity to show him some of us weren't scared of him and, as she said, grabbed it. Literally. Pam could move surprisingly fast for a larger woman.

I was gathering up my things, ready to leave, when Helen approached me.

She said, 'You're keen to be off. Our loss, Dan. I wish we could have kept you.'

'But this is the right move for me.'

'If you say so.'

She lingered. Was she going to make one last fevered bid for my body, one final wrestle, for old time's sake? I asked after her husband. Clifford had suffered a stroke the previous July. He'd been in rehab for a while and now he was back at home. She said they were having a lift installed.

'Are you getting help?'

'Yeah, yeah. Carer comes in twice a day to do the toileting and lifting. That's all manageable. It's his mind that's the problem. He really thinks he's going to walk again.'

'And he's not?'

'Dan!' she said, 'you know the score. Of course, he's not going to walk. Still got the use of his throwing arm, though.'

Poor Helen. Stuck with an angry, frustrated paraplegic.

'Does Miles help out?'

'Miles? He's fucked off to London. I can't blame him.'

'Will you take on another trainee?'

'Haven't decided,' she said. 'Maybe. Mentoring, it's not really my scene.'

As I had discovered.

'It's more Trevor's thing than mine but God knows how much more mileage we'll get out of him.'

That's what everyone said. She shook my hand, then went all out for a kissy hug.

'And if you ever change your mind,' she said. I wasn't sure if she meant the job or the other thing.

I drove home to an empty flat. Chloe had left that morning with two big suitcases of clothes and her stuffed Eeyore. We promised to talk every evening and for her to come to Colwyn Bay at the very latest on my second weekend there. By then we'd have a better idea how the renovations were going and when we'd be able to move in. My guess was that after ten days, Dee's hospitality would be wearing a bit thin and lodging at Bethan and Merv's wouldn't seem so bad after all.

So that was my last night in our first home. Sitting alone among the boxes packed for storage, eating a microwaved curry.

Chapter 3

The Lewises' granny annexe was very pink, even down to the toilet roll. The bed was covered with a shiny pink quilt that kept sliding off in the night. It was just as well Chloe wasn't with me. I didn't sleep well and if Chloe had been there, cursing and complaining, I wouldn't have slept at all.

Bethan and Merv were lovely people but, all said and done, I was still a lodger. They insisted I eat with them in the evening and their dinners were hurried affairs conducted mostly in silence. I brought a bottle of wine my first evening there, but it turned out they were teetotal. The aim seemed to be to shove the food down the gullet as fast as possible in order to get on with the evening. Bethan had a list of programmes she liked to watch and Merv needed the kitchen table for his hobby, tying fishing flies. The only evening Merv didn't tie flies was Tuesday, when he had choir practice.

By 6.30 I'd be fed and at a loose end, so I'd drive over to Rhos and sit outside the house, *our* house, and make phone calls.

Mam said, 'Why don't you go inside?'

'Because the power's off. And anyway, it's warmer in the car.'

'So, when do you reckon you'll need me?'

Mam, who'd just retired from thirty odd years as a midwife, had offered to come and help get the house straight once we could move in. To give it what she called 'a good bottoming' before the furniture arrived and we unpacked.

'Hard to say. End of February, beginning of March? You do know you don't have to do it?'

'I know, but I'd like to. You won't have time and I can't see Chloe rolling her sleeves up. No offence Dan, but she's handier at making a mess than clearing up.'

It was a brilliant offer and not without some benefit to Mam too. There had been a long-mooted plan to move my Nan in with Mam and Da, after Mam retired, and now that time had come, Mam was dragging her heels. Committing to coming to Rhos gave her the perfect excuse to delay.

My friend Vaz had called me several times, fretting about Teresa and the imminent arrival of their first baby. Her due date came and went. Vaz was beside himself. Teresa was only two days overdue and as a doctor Vaz knew the drill perfectly well, but I suppose it's different when it's your own wife and child.

'The baby's head is not engaged,' he said. 'This must happen by 36 weeks.'

I'm no obstetrics expert but even I know that not all babies follow the textbooks. I ran it by Mam.

'Is it breech? Is it a posterior presentation?

'I think Vaz would have said. He is a doctor.'

'In my experience doctor dads can be the worst. They flap about everything. How's work?'

My first week had started well. There hadn't been anything to challenge me and I got the feeling a lot of the patients had only come to check me out. People like Dennis and Beverley Underhill, a couple who'd moved to Wales for their retirement. They were from Acocks Green in Birmingham and were delighted that I knew exactly where that was. What could I help them with? Nothing.

Beverley said, 'No, we're alright, aren't we Den? We thought we'd just say hello.'

They were both on statins, Dennis was also taking a diuretic and Beverley was prescribed diclofenac for her arthritis. A modest amount of medication for people in their early seventies. They wished me well, said I was going to love Colwyn Bay, guaranteed. I already knew that, but it was nice to be told.

The practice had a very different feel to Weirdo Pants. For one thing it wasn't a custom-built surgery. The floors and doors creaked. Three of the consulting rooms were upstairs, the nurse's room was in what had been a kitchen, and Delyth, the receptionist, sat in a very small booth carved out of the entrance hall.

Delyth was pleasant enough and apparently efficient, but she was deaf, so she tended to sound very loud and fierce. I knew this because my consulting room was directly above her.

Wednesday was my half-day, my afternoon off. I was free to go home while Iestyn's wife, Aggie, held her ladybits clinic. Except I had no home to go to. Our house was still an unfurnished building site, and my room at Bethan's was just a bedroom that smelled of new carpet. It looked like I'd be spending the afternoon sitting in the car, listening to radio.

If you're lucky, each surgery has one bright or interesting spot. That Wednesday morning it was Leon Caddick. He was my 11.30 appointment. Leon was in his twenties, but with the teeth of a much older man. He was wearing the uniform of his tribe: trackie bottoms at half mast, NYPD hoodie, puffa, beanie and knock-off Nikes.

'All right, then?' he said.

I said, 'I'm all right. How about you?'

'You're new,' he said.

'I see from your file that you usually see Dr Parry.'

'Heard there was a new face. Thought I'd give you a try.'

Yes, I'll bet you did. Start as you mean to go on, Dan.

'It's about my pills.'

Leon had long-standing prescriptions for temazepam, Ritalin and Prozac. All nice little earners on the street, if he'd decided to go into business.

I said, 'This is a lot of medication. We should see about reducing it.'

'Reducing?' he said. 'No way. I'm thinking we might need to up them.'

I loved the matey 'we'. What Leon saw as our doctor-patient partnership.

I asked him to tell me how he'd come to rely on so many pills.

'Well,' he said, settling in to spin me his yarn, 'They put me on the R when I was thirteen.'

Vitamin R, the street name for Ritalin.

'And why was that?'

'They couldn't control me, see? If I had to sit down, I was liable to go off on one. So, it was take the R or get excluded.'

'And the Ritalin helped?'

'A bit. I still got excluded. But I have to say, I think there was an element of racism to it.'

I looked at him. He had black hair and a heavy shaving shadow but so do a lot of Welshmen. I do myself.

I said, 'Racism? Why would that be?'

'Because I'm Kale. Half.'

'And what's that?'

'Pikey. Travellers. Welsh.'

'You moved around a lot?'

'Not really. Mum got a council flat. It was Dad who was Kale and he fucked off.'

'Let's get back to your pills. Why are you taking temazepam?'

'Okay, so the tams are to help me sleep, the smilies are to stop me feeling like topping myself and the Rs are to stop me going off on one.'

'Are you working, Leon?'

'With my nerves? Anyway, there's nothing round here. Nothing I'd be cut out for. People say, get on your bike, but then I wouldn't see my kids, would I?'

'How many children do you have?'

'Five. Or it might be six. No, five. That one in Prestatyn's never mine. She reckons it is, but she's dreaming. You're not going to up the tammies, then?'

'No. If anything I'm going to reduce the strength.'

He said, 'I reckon you're playing the hard man with me. I might have to take my custom somewhere else.'

I sort of hoped he wouldn't. My chances of weaning him off his pills were negligible, but I knew he was one of those patients I'd look forward to seeing. Leon Caddick, the Kyle Bibby of Colwyn Bay.

Bethan insisted on making me a packed lunch every day. I'd quite have liked to walk down to Blod's cafe for a jacket potato, but I didn't want to offend. She was taking a motherly interest in me. I was at my desk, doing letters and eating my Bethan sandwich when David Parry looked in on me.

'Settling in? No problems?'

'No problems. I met Leon Caddick this morning.'

He smiled.

'Your wife coming for the weekend, is she?'

23

'Arriving Friday afternoon.'

'Good, good. You'll probably want to take her for a nice romantic dinner.'

'Any suggestions?'

'Only Miriam said to tell you, you're welcome to come to us, Saturday evening, if you're free.'

'It'd be nice for Chloe to meet you.'

'Right you are.'

'And any suggestions for Friday? For a romantic dinner?'

He thought.

'There's a seafood place at Port Eireas. I'm not sure it's open this time of year though.'

At that moment there was an explosion of noise from downstairs, directly beneath us. Raised voices, doors banging.

'That'll be Aggie,' he said.

I had yet to meet Iestyn's wife, Aggie. Her clinic was due to start at 2 o'clock. She'd arrived with five minutes to spare. She burst into my room without knocking and the first thing she said was, 'But you've moved desk.'

I had indeed. I'd swung it round to face the door, just as I had with Trevor Buxton's desk when I took over his office. I like to watch patients from the moment they walk in, and then again as they're leaving. That was a tip Trevor had given me. Watch for the lingering exit. Is there something else on their mind? Something they've been too embarrassed or frightened to mention?

I introduced myself. Aggie was blonde, small but fizzing with energy. She had a rather beautiful face.

'Yes, yes,' she said. 'I know what is your name. Quick, quick. Move desk to proper position. I have to start clinic.'

24

I put my coat on. I said, 'There's no point. I'm in this room for nine surgeries a week and I want the desk to face the door.'

'What a cheeky boy,' she said. 'David, kindly to move desk.'

Which he did, and because it seemed churlish to let him struggle alone, I helped him. It appeared that David Parry, senior partner, was afraid of Aggie Hughes, part-timer.

Then she said, 'I'm Agnes. You are Daniel. Welcome at Colwyn Bay. How you are doing?'

As soon as the desk was where she wanted it, she was prepared to be friends. More than that, she was prepared to ask an enormous favour.

'Daniel,' she said, 'boys are downstairs in stroller. You will take them, please, until 3.30. Iestyn has driving lesson. He will meet you at Argos shop.'

'You want me to babysit your children?'

'Only till 3.30.'

'But they don't know me, and I know nothing about small children.'

'Isn't matter. Push them in stroller and they will go asleep.'

David walked downstairs with me. Aggie and Iestyn's children were parked in their stroller in a crowded waiting room.

I said, 'What would she have done if I'd said no? If I'd had other plans for the afternoon?'

Delyth answered that. 'Left them with me, that's what.'

'Is this a regular thing?'

'Only since Iestyn started learning to drive.'

'And when is he likely to pass his test?'

'Never.' David and Delyth answered in unison.

25

I said, 'Well I'm not babysitting every Wednesday afternoon.'

'In that case,' says Delyth, 'in future you'll know to be gone from here by half past one. Aggie never gets here before ten to two.'

'And I'm not moving my desk every week either.'

'Ah,' says David. 'That'll be a war of attrition.'

'Why doesn't she use Iestyn's room?'

'She doesn't like it. Oh and for a place to take your wife for dinner? Try the Pen-y-Bryn. It's a pub but the food's good.'

There I was, in charge of two small children who'd never seen me in their lives before, with more than an hour to kill until I could hand them over to their father. It was also starting to rain and when I got to the bottom of Coed Pella I realised I didn't even know their names. I phoned the surgery. Sion and Aled.

I asked the one who wasn't grizzling if he was Sion. He nodded. I asked the grizzler if he was Aled. He shook his head.

'No,' says the non-grizzler. '*Dat* Sion. He did a poo.'

Great.

I took shelter in the shopping centre, to be in pole position for the handover to Iestyn. The non-grizzler, who I believed to be Aled, kept asking to get out of the stroller, but I didn't dare let him. What if he ran off? How fast can a three-year-old run? My refusal to release him brought him to grizzling-point. I thought I'd buy them something to keep them amused, but I had no idea what three-year-olds like. Should I ask someone to advise me, some grandmotherly figure? No, too suspicious. They'd assume I was the daddy and what kind of father doesn't know what his kids like? Also, Sion and Aled were both ginger, like Iestyn. People might think I'd kidnapped

26

them. Although who in their right mind would kidnap a borderline grizzler and a full-blown grizzler who'd poo'd in his pants? I bought two comics and wheeled them into Costa.

It was the longest hour of my life. I fed them on chocolate chunk shortbread, read to them from the Peppa Pig comic and hoped no-one sitting nearby complained about the smell rising from Sion's dungarees. At 3.15 we headed to Argos. Time stood still. Several hours later, when the clock showed 3.35 and there was no sign of Iestyn, I began to formulate a plan. If he hadn't arrived by 3.45 I'd wheel the boys back to the surgery and dump them on Delyth.

At 3.44 Iestyn appeared and his children immediately stopped grizzling and snotting. They turned into quite cute little chaps.

'Comics!' he said. 'Aren't you lucky boys! I hope you said thank you to Uncle Dan.'

Uncle Dan. I wasn't sure I cared for that. It suggested the boys and I might be heading for a close, ongoing relationship. Chloe's nieces just call me Dan and they're actual family. I asked how the driving was going.

'Tough,' he said. 'There's so much to remember. A day like today particularly. You've got the pedals to think about and signalling, and with the windscreen wipers going ten to the dozen.'

I said, 'You'll find things'll come more naturally when you've had a few more lessons. By the way, I think Sion has had a bit of an accident in his trousers.'

He said, 'I don't know, Dan. I've had twelve lessons now and I still get in a muddle.'

I was exhausted. I picked up my car, drove back to Merv and Bethan's and fell into a deep sleep. It was nearly six o'clock when I woke. My hosts would be home any minute and tea would be on the table. I phoned Miriam Parry's practice in Llandudno.

'Dan,' she said. 'Will we be seeing you on Saturday?'

'I just wanted to check with you. Dinner, right?'

'You and Chloe.'

She'd remembered Chloe's name. That was nice.

'David was a bit vague.'

'He would be. Come about half past seven, and it won't be anything fancy. Just us and a couple of my partners in crime. Harry Shepherd and Hilary Mostyn.'

Miriam's practice was called Parry, Shepherd, Mostyn and Tate.

'What happened to Tate?'

'Got a hot date. Hotter than dinner at our kitchen table, at any rate.'

All evening I kept calling Chloe and all evening I kept getting her voicemail. I drove to the house, checked the radiators had been installed, went back to my pink nightmare bedroom and watched *Line of Duty*. I was sound asleep when my phone woke me.

I said, 'what time do you call this?'

There was silence. Then I heard Vaz say, 'I'm very sorry, Dan. I forgot. When I phoned to India it was already morning.'

'The baby arrived?'

'We have baby daughter.'

I was wide awake.

'That's wonderful news. Is everything all right?'

'Everything. Three kilograms. It was ventouse delivery but all is well.'

'What's her name?'

'Margaret Mariam. Mariam is my mother's name. I'm sorry I have woken you, Dan. I was excited to tell you. You are my very good friend.'

Dear, dear Vaz. I felt quite emotional. It was 4 a.m., I still hadn't heard from Chloe, and the damned quilt was on the floor again.

Chapter 4

Thursday morning. Chloe checked her phone, which she said she'd left overnight in her car.

'Ten messages, Dan,' she said. 'I thought at least someone must have died.'

The very idea of Chloe being separated from her phone for all those hours was ridiculous, but I didn't want a fight. Merv was within earshot, demolishing his boiled eggs.

I said, 'What time do you think you'll get here tomorrow?'

'Oh, right,' she said. 'Slight change of plan. I'm coming on Saturday morning instead.'

'That means you'll only be here for one night.'

'No, two. I'll stay till Monday morning then drive to Wrexham. I've got an interview.'

That was good news. A job interview meant she was ready to make the move.

'Which hospital?'

'It's a private clinic.'

'Teresa and Vaz had a girl.'

'That's nice.'

'We should send a gift.'

'Okay.'

'And we're invited to the Parrys' for dinner on Saturday.'

'Really? You've only been there five minutes. I hope you're not getting us into a dinner party crowd. It's so last century.'

'It's not a dinner party. It's just dinner. They'd like to meet you, make you feel welcome. I think it's rather nice of them.'

'All right. Keep your hair on. Anything I should bring? Decent coffee? Almond milk?'

'Nothing. This is North Wales, not a desert island.'

When I was at The Lindens, aka Tipton Road West aka Weirdo Pants, I always had at least three more experienced doctors I could call on, if I wasn't sure about something. They'd known me as a trainee so even after I was fully-fledged, I was the junior. Things were different at Meddygfa Parry, Hughes and Talbot. Clearly, I could ask for a second opinion, but David Parry was shy to the point of being almost mute and Iestyn often seemed harassed. He started his surgeries late and over-ran every consultation, so he barely had time for a lunch break before it was time for the afternoon list.

On Friday I had a case that troubled me slightly. Pauline Coslett. Pauline didn't look her 70 years and from her notes I could see she was a rare visitor to the surgery. She had back pain, just below the bottom of her ribcage.

She said, 'Everybody says I must have pulled a muscle, but I haven't done anything to pull no muscle. Any road, I tried that Deep Heat, but it didn't help.'

I said, 'Is that a Birmingham accent I hear?'

'Castle Bromwich. But I've been here donkey's years.'

Was the pain sharp, spasmodic? No. It was there all the time and it was getting worse. It didn't sound like a kidney stone. Was she urinating normally? Yes, she thought so. I took her along to the nurse's room, asked Bethan to dipstick a urine sample. But what was I looking for? Blood maybe, or signs of an infection? I was hoping for something to nudge me in the right direction.

I said, 'I'll see my next patient while you're doing that.'

Bethan said, 'Dan, did you notice her wedding ring? How it's digging into her finger? And she's not a chubby person.'

I hadn't even looked at Pauline's hands. Basics, basics. Trevor Buxton was a great one for taking a patient casually by the hand, particularly women, but you have to be so careful these days. Hands can tell you quite a lot. Bethan was right on the money. Nurses so often are.

Pauline's urine sample was dark, frothy and loaded with protein. Her kidneys weren't working properly and she was retaining water. Fat fingers, swollen ankles. Was her face puffy? Perhaps if I'd ever met her before I might have noticed. Perhaps I might not.

I checked with David.

'I've got a 70-year-old with what looks like nephrotic syndrome. Is Bangor the place to send her?'

'Yes. You don't think it's a kidney stone?'

'Persistent flank pain. Albumin in her urine and she's oedematous.'

'Who is it?'

'Pauline Coslett.'

'Don't recall her.'

'You wouldn't. She's not been in for years.'

'Dan,' he said. I was halfway out the door. 'Maybe get her an ambulance? It's more than twenty miles to Bangor.'

Pauline didn't want an ambulance. She said her friend would drive her. I wrote her a referral letter and told her to go to A&E.

'Righty-o,' she said. 'Righty-o.'

The last thing I did before I finished for the weekend was call Bangor. They had no record of Pauline Coslett. Maybe she was still waiting to be seen. But she would surely have checked in. They should have had her name on their list. What to do? Phone her, chase her, find out what was going on? Or mind my own business, allow a grown woman to make her own decisions and just enjoy my weekend? After all, I hadn't seen Chloe in nearly two weeks. That was the basis of my decision.

'Never take your work home with you,' had been one of Pam Parker's golden rules and Pam was a relatively sane GP. She had a job, a happy marriage, a family and a sense of humour.

I got my hair cut, bought flowers and drove out to Rhos to make sure there were no nasty surprises at the house. No floorboards up, no wildlife in residence, no squatters. All was well. There was a smell of fresh plaster, but things were taking shape. We'd soon be able to move in, and just as well.

Back at Colwyn Bay, Bethan seemed slightly peeved that I was late for dinner. She said it was in the oven, probably ruined, and I'd have to eat it on a tray because Merv was already at work on the table. He was tying a Black Zulu.

She said, 'What happened about the kidney woman?'

'I sent her to Ysbyty Gwynedd but she never turned up.'

'I hope she's alright. I didn't like the look of her urine, not a bit. If it had been up to me, I'd have put her in an ambulance.'

That needled me. I valued Bethan's years of experience, but not when I was off-duty. Not when I was trying to eat dried up liver and onions.

Chloe arrived around twelve on Saturday morning. She looked beautiful. I'd missed her so much and she, it seemed,

33

had missed me. She wanted us to go straight to the house and have sex.

I said, 'There's no furniture. It's just bare boards.'

She said, 'I thought you were a boy scout?'

She always gets that wrong. I was a St John's ambulance cadet. But Chloe had come prepared. She'd brought a sleeping bag and a kind of camping mattress, both borrowed, and a half bottle of New Zealand sparkler. I got merit points for the jam jar of tulips.

It was so cold you could see your own breath. We dozed a little, played house a little, deciding where the furniture would go. There were things we needed to buy. More chairs. Beds for guests.

Chloe said, 'No hurry for that.'

'Mam'll need a bed when she comes to help us move in.'

'She could stay at the Travelodge.'

'No, she couldn't. It's a bail hostel.'

'Then she can use this camping stuff. If we buy extra beds you know what'll happen. We'll have Flo and the yoblets descending on us every school holiday. We need to buy units for my dressing room, though.'

'What dressing room?'

'The little room next to our bathroom.'

'I thought that was going to be the nursery.'

'Really? Where did you get that idea? We don't need a nursery. Anyway, it's perfect for a dressing room.'

A very dirty 4-wheel drive pulled in ahead of us at the Parrys. As we parked, the driver was unloading, trying to balance a cake tin, a bottle of wine and a rolled-up duvet. A woman in jeans and a stripey jumper. Too old to be the Parrys' daughter.

34

Chloe said, 'I hope that's the caterer, not a guest.'

'I don't think there'll be a caterer. It's a kitchen table evening. I did tell you.'

'I'm over-dressed.'

I assured her she wasn't, although she was, a bit. I rescued the duvet the woman had dropped and introduced myself.

I said, 'You must be Hilary.'

'I'm Harry, actually,' she said. 'Probably best if you take the cake tin and give me the bedding. You'll get covered in dog hair and your wife won't thank me.'

David was on his knees in the living room, trying to coax a fire into life. Miriam was in the kitchen with a man who turned out to be Hilary and young Joe Parry who was getting under everyone's feet making himself a bacon sandwich. Someone handed Chloe an apron and a salad spinner. It was their way of making her feel welcome. They weren't to know Chloe doesn't really do aprons. I washed the salad.

So, the other guests, who I'd got completely mixed up, were male Hilary Mostyn and female Angharad 'Harry' Shepherd, both partners in Miriam's Llandudno practice. Hilary lives with Ebbe, also male, and Ebbe works out of Holyhead, for one of the ferry companies and couldn't be with us that evening. Harry seemed to be unattached. She was staying over because she lived out in Llanfairfechan and on Sunday morning she was taking part in a needle clean-up on the Great Orme. She invited us to join her. Not the greatest selling point for our new neighbourhood, but I don't think Chloe heard.

Miriam said, 'Dan, I hear you went head-to-head with Aggie over furniture privileges.'

'Yes, and she won. David humoured her and moved my desk. He didn't help me move it back, either. And then she dumped her twins on me. She expected me to babysit while Iestyn had a driving lesson.'

Harry said, 'Well there's money wasted. They'll never let Iestyn out on the roads on his own.'

'You know him?'

'It's worse than that. We're related. He's my cousin.'

'Not a good driver, then?'

'Terrible. I don't know why he perseveres with it. Aggie's got a licence and he's got his bike. It'd do us all a favour if he gave it up as a hopeless cause.'

It was a lovely, relaxed evening. Mainly. Chloe got a bit touchy when they asked her about her job interview. The Gresford Vale Private Clinic.

Hilary said, 'I've heard of the place. Don't they do bum lifts and stuff like that? I thought you were a cardio.'

'I am,' says Chloe.

He said, 'Then you ought to be going to Glan Clwyd. What will they have you doing at this private place? ECGs on worried businessmen?'

I said, 'Chloe did try for a job at Glan Clwyd, but it didn't work out.'

Chloe butted it, 'They did offer me a registrar position, but I didn't like the consultant.'

Which wasn't remotely true. Glan Clwyd had offered her nothing.

Miriam said, 'Well there's always Bangor. They do cardio at Ysbyty Gwynedd. But you'll probably want to settle in first, get a feel for the area.'

'Yeah,' says Chloe. She saw an opportunity to change the subject. 'And what I'd like to know is where people round here go to shop?'

'You mean, like, supermarkets?'

'No, I mean clothes!'

'Chester,' said Miriam and Hilary, in perfect unison.

'Chester? But isn't that in England?'

Hilary said there were some designer outlets around Chester and Ellesmere Port and it made a nice day out.

'Chester, though,' says Chloe, pouring herself more wine. 'God, Dan. What kind of a shopping desert have you dragged me to?'

Everything went quiet for a moment. I caught a little look pass between Miriam and Harry and I felt something squirm inside me. I didn't like what I'd felt, but there was no denying, sometimes Chloe came across as a total airhead.

Miriam opened the cake tin.

'Harry, you baked! And it's Lemon Drizzle. Is it someone's birthday?'

Harry said, 'I heard a rumour it was Ebbe's, but seeing he's not here, let's call it a welcome cake. Welcome, Dan and Chloe, to the Bermuda Triangle of Designer Labels.'

And she gave me a very cheeky look. She has green eyes.

Chapter 5

Chloe got the Wrexham job, the work on the house was completed and Mam arrived with her Marigolds and the boot of her car stacked with mops and cleaning materials. It was all coming together. The Parrys had offered to put Mam up, rather than her having to sleep on the mattress Chloe had borrowed, but she wouldn't hear of it. She'd brought Aunty June's ancient airbed with her.

'I'll be right enough on this,' she said. 'And when I'm done here, it's going to the council dump. She's had it since the Silver Jubilee.'

'When was that?'

'Summer of 1977. June's trouble is she will hang on to things.'

'Except for husbands.'

'Well that's true.'

Aunty June, who isn't really my aunt at all but a very good friend of Mam's, has had two husbands. One died, one disappeared and left no forwarding address.

'What did her first husband die of?'

'Stupidity. He jumped in the Usk one afternoon. We were having a hot spell.'

'And?'

'Drowned. He couldn't swim. He was one of those people, Dan. Always knew best, always knew where you could get something cheaper. No need for swimming lessons. Just jump in and it'll come naturally. What it is, June's always gone for looks, which is all very well when you're seventeen, but for the long haul you need a man with a brain between his ears.'

'And his heart in the right place.'

'That too. So now she's giving this Internet dating a go.'

'Isn't she a bit old for that?'

'I don't know. Is there an age limit? She says she gets lonely, Bank Holidays, Christmas. I don't know why. She knows she can always come to us. I've told her to be careful. If she's going on one of those dates, I'll want to know all the particulars and she's to phone me as soon as she gets home. I mean, he could be anybody. He could put a picture of Pierce what's-his-name on there and June'd be daft enough to believe it. This is a lovely house, Dan. You've done well. I just wish you were nearer to us, I won't pretend I don't, but this is smashing. Sea views, good clean air. Plenty of room to start a family. I can't wait for your Da to see it.'

Mam tended to side with Chloe regarding the room I'd seen as a potential nursery and Chloe was determined to have as a dressing room.

She said, 'Co-sleeping, that's all the rage now. When I had you and Adam you went straight into your own room, the day you came home from hospital. It's hard enough doing the night feeds without waking up every time they make one of their snuffly little noises. But that's the trend now. Sleep with them right beside you. Is Chloe alright? She doesn't seem very keen to move down here.'

It was a sore point. Chloe had suddenly announced her Terms & Conditions. She'd given her notice at the Arden Clinic and promised to arrive the same day as our furniture but she'd also stipulated that once a month she'd be spending the weekend in Birmingham, staying at Dee's and seeing old friends. I didn't think she had that many old friends.

Mam said, 'She'll do it a couple of times and then she'll be too busy with her new life here, you'll see. Be patient with her, Dan. She's had a lot of upheaval this past year. Getting married. Losing her mother. And there was that business with her brother.'

Chloe's brother, Charlie, was actually due for release from HMP Coldingley any day, having served half his time.

'There you are then,' she said. 'She'll probably want to go down to London, make sure his place is shipshape for when he gets out.'

Mam doesn't know Chloe very well yet.

Pauline Coslett had sort of slipped my mind. Then we got a discharge letter from Glan Clwyd hospital. She'd been admitted with a renal vein thrombosis, treated with an intravenous thrombolytic but had required surgery to remove a large, persistent clot and then temporary dialysis. She was now discharged to the care of her GP. Me. But why Glan Clwyd? I'd sent her to Bangor. I asked Delyth to phone and get her to come in.

'What's it about?'

'Her recent discharge from hospital.'

'When do you want to see her?'

'As soon as. But not Wednesday. I'm out all day this Wednesday.'

'Avoiding Dr Aggie.'

'No, I'm moving into my house.'

'You just happen to be moving into your house on a Dr Aggie clinic day.'

Delyth certainly doesn't have a reverential attitude to her doctors.

'As a matter of interest, what's going to happen to her clinic when she has the baby?'

'We'll get Dr Shepherd. She's with Mrs Parry's surgery in Llandudno, but we borrow her. That's what we did when Aggie had the twins.'

Angharad 'Harry' Shepherd, baker of top lemon drizzle cake. I acted dumb.

'What's she like?'

'Normal.'

I told myself that the pleasure I was feeling was simply relief. For a while there'd be no more dodging Aggie in case she expected me to babysit. No more coming in on Thursday morning to find she'd moved my desk again. It was only natural that I welcomed the prospect of a few months of seeing Harry Shepherd every Wednesday. That was what I told myself.

Delyth said Pauline Coslett wasn't answering her phone. In my lunch break I drove out to check on her. She lived on what Delyth called a caravan site, except that all the caravans stood on breeze blocks. The Willows Mobile Home Park. Pauline wasn't at home. Neighbours popped up on both sides, checking on who I was and what I wanted. Even when I told them I was her doctor, they reserved judgment until one old boy came over and looked into the car. I pointed to my bag. I damned nearly got out my stethoscope to show him, but then he said, 'She'll be at Deana's. End of the row, turn left, number 37.' And true enough, that's where I found her, watching telly with her friend Deana.

Pauline said she was fine. A bit tired still, but on the mend.

41

'How did you end up in Glan Clwyd?'

'Collapsed in Rhyl, didn't I? In the shopping centre.'

'You were supposed to go straight to the hospital in Bangor.'

'We was going to. Deana was going to drive me, only she needed to go to Bright House first because she owed them two weeks on her settee. We was just parking up and the pain come on much worse. I was doubled up, wasn't I, Deana? I've never known pain like it. They fetched the First Aid people out to the car park and they rung for an ambulance.'

'You know you were very lucky not to lose a kidney?'

'That's what they told me. But how was I to know? You didn't tell me it was serious.'

'I did offer to get you an ambulance.'

'Yes, well,' she said, 'I'm all right. And Glan Clwyd suits me better, actually, because when I have to go back for a check-up, Deana can drop me and then go and pay her settee money.'

Not a word of thanks for my concern. And the neighbourhood watch had their periscopes up, making sure I left their park. I had my Bethan sandwich with me in the car, but I tossed it and went to Blod's for a bacon sambo. I had a full list for the afternoon. I needed sustenance.

The first flurry of interest in me as a new face had died down. The curious had come and gone and now I was seeing patients who'd been Aggie Hughes's regulars or overspill from Iestyn's list. They were mainly older people. The young left Colwyn Bay. They went south to Cardiff or Newport for jobs or left Wales altogether. I remember Paton Fenner because a patient under thirty was quite a rarity. Also, according to her notes she was epileptic and epilepsy has always fascinated me.

There was a boy at school who suffered from what they used to call grand mal fits. Nowadays we call them generalised tonic-clonic seizures. It was all very exciting, teachers screaming at us to stand clear when obviously what we wanted to do was crowd round and watch. Somebody trying to force something between his teeth to stop him swallowing his tongue. All nonsense, as I now know. He did bite his tongue one time, but it soon healed.

Paton had a history of absence seizures since childhood. Quite often they disappear in your teens, but in her case they hadn't. She'd come to see me about a rash on her neck, self-diagnosed as eczema but it looked to me like contact dermatitis. Had she been wearing something around her neck? A new necklace, maybe? She had. A locket on a chain, a Christmas present from her husband.

She said, 'He won't be happy if I can't wear it.'

Chloe had some cheap earrings that gave her a rash but she didn't want to stop wearing them, so she coated the metal with clear nail varnish and that seemed to fix the problem. I was telling Paton this when she had one of her absences. Her gaze wandered away from me across to the painting of the Brecon Beacons. Her eyelids fluttered and she smacked her lips a little. I timed her. She was gone for about twenty seconds. Then she was back.

'Clear nail varnish,' she said. 'Okay.'

Did she know she'd been absent? I had to ask her.

'Kind of,' she said. 'Sometimes I know. Sometimes I think I might have been. If Lee's with me, he tells me. He says, "You left me there for a minute, girl. Where to you been, then?" At work they don't tell me. They just look at me funny, so then I know.'

She wasn't taking any medication. She'd been prescribed sodium valproate when she was a kid and it had made her put on weight.

43

She said, 'You're not putting me back on pills. I only came in about the rash.'

'Fine. I'm just interested. No pills, if you don't want them.'

'See, most everybody knows what I've got, so I just get on with it. Can't drive, of course.'

And with that she seized again, lips moving, eyes rolled over to my painting again and her left hand fidgeting, clenching and unclenching. Had the thing with her hand happened the time before? I hadn't noticed. Twenty seconds again.

'But I don't really want to.'

'Don't want to what?'

'Drive.'

She'd picked up the thread of the conversation again perfectly.

The human brain. We know so little about it.

Paton was the highlight of my afternoon. It was close run thing between her and Leon Caddick who came in with two beautiful shiners, but I had to award it to Paton for being a pleasant, articulate patient with an interesting clinical history. Every GP needs one of those a week.

Had Leon walked into a wall? No, he'd walked into Pug Boswell.

'Head-butted me,' says Leon. 'In the Prince Madoc. Said I was looking at him. He's a fucking lembo.'

Lembo. That was one to check with Iestyn, one to add to my collection. I already had cont and fwcar, which were easy enough to translate, and sach blewog, Celyn Thomas's description of her ex: a scrote.

I said, 'Leon, from what you tell me, you've had no signs of concussion and those black eyes look a few days old. They'll fade. Nothing I can do about them.'

'Well I know that,' he said, as though Pug Boswell wasn't the only lembo in Colwyn Bay. 'But I want it put on record, for when I sue him.'

'Then you should have reported it to the police.'

'Police!' he said. 'You're having a laugh. They won't do nothing. They'll just say I should drink in a different pub. I've taken a selfie, for evidence. Now I need you to put it on record. Worst black eyes you've ever seen. Lucky not to have been brain-damaged. You'll know how to write it, with the proper medical words.'

How I missed Trevor at moments like that. I'd have loved to stroll round to the Black Bear and tell him Leon's story. But there was no after-hours drinking with the Meddygfa Parry, Hughes and Talbot crowd. Everyone went straight home. Iestyn confirmed that 'lembo' meant an idiot. He said he'd been called worse things. Such as?

'Pen coc.'

I knew pen was Welsh for head. Our house was called Pentraeth. Top of the beach. So pen coc wasn't hard to guess.

On Wednesday morning our furniture arrived before Chloe did. Stuck in traffic, she said. By the time she got to us, the removal men were closing up the van, ready to leave. We walked around the house together and her first words were, 'We need more furniture. Lots more.'

It was true. We'd moved from a small flat to a five bedder. Some of the rooms had nothing in them. But like Mam said, all in good time. We sat down to a late lunch. Our first proper meal in our new home.

Chloe said, 'You know what we should do? Hire a van, drive to Bishop's Wapshott. We could nab some furniture from the Chummery while Daddy and the Jen bitch are in London. Mummy would have wanted me to have something.'

I said, 'That'd be breaking and entering.'

'No, it wouldn't. I still have keys. Unless the bitch has changed the locks.'

I don't know which was harder for Chloe: the fact that her beloved and revered father had had a bit on the side all those years, or the fact that everyone else, her mother included, had apparently known about it and thought it wasn't exactly the end of the world. Jen seemed like a nice woman. Hardly the wicked stepmother. And Laurence was happy.

I said, 'Here's a less criminal option. Why don't you talk to your father, see whether there's any furniture we can have?'

She scowled, then she had an idea that made her brighten up.

She said, 'I'll get Flo to do it. She can load stuff into their trailer, take it to the farm and we can collect it. We need chairs. And a bigger table. There's a sleigh bed in Slow's old room. It'd be nice to have that.'

I started to say that Charlie's sleigh bed had woodworm, but Chloe was already on the job, calling her sister. Mam put the kettle on.

After a bit of furniture talk, I heard Chloe say, 'Oh Flo, no! How awful. I'm so sorry. When did you find out?'

Mam and I both stopped what we were doing. What was Flo's bad news?

Chloe said, 'Is there anything I can do? I do know a few people, obvs. Really? Really! Gosh, that's terribly brave of you.'

She signed off with 'Big love. Here if you need me.'

I had never heard Chloe speak to her sister so affectionately. She came back to the table and grabbed a Penguin.

'Well that was a shocker,' she said. 'Flo's pregnant.'

I said, 'But that's wonderful news. Listening to your end of the conversation, I thought someone had cancer.'

'Lovely news? She's 38, Dan, and they already have the three demons. It's so irresponsible.'

'I don't think it is. Plenty of people choose not to have children. Flo's just using up their quota. I imagine Henry's hoping for a boy this time.'

'Ugh,' she said, 'Don't mention Henry! The very thought that he's still at it, huffing and puffing on top of poor Flo, it makes me sick to my stomach. Do we have any ice cream?'

'No. We only turned the freezer on a few hours ago. I think you should call Flo back, right now. Tell her that now you're over the surprise, you're delighted for her.'

'But it wouldn't be true.'

'It'd be a worthy lie.'

'I suppose.'

'Do it now, while Mam and I wash up.'

'When are they delivering the dishwasher?'

'Tomorrow,' says Mam. 'And just as well because this old dishwasher's leaving here first thing and going home. It's time to get cracking with Project Deryn.'

Deryn's my nan, my Da's mother, and the time had come to move her in with them. She was still nifty for her age but getting forgetful and very paranoid. After Grandad Talbot died, she got into the habit of undressing and putting her nightie on in front of the telly while she watched the 10 o'clock news. But lately she'd become convinced that Huw Edwards could see her in her bra and knickers.

Mam and Da had already put in a small downstairs bathroom, with a loo and a sit-in shower. The next job was to install Nan in their rarely used dining room, then clear out her maisonette and return the key to the Council.

'Does she know what's going to happen?'

'She's been told. Whether she remembers is a different matter.'

'She'll drive you nuts.'

'Oh yes. But what it is, Dan, we're all she's got. It's our duty. Is that the best tea towel you could find? I'll send you some new ones when I get home.'

'You know there'll always be a home for you with us. Down the line. You or Da, whichever…'

'Survives. I know. Well, I hope we've got a good few years yet, but thank you for saying it. I can't see Adam taking me in.'

My brother has a house, in Cardiff, though I've never seen it. Mam used to go down there every so often, to clean for him, as though he wasn't capable of pushing a mop over the floors himself, but he put a stop to it. He teaches maths, swims every morning before he goes to school. If he has a girlfriend, she's a closely guarded secret. Adam's life is a closed book. Or possibly a book of blank pages.

On the Thursday morning, Mam set off on the long drive back to Abergavenny, Chloe started unpacking boxes, and I went to work. I arrived a little later than usual, and what a greeting I got

Chapter 6

Delyth still had her coat on. The boiler had broken and the plumber couldn't get to us till mid-afternoon.

'And that's not all,' she said. 'Dr David's office, quick as you like. You are needed.'

'What's up?'

'Not for me to say. I'm just the messenger around here.'

David still had his coat on too. He said we were faced with a bit of a crisis. Aggie had developed pre-eclampsia and would be out of action until the baby was born.

I said, 'One clinic a week. I'm sure we can manage.'

'No,' he said. 'That's not the point. Aggie's in hospital so Iestyn's at home with the twins. We're down to two doctors and a nurse.'

The plan was to triage for the next couple of days. Anything that looked minor, we'd send through to Bethan. David and I would split the rest of Iestyn's list between us. After the weekend we'd review the situation. Much depended on whether Iestyn managed to make childcare arrangements.

'How many weeks is Aggie?'

'Thirty five.'

'So, we're talking about her being off for quite a long time. Is the baby okay?'

'Seems to be. They might get her to 38 weeks and then induce her.'

'We're going to need a locum.'

'Probably. We usually use Dylan Tew but he's already committed. Miriam's deciding whether we can borrow Harry for a while. She was going to cover Aggie's clinics anyway. If she can do some of Iestyn's surgeries too, it'd be something. I'll let you know.'

And as sorry as I was for Aggie and Iestyn's troubles, I found myself strangely pleased at the possibility of having Harry Shepherd on the team for a while.

David said, 'By the way, you might want to work in Iestyn's room today. Aggie vomited in yours yesterday. I'd say it needs airing.'

I went along to the nurse's room to get the full story from Bethan.

'Well,' she said, 'sit down while I tell you. Now I'd noticed last week that she kicked her shoes off the minute she got here. Feet swelling up, see? I've seen it before. Then halfway through surgery she asked me for paracetamol. Said she'd got a bit of a migraine coming on, headache like, and flashing lights. I said to her, I said, 'I'm checking your blood pressure, no arguments. 145/95. And she still wouldn't have it. "No, no," she says. "Is migraine. I'm a doctor. I know." And then she threw up, no warning, all over me, all over your carpet. I've had the window open, but it still smells sour in there. I think the carpet might have to go.'

'Where is she?'

'Bangor. And that's where she'll stay. Bed rest and beta blockers. David says I'll have to take your minors today and tomorrow. But I've got my regulars, for dressing changes and I've got a few coming in for jabs and blood pressure checks.'

50

'I know. I'll try not to send you too much.'

'Good. And whatever you do, don't send me Roy Savage.'

'Who's Roy Savage?'

'Our local flasher. He usually comes in with bum pimples but last time it was an ingrowing pubic hair. How did moving day go?'

'Like clockwork. How did you deal with Mr Savage?'

'I told him to pull his trousers up, go to Superdrug and buy himself some eyebrow tweezers.'

We battled on through Thursday. The heating was restored just before close of play, but the report on Aggie wasn't great. Her blood pressure was still high, not helped by her fury at not being allowed to go home. The news about a locum was better. From Monday we were to have Angharad 'Harry' Shepherd on full-time loan from Miriam Parry's practice. By Friday evening I was feeling great. I was going home to my house and my wife. The first weekend of the rest of our lives.

On Saturday we abandoned the unpacking, layered up and took our coffee to the beach. Then we drove into Llandudno so Chloe could have her shopping-fix. Chocolates and a house plant for us and a pink fluffy rabbit for Margaret Mariam Vaz. Sunday we walked up Bryn Euryn, to the trig point, then had a blowout lunch in the Rhos Fynach.

I said, 'Next weekend we'll go to Conwy. It's a nice little town with a proper castle.'

'Okay,' she said. 'Not next weekend, though. I'll be in Birmingham.'

'But you only just got here.'

'I can't help it if that's how things have turned out. I've promised Dee I'll help her with her birthday.'

'Why does she need help?'

'The big Three Zero, Dan. It's going to be a two-day-er.'

'Am I invited?'

'You don't like Dee.'

'I like her even less now you spend more time with her than you do with me.'

She said that I was exaggerating, as usual, and that I couldn't expect her to give up her Birmingham life just because I'd chosen to take a job in the back of beyond.

I said, 'It's my career, Chloe. You don't seem very interested in yours, so I need to get on with mine. And what Birmingham life? You used to spend most of your weekends in a onesie. As I recall, we had people to dinner just once and that was a disaster.'

'Only because your pi mate Vaz went all pro-life on us.'

'Actually, Vaz was very restrained. He was a model guest. It was Dee who got drunk and gobby.'

'Anyway,' she said. 'Having people over for dinner. Who does that anymore?'

We made up before bedtime. She was starting her new job the next morning and I didn't want us to end the day not speaking. It was a fragile peace, though. And she still planned on driving to Dee's straight after work on Friday.

She said, 'You hate parties, especially Dee-type parties. You should be glad you're not invited.'

When I got to the meddygfa on Monday morning, Harry Shepherd's muddy Nissan was in my space. I had to park on the street. She was in Iestyn's office. She had bed hair.

I said, 'If you pulled your car in closer to David's, there'd just about be room for mine.'

She sighed.

I said, 'Otherwise I'm going to have to run to the ticket machine every two hours.'

Another sigh. She went off to do it, but with bad grace. She wasn't as pretty as I'd remembered.

At lunch time she came in to see me.

'Sorry about earlier,' she said. 'I'm not at my best first thing.'

She gave me an update on Aggie. Her blood pressure had improved but they'd be keeping her in hospital until she delivered.

'And what's Iestyn's story?'

'He won't be back for a while.'

'Isn't there a granny or someone who can step in?'

'No. Aggie's mother's in Poland and Aunt Gwenny can't help. We're coming up to peak lambing season. She's needed at Nant Clir. Talk about crap timing. I had holiday booked for the next two weeks.'

'Can you get your money back?'

'It's not that kind of holiday. I always go home to help with the lambing and this year they'll really need me. My mum's recovering from a mastectomy, so it'll just be my brother and my Dad, if I can't go.'

'Then you must go. David can get a locum.'

'He could. He says Dylan Tew's not available, but there are plenty of other locums. What it is Dan, he doesn't like to spend. He can be as tight as a duck's arse. Why are you smiling?'

'You sounded like my Mam. What it is. She says it all the time.'

At the end of afternoon surgery, I went looking for Harry, to tell her an idea I'd had, but she'd already left, heading up to her folks' farm to help with the evening shift. Probably just as well. It was a dumb idea.

Chloe had had a very good first day. She'd seen a patient with query anxiety/episodic atrial flutter and discovered he was actually experiencing atrial fibrillation. She knows I'm not great at reading ECGs and I love it when she explains heart things to me like I'm a dim child.

With atrial flutter the P wave has a sawtooth outline. That much I knew.

'Is atrial fib the one where the P wave is wibbly-wobbly?'

'Yes. And treatment would be?'

'Cardioversion?'

'That's your last resort.'

'A beta-blocker?'

'Or?'

'Calcium channel blocker?'

'Yes. What else?'

'Warfarin? To prevent blood clots.'

'We prefer to use dabigatran. And?'

'And what?'

'What's the other important element of treatment?'

'Reassure? Explain? I don't know. Give up.'

'How about a drug for the arrhythmia, Dr Dan?'

'Right. I wasn't thinking. What do you prescribe?'

'Flecainide. Reassure and explain! That's GP stuff.'

'Which reminds me. You don't have one down here yet. Why don't you register with Miriam Parry?'

'Maybe. Or I could just carry on with my Birmingham one. All I need are my Pills.'

'Won't it soon be time to think about babies?'

'What is it with you and babies? Buying that bunny rabbit for Vaz's sprog. Getting all misty-eyed over Flo's pregnancy. Don't rush me, Dan.'

'I'm not rushing you, but I'm pretty sure that was the plan. Finish our exams. Buy a house. Have babies. Am I wrong?'

'No.'

'Have you changed your mind?'

'No.'

'Anyway, you can't live in Rhos and have a GP in Birmingham. What use is that if you get sick? Acute abdomen in the middle of the night?'

'If I get an acute abdo, I'll expect you to take me straight to a decent hospital. Miriam Parry seemed okay. I wouldn't mind having her as my GP. Not the other one, though. The one with a man's name.'

'Harry. Her name's Angharad. Why not her?'

'I didn't like her. She was snarky.'

'Was she? I didn't notice. She's locum-ing for us while Iestyn's off.'

'Scruffy too. Imagine going to somebody's house for dinner in a ratty old gardening sweater.'

Chapter 7

By Thursday the demand for appointments on Iestyn's list had eased. Delyth said word had got round that Harry was taking his surgeries and people were cancelling or saying they'd wait till Iestyn was back at work. Was it because Harry was a woman?

'No,' says Delyth. 'It's because she won't stand for any nonsense. They can wrap Dr Iestyn round their little finger, but not Dr Harry. She's only got a few appointments for tomorrow so if you and Dr Parry split them between you, she could have the day off. She was supposed to be starting her holidays.'

I agreed, of course. And after a morning of coughs and athlete's foot and back-aches, I looked in on Harry.

I said, 'I hear you've sorted the sheep from the goats on Iestyn's list.'

She laughed.

'Yes,' she said. 'The goats are happy to wait till they can see Dr Pushover. Which is good. That gives me three days to help with the lambing.'

Then I said, 'I'm free all weekend if you can use an extra pair of hands.' And as soon as I'd said it, I regretted it. She just looked at me, said nothing for such an age that I had to fill the silence with the lamest sign-off ever.

'It was just a thought.'

She nodded and went back to her computer screen.

All through afternoon surgery it kept coming back to me. What had possessed me? Free all weekend? Offering to help someone I hardly knew with something I knew less than zero about? She must have thought I was coming on to her. I had been. A bit. I prayed she'd leave the building without my having to see her again. By Monday she might have forgotten about it. By Monday my embarrassment wouldn't feel so intense. Fat chance. As my final patient of the day left (Sheila Benyon, eye floaters, nothing to worry about) Harry came in, pulled a chair up to my desk and said, 'So, Dan. That offer to help this weekend? Were you in earnest?'

In a rush of blood to the head I told her I absolutely was.

She said, 'You don't fancy yourself as some hero vet? You haven't been watching too much telly?'

I said I could make tea and butties. Whatever they needed.

'And your wife wouldn't mind?'

'Chloe's in Birmingham for the weekend. I'd love to help. It'd be exciting.'

Harry said it wouldn't. She said most of the ewes managed by themselves so it was like watching paint dry but sometimes it got messy, and occasionally it got urgent, usually just at the point where you thought you'd die if you didn't get some sleep.

She wrote directions on a prescription blank, drew me a little map, told me to wear old clothes and bring a sleeping bag.

'I thought I'd be helping with the night shift?'

'You will, but you can still get some kip when there's a lull. We don't want you wrecked by Monday. Can't have you falling asleep on the day job.'

'Tell me about your mum. When did she have the op?'

'Three weeks ago. Mastectomy and axillary lymph node dissection. She's doing fine, but her arm's still swollen. She's not up to wrestling with sheep yet.'

I said I'd drive up on Friday evening, stay till Sunday morning. As a newbie in the church choir I didn't like to miss any services.

'Tenor?' she asked.

'Baritone. Bethan's husband roped me in.'

'Nice. English or Welsh?'

'Both. We do alternate weeks. I'm struggling with the Welsh, to be honest. I can sing Wele'n Sefyll Rhwang y Myrtwydd, but I haven't a clue what most of it means and I couldn't order a cheese and ham toastie to save my life.'

'Well,' she said, 'if I remember rightly, they speak good English in Blod's. Now, if you change your mind about coming, fine. If you do come, please check all romantic notions at the Conwy suspension bridge. You know? Gambolling lambkins? It's cold in the lambing sheds, and smelly, and you can wait for hours with nothing occurring. Also, I should probably tell you about my brother. Some people find him difficult. Not difficult. Odd.'

'I've got one of those. What the name of yours?'

'Geth. Gethin.'

'What type of odd?'

'It's in the eye of the beholder. I think he's fine. He's just a man of few words, but then, sheep don't expect a lot of conversation.'

She was at the door when she turned and said, 'Thanks, Dan. It's so nice of you. Earlier, when you first offered, I'm afraid you got my inner grinch. It'll be great. Company. An extra pair of hands.'

Those eyes again.

I felt very happy for about five minutes. Quite giddy. Then I began to cool down. What was I thinking? Wangling a weekend working alongside a woman I hardly knew but really fancied. No I don't, yes you do. I was taking advantage of Chloe's absence. No I wasn't, yes I was. Back and forth I went. How was I going to sell this one when I got home? Darling, you know Harry, the woman you didn't like? I'm spending the weekend with her. Nothing untoward, of course. Her family will be there. It sounded like they could use some extra help. Really, Dan? Extra help from a man who never saw a lamb born in his life, a man who did as little human obs and gynae as he could get away with when he was a student. Really?

Chloe was home ahead of me. I decided to play it by ear. After all, I wasn't firmly committed to going to the Shepherds. If I didn't go, I wouldn't be missed. If Chloe smelled a rat, I would have to accept that there was possibly a rat to be smelt, just a small one, barely mouse-sized, and I'd stay home. I might creosote the garden fence.

Throughout the evening I kept not using opportunities to level with Chloe. It was easily done. When she wasn't packing and changing her mind about clothes and repacking, she was on the phone to Dee, to Hua, even to Mun-Hee.

I said, 'Mun-Hee? You vowed never to speak to her again.'

Mun-Hee had been Chloe's friend until they were competing for a registrar's job on the same cardio firm and Mun-Hee won. Maybe she was the better candidate. Maybe sleeping with the consultant had something to do with it.

She said, 'We made up. Barrington dumped her. His wife yanked him back into line.'

'So, she's not working for him?'

'No, she's at the Royal London now. I can't decide about this dress. I don't know why I ever bought it. It's a bit mumsy.'

I left half of my green Thai. My mind kept drifting to the secret I was sitting on. Chloe noticed.

She said, 'You're not still sulking about me going away?'

'Not at all,' I said. 'Just not very hungry.'

Now I needed her to ask me what my plans were.

I said, 'I hope you have a lovely time. I know you're missing your friends.'

Still nothing.

I said, 'And I'm sure I'll find plenty to do.'

'Yeah,' she said. 'Still some boxes to unpack.'

I started. I said, 'I might drive up to Snowdonia.'

'Cool,' she said. And then her damned phone rang again.

That was how it came about that my wife left the house on Friday morning unaware I'd be heading up the Conwy valley after work, with my wellies and my walking boots in the back of the car and a sleeping bag that once belonged to some friend of Dee's. I think it's what's called a sin of omission.

I wasn't sure what the catering arrangements would be at the Shepherds so I stopped off in Conwy for something to eat, then headed south. I was on the road that goes to Betws-y-Coed, where Trevor Buxton's daughter lives, and I suddenly had a strong urge to call Trevor. We hadn't spoken since I left Weirdo Pants. What was I hoping for? Some fatherly advice to turn my car round, go home and stop being so foolish? I took a right turn, then pulled over. There was no signal on my phone.

The road was empty. It was early in the year for tourists. Harry's instructions said to aim towards a peak called Tal-y-Fan, but it was too dark to make out anything. No moon. The track got narrower and narrower and just when I'd decided I was well and truly lost and I'd be spending the night in the car,

I saw the fingerpost. Maes Glas. The name of the Shepherds' farm.

As I topped a rise in the track there were lights ahead. A house, barns, sheds. Everywhere was lit, and when I killed the engine and opened the car door, I could hear bleating and the hum of a generator. The first person I saw was a six-foot version of Harry. Wild hair and a long stare, not unfriendly, just not interested. Gethin, presumably. I said my name. He nodded and went on his way across the yard towards one of the outbuildings. The next person I saw was an older model of Gethin. Harry's father, I assumed.

'All right then?' he said and walked away before I could introduce myself. It seemed I was expected. Unless strangers regularly turned up there in the dark. I put my wellies on and went in search of Harry. I found her in a barn, leaning into a pen, giving a pep talk to a very small lamb.

'You came then,' she said.

I said, 'I think I just saw your brother and your Da. I kind of introduced myself. Were they expecting me?'

'I said you might come, but most of what I say goes in one ear and out the other. Dad probably thought you were a Dead-Ender.'

'What's a Dead-Ender?'

'People who drive up here by mistake and have to make a U-turn in the yard. It happens a lot in the summer.'

She climbed into the pen. The ewe had had twins and one of them wasn't suckling. Would they bottle feed it? That was a job even I could do.

'Not if I have anything to do with it,' she said. 'It takes too much time and money. Anyway, a newborn like this one, we'd stomach-tube him first, if we really had to. But there's no need here. It's just that one of her teats is a bit small and he's having trouble latching on.'

'It's a boy?'

'Yep. Ram lamb. Mum's in the house, if you need something to eat.'

'I don't. I ate in Conwy. So, give me a job.'

'Nothing much happening at the moment. Tell you what. Go over to the house and make me a cup of tea. As soon as I get this slow learner sorted, I'll show you around.'

I did as instructed. Mrs Shepherd's first words to me were, 'Boots!'

She didn't seem interested in who I was. Only that I took my wellies off. She pointed to a kettle on the Aga and a box of teabags on the table. She was busy putting a new plug on a heat-lamp, but she anticipated my next question.

'No sugar, no milk, if it's for Harry. Three sugars and plenty of milk if it's for Geth or Father.'

'How about you?'

'No. I'm awash with tea.'

An old sheepdog collected me outside the farmhouse door and herded me back to the barn. The slow learner had cottoned on and was suckling. Harry had moved to another pen. Another ewe with twins.

'So, this is one of the post-natal wards. There's another batch penned in the tractor shed, mainly the older ewes who've done it before. We keep them here till we're sure they've bonded and the lambs are feeding. This one's a wet adoption, so I'm keeping an eye. Seems to be going okay.'

A wet adoption was where a lamb in need of a mother was soaked in the amniotic fluid of a ewe's own new-born lamb to make her think she'd had twins and convince her to adopt it. Harry said it usually worked. Had the adopted lamb been orphaned?

'No, but she's one of triplets.'

'Is that a problem?'

'You could say. Ewes only have two teats.'

I wished I'd read up a bit on the basics of sheep.

We went into another, bigger barn, more brightly lit: the labour ward. About thirty ewes standing around doing nothing, or so I thought. Harry drank her tea and surveyed the scene.

'That one,' she said. 'Back left corner. Hear her? She's muttering a bit.'

'Is that how you know?'

'It can be. Some witter and grumble, some just get restless. How's your wife?'

Was that an innocent non sequitur?

'She's well. Gone to a birthday party in Birmingham.'

'I thought she seemed a bit uncomfortable, when I met her at the Parrys. Crash-landed in small-town Wales and not happy about it.'

'She's fine. Just missing her friends. How often do you have to call a vet out to a difficult delivery?'

'Never. Between the four of us we know what to do. And sometimes there isn't anything anyone can do. Not that much different to humans, really.'

Harry has dark curls. She's pale and lightly freckled with a small white scar from a cleft lip repair, and my urgent desire to kiss her got extinguished just in time when she turned to look across the lambing shed and said, 'Water bag!'

The ewe that had been muttering had started straining and a bag of clear amniotic fluid had appeared.

'What do we do?'

'Nothing. Keep an eye. She's done it all before.'

63

Gethin joined us.

Harry said, 'We've got one with fore-waters showing and that one with the twins, face to the wall, she was pawing a minute ago. This is Dan Talbot. From the other Parry practice.'

Gethin nodded.

How did they know that particular ewe was carrying twins? I dared to ask.

'Do you scan them?'

'Scan them and colour code them. See, she's got a blue mark on her side?'

There was a man in a van who came out with a scanner.

'The one with the water bag? How long till she lambs?'

'It could be a while yet. She's still standing.'

As she said it, the ewe sank down onto the straw and a few minutes later her lamb slipped into the world, pink and glistening and she turned her head to lick it clean.

'But then again,' says Harry. 'The thing about sheep is, they never read the textbooks.'

'That looked easy.'

'Yes, she's a good mother. It's not always that simple, though. If a lamb decides to come out arse first, there's nothing she can do about it.'

The blue-marked ewe was pawing at her straw again. Gethin watched her closely. Shepherd by name, shepherd by nature.

'And he's up,' says Harry. The newborn single was on its feet, minutes old.

'Can you see it's a male?'

'No, I'm guessing. It's a good size. What do you reckon, Geth? A ram lamb?'

'I'd say.'

The evening wore on without any further action until around midnight when the twin lambs were born, about twenty minutes apart, and two other ewes started to give cause for concern. Both were on the ground, both had been straining for a while, looking up at the roof of the barn. Star-gazing, Harry called it. But no lambs appeared. It looked like they might need help.

Harry paired off with her Dad. I was to stick with Gethin. 'What should I do?'

'Not get in his way. If he needs you to do anything, he'll tell you.'

That was hard to believe. He was a silent mountain of a man. More comfortable to be around than my brother, though. With Adam you always feel being spoken to is an inconvenience. Harry's brother was just at ease with silence.

He sent me to the house for a bucket of soapy water. Mrs Shepherd was in her dressing gown, dozing by the Aga.

'Boots!' she reminded me.

Gethin scrubbed his arms, pulled on a long glove and covered it with Lubigel. In he went, fingers bunched in a cone. It was just like I'd seen on the telly one time, except he was murmuring to the ewe, in Welsh.

'Iawn cariad,' he whispered. 'Iawn, iawn.'

All right, old girl. You'll be alright.

He said the lamb had its elbows locked. He eased its body back a little, to allow the front legs to straighten. It worked, then they locked again. It took three goes until the legs being straight coincided with the mother straining and the lamb dived into the world, followed ten minutes later by its perfectly presenting twin. All was well. I felt great, even though my sole contribution had been to fetch a bucket of water and then stand around holding my breath.

Across the other side of the shed things weren't going so well with Harry's ewe. The lamb was stillborn, but the ewe didn't know that. She kept calling for it. What they needed was a triplet birth, as soon as possible, so they could try to get her to accept someone else's spare lamb. It was 2 am and none of the ewes carrying triplets seemed likely to oblige. Harry was frustrated.

'What do you think went wrong?'

'I suppose the placenta packed in. It can happen. The lamb looked fine.'

'Will you breed from her again?'

'No. This was her last time.'

'Out to grass?'

'Till the autumn.'

'Then what?'

'Rogan Josh, Dan. Why don't you go and get some sleep?'

'Why don't you? Gethin's around somewhere and I can always wake you if anything starts.'

She looked at me for the longest time. What was she weighing up? My reasons for giving up my weekend to stand in a freezing barn? Ulterior motives? Genuine interest? Insanity?

'Right you are,' she said. 'I'll grab an hour. There's a little parlour off the kitchen. I'll be in there.'

Chapter 8

I was only at Maes Glas for 36 hours but when I drove to church on Sunday morning I felt as though I'd been away for weeks. My eyes ached and I had that sour taste in my mouth that comes with over-tiredness. It brought back memories of being a junior houseman. But I felt great too. I'd seen a lot of lambs born, I'd been deemed competent to spray iodine on a batch of umbilical stumps and at first light I'd gone out in the fields with Harry, transferring ewes and their lambs from the post-natal barn to pasture. I felt kind of manly. The grilling I'd had from Mrs Shepherd had been a very minor unpleasantness.

On Saturday morning there had been a lull in the lambing shed so we'd all sat down to a full Welsh fry, with tea strong enough to stain your teeth. Suddenly, in the middle of a discussion about a promising-looking ram lamb, Mr Shepherd said, 'You courting our Harry, then?'

Harry choked on her toast.

Mrs Shepherd said, 'He's married.'

All you could hear was the scraping of knives and forks. Then Harry said, 'Dan's a friend.'

'Friend, is it?' says Mrs Shepherd, and got up to refresh the teapot.

'Yes,' says Harry. 'And he's interested in sheep. His father's a livestock auctioneer.'

That got Mr Shepherd's attention. He asked if Da ever worked at the Dolgellau sales, or at Mold.

I said, 'I'm not sure. I know he does Ruthin occasionally, but he's based in Abergavenny so he mainly works around the Brecon markets and Monmouth.'

'Oh,' says Mrs Shepherd. 'You're from down there.'

Down there. Wales may be God's own country but only the half of it that's located your side of Machynlleth, whichever half that may be.

It was an English week at church, and just as well. I went to bed for an hour when I got home but I hardly slept. My head was too full of Harry images. I phoned Mam. I needed to talk about my weekend and get it out of my system before Chloe arrived.

'Guess where I've been?'

'I'll need a clue.'

'I've been on a sheep farm, helping with the lambing.'

'Have you? What do you know about lambing?'

'More than I did three days ago. How's Nan?'

'Refusing to get rid of her sideboard. What it is Dan, there won't be space for it. Once we've put her bed in there and a tallboy for her clothes. It's not a big room. Anyway, that sideboard is full of things she's never used. Tea sets kept for best. Kept for funerals. But when your grandad died we had the tea and sandwiches at our house. She's got fruit bowls and cake stands and souvenirs people used to bring her when they'd been on holiday. A cruet from Barmouth, that type of thing. It'll all have to go. So, where's this sheep farm?'

'Edge of the Snowdonia National Park. It's the family of a locum we've got at the moment, standing in for Iestyn. They were a bit shorthanded and Chloe's away for the weekend, so I offered to help.'

'Chloe's away again?'

'At a friend's thirtieth.'

Then began Mam's usual relaying of our conversation to Da.

'He's been helping with lambing, Ed. In Snowdonia.'

Da was on the phone like a shot.

'Hill farm, was it?'

'Not exactly. Bordering on. They've got some hill grazing.'

'Welsh Half Breeds?'

'Welsh Mules. They're Beulahs crossed with Blue Faced Leicesters.'

'Texel rams?'

'Suffolks.'

'They lamb easy?'

'Most of them.'

'Keep a good hold of their udder?'

I said they did, though I wasn't sure what he meant by it. I'd exhausted my scant knowledge of sheep husbandry, but I'd had an animated conversation with my father and that didn't happen every day.

Mam said she was glad I was making new friends up here. Of course, I hadn't got round to telling her that my new friend was a woman with mad hair and green eyes.

Chloe got home around six. She said she was in bits. Too much champagne, too little sleep. I offered to cook.

'Depends what it is,' she said. 'I've got hangover mouth. What were you planning?'

I suggested a risotto. It's something she really likes but would never be arsed to make for herself, plus it'd require me to stand at the hob for twenty minutes, stirring. A perfect set up for me while I casually mentioned my weekend without having to look her in the face. She said she'd love a risotto, I was a complete angel and she was going for a quick shower. When I went to tell her dinner was ready, she was asleep, still wearing the clothes she'd travelled in. We sat down to eat with her feeling cross and bleary and me urgently needing to unburden myself. I dove straight in.

'Remember Harry Shepherd, that we met at the Parrys?'

'The gay man?'

'No, that was Hilary. Harry was the girl in the scruffy sweater. I told you she's locum-ing for us while Iestyn's off. Her family have a sheep farm. I've been up there helping with the lambing.'

'Why?'

'Why not. You were away and they were glad of an extra pair of hands. The mother's recovering from a mastectomy.'

'This Harry, did she like, just ask you? What a cheek.'

'No, it wasn't. I heard they needed help and I was happy to give it a try. It was fun.'

'Fun? I hope you haven't had your hand up any sheeps' bottoms.'

'Hardly. I was head tea-maker.'

She ate the rest of her risotto in silence. Then she said, 'This Harry clearly has a thing for you.'

'I don't think so.'

'Dan, you can be such a dope. Just because you're not film star good-looking doesn't mean there isn't something adorable about you.'

'Is there a compliment in there somewhere?'

'All I'm saying is, be careful. A woman like that. Don't get her hopes up.'

'A woman like what?'

'You know. A plain Jane. Probably never had a boyfriend. Probably fantasises about you. I bet they didn't really need help at all.'

'You may be right.'

At which point Chloe changed the subject to what colour we should paint our bedroom and I was off the hook. She didn't mind in the least where I'd spent my weekend.

Normally I wouldn't dream of answering her phone, but it had rung three times while I was ironing my shirts for the week and she'd gone to bed straight after dinner and was fast asleep. The fourth time, I picked up. I could see it was her mate, Dee.

'Hey lover girl,' she said. 'How'd it go? Can you talk?'

I said, 'It's Dan. How did what go?'

She said, 'What the fuck? Why are you answering her phone?'

'She's sleeping. How did what go?'

Dee missed a beat.

'The drive home.'

'She got here in one piece. Sounds like you had quite a weekend.'

'Yeah.'

'So what did you girls get up to?'

But Dee had gone.

Chloe didn't even stir when I climbed into bed. Eeyore, her bloody stuffed donkey, was wedged between our pillows. Hey, lover girl, how'd it go? What did that mean? Had she even been to Dee's birthday? And why couldn't we be a normal couple? Get married, buy a house, choose paint for the bedroom, spend our weekends exploring our new neighbourhood and having great sex. Possibly even making a

71

baby. What was it with Chloe? Was she unhappy? With Wales? With me?

And then again, was I blameless? Had I dragged her here against her wishes? Was I boring? Could I honestly say I hadn't enjoyed looking at another woman, even one with holes in her sweater and the smell of a lambing shed in her hair? I slept fitfully and woke up feeling crap. I had a busy week ahead. No Iestyn, no Aggie. The occasional presence of Harry, but mostly just me, David Parry and Bethan versus the genuinely ailing, the worried well and the outright chancers of Colwyn Bay.

Chloe was running late, coat on, hair still wet. She made a smoothie and hardly touched it. Couldn't find her keys, couldn't remember where she'd left her phone.

I said, 'It's next to the bread bin. Dee called last night, by the way, several times. I told her you were asleep.'

'You answered my phone?'

'Eventually. Dee seemed anxious to know about your drive home. Her exact words were "Hey, lover girl. How'd it go?"'

Cool as you like Chloe said, 'What the hell is it with you? We talked about this before. About you meddling with my phone.'

'Yes, I remember. That was when we were organising your mother's funeral, you were in the bath and your phone kept buzzing with messages. From an old lover, as it turned out.'

'Fitzie's a friend. He knew Mummy. And anyway, you still had no right. We don't do that, Dan. We don't answer each other's phones.'

'Except when it suits you. Except when it's your sister calling and you don't feel like talking to her. Or your mother, when she was alive. How many times did I field calls from her?

"Hi Vinnie. Chloe's popped out to get petrol. Can I get her to call you later?"'

'That is so cruel. Bringing up Mummy's name, and on a horrid Monday morning when it's piddling rain and I've got to drive to Wrexham.'

'I didn't mean to be cruel. I was just trying to get some facts straight. Like when is it and when is it not okay for me to answer your phone? Let's talk tonight.'

She said she had to do an evening clinic on Mondays as I perfectly well knew, and she had no idea what time she'd be home.

Morning surgery was manageable. Four no-shows. It's amazing what a good downpour does for people's aches and pains. I devoted an extra ten minutes to Ivor Dugmore and his poorly controlled diabetes, though I think I might have saved my breath. Ivor's only in his forties. He's single, between jobs, lives alone. If he'd exercised a bit of self-control when he was first diagnosed, he could have managed his blood sugars, maybe even reversed things for a while, but instead he'd piled on weight. Every time we saw him he'd gained another chin.

'Thing is, Doc,' he said, 'I'm a chocolic.'

It drives me crazy when people say that, as if a sweet tooth is a terminally hopeless condition. I mean, I'm partial to a bag of Maltesers myself.

I laid it on thick, how he was dicing with all kinds of complications. I warned him about the risk to his eyesight, told him the story of Barbara Humphries, an exemplary, vigilant diabetic who nevertheless ended up having a foot amputated. Was Ivor listening? Hardly. He was just waiting for me to stop talking so he could say, 'I know, I know. It's a terrible thing. End of the day though, something's going to get you. Brain

73

tumour. Car smash. I look at it this way, at least with this diabetes business I know what's got my name on it.'

Iestyn dropped by at lunchtime. He was hoping Delyth would mind the twins for an hour. They were asleep in their stroller but he said if they woke while he was scooting round the supermarket they could get unmanageable. I could imagine. And before long there'd be three of them to juggle. He said the plan was to induce Aggie on Monday or Tuesday. If everything went well, she and the baby would be allowed home and Iestyn might be back at work the week after next. It all depended on the Polish mother-in-law situation.

'Will she fly over?'

'She'd come like a shot, only Aggie doesn't want her. They get on each other's nerves.'

'What about your mum? Will she be able to help?'

'As soon as they're finished lambing. I heard you were up at Maes Glas. I heard Harry roped you in.'

'I don't know that I was much help.'

'Well you got a pretty good write-up.'

'I did?'

'Yes, from Aunt Grace. Harry's Mam. She told Mum you weren't bad for a hwntw townie and it was a pity you were spoken for.'

Amazing. Behind that stern façade Mrs Shepherd's only objection to me was that I was a married South Walian, with no farming experience.

That afternoon I got a couple of reminders that I was also still fairly inexperienced as a GP, that my job was to listen carefully and not jump to hasty conclusions.

Menna Rowlands, aged 72, came in with her daughter, Deb, aged 47. Middle-aged daughter concerned about the health of her ageing mother? No. The other way round.

Mrs Rowlands said, 'She's always tired. Eight hours a night and she needs a nap in the afternoon. That can't be right, at her age. She forgets things too.'

Deb had so far said nothing. I asked her to tell me how she felt. It was uphill work because her mother kept answering for her. I was wondering how to stop her when Deb did it for me.

'Mum,' she said. 'Will you please shut up. You're giving the doctor brain-ache.'

Deb said she didn't forget things, but sometimes the tiredness made her mind go fuzzy. She was single, no children, worked part-time at a garden centre, lived with her mum. She couldn't manage a full-time job because of her arthritis. There was no mention of arthritis in her notes.

'It comes and goes,' she said. 'In my knees mainly.'

She was a little on the heavy side. Thinning hair, scant eyebrows. Was her thyroid function under par? Her blood pressure and temperature were fine. She had a very healthy colour, although the insides of her eyelids were pale. I said we'd look at her bloods.

Mrs Rowlands said, 'Tell him about the rash.'

'Why? says Deb. 'It's nearly gone. You can't hardly see it.'

That wasn't quite true. Like one of those optical illusion puzzles, as soon as I was told what to look for, I saw it. Her healthy colour was actually a fading butterfly rash, across the top of her cheeks and the bridge of her nose. Did I have a case of lupus staring me in the face?

I took her through to Bethan to get her bloods taken. Full cell count, ESR, thyroid function and antinuclear antibodies. I lingered a moment, to see if Deb wanted to say anything else without her mother chipping in. She didn't. But Bethan said, 'Oh look, you've got Raynaud's finger. I get that sometimes.'

She was right. Deb's ring and little fingers on her right hand were cold and white and I hadn't even noticed. Another possible indicator of lupus. A definite indicator that I needed to raise my game.

Deb said, 'What do you think? Is it serious?'

I said I thought we'd wait and see what the bloods told us.

My 5 o'clock was another mother and daughter. Skylar Jarman was fourteen. I'd have guessed she was younger. Baby-faced, although she did have that bored look of a worldly-wise teenager. Her presenting symptom was urinary frequency. How frequent? Every five minutes, according to her mother. They'd been sitting in our waiting room for a good twenty minutes. Had she, for instance, needed to use the loo during that time? No. So Mrs Jarman was exaggerating.

Was she drinking a lot and passing large volumes? No, she felt like she needed to pee all the time even when she could only manage a teaspoonful. That tended to rule out diabetes, but we'd test her anyway. Did she have pain? Skylar said no. Her mother said, 'Skylar! Yes you do. Down below. Sunday morning you were doubled over.'

Frequency, urgency, low abdominal pain. It sounded like cystitis.

I sent Skylar into Bethan, for instructions on how to provide a mid-stream urine sample for a dipstick test. I asked Mrs Jarman if Skylar was sexually active.

'At her age?' she said. 'Course not. She only started her periods last year.'

The dipstick showed no glucose, no nitrites, but a trace of blood. The urine was crystal clear. It didn't look as though Skylar had an infection, but the nitrite strip can give a false negative so I asked Bethan to send it for a lab test. Anything else? Yes, while we were about it, bloods for a full cell count and renal function.

In the meanwhile, what to do? Prescribe antibiotics anyway? I decided not. Better to wait a few days until we had the lab results. I told them to make an appointment for early the following week.

At the end of surgery, I had a word with Bethan. What impression had she had of Skylar Jarman? Was this a girl who was having sex, whatever her mum believed? Bethan thought not. She thought Skylar had seemed quite childish for fourteen. That was my impression too.

'Mind you,' she said, 'there's no telling these days. Half the time the parents don't know where they are or what they're up to.'

David came in, looking for something in the drugs cabinet.

He has children. The son's in his teens. The daughter, Becca, is at Manchester, a second-year dentistry student. What was she like as a teenager?

'Never gave us a moment,' he said. 'Always worked hard at school. Always had nice wholesome hobbies. Pony club, tennis. Miriam predicts she'll break out when she hits forty.'

'You mean like, get a tattoo?'

'Yes. Run off with a biker gang.'

'What about Joe?'

'Nothing to keep us awake at night. He's a messer at school, but I was myself. I didn't shape up till six months before A levels.'

I like David and I'd like to know him better, but he's very self-contained. I was going to suggest we go for a drink. I was in no hurry to go home. But he seemed a bit on edge, like he was waiting for the small talk to stop and me to leave. Maybe he wanted a private word with Bethan.

Delyth called up the stairs to me.

'Dr Dan, would you be so good as to call Dr Barkham.'

'Certainly. Who is he?'

'It's a she. I don't know.'

'And it's concerning?'

'How should I know. I'm just the receptionist.'

'But you have her number?'

'No. She said you'd have it. Right, I'm off. Goodnight.'

So, a call from a doctor I didn't know, for reasons unknown, and no phone number. Brilliant.

Chloe got in around 9.30 and announced that she needed a glass of wine, something to eat and bed. She was avoiding any discussion about privacy and secrets and what she'd been up to at the weekend, and my appetite for an argument was diminishing by the hour. Hadn't I known when I married her that she could be silly and impulsive? But didn't I also know that we loved each other and when things were good between us, they were very, very good? Shouldn't I be the grownup and allow her time and space to adapt to our new life? The move to Colwyn Bay had been my decision, after all. Made at a time, yes, yet another time when Chloe had been behaving like a spoilt child and I wasn't even sure we had a future together, but I'd gone ahead and accepted the job without her full agreement. Back and forth went the cases for the prosecution and the defence. Then her phone rang.

She looked at it.

'Oh God, it's Flo. You answer it. Tell her I'm asleep.'

'Yesterday you had a fit because I'd answered your phone.'

'Because I hadn't given you permission. I'm giving you permission now.'

'Thank you but no thank you. I'm refusing the privilege. She's your sister. You speak to her.'

I gathered from Chloe's end of the conversation that a) Flo hadn't done anything about liberating certain items of furniture from the Chummery as instructed and b) she was asking Chloe for something that Chloe was reluctant to give.

'I don't know,' she said. 'I'd have to check with Dan. We've got a lot in the diary.'

Which was a barefaced lie. We had nothing in the diary.

She passed me her phone and whispered, 'Tell her we're going to your folks.'

Flo was proposing to visit us over Easter. Her and the three girls. I thought it was a great idea. It would make our new house feel like a real home.

I said, 'Of course you can come. I'm not sure what the sleeping arrangements will be. We're not fully furnished yet.'

Flo said, 'I know. Chlo keeps on at me to burgle the Chummery but I'd really rather not. It is still Daddy's home, after all.'

'Quite right. Is he there much?'

'Just weekends. They may be going on a cruise, he and Jen. So, you're okay with us descending on you for Easter? Chlo said you might be going away.'

'No, come. What about Henry? Can he get away for a few days?'

'He'd very much like to. It depends on his new pig man.'

Chloe was not pleased.

'Great. You were supposed to put her off.'

'But I didn't want to. It'll be nice to have company over Easter. We can do an egg hunt in the garden.'

'Aww. Uncle Dan's egg hunt. Why are you so saintly? You do realise Flo's just after a free holiday. All that lovely Packwood money and they never, ever go to a hotel. And she'll be wearing her ancient maternity tents, waddling around like an old walrus.'

'We need to buy beds.'

'We'll need to buy cages for the ghastly yoblets. At least Horrible Henry won't be able to come. He'll have to stay with his piggywigs.'

I allowed her to believe that, though I was rooting for Henry's new pig man stepping up. I like Henry.

It was just before the start of morning surgery. I was doing letters. Delyth, yelled up the stairs, 'It's that Dr Barkham again. You were supposed to call her.'

I said, 'Press 3, Delyth.'

'And then hang up?'

'When you hear me speaking to Dr Barkham. Not before.'

It was a tense moment. They've had a very simple switchboard for a couple of years now but Delyth has never got the hang of it.

'Dan Talbot.'

And a familiar voice said, 'For crying out loud, Dan. Are you avoiding me? It'd be easier to get through to the Queen.'

Pam Parker.

I said, 'I got a mysterious message to call a Dr Barkham. Our receptionist is deaf.'

And Delyth said, 'I am not,' and put the phone down at her end.

Pam laughed.

She said, 'I know you must be on your marks for the start of surgery, but I wanted to catch you. Dan, I'm the bearer of sad news.'

Chapter 9

The mysterious Dr Barkham turned out to be Pam Parker, calling with sad news. My heart sank. Trevor. I hadn't been prepared to lose him so soon.

But then she said, 'Mrs Buxton. Saturday night, in her sleep.'

'Mrs Buxton? You know what I thought you were going to say?'

'Of course. It wasn't what any of us were expecting. Trevor least of all. I thought you'd want to know though.'

'How is he?'

'Shell-shocked. The son's come up from London, to help him with the arrangements.'

'What about Alice?'

'No sign of her so far. She'll come for the funeral. I just hope she leaves the girlfriend at home. Mrs Buxton couldn't stand the sight of her.'

'When is the funeral?'

'Friday week, in the afternoon, Stourbridge Cemetery. I don't suppose you'll be able to come.'

'I'll try. We're a bit short-handed here, but I'd really like to.'

'You can stay with us if you need a bed.'

'Should I phone Trevor?'

'Sure. Why not? He'd love to hear from you. How's Welsh Wales?'

'It's great. Did she have a heart attack?'

'To be determined. Sounds like it though. Okay, I'll let you go. I imagine you've got the halt and the lame scratching at your door.'

Mrs Buxton was dead. It was hard to take in. Trevor was the one who was sick. He'd been worried about how she'd survive without him. And now, as it turned out, it was Trevor left on his own in that big house, disabled by COPD, semi-retired and marginalised at Weirdo Pants. How would he cope?

Delyth gave me the cold shoulder for the rest of the day. When I asked her to clear my appointments for Friday week she sighed.

'Does Dr Parry know about this?'

'He does. I'll work on the Wednesday afternoon instead, and Dr Shepherd might be back by then.'

'Might is no use to me. I can't book appointments with a doctor who 'might' be here.'

'I have a funeral to attend.'

'Yes, you already said. I'm not deaf.'

I said, 'Actually, Delyth, I think you are a bit deaf. Have you ever had a hearing test?'

She turned her back on me. But when I looked at the appointment lists later on, she'd done as I asked.

I thought Chloe would be delighted at an excuse to go to Birmingham, and on a Friday too. She said the thing was, she'd already promised to see Hua and Dee that weekend and it was kind of a girls only thing, going for spa treatments, so what exactly did I have in mind? Would I come home after the funeral? Because there wouldn't be room for me at Dee's.

83

I said, 'I wouldn't stay at Dee's if you paid me. I can stay at Pam Parker's. I'd like to spend some time with Trevor, but if he has other plans I'll drive back here and go shopping for beds. Will you at least come with me to the funeral?'

'I'll try to get the day off. I do want to. I love Trevor, the poor old sausage.'

I got to speak to the poor old sausage the following day. He said he was alright, but he didn't sound it.

'It's knocked me sideways,' he said. 'She was fine. We'd had fillet steak for dinner. Watched a bit of telly. Went to bed. Never suspected a thing.'

'You found her when you woke up?'

'Not even that. I got up and made her a cup of tea, same as usual, brought it back to bed. And there she was, cold as marble. She'd been dead hours.'

'She probably never knew anything about it.'

'That's what we tell people, isn't it? Slipped away peacefully. Best way to go. But the thing is, Dan, we'd both had a few, you know? G&T before. Wine with. And I'd had a nightcap. I was spark out. If she had cried out, I don't know that I'd have heard her.'

'So now you're torturing yourself with a lot of If Onlys.'

'Well, yes. It was good of you to phone.'

'I'll see you next week. We're coming to the funeral.'

'You don't need to do that. Driving all that way.'

'I want to. I've missed you.'

'Steady on. Talk like that, you'll start the waterworks. I'm alright until people say nice things.'

'Good. Crying's therapeutic. Isn't that another thing we tell people? Maybe we could go to the Black Bear, for old time's sake?'

'Champion. I'll look forward to it. But my word, Dan Talbot, has married life turned you to drink already? Or is it the Welsh weather?'

As it happened, the Welsh weather was nothing to complain about that weekend and neither was married life. We bought paint, walked on the beach, visited Conwy castle, bumped into Miriam Parry in Llandudno and had coffee with her. She and Chloe seemed to get on well, certainly better than the first time they met. That's what Chloe needed to help her settle: some new local girlfriends to hang out with instead of bolting back to Dee's crowd at every opportunity.

On Monday, Skylar Jarman's results came in, inconclusive. Likewise, the following day with Deb Rowlands' ANA test. People think diagnostics are like playing bingo. If the right numbers come up, Full House! Your GP now knows what's wrong with you. But quite often all the numbers do is suggest what isn't wrong with you.

Skylar did not have a UTI. Yes, she had all the symptoms of one, but her urine was sterile and her renal function markers were all normal. What next? Refer her for imaging? Wait and see? I spoke to her mother. Mrs Jarman said Skylar was much better. She was still peeing every hour, up and down at night too, but she hadn't had any more pain. I suggested we review the situation in a couple of weeks and she seemed happy with that.

Deb Rowlands' case was more complicated. For one thing, Deb didn't feel there was any cause for concern. It was her mother who was the driving force. Also, lupus, which was my strong suspicion, is notoriously hard to confirm. They call it 'the great imitator' and for good reason. It can look like fibromyalgia or like hypothyroidism, to name but two red herrings.

85

Deb had tested positive for anti-nuclear antibodies at a dilution of 1:80, which was tantamount to a negative result. Her thyroid function was normal, her haemoglobin was on the low side and her ESR was high.

I discussed it with David.

'Well,' he said, 'if it is lupus you might have tested her just as it's remitting. Equally, if it's lupus, it'll recur so you'll get another crack at it. As always, think horses not zebras.'

An old adage they teach you in med school when you think you've identified some incredibly rare disease. If you hear the sound of hooves, think horses not zebras.

I was with David when we got the news that Aggie had been safely delivered of a baby girl. She weighed an enormous 4.3 kg and they were naming her Haf, which sounds like 'have' and means summer in Welsh.

'Thank God,' says David. 'Now all we need is for the lambing to finish so Granny Hughes can ride to the rescue and Iestyn can get back to work. Miriam'll be relieved too. She'd like Harry returned to her, ASAP.'

I was happy for Iestyn and Aggie, of course, but a little disappointed to think that soon I wouldn't be seeing Harry. I liked her. I liked her ratty sweaters and her take-me-or-leave me attitude and there was nothing more to it than that. I told myself.

What I really wanted was to have a consultation with Deb Rowlands without her mother. I decided to try and speak to her at work. There were two likely garden centres. The first one didn't know her, the second one said she only worked mornings. It was Thursday before I caught her.

'Who is it?' she whispered.

'Dr Talbot, from the surgery.'

'The doctor?'

'Yes, I'm sorry to call you at work but I just wanted a quick word.'

'Is it cancer?'

'What? No, no. I've got your results here and there's nothing to worry about but I would like to talk to you, about your symptoms, and I wondered whether you'd like to come in, maybe without your mum?'

She said, 'She won't like that.'

'No? Well it's up to you. Sometimes it's easier to talk if you don't have somebody trying to speak for you.'

'She doesn't mean any harm.'

'Of course not. She's being a mum.'

'I would though. Like to come on my own.'

We made an appointment for the next week.

'And it's not cancer?'

I promised her it wasn't, though that's the kind of blithe assurance no doctor ever wants to give. Just because you have one condition doesn't mean you don't have others. None of us knows what's lurking until we start looking.

The plan was, drive to Birmingham on Friday morning and rendezvous with Chloe at the funeral. On Saturday I'd spend some time with Trevor and go to see Vaz and Teresa's baby. Then on Sunday morning I'd head home, stopping off in Connah's Quay to order furniture. It was only three weeks till Easter and we couldn't have the Packwoods sleeping on the floor.

I left my car and my overnight bag at the Parkers and rode with Pam to the cemetery.

She said, 'The moment of truth approaches.'

'Moment of truth?'

'We get to find out her name. Care to place your bet?'

87

The great mystery of the first name of Trevor's wife, only ever referred to as Mrs Buxton, even by Trevor himself.

'Winifred?'

'That's a good one. I don't think that's on the list.'

'There's a list?'

'Nurse Linda organised a sweepstake at the surgery. Five quid a go. I drew Gertrude, but my gut tells me it's going to be Gladys.

'What's the favourite?'

'Beryl. Harold Boddy drew that.'

'And what else is going on at Tipton Road? Anything I should know?'

'We've got a new trainee. Bishan Gill. Punjabi Indian. Nice girl but she's very timid. On paper Helen's her supervisor but the reality is as per. She gets passed around between me and Trevor and the Boddys. It's probably better that way. She sees different styles of doctoring.'

'Is Helen coming to the funeral?'

'Yes. And Mary. They're the only two who really knew her. Gladys.'

'Or Winifred.'

'Or Beryl.'

'Nurse Chris is doing drinks and stuff at the house afterwards but if it's all the same to you I'd rather not. Standing around, trying to be cheerful but not too cheerful. Tell me about your new place. How are you getting on?'

'It's different.'

'Is that good or bad?'

'I mean, the patients are pretty much the same kind of mix, but the staff are nothing like. There's no congregating, no hanging out in the kitchen. I can go for days without speaking to the other doctors. They're not unfriendly. Lunchtime, they just grab a sandwich at their desk. Six o'clock, they shoot off home.'

'Maybe you need to set a new trend. Buy one of those fancy coffee machines and a tin of nice biscuits. That'll lure them out of their caves. Has Chloe settled?'

'We're getting there. She misses her old life. She'll feel better once she's made a few friends.'

That was what I was telling myself. And I was saved from the foolishness of burbling to Pam about Harry Shepherd and lambing at Maes Glas because we were about to join a queue of cars snaking in through the entrance to the cemetery. There was a big turnout for Mrs Buxton. It had started to rain.

Chloe had already arrived. I spotted her car though I couldn't see her in the crowd milling outside the chapel.

Pam said, 'There's a waiting room, apparently, if you want to go and find her. I like to wait outside till the coffin arrives. I've got my brolly.'

I waited with Pam and on the stroke of three the procession arrived. A hearse and two limos. Trevor was in a dark suit. The only other time I'd seen him wear a suit was when he went to Jimmy Riley's funeral. There were four people with him in the car. His son, James, with a stunning blonde and the daughter, Alice, with her partner, Micky.

I knew more than I wanted to about the Alice and Micky relationship. It was volatile and Micky was very much in control. She was a tiny, wiry woman and yet there had been episodes of real violence. But again and again Alice went back for more.

Pam said, 'Can you frigging believe it? The wife-beater's turned up, riding in style. Trevor must be fit to be tied.'

The chapel was packed. We got seats right at the back.

Pam said, 'Can you see your missus anywhere?'

'Other side, three rows from the front. Blue jacket and her hair's in an up-do. She's sitting next to an older woman.'

She said, 'That's not an older woman, you twit. That's our dear Helen.'

She was right. The auburn had grown out and the strangely sexy Helen Vincent now had short, white hair and glasses.

'What happened to her?'

'Life. Oh, here we go.'

The funeral started. A clergyman led the way. *I am the resurrection and the life, saith the Lord.* Then the coffin, then the family. It was the sight of Trevor that brought on my tears. He'd shrunk. He looked defeated. He was there to bury his beauty queen.

Alice was sobbing loudly. She seemed on the point of collapse. Micky was weeping too and holding Alice tightly in her arms.

Pam muttered, 'Look at her. The pit-bull dyke. What an actress. What an ocean-going hypocrite.'

A woman in front of us told her to shush.

We brought nothing into this world and it is certain we can carry nothing out. The Lord gave and the Lord hath taken away. Blessed be the name of the Lord.

The priest told us that we were gathered together to remember before God our dear departed sister Olive.

Pam whispered, 'Olive. Ah well. Forty quid to my husband.'

'Bob took part in the sweepstake?'

'The man throws his money around.'

She passed me a tissue and a tube of mints.

James Buxton read Matthew 5, the Beatitudes. Then Alice struggled to her feet to give the eulogy. Pam groaned. Mrs

Buxton didn't have a long CV. She'd gone from copy typist and Miss Cannock Chase to doctor's wife and then mother. The best mother in the world, Alice said. Always kind and patient. Always there with good advice.

'Which you repeatedly ignored,' muttered Pam.

She got shushed again.

Chloe waved to me on her way out. By the time Pam and I had struggled through the crush of people, she'd gone. I phoned her. She said she was on her way to Dee's.

'Did you even speak to Trevor?'

'Yes. I gave him a big hug and told him to come and visit us.'

'Good. Still, you might have waited for me.'

'Why? I wanted to get ahead of the traffic. Anyway, you and Fat Girl will be going back for the sherry and peanuts.'

I grabbed a minute with Trevor.

'Ah young Talbot,' he said. 'Am I glad to see you. Tea and cake at my place? There'll be something stronger as well.'

I said, 'Counter-offer. Lounge bar of the Black Bear tomorrow? One o'clock?'

'Done,' he said. 'Now bugger off. I think Dr Vincent would like a word with you.'

Helen, almost unrecognisable Helen, was waiting for me.

'Hello Dan,' she said. 'Doesn't your old boss get a kiss?'

Was it just Helen who'd changed? She said I had. That I'd grown up. A bit patronising of her but maybe she was right. She didn't make me nervous anymore. I asked after her husband. I knew his rehab hadn't gone brilliantly.

'Paraplegic, doubly incontinent, wishes he was dead. Apart from that, he's fine.'

I didn't know what to say.

She said, 'Don't look so shocked, Dan. Cliff and I never had the best of marriages. You know that. And look at us. I can hardly divorce him now, can I? We're trapped with each other.'

I could have felt sorry for her, but her timing was so off. We were there because of Trevor's loss and she hadn't said a word about that. It was all about her.

Pam and I set off for Himley Green.

'With a brief stop in Kingswinford to buy bog roll and alcohol. So, it was Olive. Now we know. Bit of an anti-climax really. Like finding out who dunnit. Well, I shall always think of her as Mrs Buxton.'

Chapter 10

Pam and Bob Parker have two daughters, Melissa and Hannah, both teenagers, silent, spotty, one anorexic, one bulimic. They also have Bob's father living with them. Bob Senior, afflicted by dementia and prone to wander, but benign.

Pam said, 'I'm putting you up in the loft conversion. The stairs are too steep for him so you should be safe from him up there.'

Bob Senior sometimes goes walkabout in the night and climbs into bed with Pam and Bob.

'What do you do?'

'I get up and leave him there. Let him snuggle up to Bob.'

'He doesn't try it with your girls?'

'No, pet. He may be demented but he's not lost all power of discrimination. Nobody in their right mind would go into the girls' rooms without full hazmat gear. What did Helen have to say for herself?'

'Just a little rant about her ruined life. She's so bitter.'

'Oh yes.'

'She says Cliff wishes he hadn't survived the stroke.'

'Poor sod. He's lost his main interest in life: afternoon sex with impressionable young bits of stuff. And of course, they've taken quite a hit financially. I feel sorry for both of them, Dan, but I've reached the point where I avoid Helen. All that self-pity gets boring. Tell me about your new life.'

'Tell me about Weirdo Pants first.'

'What?'

'The day I left the surgery sign said Weirdo Pants.'

'Oh no,' she said. 'The latest is Toe Warts. Do keep up.'

'How's Amber Evans?'

'I haven't seen her recently. Maybe she's lost her lust for per vag exams now you're no longer with us. Think about it. We've got Harold Boddy, who is no woman's sexual fantasy, not even Amber's, and we've got Trevor, who's older than Moses.'

'What about Dawn Beamish? Did she ever conceive?'

'No, she did not. So, God is good.'

'That was the name of her boyfriend. Godwin. She called him God.'

'You're right. I'd forgotten that. So, God Almighty, in his wisdom, made sure that God the Toyboy's Fed-Exed jizz didn't arrive in time to be viable.'

Hannah and Melissa didn't join us for dinner. They appeared briefly, in the kitchen, both in over-sized sweaters, hands tucked inside the dangling sleeves. One retrieved a tub of carrot sticks from the fridge, the other took a tub of ice cream from the freezer. Bob Senior wanted cornflakes in front of the telly. Bob Junior came in late from doing two emergency extractions.

'Friday afternoon,' he said. 'Toothache always feels worse when it's almost weekend.'

He fell asleep after dinner. His father was already unconscious. They were in matching armchairs, mouths wide open, both gently snoring.

'Look at them,' says Pam. 'Like bookends. Bless.'

I was telling her about some of my new patients. Skylar Jarman interested her. A 14-year-old year old with classic UTI symptoms but no detectable infection.

'Blood in her urine though.'

'Only a trace.'

'And she's not having sex?'

'Her mother says not.'

'Her mother? Like she'd know. What was your instinct?'

'The girl seems immature.'

'Sometimes they are, but they'll do things to impress the boys, or to trade.'

'Trade?'

'You know? Pills, for a blowjob? It's a currency. Like bitcoin. What's your drug scene like?'

'We've got two methadone centres nearby.'

'No, I mean party drugs. The kind of stuff a kid like that might get her mitts on?'

'I don't know. Colwyn Bay's full of old people. The Zimmer frame shuffle to the post office on pension day. I don't think there's a teenage drug scene.'

Pam said, 'Really, Dan? You amaze me. Everywhere has a teenage drug scene. Top drawer schools, nice middle-class families, villages with roses round the cottage doors.'

She fetched her laptop, searched for something, then slid it across to me.

Ketamine-associated urinary tract dysfunction.

Ketamine is an anaesthetic and a sedative. I'd seen it used in A&E when someone was in traumatic shock and I'd read of people taking it recreationally, but not as a major cause for concern, not readily available, like Ecstasy.

According the article, ketamine abuse could lead to the bladder shrinking and becoming fibrotic. It presents like cystitis, but there's no sign of infection. Worse still, the damage can be irreversible. If this was what was wrong with Skylar, she could be facing life-changing consequences.

Pam called upstairs.

'Hannah.'

Silence.

'Hannah!'

'What?'

'Would you come down here for a minute?'

'What for?'

'We need to pick your brain.'

Hannah came halfway down the stairs and sat.

'Tell us about ketamine.'

'What?'

Ketamine. What do they call it? Kit-Kat?'

Hannah laughed.

'That's a biscuit, Mum. You mean Kitty.'

'Well excuse me. So, is Kitty around, is it generally available?'

'Yes.'

'See, Dan? No expense was spared in educating my daughter. She knows what's what. Is it easy to get?'

Hannah shrugged.

'Is it expensive?'

'No.'

'How much, roughly?'

'I've never bought any.'

'Good. But is it affordable for kids?'

'Probably like, £2 for a bump. Might be less for a wrap. I don't know.'

She got to her feet, ready to retreat to her bedroom.

'Hold on,' says Pam. 'You're talking to the uninitiated here. What's the difference between a bump and a wrap?'

'A bump's when you snort it. A wrap's in paper. Like a roll-up paper. You swallow it. Can I go now?'

Pam said, 'You can. Thank you very much, darling.'

The two Bobs had woken up. Bob Senior was looking for somewhere to pee and already had his tackle out. Bob Junior was topping up his wine glass.

He said, 'Was that Hannah? What are we thanking her for?'

'Information. Depressing information from the streetwise. Dan, are you sure you want to have children?'

It did make you think. I mean, I could kind of imagine myself with a smiley little one, but a teenager? How would I cope with a Hannah or a Melissa? Sitting in her room, bingeing on ice cream then throwing up. Or with a boy like Helen Vincent's Miles? Drifting and dangerous when wired.

All this was forgotten the next morning when I delivered the pink fluffy rabbit to Margaret Mariam Vaz and was allowed to hold her for five minutes. Teresa's a very relaxed mother. Vaz is a fusspot father. Was she warm enough? Why did she get hiccups so often? Support her head, support her head!

Margaret has Vaz's colouring and Teresa's features and she gripped my thumb with her tiny fingers. The Vazes were the very picture of a happy family. A few years of that, and then what? Would she grow into a nightmare teenager? It was hard to imagine. Would she be kind to her parents in their old age? Look at Trevor. He had a son and a daughter and yet there he was, the day after his wife's funeral, sitting alone in the pub. James and his girlfriend had returned to London. Alice and Micky had gone back to Wales.

'It's coming up to the start of their busy season,' he said. They have a kind of gift shop in Bettws-y-Coed.

'Anyway, I don't want people fussing around me, putting me on suicide watch.'

'Are you working?'

'Back on Monday. I've promised the trainee I'll squire her around the twilight facilities. Tell me about Parry, Hughes and Talbot. Have you made your mark yet?'

'You'd have to ask Parry and Hughes about that. As far as I know I haven't dropped any clangers. They kind of leave me to my own devices.'

'That's a good sign.'

'I was shocked to see Helen yesterday.'

'You mean her hair?'

'I mean everything. It's like she's aged ten years in a few months.'

'That's what misery can do to you. She should have divorced Clifford years ago. Now you're going to ask me what my plans are.'

'I was wondering, but I wasn't going to ask.'

'Everybody and their Uncle Bill is telling me I can't stay in the house by myself. I don't see why not.'

'It is a big house.'

'We've got a cleaning lady. Had her for years.'

'Can you cook?'

'I can boil an egg. I can make Beans On. It was nice of Chloe to come to the funeral. What's she up to today?'

'Seeing old friends. She still comes back to Birmingham a lot.'

'Not settled in your new place?'

'She hasn't tried. She hasn't even spoken to our neighbours. How long were you and Mrs Buxton married?'

'Nearly 45 years. I still expect her to be there, you know? When I wake up.'

'Of course you do. I hope you'll come and visit us. We've got stacks of room.'

'Thank you. Chloe said the very same thing. Now allow me to regale you with titbits from the coal face at Tipton Road West. Guess who's getting married? Maybe.'

'A patient?'

'A colleague.'

'Has to be Nurse Linda then. It can't be Mary.'

'Don't you be so sure. Mary might make a late surge. All those years boxed in on the rail. Now her sister's gone and her old mum's shunted into care, she might surprise us all. But no, you're right, it's Linda. She met him on this Internet business.'

'But she has met him in person?'

'Oh yes. He drove all the way from Ipswich. The wedding talk seems a bit premature to me, but what do I know?'

Nurse Linda had always seemed to have a busy love life but nothing that lasted. It'd be nice if she'd found someone.

'In other news today, guess who sent me a lavish condolences card, probably liberated from Karim's Kabin?'

'Kyle Bibby?'

'Bullseye. And guess who, and I doubt you'll get this, has gone into wholesale, back-of-a-lorry fragrance distribution and gave me a bottle of Jimmy Choo Man cologne?'

'Female?'

'Male.'

'But not Kyle?'

'Not Kyle. Stinky Hodge. A man impervious to irony. And immune to his own body odour.'

'Any news of Ron Jarrold?'

'He's still with us. Palliative care only. Perhaps I could come and see you at Easter. I told Alice I'd go and stay with them. Thought I'd better make an effort. I could drive over to see you one evening. I don't think it's far.'

'About twenty miles. How did you feel about Micky coming to the funeral?'

'Look, I didn't like it, but Alice appears to need her, so what can you do?'

'I have a better idea. Why don't you stay with us and drive over to call on them? That way you can control how much time you spend with them.'

'I don't know. They might be glad of a hand in the shop. They get busy on Bank Holidays.'

'Trevor Buxton selling love spoons and postcards of Snowdonia?'

He laughed.

'Twenty miles?' he said. 'Is that all? Well I might just take you up on that.'

And that was how it came about that on the way back to Rhos I bought a king-size, a standard double and two sets of bunk beds for delivery the following week and when Chloe got home, late on Sunday, she said, 'Are you out of your tiny mind? What, are we running a hotel now? The Packwoods *and* Trevor?'

'Why not?'

'My pregnant sister, her odious husband and three brats plus a chronically ill and recently bereaved senior. Really, Dan? Seriously?'

'Henry isn't odious. He's meek and mild. His only crime was to call you a spoiled child, when in fact you were behaving like one. Anyway, he might not come. And as for Trevor, company is what he needs. He might enjoy being around Flo's children. What did you girls do all weekend?'

'Shopping. Got slightly wasted on tequila on Saturday night.'

'Do you know anything about ketamine?'

'Obviously. It's an anaesthetic. Some surgeons use it combined with propofol in coronary bypass surgery. It's supposed to boost cardiac output, but the jury's still out. And I've seen it used on a kid in A&E while they manipulated a dislocated shoulder. That worked a treat. Eyes open but no-one home.'

'What about recreational?'

'What about it?'

'I think we might have a case of ketamine-related bladder damage. A teenage girl. She doesn't look like she does drugs but these days, how can you tell? You don't look like a woman who does drugs.'

'I don't.'

'No spliffs this weekend?'

'Spliffs don't count.'

'Actually, they do. And what about those legal highs Dee dishes out? Bounce, wasn't that one?'

'It's legal, officer. Like it says on the tin.'

'Just because it's legal doesn't mean it's safe. What's in those things? Do you have any idea?'

'I'm not going to be interrogated.'

'How can we even think of trying to get pregnant when you're drinking so much and taking God knows what?'

'Oh, not that again,' she said. 'So, telling me about your ketamine girl was just a ruse to talk about babies. I knew you'd get all clucky if you went to see the Vaz kid. I'm going to bed.

And I hope Trevor knows he's not allowed to smoke in the house.'

'He can smoke in the garden. And by the way, I also ordered a slide, a climbing frame and a swing.'

'You did not.'

'No. But I still might.'

Chapter 11

I started the week knowing I had a couple of diplomatic hurdles to clear. How to free Deb Rowlands of her mother's apron strings. And what to do about Skylar Jarman. I thought a conversation with a urologist might be in order before I saw the Jarmans again. They were booked in for Tuesday afternoon.

Deb Rowlands came in on Monday, very anxious about her mother being cut out of the loop.

She said, 'She'll go spare.'

I said, 'Mums never stop worrying, doesn't matter how old we get. But you're a grown woman and it's your health we're talking about. Only you can tell me how you're feeling.'

'I'm not too bad. It comes and goes.'

'Do you think it gets worse if you're feeling stressed?'

'I'm always stressed.'

'Are you? What can we do about that?'

'Nothing. It's just the way I am.'

'Have you tried relaxation classes? Or meditation?'

'Is that the same as yoga?'

'Not exactly.'

'Because I'm not doing yoga. See, we're chapel and our minister doesn't hold with it.'

I told Deb I wanted her to start keeping a diary of her symptoms.

'What, you mean write it down?'

'Yes. The joint pain, the rash, the tiredness, the forgetfulness.'

'I don't forget. Things just get muddled up.'

'Okay. Write that down too.'

'So what's wrong with me?'

'I can't be sure, but I think you have a condition called lupus. Time will tell.'

'Is it bad?'

'It may be something you have to learn to live with. Lupus is one of those things that comes and goes. If it is lupus there are some things you can do to help yourself and one of them is to avoid stress or at least learn how to cope with it. That's why I mentioned relaxation techniques.'

'But not yoga.'

'But not yoga. The rash you get on your face is probably made worse by sunlight, so try to stay out of the sun.'

'What about my knees? Do I need replacements?'

'No. Try to lose a bit of weight and take ibuprofen when you need to. If you find you're taking it every day come back to see me and I'll give you something to stop it damaging your stomach.'

'Is that all?'

'For the time being. We need to watch and wait.'

'Don't I get a prescription?'

'Not yet. Once we know for sure what we're dealing we can review the situation.'

She looked disappointed.

I said, 'Deb, we don't want you rattling with a load of pills if they're not necessary. Let's work on this together. Keep that diary, lose a few pounds and get yourself a sun hat. Not much call for them in Colwyn Bay, but see if you can find one.'

That made her smile.

The duty urologist I spoke to said no, they hadn't seen any cases of ketamine-related damage but yes, he had heard of it and I should refer Skylar for an ultrasound of her bladder. Mrs Jarman wasn't happy.

'You mean go all the way to Bangor? How am I supposed to get her there?'

I knew it only took about twenty minutes by train.

She said, 'And then there's a bus ride. It's too far for me to walk from the station. Can't you just give her antibiotics?'

'But Skylar doesn't have an infection. As I already explained.'

Skylar herself hadn't said a word. Was this a kid who went to parties and bought drugs? She seemed so puppyish, flopped in a chair in her pink sweatshirt with a unicorn on the front.

I said, 'Skylar, has anyone ever given you pills or stuff to sniff? Say, at the park, or at a party?'

Mrs Jarman rolled her eyes. Skylar studied her boots. I asked her if she knew what Kitty was. She shrugged.

Her mum said, 'Used to have a Hello Kitty doll's house, didn't you, Sky?'

I said, 'How about Vitamin K? Have you ever been offered that?'

'Might of,' says Skylar.

'Was it a powder?'

Silence.

'Was it a little ball that you had to swallow?'

She nodded.

I asked her how Vitamin K had made her feel.

'Chill.'

'And how often have you taken it, would you say?'

'Can't remember.'

That wiped the silly smile off Mrs Jarman's face.

She said, 'Sky! What have you been doing, girl?'

'It's just vitamins,' she said.

Just vitamins.

'Here's the thing, Skylar. Ketamine isn't a vitamin. It's a powerful drug that might well have damaged your bladder. Do you understand how serious this is?'

She was red-faced, close to tears. Mrs Jarman was bobbing up and down in her seat. Suddenly she didn't care about the inconvenience of getting to an ultrasound appointment. How soon could Skylar be seen?

She said, 'We'll go private, if we have to. Just as long as we get her sorted.'

I said, 'I'll make it an urgent referral. What's crucial, Skylar, is that you never, ever again, take this so-called Vitamin K. In fact, don't take anything people offer you. You don't know what's in it and neither do the people selling it to you.'

'Selling it?' says her mum. 'Where did you get money for drugs?'

Skylar said it only cost £2 or even £1 if she got it from friends.

I said, 'They're not your friends. Friends don't sell you stuff that might make you ill or kill you.'

Mrs Jarman said, 'Are you listening, Sky? To what the doctor said?'

Now my advice was worth listening to, even if it meant catching a train to Bangor. Now I was her ally, not an annoying stickler who refused to prescribe antibiotics. We were in this together.

'Blinking kids,' she said. 'You can't turn your back for a minute.'

As it turned out, events overtook my urgent referral. That night Skylar began screaming in pain and passed visible blood in her urine. Instead of a train ride she went to Ysbyty Gwynedd in an ambulance and was admitted with a severe case of ulcerative cystitis, though the first I knew of it was a week later when Delyth waved a hospital letter under my nose.

'It's about the Jarman girl's bladder,' she said. 'I could have told you when she came in that she was on something. I've got a nose for it.'

I said, 'Delyth, whatever happened to patient confidentiality?'

'What's your problem?' she said. 'There's nobody in the waiting room yet.'

It wasn't the only time Delyth was too free with her opinions that day.

Mid-afternoon Iestyn asked me to look at one of his patients. I was a bit taken aback. Iestyn has a few years more experience than me. He said he was dog-tired, up and down all night, if it wasn't the baby crying it was the twins, and he'd welcome a second opinion.

Ffion was a walk-in. She worked in an office nearby and when she'd felt unwell a friend had walked her round to us. Delyth had diagnosed a panic attack and kept them sitting in the waiting room for more than an hour. Ffion's main symptom was breathlessness. It had come on suddenly. She also had slight pain on the right side of her chest. Nothing too bad, she said.

Her blood pressure was normal and her breath sounds were clear but her heart rate was fast and her oxygen saturation was down to 90 percent. Had she been feeling anxious? I so wanted her to say no. I so wanted to teach Delyth a lesson.

'Well a bit,' says Ffion. 'There's a rumour some of us are going to be made redundant.'

Maybe it had been a panic attack. But that should have passed. There was no significant history. A fit, healthy 32-year-old. Non-smoker. Taking oral contraception, plus echinacea because a friend had recommended it against colds.

Iestyn had checked her calves for signs of a DVT. Nothing. And yet. She was clammy to the touch and even after several whiffs of oxygen the pulse oximeter still registered 90 percent. Was it possible we were looking at a pulmonary embolism? My instinct was that we should get her to hospital.

Iestyn said, 'Possible PE?'

'Yes. Let's err on the side of caution.'

I ran down to Delyth, told her to request an emergency ambulance and in the short time I was gone the borders of Ffion's lips had turned undeniably blue and she'd picked up on Iestyn's anxiety.

She said, 'Am I going to die?'

I assured her she wasn't. It's what you do, with your fingers crossed.

I assumed the friend would go with her in the ambulance, but she said she wasn't actually a friend, they just happened to be working in neighbouring cubicles, and anyway, she really needed to get back to work. Was there someone we could call? Husband, maybe?

'Partner,' Ffion whispered. 'But don't phone him. He hates hospitals.'

Off she went with just a paramedic for company, not a bad option when you might have a life-threatening condition.

Iestyn said, 'Thanks, Dan. I was pretty sure what it was but, you know. Been at home too long. I haven't quite got my mo-jo back.'

I said, 'I dread situations like that. And not knowing the woman made it worse. No background. If I'd wanted to make life-or-death judgments, I'd have gone into emergency medicine. Now the question is, what do we do about Delyth?'

'How do you mean?'

'The length of time she kept your woman waiting. If it is a PE, the delay could have been fatal.'

'Delyth wasn't to know that. She's only a receptionist.'

'That's my point. She decided it was a panic attack and not urgent. We ought to have some ground rules.'

'You'd have to talk to David about that.'

I like Iestyn, but it was clear he wasn't a man who'd ever take the initiative. He wants a quiet working life, eight surgeries a week and no dramas. Perhaps Aggie and three small children are as much as he can manage.

David had gone home early, feeling fluey, according to Bethan.

I had a word with Delyth before she left.

I said, 'When someone walks in off the street and they're having a problem breathing, please don't just stick them in the waiting room. Call up to one of us. Leave it to a doctor to do the triage.'

'Trouble breathing?'

'Yes.'

'Including asthma?'

'Yes.'

'What about a headache?'

'What about it?'

'If they come in with a headache. You don't realise. I have to deal with all sorts.'

I said, 'You do. That's why I'm going to talk to Dr Parry and we'll draw up a list of guidelines for you. But for now, if in doubt, ask one of the doctors to come down.'

She said she'd never needed guidelines before. She had her defiant face on.

'Anything else? I've got a bus to catch.'

'One thing. Where's the best place to buy sheets and pillowcases?'

'Clare's in Llandudno.'

She didn't say goodnight. She was in a huff with me, but as Pam Parker had often reminded me, I wasn't there to be loved, not by patients and certainly not by a headstrong receptionist. I wasn't the tentative trainee anymore either. I was the real deal, supposed to be, and if I thought something needed saying, I should speak up.

The news on Wednesday was that Iestyn's walk-in had indeed had a pulmonary embolism. Two break-off clots in her lung and a big bad boy in the femoral vein, in her groin. And David Parry hadn't gone down with 'flu. He was at his desk, as usual. I caught him before I went for my afternoon off.

'We had a lucky escape yesterday. A walk-in with what turned out to be a PE. Delyth had decided it was a panic attack and kept her waiting an hour.'

He looked at me over his glasses.

'I know she sees herself as our gate-keeper. She needs some clear guidelines.'

'Okay.'

'We can sugar-coat it. Call it training. Career development. I just don't want her making clinical decisions for me.'

'Sure. Go for it. But don't call it career-development. She'll expect a pay rise.'

There was a commotion downstairs and children's voices. Aggie had come, as promised, to show off the new arrival. On the landing I met Harry Shepherd carrying a very young baby.

'Dan,' she said, 'look what I found.'

Haf was asleep. She had a pale, composed little face. Harry took off her bonnet and examined her wisps of hair.

She said, 'I see traces of Hughes ginger. Much more than the boys had at this age. Do you want a go, Dan?'

She handed Haf to me. She smelled milky. Haf did, not Harry.

Downstairs Iestyn's boys were out of their stroller and running riot. Harry leaned in close, examining Haf's little fingernails.

'I could just eat her,' she murmured. 'I want one.'

And I, flooded with ridiculous feelings and dangerous fantasies, said, 'There's something I've been meaning to ask you.'

'Is there?' she said and stepped away.

I told her about the possible but far from definite visit of Henry. Was I being a thoughtful host? Not if I'm honest. Henry was my Trojan horse.

'My brother-in-law's a pig farmer but he's thinking of trying a few sheep. He might be visiting us at Easter and I thought he'd be interested to see Maes Glas.'

'Sure,' she said. 'Bring him up.'

'You'll be there?'

'I will.'

'Only I wouldn't want to turn up if you weren't around. Your family might not remember me.'

'Oh, don't worry, they remember you,' she said. 'Now hand back that baby. I want another snuggle before I start work.'

I floated around the homewares department buying sheets and pillows. Easter was taking shape in my mind as a perfect weekend. Our house would be filled with people, the sun would shine, my slow-roasted leg of lamb would fall off the bone.

I drove home on auto-pilot. I smiled like a lovestruck loon at the bed delivery men. And all because I now had a flimsy excuse to see Harry Shepherd out of hours, maybe. Everything hinged on Henry Packwood's pigman.

Chapter 12

I called Flo.

I said, 'I hope you're still coming because I just melted my credit card buying moon and stars duvet covers and chocolate eggs.'

'How super,' she said. 'I must say I'm looking forward to a rest.'

'And Henry? Will he be able to get away?'

'He very much hopes to. The pigman's had bursitis but he's feeling better so one's fingers are crossed.'

I said, 'Tell him I have a visit to a sheep farm lined up for him.'

'Do you? Why?'

'Last summer he was talking about getting some sheep. At the wedding, he was asking my Da about breeds.'

'I see. Well he hasn't taken it any further. In fact, he's been looking into ostriches, for the exotic meats market. But it's terrifically sweet of you to think of him. How's Chlo? She always sounds so cross.'

'Unsettled. She keeps dashing back to see her old friends.'

'Yes, one rather gathered. What must she be spending on petrol?'

Chloe and I were at odds over Henry, of course. She hoped he wouldn't come. I was fervently praying he would. There was also the Trevor factor. If he came, he was guaranteed to bring out the sweeter side in Chloe.

I called him.

He said, 'Of course I'm coming. Why? Have you changed your mind?'

'Quite the opposite. I need you here.'

'Uh-oh,' he said, 'is there trouble at t'mill?'

I laid out the likely scene. Chloe might be sweet and lovely, or she might be quarrelsome. Flo planned on putting her feet up. Poppy, Daisy and Lily would be bouncing off the walls. And Henry, if he came, reserved but amiable, unless really provoked.

Trevor said, 'Sounds like a fairly normal family. It'll be better than bunking down at Alice and Micky's. A couple of hours with the bantam weight bitch will be quite enough for me. And if you're wondering how to break the news that I'm not allowed to smoke, I've already thought about that. Any time I need a cig, I'll go for a little walk. Mustn't corrupt the children.'

'You might have company. Henry enjoys a cigar.'

'Does he? Then here's to Henry. And I'll leave you on Easter Monday, if that's alright. If I don't wear out my welcome before that. There's a nice race card at Bangor-on-Dee. Perfect way to break my journey. There's no sense rushing back to an empty house.'

'How are you doing?'

He said, 'I'm doing all right. The main problem is finding where Mrs Buxton kept things. Where would you look for Sellotape?'

'Kitchen drawer?'

'Nope. In the fuse cabinet, next to the back door. Women are creatures of mystery, Dan.'

On Good Friday we were running a reduced service. A morning surgery only, no Bethan, no Iestyn. Just me and David, and Delyth on the desk. There was still tension between me and Delyth. She'd made a big production over the triage guidelines I gave her. David hadn't even wanted to vet them. If I'd suggested piping heavy metal into the waiting room and getting Bethan to dress up as Minnie Mouse, I think he'd have agreed.

'Whatever you think,' he'd said.

It was very simple. Any walk-in with 1) sudden, severe pain, 2) difficulty breathing or 3) confusion, prioritise them. Delyth had to have the last word.

She said, 'Half the people we get in here are confused.'

I said, 'You know perfectly well what we mean.'

She narrowed her eyes at me, but she accepted an Easter egg with good grace. It was the one I'd bought for Chloe, only Chloe had announced she was starting a diet and I'd promised to support her in her barmy decision to give up chocolate the very weekend the house would be full of it.

The last patient on my list was Philip Jakes. He had mouth ulcers. How long had he had them? Weeks, he said. As fast as one died down, another one popped up. Was he under stress?

'I don't know,' he said, as though I'd asked him a quiz question.

I looked in his mouth. He certainly had some livid ulcers. Also sub-standard oral hygiene. Philip takes nicorandil for his angina. He's on a low dose but it is a drug that can cause mouth ulcers. I suggested trying over- the-counter benzoin pastilles, and we'd review the situation in a couple of weeks.

He said, 'What, you mean, like buy them?'

I said, 'They're not expensive. Boots sell them. And get yourself a softer toothbrush too. No sense torturing yourself. You should think of seeing a dentist too.'

'Dentist?' he said. 'I don't know about that. They're a price.'

I was tidying my desk, ready to leave when Delyth bellowed up the stairs, 'Code 3. Dr Talbot to Reception, please.'

'Code 3?'

'Confusion. It's on that list you gave me. Not the kind of thing I can deal with.'

Leon Caddick was hunched over the counter, scratching his greasy head. He didn't have an appointment. He said he'd come over very light-headed walking on Woodland Road and he couldn't remember where he'd left the shopping bag with his prescription refills in it. I took him into the waiting room. What particular drug cocktail had he taken that morning?

'The usual.'

So, Prozac, Ritalin and temazepam. Anything else at all? Any alcohol?

'Just a can of Frosty Jack's.'

Leon's idea of breakfast.

His breathing and pulse were normal and so were his pupils. He wasn't drowsy, neither did he seem wired.

He said, 'So can I get another prescription?'

Leon was trying the old, last-minute, anything to get rid of him so I can go home ploy.

I said, 'No, you can't. You need to clear your head and remember where you left that shopping bag. Those drugs could be dangerous if they fell into the wrong hands. What if a young child found them and thought they were sweets? In fact, we should call the police. I'll do it now.'

116

'No, you're alright,' he said. 'No need to bother the plod. It's coming back to me now. I think I remember what I done with it.'

'And what's that?'

'I think I might have gave it to Kiz to take home.'

'Who's Kiz?'

'Sister.'

'Call her. Because if she doesn't have that bag of pills, you know what I have to do.'

Credit to him, he put on quite a performance with that phone call.

I said, 'Leon, you've missed your way in life. You should be an actor. You ought to be on the telly.'

He grinned. I locked the door behind him. We were done till Tuesday. Delyth could have left too but she'd waited, so she could deliver a parting shot.

'Sorry about that, Dr Talbot,' she said. 'But it'd be more than my job's worth to ignore the guidelines.'

There was a very muddy hatchback parked on our drive. The Packwoods had arrived. A smoke alarm was screeching and in the kitchen Flo and her three girls were sitting in a blue haze.

Daisy said, 'Aunt Chlo's burning our sausages.'

I hadn't seen the children since our wedding. Poppy had changed the most. Ten, going on eleven, she was pre-pubescent. Lily clamped herself to my leg.

She said, 'I got car-sick, but not in the car. I kept it in till we stopped and did it in a ditch. It was all my breakfast and it was pink because I had blueberries with my porridge.'

Flo said, 'Too much information, Lils. Anyway, you were jolly brave.'

No sign of Henry.

Flo said, 'He's following. He should be here by cork-pop. I love your house, Dan. Quite super. And you got bunk beds for the girls. So sweet of you.'

Poppy said she was too old to share a room with her sisters. Chloe called her an ungrateful wretch.

Lily said, 'Aunt Chlo's in a grump. When can we go to the beach?'

'After you've eaten your crispy sausages,' says Flo.

It had started to rain but the Packwoods don't allow the weather to change their plans. They bring their wellies everywhere. Even, as I recalled, to an elegant summer wedding.

Chloe said, 'Count me out. I don't want my hair ruined. Dan'll go with you. He's become a fresh air fiend. Country walks, clambering around castle ruins. And did he tell you about lambing? Dr Dan wading around in sheep gubbins. This is how he spends his weekends if I'm not here.'

'Well then,' said Flo, very evenly, 'if you don't approve perhaps you should stop abandoning him.'

The rain stopped and the sun came out just as we reached the Crazy Golf. Flo's a brisk walker. Not at all the waddling walrus Chloe had predicted.

She said, 'Why must she be so disagreeable? She's cross with me because I haven't broken into the Chummery and stolen any furniture, but honestly, what a madcap idea. Is it about money? Are you short?'

'No, we're not. It's not really about furniture. It's about the Laurence and Jen situation. It all came as a shock to her.'

'I know. Extraordinary. I mean, one never discussed it, but one rather assumed it was common knowledge. Mummy certainly knew.'

'Chloe idolised your father. Now she knows about his girlfriend, she's transferred your mother onto the vacated pedestal, and as Vinnie's no longer with us, she can do no wrong. As far as Chloe's concerned the Chummery is now a shrine to Vinnie and she doesn't want Jen making any changes or getting rid of anything.'

Flo sighed.

She said, 'It's still no reason for her to be permanently cross with me. She's even annoyed with me for having another baby.'

I said, 'That may be my fault. I'd like us to start a family fairly soon, but she feels I'm pressuring her. She hates any mention of babies. I'm going to shut up about it for a while.'

Flo said, 'You never know, when she sees our new arrival it may make her long for a child of her own.'

Yes, I thought. Around the same time pigs are cleared for take-off from Heathrow.

Trevor and Henry arrived together, Trevor in his weekend Jag with the top down, Henry in his RAV-4. They'd noticed each other, driving at a crawl, peering at house names, and stopped to confer. We had tea and cake and the atmosphere in the house lifted immediately. Lily, sitting across the kitchen table from Trevor, despatched the elephant in the room.

She said, 'Your mummy died.'

'My wife,' he said. 'Yes, she did.'

'What was her name?'

'Mrs Buxton.'

'Why did she die?'

'Her heart wore out.'

'My silkie bantam died. A fox killed her. My granny died too. We were driving in her car, just me, not Poppy or Daisy, and it turned completely upside down. Granny said the F word. Then a man pulled us out and we all laughed and went home, but next day Granny died because something inside her got squished.'

Trevor said he was very sorry to hear it.

He and Henry went out to smoke and inspect our garden. I lit a fire in what Flo referred to as the drawing room and prepared a tray of champagne glasses ready for the launching of Pentraeth. It felt like a home now, not just a house. Chloe called me her adorable house-husband. Suddenly she was in a better mood. We slow danced, without music.

'Henry's gained weight.'

'Has he?'

'They should call him Porkwood, not Packwood. He strolled in here, hello Chlo, like we're the best of friends, like nothing ever happened.'

'Because nothing did happen. You were messing people around, wedding called off, wedding back on, then off again. He gave you a piece of his mind. Basically, he told you to pee in the pot or get off it. It was fair comment. Anyway, we did get married and here we are living happily ever after. And Henry's a good bloke. Let it go.'

'You're so sweet. You always think the best of people. I suppose it's because you believe in Jesus and everything. Let's have sex.'

'With a houseful of guests? And children roaming around?'

'That's part of the fun. We can have a quickie in our bathroom.'

'Or how about a not-so-quickie later, in our bedroom, behind a closed door.'

'Spoilsport.'

120

Perhaps I should have humoured her. But I had dinner to prepare. Asparagus to steam. Potatoes to mash for the top of the fish pie.

'Dan Talbot,' she said, 'I hope you're not turning into a boring old married man.'

Chapter 13

I was up early. I wanted to clear up the kitchen and make a feast of a breakfast. The first thing I discovered was that the door to the children's room was open and Daisy was in there alone, bundled up under a duvet but awake. Where were her sisters? She shrugged. One of the mattresses was missing. Was she hungry? Would she like a cup of tea? I had no idea what eight-year-olds drink in the morning. Did we have hot chocolate? Yes, we did.

I found Poppy. She had dragged her mattress into the only bedroom we hadn't got round to tackling, a small, chilly room with Seventies wallpaper and no furniture.

'The bunks not to your liking?'

'Daisy and Lily are too annoying.'

'Where's Lily?'

'Don't know.'

'Would you like hot chocolate?'

'Can I have it in bed?'

'You mean room service?'

'What's that?'

The Packwoods don't pay for hotels. They stay with people.

I paused outside Trevor's door. I could hear a child's voice. I tapped and looked in. Trevor was propped up on pillows looking a bit grey and bristly. Lily was sitting beside him.

She said, 'I'm reading *The Cat in the Hat* to Trevor Buxton.'

I said, 'I see you have company. Do you mind?'

'Not at all.'

'Cup of tea?'

'Two sugars and just waft the milk jug over it.'

Chloe and Flo were the last to appear. The Swift women aren't at their best in the morning. Henry has breakfast down pat. Which daughter insists on putting the milk in the bowl and then the cereal. Which daughter prefers her toast cold and soggy. I grilled the bacon, he fried the eggs. Together we were a dream team.

Chloe had a champagne headache. She said she couldn't eat a thing, but she managed to put away three croissants.

She said, 'Is there a plan for today?'

Daisy and Lily wanted to go back to the Crazy Golf. Trevor said he supposed he'd better drive over to see Alice. He made it sound like an appointment for a rectal examination. Chloe said she felt she should take Poppy clothes shopping.

'Why?' says Flo.

'For a start, where on earth did she get that vile T shirt?'

Flo said it was a perfectly good T shirt. That many of the girls' clothes were hand-me-downs from their Packwood cousins, items that still had years of wear in them.

'But Flo,' says Chloe. 'she looks like an orphan.'

What was an orphan, Lily wanted to know. Poppy said she'd quite like some new clothes as long as they weren't sick-making dresses.

I decided to take charge. As the sky looked overcast but the forecast for the afternoon was promising, we should save the Crazy Golf for later in the day. Those who wanted to shop should shop, Trevor should go to Bettws-y-Coed, Henry and I would drive up to Maes Glas to look at sheep.

Lily said she wanted to look at sheep too and she thought Trevor should come with us because he seemed sad about visiting Betsy. Daisy said she'd rather eat frog spawn than go shopping. So, the party separated for the morning. Chloe, Flo and Poppy went to Llandudno to buy clothes, the rest of us in convoy to Maes Glas with Trevor then continuing on to his daughter's.

He said, 'All right if tag along to the farm? I'm not in any hurry to get to Alice's.'

The sun came out as we turned onto the farm track. Harry's brother Gethin stood and watched us pull into the yard. He must have thought we were dead-enders. Would he remember me? I couldn't read his face.

'Harry's friend,' he said. 'I'll fetch her.'

He disappeared into the house. The sheds and barns were quiet and empty. The lambing season was over. The ewes and their lambs were all out to pasture. Eventually Gethin reappeared.

'She's in the tŷ bach,' he said. 'She'll be out presently.'

In the toilet. Too much information, Gethin.

Harry emerged from the farmhouse. Same old sweater, same tousled hair, same silly flutter in my heart.

'What's this, then?' she said. 'A war-party? Have the English invaded?'

She said she'd take us up to see the flock, as soon as Pete was ready. She said he was just helping her mother worm the

124

cats. Who was Pete? She didn't say, but even before I'd met him, his name hit me like a cold shower.

Harry took Henry off to view the Suffolk rams. Daisy and Lily went with them, escorted by the old sheepdog, Fly.

Trevor said, 'That's the prettiest Harry I ever met.'

He lit a cigarette. There's no traffic noise at Maes Glas. You can hear the birds singing.

'Well, Dan Talbot,' he said, 'this makes a change from the concrete towers of Cherry Tree and Bonnie Brook Glen. No empty cider cans underfoot here. No Bibbys and Dearloves threatening each other with bodily harm. I can see why you like it here. Oh, here comes someone. Could this be Pete?'

Six foot and change, good-looking, pleasant, friendly even. Harry had a boyfriend. Of course, she did. Why would she not?

She had Lily in one hand and Daisy in the other as they returned from the ram pens.

'Introductions,' she said. 'Henry, pig farmer, Daisy, Lily, Dan GP and Dr Buxton, also GP, meet Pete, veterinary surgeon.'

I found myself hating Pete. Not only was he handsome and apparently spending the weekend with Harry, he was also a vet. The kind of man who heals sick kittens and women go mad for. Then a wave of self-loathing overtook me. What was I thinking? I was a married man. I had no business having a crush on anyone. Furthermore, Harry was a single woman with all her options open and zero interest in me. These were the thoughts I beat myself with as we drove up to the pasture. Gethin came with us too.

The earliest lambs didn't look like lambs anymore. Only the later-born ones were gambolling. Trevor asked Harry if she recognised individual ewes.

'Some,' she said. 'Mainly the ones who've given me grief. You know? Trodden on me. Knocked me base over apex. I can harbour a grudge. Geth knows them all. He even knows their voices.'

I longed to be gone, away from the sight of Pete, lolling comfortably over the gate beside Harry. They were an item. The body language was written in capitals. There was more sheep talk. What kind of grazing did Henry have?

'Dampish,' says Henry. 'We're in a valley.'

'Mild winters?'

'Yes. Someone suggested I try Ryelands.'

That had been Da. I remembered distinctly.

Gethin said he wouldn't give Ryelands the time of day.

'They're more of a wool breed and not much good for that either. See, we breed for meat, pure and simple. Beltexes might suit you. They won't win any beauty contests, but the rear end is where the money is.'

Henry asked if they had any experience of breeding for milk.

'Milk?' says Gethin. 'I doubt you can make money at it. You've got the expense of feeding your lambs on formula. Then you've got to milk them twice a day. That's my idea of slavery. And keeping ewes in a shed for months on end, it's not natural. Anyway, who drinks sheep's milk?'

Henry said he was thinking more of cheese or yogurt. That it might make an interesting sideline for Flo.

He said, 'The French seem to do quite well at it.'

Gethin sniffed.

'The French?' he said. 'I'd leave them to it if I was you.'

'Oh I don't know, Geth,' says Pete. 'Nothing wrong with a slice of Roquefort and a nice juicy pear.'

Pete. Gourmet, lover boy, saviour of puppies and kittens.

We parted from Trevor at the main road. He went south to Bettws-y-Coed, we turned north, for home.

Lily said, 'He doesn't want to go. Why doesn't he?'

'Because he has to visit someone he doesn't like very much.'

'But it's his little girl. He told me. Her name's Alice.'

'Yes, but she's grown up, and she lives with a friend who isn't always nice.'

'Like Pandora Sayer-Kerr.'

'Is she in your class at school?'

'Yes. She pinches, but if you tell on her she says you're a fibber.'

Daisy said, 'I'd like to live on that farm.'

Henry said, 'You already live on a farm.'

'But they had sheep. They're snugglier than pigs.'

'I beg to differ,' says Henry. 'A pig can be an affectionate animal.'

I said, 'Flo said you were considering ostriches.'

'I did look into it. It's a growing market. Very tricky though, ostriches. They can get aggressive. And you need really secure fencing. I wouldn't want the Grange looking like some top-secret MOD establishment. I don't know. One does need to diversify. Nice place your friends have. I wasn't altogether clear though, which of the men is Harry married to?'

'Neither. Gethin's her brother.'

'And Pete's her boyfriend,' piped up Lily. 'I liked that Harry lady.'

The shoppers came home laden with bags. Chloe had bought clothes for all three girls, but she'd made quite a project of Poppy. Jeans, sweatshirts, trainers. I thought it was over the top. Poppy's only ten but suddenly she was dressed like a teenager. Chloe said ten practically is a teenager.

She said, 'Flo's clueless about fashion, and so tight with money. How was your day in the country?'

'Excellent. Henry got some advice on sheep and the girls loved it. The air up there is so good.'

'Was your little admirer there?'

'I have no idea who you mean.'

'Yes, you do. Sad Harry. Seeing you must have made her day.'

'She was with her boyfriend.'

'A boyfriend? Really? Well, I suppose there's someone for everyone.'

Trevor got back from Bettws-y-Coed just as we were sitting down to drinks.

'Duty done,' he said. 'Mine's a large one.'

He said it had all gone smoothly. Micky had been cordial. Alice had seemed happy to have him there.

'Of course,' he said, 'with Alice you can never be sure. Happiness is a relative thing. It may just mean she's enjoying a post-punch-up honeymoon. That'd be the usual pattern. I couldn't see any bruises though.'

Flo was shocked.

Henry, who hadn't paid any attention when he was being briefed on Trevor's story, said, 'You mean to say this Micky fellow beats your daughter?'

Chloe said, 'Don't be a duffer, Packwood. Micky's a woman. At least, that's what she claims. They're lesbos.'

'Chlo!' says Flo. 'Pas devant les enfants!'

Which was pure Vinnie. It broke the tension and we all laughed till we cried. Tant pis! Quel dommage! All delivered with a cut glass English accent. It was like my mother-in-law had risen from the dead.

When we turned in for the night Lily was already asleep in Trevor's bed.

Chloe said, 'Do you think it's okay?'

I said, 'The pile of Dr Seuss books might cramp Trevor's style a bit, but it's a big bed.'

'That's not what I mean.'

I understood what she was getting at and though I thought it was ridiculous I knew I'd get no rest till I'd addressed it. I carried Lils back to her bunk and she never even stirred.

'Satisfied?'

'Yes. But don't you think it's weird? Why would a six-year-old choose to sleep with an old man who smells like an ashtray?'

'Maybe because she lacks a grandfather figure? Her Grandpa Packwood's dead and she rarely sees her Grandpoppa Swift these days. And anyway, Jen might draw the line at three in a bed.'

'Cheers. Thanks for bringing her name up.'

'I think Lily's got Trevor figured out. He's a lonely old wheezer who'll never have grandchildren of his own. She's very astute.'

'If you say so. What happens tomorrow?'

'Church, egg hunt, stonking great roast lunch.'

'With your guaranteed crunchy roast potatoes?'

'Obviously.'

Chloe was in a mellow mood. The yoblet nieces were growing up. They were calmer, less like a mob nowadays. At the Chummery something had always got banged into or knocked over, but maybe that was because of all the little side tables with photo frames and china bits and pieces that seemed to breed and multiply between our visits.

She'd enjoyed buying stuff for Poppy, there had been very little bickering with Flo and though she was barely speaking to Henry, he appeared not to notice. I felt she was even warming to Rhos and our lovely house. If I hadn't been required to kiss bloody Eeyore before qualifying for a spot of conjugals, it would have been a pretty good end to a mixed day. The Day of Pete.

On Sunday afternoon, Henry headed home, to relieve his pigman, and everyone else slumped into a chocolate coma. Trevor and I went for walk along the seafront.

He said, 'It's been a cracking weekend.'

'I hope you'll come again. We're handy for your Alice's.'

'You are. But I don't imagine I'll be going back.'

'I thought it went okay yesterday?'

'It did. It was a bit tense because I know what goes on and Micky knows I know. That's the trouble. You can't un-know stuff. But I think I caught them mid-cycle.'

'What does that mean?'

'There's a pattern. Things blow up every six weeks or so. It used to be three or four times a year. I think it's more frequent now. There's a big barney about something, fists fly, then it's flowers and scented candles and a few weeks of calm. I got the feeling that's where they are now. But I can't be doing with it, Dan. I used to make an effort, for Mrs Buxton's sake, but now she's gone I can't be arsed. Alice knows she has a place to run to. It's up to her.'

We sat on a bench.

He said, 'Cheer up, lad. Look at all this. Sea in front of you, mountains behind you. Didn't you do well?'

I tried to explain to him why I was feeling a bit down. All those people I knew with sweet little babies and kids who say funny things, and then they grow up and it all gets complicated. Skylar Jarman, half child, half woman, and her health very likely wrecked. Pam Parker's girls hiding in their bedrooms, logging on to anorexia websites. Even Poppy, only ten, was on the brink. Disdainful of her parents and bored with her sisters.

I said, 'Sometimes I do wonder, about having children. They're not cute for long.'

'True. You have to think of them as a long-term investment. Young Lily's a caution.'

'She wants to adopt you.'

'So she told me. She said I can have her room and she'll sleep in their tree-house. They're a nice family. Not suspiciously perfect and just enough grit in the shell to make them interesting. Correct me if I'm wrong, but I get the feeling Chloe's not quite ready for motherhood.'

'That's what she says. She's a much cleverer doctor than I'll ever be, but sometimes she's still like a child herself.'

I told him about Eeyore. He chuckled.

Then he said, 'It may just be a matter of time. Women sometimes suddenly get broody for no accountable reason. On the other hand…'

'What?'

'Nothing. Mind if I smoke?'

He took his time, tapping the end of his cigarette on the box like I remember my grandad doing, sheltering the lighter flame inside his jacket, savouring the first long drag.

'As I recall,' he said, 'you had more than your share of ups and downs when you were courting.'

Courting. It's a word my Nan uses.

'You've had a lot going on. You both had big exams. She got her head turned a couple of times. There was all that drama

131

when her brother got nicked. And in the middle of it all, there was the wedding that nearly didn't happen.'

'What are you saying?'

'What am I saying? That maybe you've been too busy to get to know each other. Maybe you haven't put in the hard yards yet.'

'I think I have. Am doing.'

'Well that's the other thing. Maybe you have but she hasn't.'

'Because she can't be bothered?'

'That's not for me to say. I like Chloe. She's a dear girl, always sweet and kind to me. But if she's not right for you, Dan, have the balls to get out of it before you have kids.'

I opened up to him, a little. I named no names, but I admitted I was feeling ambivalent.

'Yes,' he said. 'That's what I thought.'

'How come you're so wise?'

He said, 'It's not wisdom. It's just years of reading between the lines. Isn't that what we're supposed to do in general practice? We get ten minutes to listen and try to join a few dots. Ten minutes to decide whether to send them to Boots or pass them along to one of those clever blighters who made consultant. You get better at it, over the years. Not that you always get it right, mind. Oh, and by the way, did I tell you the latest on Ron Jarrold?'

'Dead?'

'Last week. He had hospice care at home.'

'Well that's something. They'll have kept him comfortable. Poor Ron. I couldn't stand him when I first met him. He was in the Patient Participation Group and he always took charge. It was supposed to be a forum, but Ron treated it like his own little committee.'

'I know. Why do you think I got you to go in my place? And now his wife's joined it. Freda. Been on Google Freda. She stepped into Ron's shoes months ago. Although recently she's probably been too busy teaching the palliative care nurse her job.'

I was sad to hear about Ron, though it was no surprise. He'd delayed coming in to see me about his bad back and when we found his cancer it had been well advanced. Ron, the officious little cock of the walk, cut down to size by pain and fear.

'Anyway,' says Trevor. 'On that cheery note, shall we be getting back? Lily Packwood still has two library books she hasn't read to me.

Chapter 14

Skylar Jarman's mother wasn't happy. The urologist had pulled no punches about the seriousness of Skylar's condition and Mrs Jarman had come to take it out on me.

She said, 'They're making her out to be a druggie. How can she be? She's only fourteen.'

I tried to be the calm and steady voice of reason. Skylar had experimented with a powerful drug, it had caused her actual physical harm and now the hospital team were doing everything they could to help her. They'd put her on ibuprofen, to reduce the inflammation. The next step would be to treat her with Cystistat, to coat the lining of her bladder and allow it time to heal, but everything depended on her never again using ketamine and it still might not be the end of the story. We could well be talking about bladder reconstruction.

Mrs Jarman said, 'She only tried it once.'

I said, 'Trying it once wouldn't have done so much damage. If I were you, I'd be trying to find out who sold Skylar the ketamine.'

'She can't remember.'

That was possibly true. I pressed on.

'Another point is that ketamine's what they call a rape drug. Once a girl's under the influence she doesn't know what she's doing. Skylar could easily have been raped and not even remember it. I think we should just be thankful she's not pregnant on top of everything else.'

'They ought to do something about it,' she said.

'Who? What?'

'About all these drugs. You never see a copper on the street. They ought to clamp down on it.'

The magic 'they.' Who were 'they' exactly?

I said, 'Easier said than done. It'd have to be a community effort. And it'd have to start with people like you. Parents.'

She got up to leave. I'd given her no joy.

'I can tell you haven't got kids,' she said.

I was glad to see the back of her. Glad to see Alun Husbands, who only had ringworm and politely and pleasantly accepted my advice to treat it with an anti-fungal he could buy over the counter and save queueing to get a prescription dispensed.

At lunchtime, remembering Pam Parker's advice, I went out and bought an espresso machine.

Delyth said, 'And where's that going?'

At the meddygfa we didn't exactly have a kitchen. It was more like a cupboard with a kettle.

I said, 'To be decided.'

I was poking around, opening doors on rooms full of junk, when Aggie Hughes arrived. She had the baby in a papoose.

'Danek,' she said, 'what you are doing?'

'We need a place we can hang out, have a cup of coffee, chat between surgeries.'

'Yes!' she said. 'Good plan. Chatting is nice.'

'There's all this space going to waste. And when you come back to work, you'll need an office.'

'I have office.'

'No, that's mine now.'

She pouted.

I said, 'Aggie, I'm here full-time. You're not. And I'm not having my desk moved by you every Wednesday afternoon.'

'We can toss coin.'

She lost the toss. I showed her a room filled with old furniture. The window needed cleaning but there was a view of trees and chimney pots. It would make a perfectly good consulting room. I could see the wheels turning.

She hollered, 'David! Come see. I have great idea.'

He emerged from his room looking like we'd woken him. Aggie and what she'd decided was *her* great idea, hit him like a tsunami.

'I will have this room. It will be my clinic. We must get big skip, throw away these rubbishes. Paint walls. Iestyn can do this. No, better I do it. Also, we must make proper kitchen. Danek has bought super coffee machine. What is in these boxes?'

David had no idea. He opened one. An old autoclave, some net curtains. He said he'd need to sort through the others. They couldn't just be thrown away.

'Not allowed,' says Aggie. 'How many years they sit here? We open them and so long they don't have patient files, we put in skip. Next door room, we can make kitchen. I will enjoy smell of coffee.'

He said, 'Aggie, it's not really a room. It's just storage space.'

'Is bigger than kettle cupboard. Here will be coffee machine, microwave and fridge.'

He said we'd managed years enough with what we'd got, but he'd caved and Aggie knew it.

136

She said, 'You are poor old stick-in-mud. I will paint my room yellow.'

I hadn't exactly welcomed Aggie's return to work. The arguments over shared office space, the fact that it meant Harry Shepherd was no longer required. But suddenly I saw things differently. Aggie was a force of nature, a can-do bulldozer of a woman. She and I were what the place needed. And my not seeing Harry was for the best. It would save me from making a total fool of myself.

I went into afternoon surgery in brighter spirits and to top it all I had my first consultation with Lilian Blacksmith.

Lilian was an 82-year-old widow with two hip replacements and a history of refusing to take statins.

She said, 'I've been hearing there's a tasty new doctor here, so I thought I'd come and have a look at you.'

'What do you think? Were the reports exaggerated?'

'You'll do. You're easier on the eye than the Dr Iestyn. He's a scruffy article. I'd like to get my hands on him, give him a shave and a decent haircut.'

Lilian was a retired hairdresser.

'And what can I help you with today?'

'Nothing. I'm just browsing.'

'Have you thought any more about statins?'

'Nothing to think about. I don't want them.'

'Your cholesterols weren't great the last time we looked at your bloods.'

'If you say so. We didn't even have cholesterol till a few years ago.'

'How are your hips?'

'Tip top. I go to Zumba Silver every week and aquarobics at the Eirias pool. My friend Jean's not been the same since she started on those statins. She's too weak to lift a feather. And that's not the only thing.'

'What else?'

'Wind. She has terrible wind. Are you married?'

'I am. Shall we have a look at your blood while you're here?'

'Can I spare it?'

I said, 'You seem in good shape, Mrs Blacksmith.'

She said, 'You can call me Lilian. I'll tell you another reason I don't want those pills. I like a Paloma of an evening, before I have my tea.'

'What's a Paloma?'

'It's tequila and grapefruit. Only they say you mustn't have grapefruit if you're taking statins.'

'That is true. Of course, you could always try a different cocktail. I've never heard of a Paloma.'

'My oldest boy got me started on them. It's from Mexico. He's been there a few times, for his holidays. Gin and lime was always my drink before, but I do enjoy a Paloma.'

I took Lilian through to get her blood drawn.

'Bethan bach,' she said, 'I'm only doing this to humour him. Hasn't he got lovely thick hair, though? If only I was fifty years younger.'

By Friday morning a small skip had been delivered to the front of the surgery and David and I had to park on the street.

Delyth said, 'Will somebody please tell Dr Aggie I can't have her carrying bags of rubbish through my reception area when I've got patients. It's not hygienic.'

David certainly didn't want to be the one to tell Aggie anything. He's slightly nervous around her, like she's a smouldering firecracker. I suggested the clearing out could wait till Saturday morning.

'No,' she said, 'is too much to do. Anywayhow, patients don't mind. Lady just took electric fire. She said it was too good for skip. When you can help me?'

'Tomorrow. I told you.'

'Good. Iestyn has driving lesson till ten o'clock. You can look after boys while I paint room.'

I stood firm. I'd help with clearing and I'd help with painting, but I was not minding her twins.

She said, 'Perhaps your wife?'

'Perhaps not my wife. Trust me.'

I did ask her, though I guessed what she'd say. Highly trained medics giving up their weekend to refurbish their own workplace? The very idea. David Parry should put his hand in his pocket and get a man in.

I said, 'It's just a few hours work and it'll make a big improvement. Come and help us. You could get to know Aggie.'

'Why?'

'Because she's fun and she's part of our little circle. Don't you want to make some friends here?'

'She's a baby machine. I'm not holding any babies.'

'Fine. If the baby needs holding, I'll do it.'

To my amazement, Chloe did turn up. She brought coffee and Danish and even helped me rip up an old carpet and carry it to the skip while Aggie fed Haf. Chloe watched her. I could tell she was fascinated.

She said, 'Doesn't doing that make you feel like a cow?'

'No,' says Aggie. 'It makes me feel like useful human being. Anywayhow, nothing wrong with cow. Milk, cheese, kefir, big juicy steak, Michael Kors handbag. Cow is very useful animal.'

I think it was Aggie's display of handbag connoisseurship that swung it. Chloe decided she liked her.

'She's a blast,' she said. 'What's she doing with Iestyn?'

'I imagine she loves him.'

'But he's like a hippy. That beard.'

'Iestyn's nice. It just takes a while to get to know him. He's quite shy.'

'He was wearing socks with sandals.'

'It's Saturday. He was dressed down.'

'And why does he need driving lessons at his age?'

'Let's say, he's not a natural. He gets his pedals mixed up.'

'What a bell-end. I wonder how he and Aggie ever got together?'

Of course, she and Aggie were never going to become besties, but it was a start. That weekend she even showed a passing interest in our garden which had suddenly become a jungle. I was thinking we should reduce the size of the lawn and grow some vegetables. Chloe wanted somewhere she could sunbathe topless without exciting the neighbours.

I said, 'Does that mean you'll be spending the summer weekends here and not dashing off to Birmingham?'

What had started as something she'd do once a month, as she eased into our new life, had somehow telescoped into twice a month and she wasn't willing to give it up. Rhos was boring, she said. It was good for us not to be always in each other's pockets, she said.

'Read your seed catalogues,' she said. 'Do your hymn singing and country walks and whatever else floats your boat and let me do my girl things. You know it makes sense.'

Choir practice was on Tuesday evenings and afterwards most of us would go to the Royal, just for a half, or in Merv's case, a bitter lemon. That was where he approached me one evening. You can always tell when somebody wants to ask you a doctor question. They come in close, say something about the weather or crack a joke, have a quick look round to make sure no-one's in earshot.

Merv said, 'I hear Dr Aggie's back at work. I hear she's had the place turned upside down.'

'She's done a good job. Chucked out a load of old junk and made herself a nice little office.'

'The feminine touch.'

'Yes.'

Where was Merv going with this?

He said, 'Very important, I'd say, to have a lady doctor on the premises. I dare say there's things womenfolk don't care to discuss with a gentleman doctor. I prefer to talk to a man, myself. Not that I've anything against lady doctors. Credit to them, I say. All those exams. How do you think she seems?'

'Dr Aggie? She's very well.'

He lowered his voice.

'No, I meant Bethan.'

That threw me. I'd been pretty sure he was about to make a round-the-houses enquiry about male waterworks.

I said, 'I'd say Bethan seems well. She works very hard.'

'Oh yes. She's a grafter.'

The Bethan question hung in the air for a moment.

'And she seems well to you?

'She does, but Merv, I can go for days without a proper conversation with her. We're like ships that pass. Are you concerned about something?'

'No, not really. You know what these women are like.'

Not really, Merv, I thought. Just when I think I'm getting the hang of them, they do something to confound me. Take Chloe. She can go from nursing a grievance to hot with desire in minutes.

'Are you worried about Bethan? Would you like me to speak to her?'

'Probably not. As you say, she seems well enough to you. Not a complainer, my wife.'

'No.'

'Nose to the grindstone. Shoulder to the wheel. And she can easily have a word with Dr Aggie.'

'Easily.'

'It's not like she'd need an appointment.'

We both laughed at the very idea.

What to do? To look at Bethan with a clinician's eyes, but discreetly? To say something to Aggie, on the QT? I decided to do both. The first part was easy. Bethan looked fine.

She said, 'Was there something you wanted, Dan? Only you're standing there gazing at me and I've got three dressing changes waiting downstairs.'

I said, 'There was something, but it's gone clean out of my mind.'

Aggie's room smelled of new paint and new carpet. Little Haf was asleep in a bouncy baby chair. I recounted my strange conversation with Bethan's husband.

Aggie said, 'Hm. How old she is?'

'I don't know. Early fifties?'

'Can be she has menopause. I will think about this.'

I was in the supermarket, buying something for dinner, when she phoned me.

She said, 'Dan, I have quite good idea. I will invent new clinic for women like of Bethan's age. It will be health check clinic. I will ask her to be hamster.'

'A guinea pig. Not hamster.'

'Is same thing. What you think?'

'It might be a good way to get her in for a chat.'

'Yes. Health chat for after menopause.'

'Bethan's not dim. You'll have to actually make something of this new clinic idea otherwise she might smell a rat.'

'Rat? Not hamster?'

And that was what happened. Aggie mentioned her clinic idea to Bethan and Bethan said she'd be happy to help but could they please have their chat in the nurse's room because the smell of paint was making her bilious. They settled on Friday lunchtime. Then Bethan got delayed, queuing at the bank, so Friday drifted to Monday and on Monday Aggie's twins had tummy upsets, so Monday drifted to Tuesday, which probably didn't matter at all because Bethan seemed just fine and whatever was worrying Merv was most likely nothing at all.

On Tuesday, just before the start of afternoon surgery, Delyth roared up the stairs, 'Dr Talbot, Dr Aggie would like a word with you.'

I said, 'Press 4, Delyth. Then hang up.'

'She's not on the phone,' says Delyth. 'Well she is, but she'd like to see you in her office.'

By this time, I was out of my chair, out of my room and staring down the stairwell at Delyth.

She said, 'It's a private matter.'

'Not anymore, apparently.'

I ran down to Aggie's room.

'Dan,' she said. 'I had chat with Bethan. Guess what? You won't never guess.'

'She's pregnant?'

'She is 55. I think this is not possible, except with Holy Ghost.'

'What then?'

'Is very exciting. She is lactating.'

'No!'

'Yes! Big time she is lactating. She has tissues in her brassieres. Is very interesting case, no?'

Chapter 15

A post-menopausal, childless woman producing breast milk? It sounded like a case history in an exam question. I knew I should know the answer, but offhand I couldn't think what it was.

'Did she volunteer it?'

'What you mean?'

'Did she tell you or did you find out by chance?'

'She told me, but not straight way. Bethan is quite shy lady.'

'So, what do you think?'

'Most likely it can be pituitary tumour.'

'Did you tell her that?'

'No. People don't like to hear word of tumour. I took blood. First we look for prolactin level and thyroid function.'

'And then what?'

'Depends. I never saw this before, did you?'

'No. Will she need brain surgery?'

'I don't think. This tumours is usually benign. When I see bloods, then we maybe get MRI. Also eye check. If there's pressure on pituitary it can affect optic nerve.'

'It's good you talked to her.'

'Yes, but is bad I had to trick her. Why she didn't come to me anywayhow?'

'Maybe she was plucking up courage. Like you said, she's shy.'

I peeped in on Bethan on the way back to my room. She had her back to me, looking at her computer screen. Nevertheless, she said, 'Help you with something, Dan?'

How do women do that?

At the end of surgery, she came in to see me.

She said, 'I suppose you've heard. I've probably got a tumour.'

I'm not much of an actor.

She said, 'I'd already worked it out. I know how to look things up. Was it Merv? Did he say something to you?'

I said, 'We were in the pub after choir practice. Merv didn't go into any details but it was obvious he was concerned about you. I couldn't think what else to do.'

'Dr Aggie and her new health check clinic nonsense. I wasn't born yesterday. And I'm sorry about Merv. He shouldn't have bothered you.'

'He was worried. You're precious to him.'

'Yes, well.'

'Did Aggie explain things to you?'

'Kind of. She talks a mile a minute, that one. If it's what she thinks it is, it won't kill me.'

'Correct. Pituitary tumours are almost always benign. But wait and see what the blood results say.'

'Yeah.'

'Are you registered with us?'

'With David. I'd sooner go to Dr Aggie though.'

'That's what she's here for.'

She sat. Usually Bethan's dashing off home to cook dinner, but she made no move to leave. I did a Trevor Buxton. Leaned back in my chair, let the silence hang. It's a thing I still find hard to do.

She said, 'Funny, isn't it? I always wondered what it'd feel like, to nurse a little one. We weren't blessed with a family, me and Merv. We don't know why. We didn't look into it. People didn't so much when we were young. We talked about adopting or fostering, but we never got round to it. And now this. Leaking milk, but no baby.'

I said, 'It can happen to men too, you know? With that kind of tumour.'

'So Dr Aggie said. Imagine. Anyway, I'd best get home.'

But still she sat.

She said, 'You going to choir practice tonight?'

'I am.'

'Don't say anything to Merv.'

'You know I wouldn't.'

'He'll get in a flap. His Uncle Wyn had a brain tumour, gone in six weeks, straight down the plughole.'

'No need to say 'tumour'. You can say your pituitary's gone haywire.'

'Because I won't need an operation.'

'Very unlikely.'

'Merv says you're a handy singer.'

'I love it. They're a friendly crowd.'

'And wait till you go to the cymanfa. It'll give you chills, all those voices together.'

I'd been instructed to put the cymanfa ganu in my diary, for October. Choirs from all around Conway, gathering to sing.

'Mind,' she said. 'They're not what they used to be. Some of them, they don't even pretend to harmonise. So, David's knocked off early again, left Iestyn to finish his list. Well he's the boss. I suppose he can do as he pleases.'

There it was, casually tacked on. The reason Bethan was lingering. She had a beef with David and she wanted to tell me about it.

'I'm sure he had a good reason.'

'I've never known a person get so many colds.'

'He wasn't feeling well?'

'Feeling fluey, he said. Again. How many times have I heard that? And it never amounts to anything. He'll be back tomorrow morning, you watch, healthy as a horse.'

Our conversation had taken a surreal turn. We'd gone from talking about her probable pituitary tumour to singing festivals to David Parry's erratic behaviour. It was true David did occasionally cut short his working day. Iestyn and I had both seen patients from the tail end of his list. It was true that in the short while I'd known him, he'd seemed about to go down with 'flu several times but then hadn't. What was Bethan suggesting? Was David bunking off? Did he have a secret life? A lover, maybe? The very idea was ridiculous. He and Miriam were a picture of long-married contentment.

I said, 'Is there something you're not saying, Bethan?'

'No,' she said. 'None of my business.'

She was on her feet.

I said, 'I'd like to think we keep an eye out for one another. We're all so busy looking after the world and his wife. Doctors and nurses get sick too.'

'Yes,' she said, 'but men always think they've got the 'flu. One sneeze and they're dying. Forget I said anything.'

She didn't mean it, of course, and anyway, I couldn't, could I? Bethan was a sensible person and a very good nurse.

What was she getting at, what was she seeing in David that I wasn't? I didn't push it.

I said, 'Okay. But you know my door is open, if ever there's anything else.'

'Yes,' she said, 'but I don't suppose there will be.'

At choir practice Merv and I ignored each other in the nicest way possible. Was he embarrassed about having approached me? Did I now know something he didn't or had Bethan rushed home and told him about her likely diagnosis? And was it ever a good idea to blur the lines between friends, work colleagues and patients.

When you're in medical school you start off with the basics: the anatomy, where everything is, and the physiology, how everything works. Then, after a couple of years they let you near actual living human beings. You draw bloods, take histories, practice your stethoscope skills, try to avoid being publicly humiliated during grand rounds. But I don't remember any training in the other stuff my work asks of me now. Be a detective, be a diplomat, keep a secret, deliver bad news, present an unhurried and non-judgmental face at all times, be empathetic even when your own life isn't exactly peachy.

Chloe and I hardly saw one another. Mondays she had an evening clinic, Tuesdays I had choir practice, Thursdays she did a Pilates class, Fridays, with what seemed like increasing frequency, she'd drive to Birmingham to see her old gang. That was what she called them, although when we were living in Birmingham, I don't recall her seeing so much of them. She didn't like Rhos or its surroundings, she actively hated Colwyn Bay and she was effectively living out of a suitcase, as if she was waiting for us to move somewhere more to her liking.

It wasn't all bad. Sometimes we'd have a cosy night in. I'd cook, she'd slop around in one of my rugby shirts. Sometimes we'd talk shop. Chloe could be really helpful on anything cardio. She'd focus on the numbers, the story the ECG told, any co-morbidities, and not get distracted by the wider human picture. She wasn't remotely interested in whether the patient was a Sunday fly-half who drank too much and only saw his kids on alternate weekends, or a spinster in her eighties who lived with a houseful of cats.

'Don't get so involved with people,' she'd say. 'Primary care is like a filter. All you have to do is identify the ones who need specialist care and send the rest on their way with a smile and a prescription.'

That was Chloe's way of looking at my job.

I told her about Bethan's case, no names, no pack drill.

'Wow,' she said. 'What's the prognosis?'

'If it's a pituitary tumour, excellent. It can be treated with a dopamine blocker. The main risk is to her vision.'

'Like papilledema?'

'Yes. And if her oestrogen levels are low, she should probably be monitored for osteoporosis.'

'What if it's not a pituitary thingy? Does she smoke?'

'No. What's that go to do with anything?'

'I mean weed.'

'Definitely not. Why?'

'Remember Kellerman?'

'No.'

'Yes, you do. He got chucked out for being stoned in the dissection room.'

'Good. But I didn't know him.'

'Yeah, he was in my year, come to think of it. South African. Anyway, he was a heavy user of weed and he developed breasts, with actual milk. So if your woman's a smoker.'

'I can tell you, she isn't.'

'You might be surprised. Just because you're Dr Straight. I'd say most people enjoy a spliff now and then.'

'I know you would. Let's agree to disagree.'

Chloe thinks I don't do drugs because of some kind of Puritan streak. She's quite wrong. Partly it's because I was hardly ever offered any. Matt did cocaine a few times when I was sharing a flat with him and Rob, and he was very protective of his stash. I suppose it was expensive. Not that I had designs on it. Matt's behaviour could be dick-ish enough without chemical assistance and I had no desire to copy him. In those days I had no confidence in my attractiveness to women and I didn't want to ruin what chances I had by being a moody, jittery asshole.

So there's that. And there was the kid I'd seen when I was doing a psych rotation. He was sixteen and swinging between feeling invincible and suffering from terrifying paranoid delusions. His parents rejected the idea that marijuana was the cause because to them it was a normal household staple, like milk or ketchup. Then while we were waiting for a bed for him on a secure ward, he got up onto the roof and threw himself off. Whether it was because he was convinced that he had superhuman powers, or because he believed all his thoughts were being broadcast on BBC television, we never found out because the fall killed him.

Those are the main reasons half a bottle of wine is my mind-altering limit, which Chloe says is merely a drug that happens to be socially acceptable and why don't I stop being a party pooper. Even her brother's time in prison hasn't changed her point of view. As far as she's concerned Charlie 'Slow' Swift was just unlucky. He was unlucky to get pulled over, unlucky that he happened to have a bag of cocaine in the cupholder of his car, unlucky that the very expensive lawyer his father hired failed to keep him out of prison.

She says, 'What earthly good did it do, locking him up in that ghastly place? Ruining his business.'

Charlie's business wasn't ruined. It was waiting for him when he was released. Laurence made sure of that. My father-in-law is a strange man when it comes to his children. Flo's just Flo. Low maintenance. Chloe is his undoubted favourite, because she's bright and beautiful and she followed him into medicine. Charlie's the only son. A bottomless receptacle for rescue money. Perhaps he's seen as the onward carrier of the Swift name, though personally I wouldn't depend on it.

My answer to Chloe is that her brother's sentence to eighteen months in Coldingley might at least make him think twice about getting behind the wheel of his Jaguar coupe after doing lines of coke. And anyway, he only served nine months.

I also think that the humiliation of having to attend his mother's funeral in handcuffs might have been the cold shower he needed, but I keep that thought to myself. Vinnie's death is still a very raw nerve for Chloe.

On Wednesday the meddygfa was running like a well-oiled machine. Bethan was bright and cheery, no doubt relieved to have shared her problem. David hadn't gone down with the 'flu, Iestyn had had a full three hours of undisturbed sleep and Delyth was in a very good mood because she was about to start a two week holiday, going down to Tenby to stay in her brother's caravan. In her absence, Iestyn's mum, Gwenny Hughes, was going to be our receptionist.

Mid-morning a very handsome chocolate cake was delivered, a thank you from the walk-in lady with the pulmonary embolism. At lunchtime we gathered in David's office because it was the nicest room.

Delyth had popped out to buy sun cream and a paperback, so we started without her. It was a rare get-together. We talked about holiday plans. Iestyn and Aggie would be taking the kids up to his parents' farm, in August. David and Miriam might go to Portugal. Bethan and Merv preferred to do daytrips, to get up in the morning and decide on the fly. I'd booked ten days off in July but had no idea what we'd do. I felt I should visit Mam and Da, maybe offer to look after Nan for a couple of days, to give them a break. Chloe wanted to work on her tan.

We heard the front door open and slam shut. Delyth was back. Then there was a strange, scuffling noise followed by a bump. Had she fallen? Iestyn called down to her.

'You all right, Delyth?'

She said, 'Could you come down, please?' Her voice was strange. Timid, measured, not at all the usual Delyth foghorn.

Iestyn was on the stairs when I heard him say, 'Oh.'

I followed him. He was stalled halfway down. When I reached him I could see her. She was on her knees, and behind her, holding something to her throat, was Leon Caddick.

'Now then,' says Iestyn, moving one step further down.

Leon said not to come any closer.

Delyth said, 'He's got a knife.'

I asked Leon what he wanted.

'Pills,' he said.

I said, 'Then there's no need for this. Come in when surgery opens. I'll see you.'

'Fuck that,' he said. 'I need them now.'

David and Bethan had joined us on the stairs. It was like the walk-down at the end of the Cardiff panto.

Iestyn took another step towards them.

Leon said, 'Come any closer and she gets it.'

153

Then Bethan joined in.

She said, 'You'd better stop this, Leon Caddick, before I phone for the heddlu.'

'Heddlu don't bother me,' he said. 'They lay a finger, I'll sue them for discrimination. I'm Kale.'

I said, 'What pills are you after, Leon? We're not a pharmacy.'

He said he knew we'd have some Oxys. Oxycodone. A powerful painkiller. It wasn't something I'd ever prescribed for him. Was he in pain?

Suddenly everyone was speaking at once.

Iestyn said, 'How about you and me sit down, nice and calm? Have a cup of coffee? Talk things over, see what we can do for you?'

Delyth was whimpering, 'the knife, the knife.' David was saying, 'You're out of luck, boy. We don't have any Oxycodone just now' and Bethan was contradicting him.

'Don't antagonise him,' she said. 'Let him have a couple.'

The phone rang and we all jumped. That was my chance. It's been a few years since I've played but even I could tackle a little weasel like Leon Caddick with his plastic picnic knife. I took him side-on and we rolled. He didn't fight me. We ended up jammed against the reception desk, me on top, looking up his nose. He started a whiny kind of crying, apologising to Delyth, swearing it wasn't anything personal.

Iestyn helped her to her feet. 'Of course it was personal,' she said. 'You followed me here. I saw you in the chemist's, skulking around. They ought to ban you.'

The phone stopped ringing, then started again. I pocketed the plastic knife, picked up Delyth's scattered shopping. David told her to take the afternoon off. Bethan said she'd need hot, sweet tea, for the shock, and Delyth said she wasn't going anywhere until she'd had her slice of cake. Iestyn took a defeated Leon into the waiting room.

Oxycodone addiction? I knew of it but not much about it.

Upstairs, Bethan and David had started a whispered argument.

'I've asked you and asked you,' she said, 'if you take stuff from my drugs cupboard, tell me, or sign it out.'

David said, '*Your* drugs cupboard? Whose practice is this?'

'Don't get ugly with me,' she said. 'All the years I've worked here, and for two pins I'd walk out, right now.'

'If that's how you feel, you know where the door is.'

'Face it, David,' she said. 'You've got a problem.'

He told her to keep her voice down, but it got louder. She was close to tears.

'I used to enjoy coming to work,' she said. 'But not anymore. I never know where I am with you. You're moody. You're unreliable. You're a flipping drug addict and it's about time you admitted it.'

The front door opened again. Aggie had arrived.

'Iestyn,' she called. 'Why you are late? Twins is in car and Aled has tummy ache.'

It was time for the regular Wednesday lunchtime handover. Iestyn home, to look after his kids and Aggie to do her afternoon surgery. She met me on the stairs.

'What?' she said. 'Why Delyth is crying? Why you are looking at me?'

'Drama,' I said. 'Ask Iestyn, but not now. He's with a patient.'

She started to protest.

I said, 'Go back to your car. If your clinic's a bit late starting it won't be the end of the world.'

Delyth was my priority. I wanted to put her in a taxi but she refused. She said it'd take more than Leon Caddick to stop her working. Bethan brought her a mug of tea. She had her jacket on. Was she really going to walk out? No, because she had an afternoon list and she didn't let people down. 'Unlike some,' she said.

Did she want to talk?

'Later,' she said.

That left David. I had to say something. He was standing in the doorway to his office, grey and sweating.

I said, 'Shall we talk?'

'Fuck off,' he said, and slammed the door in my face.

Iestyn appeared.

I said, 'David's not in any state to take afternoon surgery.'

He said, 'Well I can't do it. I've got the children. I'm going to put the boys in their stroller, then I'll walk Leon round to the mental health place.'

Bethan said, 'Looks like you just lost your afternoon off, Dan.'

So that was what happened. I took David's list and the no-shows gave me time to talk to a prescription drug addiction helpline. Detox, they said. Closely supervised detox, followed by rehab. I suppose they thought I was the addict. They must get a lot of people pretending to be calling about a colleague. Asking for a friend.

At around four o'clock Delyth came in to see me. She said David had just left, very quietly, without speaking to anyone.

'How did he look?'

'Same as usual.'

'How are you feeling?'

'Shaky.'

'As soon as the last patient's booked in, you can put the machine on and go home. Do you want something for the shakes?'

'No thank you,' she said. 'I reckon we've got enough drug addicts around here.'

'It's good you're going on holiday.'

'Yes. Thank you for, you know? Saving me. I thought it was a real knife.'

'I could see it wasn't. I wouldn't have tackled him if he'd been dangerous. I'm not one for heroics.'

'That's nice,' she said. 'So you'd have let him cut my throat?'

I said, 'No. I'd have run for my prescription pad and written him up for Oxys.'

Bethan sat down with me as soon as surgery finished. I asked her to tell me everything she knew.

'David's been helping himself to the OxyContin for a long time.'

'Was that what you were getting at? When you mentioned how often he gets 'flu symptoms.'

'Yes. Chills, aching muscles. That's when he needs a fix, and if I'm in my room he can't just walk in and help himself. Well he could, but he likes to think nobody knows.'

'Who does know? Do Iestyn and Aggie? What about his wife?'

'You'd have to ask them.'

She though it had started after he hurt his back, more than a year ago.

'And you hadn't confronted him about it, until today?'

'I told him to watch his step a couple of times, if I saw him at the cupboard. He just laughed.'

'You weren't serious about leaving?'

'I could do. I could get another job, easy. Are you going to report him?'

'Ideally he has to report himself.'

'Yes. Don't worry, I'm not going to leave. I love my job. I like Dr David. It breaks my heart to see him like that. Something has to happen, though, after today. The cat's out of the bag.'

I was quite hoping David might come back, so we could talk. He didn't.

I parked on the seafront for a while, wondering what my next step should be. As the most junior member of the practice, did I even have a next step? A big, ugly seagull came and sat on my bonnet and took an enormous dump. I couldn't have put it better myself.

Chapter 16

Chloe had bought new shoes. She asked me what I thought.

'Very glamorous. Are they for anything in particular?'

'Not exactly. They were reduced. I might wear them to this thing on Sunday.'

'What thing?'

'This thing at the Parrys.'

I had completely forgotten. David and Miriam were having a lunch party to mark their silver wedding anniversary. An awning in the garden, a caterer, the works.

'What do you think about the shoes? They were a real bargain.'

'I like them. Won't the heels be a problem on grass?'

'Heels are only a problem if you let them be. So, you only like them? You don't love them?'

'I absolutely love them. I should phone Miriam, make sure it's still on.'

'It had better be. I rearranged my weekend for it. Anyway, why wouldn't it be? How many years is silver?'

'Not sure. A lot. What about a gift?'

'I leave that to you. I hardly know them.'

I decided against phoning Miriam at home. David would be there. He'd know I was checking up on him.

Chloe said I was walking around like a zombie. I told her about the Leon Caddick incident, but not about what had followed. I had to keep the lid on that for the time being.

She said, 'What did the police do?'

'We didn't call the police. We kind of de-escalated things ourselves, then Iestyn took him to the Mental Health Centre.'

'What do you mean, de-escalated things?'

'Distracted him, tackled him. He's not a big guy.'

'Dan!' she said, 'you could have been injured. Why do you insist on working in such dangerous places? Why couldn't you take a job somewhere nice? Daddy could easily have fixed you up. He told me so. He knows heaps of useful people.'

I said, 'Chloe, my work's not dangerous. It's interesting. So was Weirdo Pants. And I'm sure they have OxyContin addicts even in Leamington Spa or Kenilworth or wherever it is your Dad's friend has his practice. Besides, I really object to the assumption that I need anyone to fix me up. Your father is so full of it.'

That silenced her.

The price tag was still on the sole of her new shoes. I guess 'a real bargain' is a relative concept.

David was back at work on Thursday morning. He came in without speaking to anyone, but there was nothing unusual about that. He's not a morning person. I called Miriam just before the start of surgery, on the pretext I was checking on the arrangements for Sunday.

'Any time after 12.00,' she said. 'Hot food's being served at 1.00. Come as you are. No need to dress up and please, no presents. After 25 years we have everything we need.'

160

She didn't sound like a woman who'd been up all night, listening to the confessions of a drug addict. Was David brazening it out? Or had we all been overwrought the day before, misreading stories we didn't know in full? Was I indulging in wishful thinking?

I grabbed Iestyn on his way in.

'About yesterday.'

'Yes,' he said, 'Looked a bit hairy for a minute, didn't it? Well now, I took Leon round to Mental Health and they said they'd have a chat with him. He's a nice enough bloke, just not very bright. I'd say he has a lot of issues. People don't always realise how powerful those pills can be.'

'Leon's a hopeless case. What about David?'

'I heard him shouting.'

I said, 'Come on, Iestyn. You must have heard what Bethan said.

'We were all a bit het up.'

'She wasn't het up when I spoke to her later. She was calm and collected and in no doubt that David's addicted to painkillers.'

'Right.'

'Did you know?'

'Not really.'

'Do you have any difficulty believing it?'

'Anything's possible.'

'In which case, what are we going to do about it?'

He scratched his beard.

He said, 'I suppose you could have a word.'

'Me? You know him better than I do. I'm the recent arrival. Besides, I tried yesterday. He told me to fuck off.'

'You could speak to Miriam.'

161

'I already tried that. I don't think she knows. She didn't even mention the Leon drama. What does Aggie think?'

'I don't know.'

'You must have talked about it.'

He said, 'We don't have a lot of time, Dan, with three little ones.'

'She saw David slam his door in my face. Didn't she think that was something worth talking about, you know? Over dinner?'

'Well,' he said, 'Aggie slams a pretty good door herself. She probably didn't think anything of it.'

'We have to do something before the Parrys' party. Are you and Aggie going?'

'I think so.'

'What will Mental Health do with Leon?'

'I couldn't say. They're very stretched, with the cutbacks.'

Delyth shouted up the stairs, 'Dr Hughes, Dr Talbot, it's ten past nine and the waiting room's full.'

I said, 'Delyth seems back on form, considering her ordeal.'

Iestyn said he was just grateful it hadn't happened next week, on his mum's watch.

'Although,' he said, 'Leon might have bitten off more than he could chew if it had been Mum. She handles 90 kg of sheep without too much bother.'

'Won't she go crazy, stuck indoors here all day?'

'No, she loves it. She does it every year. It makes a nice change for her, a week in the big city. Like a proper holiday. She doesn't get to see many people, up at the farm.'

Colwyn Bay, the big city? Perhaps Gwenny Hughes included Llandudno and its conurbation.

Regarding the David situation, it seemed I was on my own. Bethan had spoken up and got nowhere. Miriam was apparently in the dark, and Iestyn didn't want to know. Aggie was an unknown quantity, but she'd been willing to take on David in smaller matters, and she wasn't afraid to speak her mind. She was my best hope as an ally. I cracked on with my morning list.

Some days you feel as though all you see are bad backs and coughs, with maybe a few rashes and low spirits thrown in. Not that I wished serious conditions on my patients, but you need the occasional challenge to keep you on your toes. Bad backs can be significant and so can coughs.

Emlyn Gadd was a solid figure of a man, good-looking, for a senior. He was wearing a jacket and tie. There are still a few patients who dress up for a doctor's appointment. Nan Talbot used to do it when she was going to the bank as well. Hat and gloves. Shoes polished.

According to Mr Gadd's notes, he'd suffered from bronchitis, the past two winters, though this was the first time I'd seen him.

'You're new,' he said.

Emlyn had a cough that had never quite gone away since the previous December's bout. Any sputum?

'Oh yes.'

'Any blood?'

'No.'

He found he tired easily, but he had no pain, no unexplained weight loss.

He said, 'My dear wife won't allow weight loss. She keeps me well fed. I will admit, though, I'm not the man I was. But I'm 71, near as makes no difference, so what can you expect?'

His breathing was laboured. I could hear a little squawk at the end of each inspiration. And was he a bit cyanotic or was it just that Welsh, blue-black shadow around his mouth and chin?

I said, 'I see you were a stonemason.'

'Forty one years. I went straight to that after Dinorwic closed.'

'Dinorwic? Was that a slate quarry?'

'Not *a* slate quarry. It was *the* slate quarry.'

I apologised. He laughed, which set him off coughing.

He told me he'd started working at Dinorwic the day after he left school.

'Followed my father into it. He was a splitter, highly skilled. It was Dinorwic quarry made the dais for your Charlie Boy, when he come to be invested Prince of Wales. July, 1969. And that was about the last job we did.'

My Charlie Boy! Emlyn thought I was English. I put him straight.

'Is that a fact?' he said. 'Well you sound like you've been too long away from the Principality. We'll have to reclaim you. Do you think it's the silicosis I have?'

It was exactly what I was thinking.

I said, 'It could be. You've probably seen a few cases of it?'

'Oh yes. My Da and two of his brothers. They got compensation. Not a lot. I thought I might get away with it, seeing I was still a young man when I left the quarrying. I suppose you'll be sending me for an X-ray?'

'Yes, that's the next step. I'll do the letter today.'

'Right you are. Might as well find out what the damage is. Now tell me, if you're from Abergavenny, what are you doing in Colwyn Bay?'

164

'I could ask you the same thing. Isn't Dinorwic over by Caernarvon?'

'Llanberis. But my wife's from Colwyn. I always promised her we'd retire here.'

'I'm new to the area and fairly new to marriage. It seems like a good place to settle down and raise a family.'

'Da iawn ti,' he said. 'We've got four daughters and eleven grandchildren. And I'll tell you something, all those years I worked, now I look back it doesn't amount to much. Food on the table, that's all. It's the faces *round* the table. That's the achievement. It'll be different for you, of course. You're in the business of saving lives. Well, I'll bid you good day. It was very nice to meet you.'

A patient like Emlyn Gadd can lift a doctor's spirits. Someone who gives a good account of their symptoms, to the point, no rambling, but chats about themselves a little too, allowing you a peek at the bigger picture. Are they lonely or bored? Are they frightened? Or philosophical, like Emlyn. His consultation put me in such a good mood for a moment I forgot about the David Parry cloud hanging over me. Then I ran smack into David at the end of afternoon surgery. Perhaps that was the best way. I had no time to prepare.

'All right, Dan?' he said. His usual greeting. I gave him my usual reply.

'All right.'

'Weather's set fair for the weekend.'

'That's good. Are you looking forward to your party?'

'I am.'

'Twenty five years is an achievement.'

'Oh yes,' he said. 'Passes in a blink, mind. Seems like only yesterday. See you.'

He was out the door and gone. The cloud returned.

165

That had been a normal-for-David conversation. No embarrassment, no awkwardness. Was Bethan delusional? Was I? Had yesterday even happened? I started trying to reframe it. David's a regular guy, a family man, a respected member of the community. What if Bethan's adenoma was affecting her judgment? But no, much as I wanted to, I couldn't buy that. Addicts are slippery and deceitful and the more intelligent they are, the cleverer they are at living two lives. They may wear Burberry ties and drive a nice car. As long as they get their fix, they are masters of concealment.

Sunday dawned clear and sunny, a perfect day for a garden party. I'd been looking forward to it, until Wednesday's drama. Meeting some more locals, getting to know people like Iestyn and Aggie socially, perhaps even seeing Harry Shepherd with Pete and feeling totally okay about it. Chloe looked fabulous. Boat-neck dress and those bargain killer heels.

I said, 'I think most people'll be casual. It's a come-as-you-are.'

'I know,' she said. 'You already told me. This is as-I-am.'

The Parry's daughter, Becca had come home for the weekend. She's a dentistry student, just finishing her second year at Manchester, a pretty girl, a younger version of her mother. Joe, the son, put in his required appearance, mumbled hello and made his escape.

There were some neighbours and some old friends, including a GP from Chester, John, who had been David's Best Man. Aggie and Iestyn had cancelled. One of the twins had a temperature. I knew Bethan and Merv weren't coming.

'I can't face it,' she'd said to me. 'I'm sorry but I just can't. I'm fond of David and I think he has a smashing little family, but I know what I know.'

Miriam's co-workers were there. Hilary Mostyn, with his Swedish boyfriend, and Giles Tate, the junior of the practice, who I hadn't met before. He made a beeline for Chloe. There was no sign of Harry Shepherd.

We were an hour into drinks and just making a start on the buffet when she arrived. I heard Miriam say, 'You poor thing. Do you need a shower?'

Harry had had to change a flat tyre. Her T shirt was filthy.

'A shower and a change of clothes. Can you lend me a shirt or something?'

She and Miriam went indoors. I sat with GP John. He was watching David.

'Lucky man, that,' he said. 'Drew a winning ticket in the marriage lottery.'

John told me he was divorced, twice.

'Can't seem to keep them,' he said.

He'd known David since their first day in medical school, like me and Rob and Matt, except that neither of them is likely to make it to my silver wedding. Rob's well and truly settled in Australia. He's just a Skype buddy now, and Matt's completely dropped out of my life. Since he qualified, his prick tendencies have flourished. A surgeon prick. He reckons surgical scrubs are the ultimate babe-bait. Chloe can't stand him.

'My word,' says John, 'look at that! Parry's recruited some gorgeous-looking ladies for his party.'

I thought he might be referring to Chloe or Becca Parry, but he wasn't facing in their direction. He was looking at Harry who had rejoined the party wearing a dress, white, sleeveless, with a thin gold belt. The beat-up trainers made for an interesting contrast. It was the first time I'd seen her legs.

I waved to her.

'You know her?' says John. 'Is she single?'

I introduced them.

'Stunning dress,' he said.

'It's Miriam's,' she said. 'White? I mean, honestly! I'd say there's a ninety percent chance of me spilling food down the front of it, but she insisted. How are you, Dan Talbot?'

'I'm very well. No Pete today?'

'Pete? Oh, Pete. No, he's probably working. Probably doing CPR on somebody's pet gerbil. Actually, I could have done with him an hour ago when I was trying to loosen the wheel nuts. I'm going to get food.'

GP John was clearly interested in her.

He said, 'What's a divine creature like that doing unattached?'

I told him she was career woman.

'Damned waste,' he said. 'I'd loosen her wheel nuts any day. She's not a lesbian by any chance?'

'I don't think so.'

'It can be hard to tell these days,' he said. 'As if dealing with the fairer sex isn't difficult enough.'

The fairer sex. I could see how he'd struggle with any woman under the age of 40. He spoke an ancient language.

I caught up with Harry over dessert.

She said, 'You look like a man on a mission.'

'I am. Two things. The bloke I was sitting with is wondering whether to ask you for a date.'

'What's the other thing?'

'Seriously. He's 54, single, GP with a two-man practice in Cheshire.'

'What's the other thing?'

'So, you're not interested?'

'Dan,' she said. 'If he's single at 54, there's a reason. Anyway, he's asked me before and the answer's still no.'

'He asked you before? You mean, today?'

'No. The last time the Parrys had a party. He's a bottom-squeezer. And he's obviously forgotten he already met me, or just not recognised me. This isn't my usual style.'

'It should be. You look lovely in that dress.'

'Thank you. I will admit, I do feel a tiny bit fab. Miriam's so good at clothes. And for the final time of asking, what was the other thing?'

'It's difficult.'

'Spinach on my front teeth?'

'It's about David.'

'Oh. That kind of difficult. Is this the place to talk?'

'Just one quick question. Has he ever had any problems that you know of? Nervous breakdown? Alcohol, drugs, anything like that.'

She gave me a long, steady look. Those eyes. In some lights they're grey, in most lights they're green.

'Not here,' she said. 'Meet me for a drink one evening?'

Chapter 17

I met Harry in the Toad on Monday evening. I'd suggested meeting somewhere out of town, in case we were seen but Harry said, 'No, that'd make it look like we had something to hide, like we're having an affair. Anyway, don't worry about David seeing us. He doesn't go to pubs.'

I told her the story. Everything that had happened from the minute Leon Caddick had seized Delyth and demanded drugs, right up to Sunday's party when David had been his usual self. We shared a bag of pork scratchings while she thought.

Then she said, 'A couple of things I should tell you. David has been prescribed OxyContin. I know because I wrote one of the prescriptions. Hilary's his GP but he called me once for a repeat, when Hilary was away. It was for back pain. An old ski-ing injury. Also, I gave him more than I probably should have because Hilary was gone for two weeks. I trusted David to be careful. Obviously.'

'What do you think?'

'It does sound like he might have a problem. That nurse, Bethan, never struck me as the fanciful type. Not a trouble-maker.'

'Not at all. Bethan gets on with everyone, David included. But now, there's an atmosphere between them. I honestly don't know what to do. Iestyn's downplaying it.'

'Forget Iestyn. He wouldn't say boo. If it comes to a battle, Aggie'll be your surface-to-surface missile, but we have to tread carefully. We need be sure of our facts. Are you keeping an eye on the drugs cupboard?'

'Bethan was doing, but there's no OxyContin in there at the moment. If Hilary's his GP, should we talk to him?'

'I'll do it. Delicate, though. Patient confidentiality and all that. The other thing I'll do is check with a couple of pharmacists I know, to see if he's been self-prescribing. It's not against the law, but that doesn't mean it's a good idea, especially for opioids. Hell Dan, I hope you're wrong. It's not an easy addiction to treat.'

'An intervention?'

'Let's not run ahead of ourselves. That's the last resort. An intervention can be brutal.'

'But if he needed help? Where would he go?'

'As far away as possible. Abroad even. You wouldn't want to bump into anyone who knew you. Like the bloke with the plastic knife, for instance.'

'Leon.'

'I'm surprised Delyth didn't deal with him herself. You know, whump, whump, a double knee face-breaker? She terrifies me.'

'She was pretty shaken. But she's on holiday for the next two weeks. We've got Iestyn's mum in her place.'

'That's my Aunty Gwenny.'

'I know. She's nice.'

'She's a sweetheart. Everybody should have an Aunty Gwenny. Staying at Iestyn and Aggie's and doing Delyth's job, it's her idea of a summer holiday. To her, it's like staying at the Ritz. No drenching for worm, no dipping for fly-strike, no listening to Uncle Rhys snoring.'

'Bad, is it?'

'Enough to wake the dead.'

I could happily have sat all evening with Harry, but I didn't. Chloe worked late on Mondays and she always came home in need of food, wine and tender, loving care.

I said, 'So we'll talk again? You'll let me know if you find out anything?'

'I will. And you do likewise.'

I kind of wanted to tell Chloe what was going on, but I hesitated. She could be such a drama queen. When I was working at Weirdo Pants and that little baby died of a botched circumcision and the shit hit the fan, she'd overreacted. Even though we weren't in any way culpable, to Chloe it confirmed what she'd always thought: that I was training in a substandard practice in a dodgy area. She'd been on the phone to Daddy Laurence like a shot. I decided not to say anything for the time being.

Gwenny Hughes was quite a contrast to Delyth. She didn't shout, she understood how to put calls through without cutting people off and a couple of times she brought in doughnuts from the van on the promenade. She said I looked like I needed feeding up. I told her she needed new glasses.

'Get away now,' she said. 'I like to see a bit of flesh on a man. Now you're the one that went up to Maes Glas for the lambing.'

'I am.'

'What did you want to do that for?'

'I thought it'd be interesting. It was interesting. Harry mentioned they were a bit pushed because her mum was still recuperating, so I offered to be head tea-maker.'

'And how come you know our Harry?'

'She was doing clinics here, while Aggie was away.'

'That's it,' she said. 'It comes back to me now. See, Grace, Harry's mother, she's my sister. Well you must have a very understanding wife, that's all I can say. Lending you out for a whole weekend.'

'I have,' I said. 'Very.'

I tried to keep Chloe's frequent absences a secret. I felt embarrassed by them. What did it say about me, if my wife kept running back to her old haunts? If people ever asked about my plans for the weekend, I kept it vague. A bit of gardening, weather permitting. Maybe a pub lunch.

On Friday evening, I called Mam. Da answered. Da never answers. He said Mam wasn't feeling so good and she was asleep.

I heard her say, 'No I'm not. Give me that phone.'

'What it is,' she said, 'I've got the shingles again.'

Again? I couldn't recall her ever having shingles. She said it must have been when I was away at medical school.

'Where have you got it?'

'All over my scalp and down the back of my neck.'

'C2 and C3 dermatomes.'

'If you say so. It's a blummin' nuisance, I know that much. I can't wash my hair. I do look a sight.'

'You're rundown.'

'Can't imagine why,' she said.

I knew if Da was listening she wouldn't complain about having to look after Nan.

173

'Is Da taking care of you?'

'Oh yes.'

Which probably meant, not really. Da worships Mam but he doesn't have a clue about putting a meal on the table or some nice clean sheets on the bed.

'How about Aunty June?'

'She's away. Two weeks in the Canaries.'

I said, 'Shall I come?'

'Bless you, no,' she said. 'It's a long drive. Come when I'm better. I wouldn't want Chloe to catch it.'

Chloe? Why Chloe? Then I understood. The unspoken 'in case she's pregnant.' Fat chance.

She said, 'Has she had the chicken pox?'

'I imagine so. You will tell me if you change your mind?'

'I will.'

'How's Nan?'

'Thriving. This morning she took all the teaspoons into her room, swore I'd stolen them from her.'

I called my brother.

'Talbot.' That's how he answers his phone.

'It's Dan. Did you know Mam's not well?'

'No.'

'She's got shingles, she's trying to cope with Nan, and Da's a bit out of his depth.'

Silence.

I said, 'They need help, Adam. Can you drive over?'

'I don't know about that,' he said.

'What does that mean?'

'I'm pretty busy.'

'How? It's weekend and anyway you've broken up for the summer.'

'I've got things to do. I'm training, for the Wild Wales.'

'What's that?'

'Cycling challenge.'

'You can't train every day, even I know that. Will you please call Da and offer to help? Mam needs to rest and Nan's running them ragged.'

'I can't look after Nan.'

'Why not? You can sit with her for an hour or two. Take her out for a drive.'

'What if she needs the lav?'

He agreed, reluctantly, to make the offer but I knew exactly how that would go. When I called him on Saturday night he was at home. He said he'd spoken to Mam and she'd told him she was feeling better and there was really no need for him to give up his weekend.

Adam's two years older than me, so he's always been in my life and as far as I can remember he's always qualified for special dispensations. He was gifted, they said. Not true. He has a knack for maths, but he's no Einstein.

He was special, they said, he was a strange one. That bit's right. He doesn't have mates and as far as we know he's never had a girlfriend. He goes to work, comes home, has obsessions. Cycling challenges are the latest one. Before that it was long-distance swimming and achieving Platinum level in the Three Peaks hike. Adam likes pushing himself, but not when it comes to family. We don't interest him.

Chloe says I should just forget he exists. She's never forgiven him for turning up to our wedding in an anorak.

Sunday, it rained all day. After church I went to B&Q and bought paint. Chloe's original choice for our bedroom had been a sludgy pink mistake. Our windows faced north. We needed something more cheerful.

175

I was making great progress. I had a few beers in the cool-box, the Lord's Test was on the radio, and a sunny shade of yellow was taking over the walls. I heard my phone ring and couldn't get to the damned thing in time. It wasn't a number I recognised.

Harry Shepherd said, 'Yes, it was me. Is this a bad time?'

She had some news. Hilary Mostyn was still prescribing OxyContin for David. And a pharmacist in Rhyl had filled several self-prescribed scripts for him.

'He's been going to Rhyl?'

Harry said, 'Well he's not going to go where he's known, is he? So that's two sources, and if he's been dipping into the cupboard at your place, that makes three. Has he taken anything this week?'

'We haven't restocked yet. What's the next step?'

'I think we've done all we can for now. Hilary won't give him another prescription without seeing him and if there's a confrontation, that'll be the trigger to take things further. Get Miriam involved. I don't know, Dan. I've never had to deal with an educated addict. Is that the cricket I can hear in the background?'

'India versus England.'

'I know. Geth's listening to it here.'

'You're at the farm?'

'I'm here most weekends. Mum's not great. This surgery's knocked the stuffing out of her. Do you think India can win?'

'Only if England throw it away.'

'Geth would enjoy that. He's not a fan of the English.'

It was late when Chloe got home. She loved the buttercup walls, but she said she couldn't sleep with the smell of paint. She bunked down on a sofa with tea and toast.

I said, 'Let's plan some things to do together the next few weekends. I'm fed up with being on my own and there's so much around here you haven't seen yet.'

'Such as?'

'Anglesey, the Lleyn.'

'What's there?'

'Scenery, little towns, beaches. We can just take off and explore. Find a nice B&B. Do a boat trip. They have dolphins and seals in Cardigan Bay.'

'Okay. Not over the Bank Holiday though.'

'Why?'

'I'm going to a music festival. Mandala.'

'What, for the whole weekend? Did I know that? Where is it?'

'Northamptonshire.'

'I'll come with you.'

She made a face.

'Not poss,' she said. 'Sorry. We already booked our tents.'

'You're camping? You? Sleeping in a tent?'

'It's a yurt, actually. It's called glamping. You get your own toilet and nice towels and a fire pit and everything.'

'Didn't it occur to you to include me?'

'You'd hate it. It's not your scene, Dan. Not your kind of music.'

'What's my kind of music?'

'You know. Holy Joe stuff.'

'That's so ridiculous. I like Bear's Den. I like Mumford and Sons. I'll tell you what I hate, Chloe. This semi-detached marriage. You're hardly here.'

She said it was keeping our love fresh. She said she was too tired to talk.

I said, 'Mam's not well. She's got shingles.'

177

She said, 'There you are then. While I'm at Mandala, you can go and visit your rellies. Perfect.'

Chapter 18

Gwenny Hughes said, 'Dr Dan, I wonder would you be able to visit Professor Lloyd Humphreys before afternoon surgery? She's between Old Colwyn and Llanddulas.'

The professor's name meant nothing to me.

'I can. What's the problem?'

She said, 'I think she's had a fall. It was her foreign carer lady who telephoned. It was hard to understand what she was saying.'

I looked at the file. Buddug Lloyd Humphreys. Born 1933. Last seen by Iestyn nearly two years ago, treated for a possible tick bite.

I said, 'I don't mind going, but she usually sees Iestyn.'

'I know,' she said, 'but it's a long way for him to go, on his bike.'

Iestyn had failed his driving test again.

It was a rundown, detached house. The garden was overgrown, except where a battered old Ford Capri was parked. A voice inside the front door said, 'Can't open. Come backside.'

The owner of the voice was a tiny woman in a nylon overall. Benilda, the home help. She let me into the kitchen. Every surface was covered with stuff. Empty jars and bottles, newspapers, foil food containers. There was a powerful smell of mice. Benilda smiled. She had a pretty face.

She said, 'Professor don't like throw things away.'

'And she's had a fall? Did you see it happen?'

'No. It was happened in the night. I go home in the night.'

The messy kitchen was but the tip of the iceberg. Dr Lloyd Humphreys was in the living room and to get to her I had to squeeze through a canyon of bookshelves and bookshelf overspill. There were books everywhere.

The patient was on the sofa in a nightie. She was a tall woman and the sofa was small.

I said, 'That doesn't look very comfortable.'

She answered in Welsh.

I said, 'It'll have to be in English, I'm afraid.'

'Ha, Saesneg!' she said. That much I could understand. 'An Englishman.' Her opinion of the English was clear. Better to take the insult on the chin and keep quiet about my true roots. If she was scornful of the English, I could imagine what she'd think of a Welshman who couldn't understand Welsh. I decided to take a firm line.

I said, 'Tell me what happened. In English, please.'

'Where's Iestyn Hughes?'

'He's not available today. Benilda says you fell. When was that?'

'Middle of the night. I don't know. What does the time matter? Don't ask stupid questions.'

'Professor Lloyd Humphreys is a bit of a mouthful. May I call you Buddug?'

She didn't say I couldn't. She had a magnificent face, like a Sioux warrior, and a shock of white hair.

Benilda said, 'Professor fell down on stairs. There is too much books.'

Gradually I pieced together the story. At some point in the night she'd come downstairs, searching for a particular book, tripped, fallen from about halfway down and banged her side hard against the bannisters. Then she'd dragged herself to the sofa, too shaken to climb the stairs and go back to bed. Benilda had found her when she arrived to make breakfast. Cold, cross, in a urine-stained nightdress and grey with pain.

'Where does it hurt?'

'Chest. Broken a rib, I think.'

There were bruises on her left cheek and along the side of her left leg.

'Can I examine you?'

No answer.

'What was the book you were looking for?'

'Commentary on the poems of Iolo Goch.'

'What does it look like?'

'Quarto, clothbound, brown. Slim volume.'

I asked Benilda to look for a thin brown book. Underneath the nightdress, Professor Lloyd Humphreys was wearing a grubby thermal vest.

'Who was Iolo Goch?'

'Bard. 14th century.'

'Is that your field?'

'Yes.'

'I might need to cut your vest open. It's going to be hard to examine you otherwise.'

'Nonsense. It's a perfectly good vest. Just strap me up.'

'Where did you teach?'

'Bangor.'

I didn't cut the vest. Peering down it I could see all I needed to. Her breathing was shallow and guarded and her chest was moving like a crazy accordion.

181

I said, 'You need to go to hospital.'

'Why?'

'Because not only have you broken your collarbone and some ribs, it looks like they're broken in more than one place. The left side of your chest is shattered. It isn't working in concert with the right side. It's what we call a flail chest.'

'Never heard of it.'

'Also known as paradoxical breathing.'

'Won't it heal itself?'

'No, and there's a high risk of a pneumothorax. Do you know what that is?'

'I suppose you're going to enlighten me.'

'It's when something like a broken rib punctures your lung, air leaks into the space between the lung and the chest wall and the lung collapses. Trust me, you don't want that to happen. I'm going to call for an ambulance.'

'Don't bother. Just shoot me.'

Benilda had found several slim volumes, blue, red, black.

Dr Buddug was exasperated. 'Brown,' she said. 'I distinctly told you it was brown.'

She was wrong. The Iolo Goch book was red.

'Well it looks brown to me,' she said.

Cataracts, probably. Another curse of old age, making every colour look muddy.

We draped an old-fashioned man's dressing gown around her shoulders.

I said, 'You've had this a few years. Was it your husband's?'

'Husband?' she said. 'Never had one. Never had time for one. This was my father's robe.'

'It's lasted well. Do you have any family?'

'None.'

Benilda put a few overnight things in a carrier bag. A spare nightdress, reading glasses, the little red book, a sliver of soap wrapped in a disgusting old face flannel. I waited with them until the ambulance came. I could quite imagine the old lady telling Benilda to cancel it the minute my back was turned.

I said, 'This Iolo Goch. Am I right in thinking the 'goch' bit means red?'

'Correct. Coch, mutated to goch. How long have you lived in Wales?'

'Thirty years, apart from medical school.'

'Shame on you,' she said. 'Thirty years and barely a word of your own language. Iestyn Hughes has excellent Welsh.'

The paramedics had to go through the 'come backside door' routine. Samantha and Will. Samantha made the mistake of addressing her as 'darling.'

'Professor Lloyd Humphreys to you,' she said. 'I'm not anyone's darling.'

They started her on oxygen, put a pillow against her injured side and strapped her left arm to it. She winced and groaned and swore at them.

Would they be taking her to Bangor? No, to Glan Clwyd. It was closer.

Would it be possible, Will asked, to open the front door? Otherwise it was going to be very difficult to manoeuvre a wheelchair. Benilda said that door hadn't been opened in the three years she'd been coming to the house. I pulled from the inside, Will put his shoulder to the outside and eventually we got it open.

The professor said, 'I hope you haven't damaged the paintwork.'

I could honestly say we hadn't. There was no paintwork to damage.

'And mind my car!' she said.

Samantha said, 'Does it go? Are you still driving it?'

'Of course. How else would I get about?'

'You didn't have any trouble renewing your licence, then? My grandad had to be assessed, because of his eyes.'

'Assessed?' she said. 'I refuse to be assessed. I'm Emeritus Professor of Medieval Welsh Literature.'

I saw her loaded into the ambulance, wagging her big, bony hand, still giving orders to Benilda. Secure the front door, return the blue and black books to the place you found them, do not, under any circumstances, throw anything away.

Will said, 'She's got vermin in there. I could smell it the minute we walked in.'

Benilda asked, 'What is vermin?'

'Mice.'

'Oh yes. Dr Buddug talks to them. She tells them not eat her books.'

Iestyn said Professor Lloyd Humphreys was an amazing character, a famous scholar, very highly thought of.

I said, 'That may be so, but she's living in terrible conditions. She hoards rubbish. The house is infested with mice.'

'Can we get her a home help?'

'She already has one, a nice Filipino woman, but she's struggling to do anything useful. Toasts her a Pop Tart. Washes her hair. That's about all. If she tries to throw anything away, your famous scholar retrieves it. And see what happened last night. She came down the stairs, probably half-cut on gin, piles of books on every step, missed her footing and ended up with her chest stoved in. When the home help arrived and found her this morning, she was hypothermic and damned lucky not to have a collapsed lung.'

Iestyn said nobody knew more about the 14th century bards.

Holding Chloe to what we'd agreed, I booked us two nights in a hotel in Aberdaron. It was a long drive and personally I'd have been just as happy having a lazy weekend together at home, but Chloe likes hotels. Usually.

She was quiet, distracted even, and very frustrated with the patchy Wi-Fi service.

I said, 'We don't need it. It's not as though either of us is on-call. Let's just put our phones away.'

She didn't, though.

We rented bikes and cycled to the Whistling Sands beach. It was a nice day. Cloudy but warm.

I said, 'You seem miles away. What's up?'

Just tired, she said.

I said, 'You're doing a longer commute than I'd hoped. Do we need a rethink?'

'You mean, like, move?'

'No. I mean rethink your job.'

'Such as?'

'Try for something at Bangor. Or take a break. Have a baby, then find something nearer home.'

Eventually she said, 'You're dead keen on babies, aren't you?'

'I'd certainly like us to have a few.'

'A few?'

'At least two. Isn't that what we always said?'

We were sitting at a beach café, looking out across the water.

'That's Ireland over there,' she said.

The sun disappeared behind a black cloud.

She said, 'Let's go home.'

'You mean to the hotel?'

'No, home home. I don't like having sex at the hotel. The bed squeaks.'

The hotel manager was annoyed. I had to pay for the extra night, but it was a small price to pay to see Chloe cheerful again. If we hadn't had crab sandwiches for lunch I probably wouldn't have needed to floss, and if I hadn't gone looking for floss in her toilet bag, I wouldn't have found the pregnancy test kit.

Could that be why she was feeling tired all the time? Why hadn't she said? Part of me wanted her to take the test there and then. Part of me knew better. Chloe has to do things her way. She wanted us to have a loved-up evening at home and then, ta-da!

I thought I played it pretty cool but a couple of times on the journey back she asked me what I was smiling about. Just remembering a funny patient, I said. An old lady who'd warned the paramedic not to scrape the paintwork on her dented old banger that had to be at least twenty years old.

'You are one weird guy,' she said. 'How do you remember all those irrelevant details about your patients? I hardly even remember the names of mine.'

I suggested a caprese salad and an early night. She wanted Chinese. Crispy duck, hoisin sauce, pancakes, the works, and cold white wine. Monosodium glutamate, alcohol. All I could think was, was that advisable? What about our possible unborn child? But I said nothing. I wanted Chloe to have her moment, her big reveal.

The end of July. Say she was six weeks pregnant, that'd be a February baby, like me. It might be my 32nd birthday present. We probably wouldn't tell anyone until she was past the crucial

12 week point. Except Mam. I don't know if I'd be able to keep it from Mam for that long.

Flo would be pleased too. Her baby and ours would only be a few months apart. Next summer we might have two strollers parked under our pear tree and at long last Chloe and Flo would have something in common, something they could talk about. Motherhood.

When I got back from picking up our order from the Kwong Chow, Chloe was curled up in an armchair, on her phone, talking ten to the dozen about the Mandala festival.

'I am so going to get a Dead Sea mud wrap,' she said. 'It's going to be wild.'

I'd forgotten about Mandala. If she was pregnant, should she still go? What if something went wrong? She'd be stuck in some field in the middle of nowhere with thousands of doped out strangers. And the drugs. Could I trust her not to smoke any dodgy weed or pop any pills? She might promise not to and then she'd cave in. I didn't want to spoil our joyful news with an argument, but this was my unborn child we were talking about. I might have to put my foot down.

I unpacked our Chinese, laid the table, poured the wine.

She said, 'What's with the kiddie grape juice?'

'What do you mean?'

'You bought Natureo. It's zero alcohol.'

'Did I? I hadn't noticed. I thought it was cheap. Never mind. A night off the booze won't hurt us.'

'Maybe so,' she said, 'But not tonight. I want a proper drink.'

She went to the fridge and found half a bottle of Chenin Blanc. Then she came to the table. She was clutching a hot water bottle.

I said, 'Are you cold? Are you ill?'

187

'Period pain,' she said.

I'm not great at hiding my feelings. Poker wouldn't be my game.

She said, 'What? Why are you looking at me like that?'

Out with it, Dan, I thought. Nothing wrong with a bit of honesty.

I said, 'I saw the test kit in your bag. I was hoping you might be pregnant.'

'Wow,' she said. 'Just wow. You do go poking around, don't you?'

'I was looking for dental floss. Did you think you might be pregnant?'

'No,' she said. 'It's a free sample.'

She was floundering.

'They give out free sample pregnancy tests at a cardio clinic?'

'Dee gave it to me.'

'So, like, just to keep in your kit bag on the off-chance? Although I'm sure Dee knows you have zero interest in getting pregnant at the moment.'

'Jeez, Dan,' she said. 'Lighten up, will you. You're like the Spanish fucking Imposition.'

'Inquisition.'

'Whatever. I'm going to bed.'

I don't think I'll ever touch another prawn cracker as long as I live.

Chapter 19

Professor Lloyd Humphreys was in the ICU but doing well. They were giving her intravenous analgesics and had her on a sleep apnoea machine, to keep her respiration as normal as possible. The risk of her developing pneumonia was significant. Would they operate, to repair her ribs? Unlikely, according to the senior registrar.

'Five ribs broken, three of them have multiple fractures. Given her age, we're probably not looking at a great outcome. It's a case of wait and see.'

So many things are. Deb Rowlands was still a possibly/maybe case of lupus but when she came in with a livid, scaly butterfly rash on her face, I upgraded that to 'likely.'

Deb had been working outdoors at the garden centre.

I said, 'I did warn you to stay out of the sun. Can't you wear a hat?'

'I keep forgetting,' she said. 'Makes you feel better though, doesn't it, a bit of sun? I've been putting proper medical cream on it, but it won't budge.'

'What cream?'

She fished it out of her bag. Betnovate.

'Where did you get this?'

'Bathroom cupboard. My dad had it for his dermatitis.'

189

If I ruled the world, I'd make everyone clear out their bathroom cabinets. There'd be an amnesty, a few weeks when they could turn in their old medicines without a penalty. After that, I'd throw the book at them.

I took the Betnovate and tossed it in my bin. She was shocked.

I said, 'Two reasons I did that. Number one, Betnovate is too strong to slap on a rash without a very good reason. It's not Nivea, Deb. Number two, how long has it been in your cupboard?'

'Don't know.'

'Does your father still have dermatitis?'

'No. He's been dead seven years.'

'In which case, the Betnovate's probably lost its potency by now.'

'So, I can still use it?'

She's not a stupid woman. She just doesn't listen.

'No. I'm going to give you a prescription for a mild hydrocortisone cream. Use that and nothing else. And stay out of the sun. Apart from the rash, how are you?'

'Yeah, alright. My mum's got chronic indigestion. We've tried everything. Rennies, Alka-Seltzer.'

'She should come and see me.'

'Can't you give me something for her?'

'No.'

'Why?'

'Because I'm a doctor, not a convenience store.'

'Nice mood you're in,' she said.

I didn't argue.

Freddie Scurlock had earache. He was four years old and he'd been grizzling on and off all night. He sat on his mum's lap, pulling at his ear.

I said, 'I like your shoes. Do they light up?'

He buried his face in his mum's chest.

'This isn't like him,' she said. 'Normally he'd be running around. He'd be into everything.'

His temperature was 39 degrees, but his eardrum looked normal and there was no discharge.

I said, 'Let's try Calpol and a heat pad. I don't like giving kids antibiotics unless there's a very sound reason.'

'Me neither,' she said. 'What about garlic oil?'

'I put it on pizza, myself.'

Freddie's mother said I ought to know about essential oils. Nature's pharmacy, she called them. Maybe she was right. There are a lot of things I should probably know about.

Freddie slipped down off her lap to show me how his shoes lit up.

I said, 'I'm going to get some of those. What do you think?'

He said I was too old.

'How old do you think I am?'

'Four and ten and a hundred million.'

'Would you like a sticker?'

He nodded. But when I got out my sheet of stickers the only ones left were pink, girlie ones. I did an old Trevor Buxton trick and drew a smiley face on a tongue depressor instead. He liked that. Then he wanted one for his mum, one for his dad and one for his gran. He ended up with a full set, including a dog. And he took a pink sticker. Freddie left my office laden with Dan Talbot merchandise.

Mrs Scurlock said I seemed good with the little ones.

191

She said, 'How many have you got yourself?'
Ouch.

Bethan had taken to giving me a daily update on the drugs cupboard. Since the Leon Caddick episode and a restock of OxyContin, nothing had gone missing.

She said, 'It looks like he's come to his senses. I'm glad I spoke up. I didn't enjoy doing it. He's a very nice man. But sometimes a person needs a jolt.'

I went through the motions, agreed the signs were encouraging. Bethan didn't need to know she was far from being the only one keeping an eye on David.

'And what's happening about your adenoma?'

'They've started me on some pills. Caberlin. I have to take them twice a week.'

'Any side effects?'

'Not so far. They said I might get hot flushes. Well I've been through that before. I'm getting first class treatment at home, though. Merv's waiting on me, hand and foot. I mean, they explained it all to him, at the hospital, how it's not a bad kind of tumour, but he's still on pins. He still keeps telling me to put my feet up.'

It was Thursday lunchtime when things began to unravel. Delyth had taken a message for me to call Miriam Parry and I had my hand on the phone when David walked into my office, without knocking.

'I'll be taking some time off,' he said. Straight in, no preamble.

'Okay. You know I have some holiday booked? Like, tomorrow afternoon, for instance.'

'It won't affect you,' he said. 'Dylan Tew is going to locum.'

'And that'll be when?'

'Immediately.'

I said, 'This is very spur of the moment. Are you alright?'

'I'm fine,' he said. 'I just need a bit of time off.'

'Are you going away?'

'Possibly,' he said. He was shifting from one foot to the other, more like a schoolboy who'd been hauled in before the headmaster, than a boss telling his junior about his holiday plans. With Trevor Buxton this would have been a clear signal to go to the Black Bear.

I said, 'David, you have me worried.'

'So I gather. You and half the town. It's a shame you didn't talk to me, a shame you didn't check your facts before you started gossiping.'

I wasn't having that.

I said, 'I tried to talk to you. You told me to fuck off.'

That threw him for a moment. I don't think he remembered. He said he had a few things to sort out.

I said, 'Then time off seems like a good idea.'

He turned to go.

'All the best,' I said, to his back. 'Whatever you decide to do.'

The moment he'd gone, Iestyn appeared, even paler than usual. Downstairs the phone rang, then Delyth yelled, 'Dr Talbot, I've got...'

I said, 'Press 3, damn it. How many times do we have to go over this?'

I picked up. The call dropped. Iestyn sat down.

'Who was it, Delyth?'

She thundered up the stairs. 'It was Dr Miriam,' she said, in a whisper that you could have heard in Llandudno. The phone rang again.

All Miriam said was, 'You knew.'

'Tell me what's happened.'

'What the hell, Dan? He was dealing with it himself. You've backed him into a corner. You and Harry and Hilary. I hope you're satisfied.'

I said, 'It wasn't my intention. Frankly, I didn't know what to think or who to turn to.'

'You should have talked to me. Not gone behind our backs.'

Her voice was thick with tears. She said, 'I thought you were a friend, Dan.'

And she was gone.

Iestyn had his head in his hands. That really pushed my buttons.

I said, 'I don't know why you're acting so tragic. We both know David needs help. The pilot has now abandoned the cockpit, so that leaves you in charge. Do you know this locum?'

He sighed. Dylan Tew had apparently locum'd for us on a couple of occasions, before my time. What was he like?

'He's an older person,' says Iestyn. 'Not easy. He doesn't believe in ADHD and he thinks anti-vaxxers should be shot.'

If I hadn't been feeling so upset about Miriam and David and the whole horrible mess, that information would have cheered me up.

I met Dylan Tew five minutes before the start of afternoon surgery. He was short, round and red-faced. Like a billiard ball in baggy suit and a strange embroidered hat, the kind of thing an African chief might wear.

'Tew,' he said, and shook my hand. 'You're the new face. I gather Parry's gone off the deep end.'

I said it was a delicate situation.

'Often is,' he said. 'Questions. Does the mad Pole still work here?'

'Aggie? She does a couple of surgeries a week. She had a baby not long ago.'

'Another one? Good grief, the woman must be permanently in calf. You wouldn't think Ginger had it in him. Second question, are you a drinking man?'

'As long as it's close to home.'

'Friday, after the shop's closed? In the Toad?'

'Any other day. I'm leaving early tomorrow, going to see my folks. Making the most of the Bank Holiday weekend.'

'Tuesday, then. Where's home?'

'Home's Rhos. But I'm from Abergavenny originally. That's where my parents are.'

'Ah,' he said, 'the mighty Usk. Where I once caught an 8 lb salmon.'

Bethan thought Dr Tew's arrival was a good sign. It meant David had accepted he needed treatment. I wasn't so sure. Delyth said it was all over Colwyn that Dr Parry had cancer and wasn't expected to live.

I said, 'That's not true. He's just taking some time off.'

She said, 'I'm only telling you what Joan Toplady said, and she heard it in the Co-Op. And another thing. I shall be finishing work on the dot while that Dr Tew's here. I won't be hanging about if he's in the building.'

'You always finish on the dot. What's Dr Tew done to offend you?'

'I don't like the way he looks at me.'

'And how's that?'

'He looks at my bosom.'

Delyth is quite well-endowed, although more matronly than pneumatic, I'd say. Also given to delusions.

I said, 'There's a good reason he looks at your bosom. It's at his eye-level.'

She said I had no idea what women have to put up with.

Iestyn hid in his office until Dylan Tew had left the building. I was about to call it a day myself when my mobile rang.

Miriam said, 'I'm so sorry, Dan. I was horrid to you. I didn't mean what I said.'

We talked a little. David had asked Hilary for more pills, Hilary had challenged him about how much OxyContin he was using, they'd got into an argument and David had thrown a punch. It was hard to imagine. He was such a mild-mannered man.

'Is Hilary hurt?'

'No. David missed.'

'What happens now?'

'He's agreed to go for detox, but only because Hilary hasn't given him much choice. I don't think he accepts that he has a problem.'

'That was the impression I had. Did you have any idea?'

'None. I knew he'd tried Oxys, for his back. I didn't know he was still taking them. What does that say about me? Some doctor. Some wife.'

'If it weren't for Leon Caddick, I don't think anyone here would have realised either. Well, Bethan had her suspicions, but I certainly didn't.'

'Who's Leon Caddick?'

'One of our regulars. He took Delyth hostage and demanded oxycodone. Only the cupboard was bare. David didn't tell you?'

'No. I wonder what else he didn't tell me?'

'Where will he go to detox?'

'Some place in Cheshire, on Saturday, if they'll take him. And if he keeps his promise. I won't believe he's going till he's gone. Hilary's organising it.

'Will you be okay?'

'Have to be, won't I? Harry's coming over to keep me company on Saturday night, which is very sweet of her considering the names I called her yesterday.'

'It's my fault Harry got embroiled.'

'I know. But fault's not the word, Dan. You're the *reason*.'

'Do your kids know what's going on?'

'Joe does. I'm afraid he witnessed the big confrontation and it wasn't pretty. At the moment he won't even speak to David. He's processing it, I suppose. Dad, the drug addict. I'm trying to keep it from Becca at least until he's completed the detox. She's a real Daddy's girl and Liverpool's a bit too close to this Warrington clinic. She'll want to visit him and that wouldn't be a good idea.'

What could I say? You'll get through this? Patronising. Don't forget to take care of yourself? Very patronising. I settled for, 'If there's anything I can do.'

'There is,' she said. 'Keep your hand on the tiller. Iestyn's not great in a crisis. Aggie's better but she's not around much.'

'We've got Dr Tew.'

'Dylan. Yes, I know him well. He's a good doctor, but best to keep him away from the controls. It won't be difficult. He's a nine till five man, but he can be a wild card. He has strong opinions. You're the safer pair of hands. And I know that's David's opinion too, though I doubt he'd ever tell you.'

Only seven months into my first post-reg job and it was my shaky hand on the tiller. After what Miriam had said, I didn't take Friday afternoon off. I could have done. There were no dramas, no majors, just the usual parade of niggles and twinges that suddenly seem worse before a three-day surgery shutdown, but I felt I should stay till closing time. It was late when I got to Abergavenny and I was knackered.

Nan was already asleep, so we sat in the kitchen and spoke in whispers.

Mam said, 'What it is, she's looking for her bed by half past eight. Then she's up at five, wanting her breakfast.'

I said I'd do the early shift so Mam and Da could sleep in.

'Maybe on Sunday,' says Mam. 'You look like you need a good night's rest yourself. And where's Chloe this weekend?'

'At a music festival. There's a crowd of them going. Not my scene though.'

Mam said she thought only teenagers went to that kind of thing. Queuing for the lav and getting silly on wacky baccy.

I said, 'I'm told it's a bit more refined than that. The tents have proper beds and everything.'

'I see,' says Mam. 'Well I suppose it'd have to be. She's not exactly one for roughing it, is she?'

It wasn't like Mam to say anything negative about Chloe and I caught Da shooting her a little look, as if to say, 'Steady on, Eirwen.'

But Mam was at the end of a frayed rope, tired from keeping Nan Hours, still drained by the shingles, and not inclined to mince her words.

'That beautiful home you've made for her, and she never seems to be there. Call me old-fashioned but sometimes I wonder why you got married.'

We crept past Nan's bedroom door. There was a night light burning in her room and you could hear her gently whiffling in her sleep. I was bone tired. I didn't hang up my clothes, didn't read. I just put my head on the pillow and passed out. The next thing I knew, someone was trying to climb in beside me.

Nan said, 'Budge over, Edwin. I've been to the kitchen and there's no sign of any breakfast yet.'

She thought I was my grandfather. I made room for her and just hoped the only thing she wanted was someone to warm her feet on.

I looked at my phone. I was 4 a.m.

Chapter 20

I'd planned to take Nan out for a few hours. Maybe drive to Crickhowell, find a tearoom and get her talking about the old days. Mam said I'd never be able to manage her on my own. That she'd try to open the car door while we were still moving, or she'd go to the Ladies and come out with her skirt tucked in her knickers.

'Besides,' she said, 'I don't want your Nan hogging you. I'd like to spend some time with you.'

In the end, Aunty June was the solution. Just back from the Canaries and as brown as a hazelnut, she said she'd sit with Nan while Da mowed the lawn and I took Mam into town. She got a cut and blow-dry, then we went for afternoon tea at The Angel where Mam insisted on telling the waitress, 'This is my son. He's a doctor.'

I said, 'Cheers for that. Now I'll be on call for a Heimlich manoeuvre if anyone starts choking on their cucumber sandwich.'

We talked about Nan.

Mam said, 'I know what you're going to say. We'll have to put her in a home.'

'Have you started looking?'

'Not really. We do talk about it, but then your Da back-pedals.'

'All very well for him. He's not there half the time. When's he retiring?'

'End of the year.'

'End of which year?'

She laughed.

'Look,' she said, 'I'll do it while I can. It's not a lot for an old lady to ask. She can't help the way she is, and I can manage. I just get a bit rattled sometimes.'

My brother, Adam, is a no-go topic with Mam, but I always try. He's her son, for crying out loud, and I know she'd like to see more of him. I suggested we drive down to Cardiff the next day for a surprise visit. I knew what she'd say. Adam hates surprises.

I said, 'Do you know I've never set foot in his house? Isn't that weird?'

'He's not the type for socialising.'

'Hardly socialising. I'm talking about a cup of tea and hello bro, what's new with you. How long did he stay at my wedding? An hour at most.'

'You don't understand him.'

'I shared a bedroom with him for sixteen years. One of these days I swear I'm going to doorstep him.'

'Not with me in the car you won't. He'd be furious. He'd go off on one and then you'd be sorry.'

I said, 'Mam, are you frightened of him?'

'Don't talk so daft,' she said. But I think she is scared of him, just a bit.

'Anyway,' she said, 'On a Sunday he'd be out on his bike or something. It'd be a wasted journey.'

'I think he's got a woman we don't know about. Or a man.'

She refuses to entertain that possibility. It's not that she minds men in general being homosexual, but Adam doesn't fit her view of a gay man. Her trump card is that he used to play prop forward. Therefore, he cannot be gay. QED.

She said, 'I'm not rising to it, Daniel. You're just trying to wind me up. Let's talk about you. Are they working you too hard? You looked all in last night.'

I told her about David Parry. I thought she'd be shocked.

'No,' she said, 'It doesn't surprise me. I've seen it happen. I've seen midwives helping themselves to pethidine. It's an easy thing to start and the hardest thing to stop. They must think very highly of you, though, putting you in charge.'

'It's not an official thing. I don't know if David or Miriam told everyone else, or even if it's just Miriam's idea. I feel like a bit of a fraud, to be honest. I can't even sign death certificates yet. Iestyn's older than me and more experienced. The locum's much older than me. Sometimes even the nurse seems to know more than I do.'

No bad thing, Mam said. It'd stop me getting too big for my boots.

We didn't go to Cardiff. All things considered, I didn't want to see my brother's cross face and shiny, shaved bonce. I'd just have liked to remind him that Mam loves him, and she'd like to see him once in a while.

At the meddygfa, my hope was that we could get through David's absence without me having to exert my authority. I hadn't allowed for the Aggie Factor. On Tuesday morning she was on my case.

'Why you are boss? Iestyn should be boss.'

202

I said, 'I'm not the boss.'

'Yes, yes,' she said. 'Miriam has said. Dan is in charge.'

'But we don't really need a boss. We're a team. She only said that in case there's a decision to be made quickly, and it's unlikely there will be.'

'What decision? Iestyn can make decision.'

I was quite surprised by what I said next.

I said, 'Actually, Iestyn doesn't like making decisions. Shall I give you an example?'

'What example?'

'He had a patient presenting with signs of a pulmonary embolism, but he left it up to me whether we called an ambulance.'

That got her off my back. She went to give Iestyn an ear-bending instead, poor guy.

Dylan Tew and I had agreed to meet for a drink after work. He was at the pub ahead of me, halfway down his pint, and he was wearing another exotic-looking hat, like a skull cap covered with little beads. I asked him about it. He took it off and looked at it.

'Turkmen, this one, I think. Or is it Uzbek? I've got so many I get them mixed up.'

'Collected on your travels?'

'No, no,' he said. 'I don't travel. I don't have a passport. I just like collecting hats.'

Each time I'd looked at Dylan I'd revised my estimate of his age. My first guess had been a well-preserved seventy. Then I thought early sixties. Now, sitting with him, he could have been anything over forty. His face was boyish, his style was old man. He recommended the Wild Horse and gestured to the barman to bring me a half. It seemed he was a regular.

How was his locum-ing going? Nothing to it, he said. He knew the practice well. He'd known Iestyn's predecessor and the predecessor's predecessor. I asked him when he'd retired from his own practice.

'Never had one,' he said. 'Never wanted the worry of it. Look what's happened to Parry. I like the locum life. The phone rings, they have a job for me, I can say yes or I can say no.'

No passport, no fixed job, a man who preferred a modest but varied life. I was starting to take to Dylan. He was from Hereford originally, trained in Manchester, and was now living in Llandudno. His view of primary care medicine was simple. If there's a red flag, fast-track them to hospital. If they're malingerers, give them a kick up the backside and send them on their way. Everything in between, wait and see because time will usually tell.

'You don't think we should give all patients the benefit of the doubt? Because one day a malingerer or a hypochondriac may present with a red flag.'

'But not to me,' he said. 'They'll decide they don't like me and go to a different doctor, someone like Iestyn Hughes who'll listen to them whining and wittering till the cows come home. Personally, I'd charge people to see us. Not a lot, but enough to make them think twice before they waste our time or don't even turn up.'

'What about the people who can't afford to pay?'

'No such animal,' he said. 'They can afford their smokes and their scratch cards. Go to their houses and you'll find they have a telly the size of a billboard. I don't buy this 'can't afford it. So Parry's got himself hooked on opioids. That's a tragedy.'

'It is. You know him well?'

'Miriam, more than him. But I've locum'd for both of them. He's a reserved man. I hope they haven't sent him somewhere he's expected to sit in a circle and 'share."'

'You don't think sharing helps?'

He thought for a minute.

He said, 'For some. Alcoholics Anonymous, some people swear by it. But I'd imagine David Parry's feeling too mortified to open up. Does he even accept he has a problem? He told me he was just tired and needed a proper holiday. What's your story? Wife? Kids? Addictions?'

'Wife yes, no kids and no serious addictions. Crisps. Seed catalogues. Chloe's a cardiologist. We moved here from Birmingham earlier this year and bought a house in Rhos.'

'Nice,' he said. 'Rhos is nice.'

'And you fly fish? Did you know Nurse Bethan's husband ties flies?'

'Yes, I've met Merv. Of course, he's more of a trout man. Salmon's my fish. I go to Bangor-on-Dee when I get the itch. Well, I'm glad to know you, Dan Talbot. I don't mind a quiet life but sometimes that surgery feels like a graveyard.'

'Unless Aggie's in.'

'Ah yes. Aggie. Funny, isn't it, how people pair off? Iestyn's as quiet as a chapel fart and he married a woman who never stops talking. But as my old mother used to say, as He hatches them, so He matches them. Well, I should be getting home to my boys.'

I thought he was about to reveal the existence of an unexpected wife and family, but he was talking about his cats. Dylan has three rescue toms. Also, a lot of strong opinions and a collection of snazzy, embroidered hats.

Chloe had come back from the Mandala Festival with the runs, caused, she thought, by a suspect kebab. I had the impression the weekend hadn't been a brilliant success. It had rained on Saturday night and their yurt had sprung a leak. Then Dee had found an old Elastoplast in their hot tub. And a dog from one of the neighbouring tents had nicked all their Iberian ham.

I said, 'That's what's known as a First World problem.'

'Why?'

'Because if that's all you had to worry about, life was pretty good.'

'Do you know how much Iberian ham costs?'

'You haven't asked me my news.'

'What?'

'David Parry has an opioid addiction. He's in a clinic, detoxing.'

'No! For real?'

'For real. Also, my Nan kept getting into bed with me.'

'David Parry? Dr Straight and Boring?'

'He'd been prescribed oxycodone for back pain. You know how easy it is to get hooked.'

'Shit. So, he like, just announced it? My name's David and I'm an addict?'

'No. There was a kind of intervention. Hilary, his GP, and Miriam. I sort of knew. We'd had pills go missing at the surgery and then Harry did some investigating. David had been self-prescribing.'

'Wait, what? I'm confused. Is Hilary the fashion train wreck who has a crush on you, or the fit gay guy?'

'Hilary's the man. Harry's the woman. And she does not have a crush on me. So, David's gone for a while. We have a locum called Dylan Tew and I'm the designated decision maker.'

'For real? Does that mean you get more money?'

'No, it means I get more sleepless nights. Is Hilary what you'd describe as fit?'

'Six pack, defo. What a waste. Why did your Nan get into bed with you?'

'She mistook me for my grandad. That's what happens with dementia. It's horrible.'

'They'll have to put her into a home. I need more Lomotil.'

I said I'd go to the pharmacy.

'And I need wet wipes, and hair scrunchies. And if you're going into town, get some chocolate biscuits.'

'I thought you were feeling ill.'

'Not chocolate biscuit ill. Charlie's buying a flat in Dubai.'

Charlie 'Slow' Swift had apparently bounced back from his stint behind bars. Not that Coldingley had been that kind of prison. He hadn't had to wear a ball and chain.

'You spoke to Charlie?'

'No, Flo told me. It's in a building with its own swimming pool and gym and everything. I can't wait to go. He'd damned well better invite us.'

'What is there to do in Dubai?'

'I don't know. Shopping. The flat's on a high floor so it'll have wowser views.'

'We've got a wowser view here, in case you hadn't noticed. How was Flo?'

'She phoned to tell me Grandpa fell out of his wheelchair.'

'Wasn't he strapped in?'

'I don't think they're allowed, unless he's been sectioned or something. It's to do with his human rights. Anyway, he's okay. Just bruised.'

'And Flo's well?'

'Why wouldn't she be?'

'Well she is very pregnant.'

'Oh that. Yeah, she's fine. I'm going to call Slow about Dubai, before he promises it to all his mates. We could go for Christmas.'

'No thank you. I don't want to go to Dubai any time soon and definitely not for Christmas. And while we're on the subject of going away, now you've done the Mandala thing, I'd like you to spend more time at home. You did say you would.'

'Did I?'

'I miss you. And people are starting to talk.'

'What people?'

'Mam, for a start. She can't understand why you keep going away. And neither can I.'

'You want us to turn into a boring married couple.'

'Yes.'

'Going to garden centres. Visiting stately homes.'

'Sounds good to me.'

'Next thing you'll be wearing a blazer. And a cravat.'

'No, I won't. But seriously, no weekends apart for a while. If you're that desperate to see people, invite Dee and the others to come here.'

She gave me her You Can't Be Serious face.

'A month with no disappearing on Fridays. Agreed?'

'Three weeks. Marriage is about compromise, remember. His Holiness Spud-u-Like said so.'

I was surprised Chloe remembered anything from our Preparation for Marriage session with the Reverend Spedlow.

But we struck a deal and the next three weekends were blissful. We'd sleep late, eat a huge breakfast, walk on the beach a bit and then decide what to do. We went to the Swallow Falls and to Caernarvon. One Sunday Chloe actually came to church with me, but only on condition she could sit at the back and we could leave as soon as the service ended. She said if we lingered, they'd try to rope her in for something.

'You mean, like, take up the collection plate? Make the coffee once a month?'

'That's how they start. I know what those places are like. One time, St Bot's tried to get Mummy doing altar linens.'

That was a comical notion. Vinnie, a conscientious objector to ironing, a woman whose towels had been like sandpaper.

I said, 'Chloe, no-one is going to press-gang you. They know you're a busy doctor with a long commute. But it's nice for me if they can put a face to the name, otherwise they might think you don't exist. Dan's imaginary wife.'

Chapter 21

I'd heard the name Roy Savage several times, but I'd never met the man. According to Bethan he was an incorrigible flasher who made appointments to see her on some genuine pretext, like having the dressing on a deep cut changed, and then found a reason to get his tackle out. I'd pictured an old man in an Inspector Colombo raincoat, so when Roy's name appeared on my afternoon list and a good-looking, youngish bloke walked in, I was surprised.

Roy was built. His arms were so muscular they didn't sit normally. He carried them like bulging wings hung out to dry. I guessed him to be forty. According to his notes he was 42. How could I help him? He had lumps, he said, in his neck. His voice was a shock too, light, almost feminine.

The lymph glands above his right collar bone were enlarged. Had he been ill recently? An infection of any kind?

'No,' he said. 'I've just been feeling a bit humpty.'

Humpty is one of those words they don't teach you in medical school. Also, ropey, crummy, peaky, iffy. But you get the picture.

He said he'd lost a bit of weight, hadn't been sleeping well, felt tired all the time.

His temperature was 38.4. Slightly elevated. Had he noticed lumps anywhere else? No. Would he mind if I examined him? No.

He peeled off his T shirt. The man's pecs were enormous. I found two lumps in his right armpit, but only after a struggle. Roy was extremely ticklish. His spleen felt normal. The next challenge was to check his groin.

'What?' he said, 'You mean down below?'

'It'll be over in no time.'

'Important is it?'

'Yes. Very.'

I discovered two things during the examination. The lymph glands in his groin were not enlarged, and Roy had a very small penis.

The inside of his eyelids suggested he was slightly anaemic.

I said, 'About the sleepless nights, have you noticed any sweating?'

'Terrible,' he said. 'Well, we have had a hot spell. Mam's had to change my sheets a few times.'

Roy lived with his mother. He worked as a bouncer at a club in Llandudno and by the look of him he spent all his free time in the gym.

I said, 'The next thing is to take some blood and get it checked.'

'That nurse doesn't like me,' he said.

'Why do you think that?'

'I can just tell.'

'I think you're mistaken. She has a very professional attitude towards all her patients. And she's a lot better at taking blood than I am. It'll be done before you know it.'

I asked Bethan to come into my office to draw Roy's samples. Full cell count plus flow cytometry. She thanked me afterwards.

She said, 'That was very considerate of you. I'm in no mood to be looking at his John Thomas.'

I said, 'I wonder you even noticed he was flashing at you. It's not very big.'

'I'm sure I wouldn't know,' she said. 'It's not a thing I've made a study of.'

Generally, I saw more female patients than male. We served a mainly ageing population, so there were a lot of widows on our books, but that afternoon I had three male patients in a row.

Emlyn Gadd came in after Roy Savage. We'd had his silicosis confirmed by the hospital. I talked to him about using a bronchodilator and then having an oxygen cylinder at home, as things progressed. He chuckled.

He said, 'I don't know that 'progressed' is the right word. Deteriorated, more like.'

'Have you talked to an industrial injuries lawyer?'

'Lawyers!' he said. 'I've avoided them all my life.'

'But you could be entitled to compensation. Down the line you might be glad of it. And if not you, your wife.'

'I know, I know. As a matter of fact, it's the wife I wanted to ask you about. She's getting very forgetful.'

'Will she come in, so I can meet her?'

'That's the trouble. She says I'm imagining things, but I'm not. Our girls have noticed it too. I'm that worried about her.'

'What if I did a home visit? You could tell her it was for you.'

'Would you do that?'

'Of course. I could come out to give you your PPV.'

'What's that?'

'It's a vaccination against pneumonia. It's important you have it, with your lungs not being in great shape.'

'Like a 'flu injection, then.'

'Yes. Except the PPV is a one-off. I can come on Wednesday afternoon, if your wife's likely to be there.'

'She will be,' he said. 'These days she hardly goes out.'

He made me think of Trevor. Everyone's eyes on his progressive lung disease and no-one anticipating Mrs Buxton would be the first to go.

And then came Leon Caddick. It was the first time I'd seen him since the Delyth incident.

He opened with, 'She's got a face that'd stop a clock, her downstairs.'

'You mean our receptionist?'

'Yeah.'

'It's hardly surprising. The last time you were in you held a knife to her throat. You're lucky we haven't taken you off our list.'

'Naah,' he said. 'Not me.'

'Yes, you. You were demanding oxycodone pills.'

He scratched himself.

'You sure?'

'As I sit here. You didn't get any. Dr Iestyn took you down the road to the Mental Health Centre.'

'Oh yes,' he said. 'I think I remember that. He had his kiddies with him.'

'What did they do with you at the centre?'

'Now you're asking. Gave me a cup of tea, I think.'

'They didn't offer you a detox programme?'

'Don't think so.'

213

'How often do you take oxys, Leon?'

'Hard to say. When I can get them.'

'You know they're very powerful and very addictive.'

'Oh yes. It's my toe I've come about.'

Leon peeled off his cheesy white socks. He had three infected toenails. The one on his big toe was yellow and crumbling.

'You've got a fungal infection. How long have they looked like this?'

'Quite a while.'

'If you'd come as soon as it started it might not have spread.'

He said he'd kept meaning to, but he'd had a lot on.

'So, what can we do about it?'

Leon likes to use the inclusive 'we'.

I said, 'One option is to remove the infected nails, but I'm not doing that today. You'd need a local anaesthetic'

'Put me under, like?'

'No, put your toes under. I'll prescribe a cream first. Follow the instructions carefully, and make sure you wear clean socks every day.'

'Can I get them on the Health?'

'The cream? Yes. You could buy it over the counter, but I know you won't so I'm giving you a prescription.'

'No, I meant the extra socks.'

'You're taking the mickey. Use the cream. Change your socks. Come back in six weeks.'

He said, 'You don't think pills'd be better than this cream?'

Leon might not always remember where he'd been and what he'd done, he might not own a well-stocked sock drawer, but he knew a tube of clotrimazole had zero street value, whereas there was always a market for pills of any kind.

'No pills. And on your way out, you might apologise to our receptionist.'

'Consider it done,' he said. 'Consider it done.'

Roy Savage's groin, Leon Caddick's manky toenails. A GP never knows what he'll be exploring next. I'd certainly developed a stronger stomach. The first time I had a close encounter with a gangrenous diabetic foot I'd almost gagged. That was Barbara Humphries. Trevor Buxton had stepped in and done a closer examination, then he'd lit a cigarette as soon as Barbara had left the room. Better than any air-freshener, he reckoned.

I opened my window wider and sprayed a couple of squiffs of Glade, but when Lilian Blacksmith came in the first thing she said was, 'Someone's been eating Danish Blue.'

I said, 'Tell you what, Lilian. Let's check your blood pressure in Nurse Bethan's room. It's more fragrant in there.'

Her pressure was a bit high. It sometimes is, but she refuses to take anything for it.

She said, 'Course it's up. Handsome young doctor like you bending over me. What can you expect?'

Bethan smiled. She said, 'Do you have a gentleman friend at all, Mrs Blacksmith?'

Lilian said she had several, but none of them were up to standard.

Bethan said, 'What does that mean?'

'You know. Don't make me spell it out. You'll have Dr Dan blushing.'

'I'd have thought at your age you'd just be glad of a dance partner. No need for any extras.'

'Well you'd have thought wrong. You're never too old for a kiss and a cuddle. Now what's going on with Dr David? I heard he's ever so poorly, not expected to live. Then at aquarobics somebody said he'd been found to be an alcoholic and they'd had to put him away.'

'All gossip. There's no truth in either story, Lilian. He's taking a well-deserved break and he'll be back.'

'Good. Because I like him. He's another one that gives me blood pressure.'

'How long have you been a widow, Lilian?'

'Too long,' she said.

When I went down to Reception at the end of the day, there was a box of chocolates on the desk.

I said, 'What's this? Do you have an admirer?'

Delyth said she was ignoring it.

'Who's it from?'

'That worm.'

'Does the worm have a name?'

'Caddick.'

'I think he's trying to apologise for the knife business.'

'I'd as soon he got a new doctor. I'd as soon he went to a different surgery. He gives me the heeby-jeebies.'

'He doesn't remember attacking you.'

'So he says. Nice for him. Well *I* remember.'

'Give them to Bethan if you don't want them.'

Bethan was right behind me.

'Give me what? That box of chocolates? No thank you. I've just started Weight Watchers.'

Delyth's final word on the subject was, 'Take them for your wife. She won't know where they came from. More than likely he nicked them from SPAR anyway.'

216

So Chloe got a second-hand box of Ferrero Rocher, possibly shop-lifted but no questions asked, and when Bethan went to Weight Watchers, though she hadn't lost any weight she hadn't gained any either.

Emlyn Gadd and his wife lived in Old Colwyn. I was expected, but Emlyn had asked one of their daughters to happen to drop by while I was there too.

'That way,' he said, 'you'll see April more natural. She'll be so busy nattering to our Katie, she won't notice you're studying her.'

Mrs Gadd said Emlyn was getting Rolls Royce treatment, having a vaccination done at home. She was still a pretty woman, very soft and smiley. We chatted a little before I gave Emlyn his shot. The daughter arrived.

Mrs Gadd said, 'Daddy's getting the Rolls Royce treatment.'

I said, 'Your garden's a picture. Who's the gardener?'

'That'd be April,' says Emlyn. 'She's the gaffer. I just follow orders. Should you like the guided tour? There's no charge.'

April could tell me the names of every plant in the flower beds and which variety of peas I should try in my plot. Kelvedon Wonder, apparently. But several times she whispered to her daughter, 'who is he?'

We went back into the house.

There's no easy way to do the next thing.

I said, 'Mrs Gadd, you seem like you might be having a bit of trouble with your memory. Not all the time. Just some things. What do you think?'

She said nothing for a moment.

Then she said, 'So this was all a put-up job. Injections done at home. I thought as much. I'm not so green as I'm cabbage looking.'

Their daughter said, 'Mam...'

'I know, I know,' she said. 'There's no need to ambush me.'

Emlyn had tears in his eyes.

'Cariad,' he said, 'As if we would. But you're a stubborn woman. I should know. Why don't we just listen to what the doctor has to say?'

She listened, but with a face that said, 'you're wasting your time.'

The next part is easier. You can talk about some of the fixable reasons a person's memory might be failing.

'And?' she said. 'What if it's not anything like that? What if I've got softening of the brain?'

'Did you know someone who had that?'

Her mother and an aunt had been diagnosed with senile dementia, back in the day. I said we'd made progress since then. That there was medication. I didn't talk it up too much. April was an intelligent woman. If she ever opened a newspaper, she knew there was no cure for dementia. Only a way of slowing the descent. A parachute pill.

I suggested the first thing we should do was to make sure her thyroid was functioning properly. She said yes, she'd come in for a blood test, but she couldn't say when it would be.

'How about next week?'

'I don't know,' she said. 'There's a lot to do this time of year. You're a gardener. You should know.'

Her daughter said, 'Mam, you're going into town next week to get your hair permed. You can easy drop by the meddygfa. Let the doctor take some blood.'

'There you go again,' says April. 'Do this, do that. I won't be bullied, Katie. I'll think about it.'

It was fair enough. Whatever was causing Mrs Gadd's problem, it wasn't likely to be life-threatening. A week here or there wouldn't make a difference. She was entitled to some thinking time. With her family history, maybe she felt she already had dementia in the bank. Maybe *I* do. My Nan has it. Would I want to be told as early as possible? Hand on heart, I really don't know.

All I can say is that the following week, a newly-permed April Gadd came in with her daughter and as well as having some blood taken she agreed to let me do the mini mental status exam.

'Go on, then,' she said. 'If I don't, I shall never hear the end of it from Emlyn.'

She was perfectly oriented as to time and place, named the objects I pointed to and managed the backwards counting faster than I could. When it came to recalling the five words I'd asked her to remember she was completely lost and the clock face I asked her to draw, with numbers and the hands pointing to three o'clock, defeated her, though she didn't seem to realise it. She handed me back the paper and pencil and all she'd drawn was a circle.

'Well?' she said. 'How did I do?'

'Not bad. But could have been better. There's a pill that might help. Would you like to give it a try?'

She said she might.

She said, 'My husband's not well.'

'I know. It's caused by the dust from his work.'

She looked at me.

She said, 'Do you know my husband then?'

'I do. I'm his doctor.'

'That's right,' she said. 'I knew that.'

I wrote her a prescription for Aricept.

They were leaving and her daughter said, 'Mam, haven't you got something for Dr Talbot?'

''What?' she said. 'Am I supposed to pay him?'

'No,' says Katie, 'you brought him something. In your bag?'

Mrs Gadd had brought me pea seeds.

She said, 'You're too late for Kelvedon Wonders this year, so I brought you these. They're called Feltham First. You can sow these in October. You can't beat peas fresh from your own garden.'

Chapter 22

Chloe was going off for a girls' weekend, her first for a while. She started packing on Tuesday evening. You'd have thought she was about to be released from prison, she was so eager to be gone.

I said, 'It's a good job I'm not an over-sensitive guy.'

'But you'll be free to have your own kind of fun,' she said. 'Hoeing and stuff.'

'One of these days I might drive to Birmingham and surprise you. See what it is you women get up to.'

For a moment she thought I was serious.

'Don't you dare,' she said. 'That'd be like parents snooping around their teenagers. Locking away the booze. Sniffing for weed.'

'Did Vinnie and Laurence snoop around you?'

'Mummy did, a bit. She was mainly worried about heavy petting although I don't think she knew exactly what that was.'

'Of course, she did. It wasn't invented yesterday. Vinnie was a teenager in the Sixties, for heaven's sake.'

'I suppose. She had a kind of tariff. Snogging with mouths closed, fine. Snogging with mouths open, riskier. Getting fresh, which was okay as long as there were other people around.

Heavy petting, uh-oh, because it might lead to Going the Whole Way.'

'I miss your mother.'

'Do you? I hardly know yours.'

'That's not her fault. You're the elusive daughter-in-law.'

On Saturday I went to a barbecue at Liz and Jim Morgan's. He sings tenor in the church choir, she's a soprano. They live in Mochdre.

'Wife working?' everyone kept asking. I said she was.

Merv and Bethan were there.

Bethan said, 'Guess who I saw in the Victoria Centre this morning? David. He's back.'

She'd spotted David and Miriam going into Boots. They hadn't spoken but they'd waved. How had he seemed?

'He didn't look any different,' she said. 'Dressed in his usual. I wonder if he'll be at work on Monday? Dr Tew didn't say anything.'

On Sunday I'd just got in from church and turned my phone on. There was a missed call, but no message. I called the number.

'Packwood,' said a familiar voice. It was Henry.

I said, 'It's Dan. Has the baby arrived?'

'Ah,' he said. 'Dan. No, no baby. Any day now. I was calling regarding another matter.'

Silence.

'It concerns Chloe.'

Another silence. I got the feeling Henry needed help.

'Have she and Flo had another quarrel?'

'Not at all. Well here's the nub of it. Flo received a call this morning, from the University Hospital in Coventry. It seems Chloe has been in a bit of a prang.'

My heart started pounding.

'Is she badly hurt?'

'No, no. Just a little battered, I think. The thing is, Dan, they've asked whether a family member might attend and as Flo is about to farrow, I fear she can't help. I'd go myself but one's presence would be of little comfort to Chloe. Anyway, I prefer not to venture far from the farrowing stall at this time. You'll understand?'

About to farrow. Sometimes I wish I could bottle Henry's language. Is there another man alive who talks about his wife as though she's a pig and means no disrespect?

'I do understand. What about her father?'

'Laurence and his friend are away. A cruise on the Danube. I wondered about one of Chloe's doctor chums. Might there be someone in the locality?'

'Dee would be the nearest. Hang on though. Why is Chloe at a hospital in Coventry?'

'I really have no idea. One imagines they were driving nearby.'

'They?'

'Chloe was a passenger. Which is as much as I know.'

'Then Dee must be with her. She's been staying at Dee's over the weekend.'

'Perhaps,' says Henry, 'you might phone this Dee person. Or indeed the hospital.'

'I will.'

'Sorry to be the bearer of bad news.'

I said, 'Henry, why did the hospital call Flo instead of me?'

223

'No idea, old boy,' he said. 'But do let us know how you get on.'

I called the hospital. It took forever to speak to someone. Sunday lunchtime, A&E would be busy with sports' injuries and DIY mishaps. Chloe wasn't in A&E. Apart from some minor lacerations, she'd been slightly concussed, so she'd spent the night on an observation ward. Spent the night? The accident had happened on Saturday afternoon, and I was apparently the last to be informed.

I said, 'I'm in North Wales. Do I need to come?'

'Only if you want to.'

'What about getting home tomorrow? Is she fit to drive?'

They said the friend who'd been with Chloe in the car had been discharged and had mentioned coming to collect her.

I called the Queen Elizabeth. Eventually, reluctantly, they gave me Dee's mobile number. It rang for ages. She sounded as though I'd woken her.

I said, 'It's Dan. Are you okay?'

'Who?'

'Chloe's Dan. Are you going to the hospital?'

'No, I'm at home and I was asleep. It's Sunday, for fuck's sake.'

Then things began to unfold in small, slippery steps.

'So, you're not going to see Chloe?'

'Oh, I get it,' she said. 'You're checking up on her again.'

'She's in hospital, Dee. She's been in a car crash and she's in hospital, in Coventry.'

'Shit,' she said. 'Is it bad?'

'Mild concussion. She was a passenger. I assumed you were the driver. But I guess not. Now the question is, who was she with?'

'How should I know?'

'You must know. You're her cover story. Another girls' weekend at Dee's. That's what she told me.'

'Hey,' she said, 'leave me out of this.'

'You're not going to tell me who she's with?'

'I think that's Chloe's job, don't you? It's not my fault if you can't keep your wife happy.'

'I suppose I'm just going to have to drive to Coventry and find out for myself.'

There was a pause. Dee was calculating how much of a friend to be to Chloe.

'Okay,' she said. 'I'll go. Give me an hour to shower and get coffee.'

I said, 'Don't bother. I'm on my way.'

Which wasn't quite true. I needed to close up the house, get petrol, warn Iestyn I might not make it back in time for Monday morning surgery. I had a three-hour drive ahead of me, and then what? Why hadn't Chloe asked the hospital to call me? Didn't she want me there? And as she hadn't been with Dee, who had she been with? I was going because I was Chloe's next of kin. But mainly I was going because I had to put a face to what I'd sort of guessed for a long time.

I stopped at the Sandbach Roadchef for a cappuccino and a muffin. The closer I got to Coventry the less I wanted to arrive there. Part of me wanted to talk to Mam, or anyone else who might offer me words of wisdom. Part of me wanted to crawl under a rock. I rehearsed several versions of the conversation I was likely to have with Chloe, gave it up as a bad job and set off on the final leg.

Chloe was on Ward 12. Was I a relative?

'I'm her husband.'

I registered a little flicker of something from the charge nurse. What was it? Amusement? Interest? Did even he know more than I did? Or was my imagination working overtime?

'Right,' he said. 'Let me just check if she's decent.'

'Tell me about her condition first. Has she had a CT scan?'

He looked at me.

He said, 'You'd need to speak to a doctor.'

I said, 'I am a doctor.'

I didn't feel like a doctor. It wasn't my territory. I was just a relative, the kind of person I'd had to deal with when I was training. Nice normal people made narky and demanding by fear for their loved one.

I said, 'All I want to know is what was her GCS score on admission, what is it now, and has she been scanned?'

He checked Chloe's notes. On admission she'd scored 13/15 on the Glasgow Coma Scale. There had been transient loss of consciousness and mild verbal confusion. Her motor responses had been normal. The confusion had resolved and she was now fully conscious, scoring 15/15. There was some neck tenderness, but she had a normal range of rotation and there was no peripheral neurological deficit.

'Sounds like she's ready for discharge.'

He said, 'I think she may be staying with us for another night. But as I said, you'd need to speak to a doctor.'

I said, 'Then I'd like to do that. As soon as possible.'

Chloe was in a bay with two other women. She was looking at her phone. She jumped when she saw me. I wasn't who she was expecting. She closed her eyes and said, 'Where's Flo? I asked Flo to come.'

'Flo's due to give birth. Why should she trail over here when you have a husband?'

'You were in Wales. I didn't want to bother you.'

226

'It's not a bother for a man to rush to his wife's side when she's been injured. Not under normal circumstances, anyway. Who were you with?'

'Don't start,' she said.

We sat in silence. Probably two or three minutes, but it felt like hours.

'How did you get here so fast?'

'With my foot to the floor. Who is it, Chloe? I know you weren't with Dee. Let's get this over and done, then I'll leave you to sleep.'

It was a moment she must have prepared for, though with Chloe you could never be sure. She often didn't think things through. Maybe she'd imagined she could get away with it. A bit of fun, with Dee as her cover. It would run its course, then she'd be back to playing house with good old Dan. Until the next time.

Her lips looked pinched and dry. The woman in the next bed was talking loudly on her phone.

'God,' says Chloe, 'this is torture. Can't I get a private room?'

I said, 'Here's what's going to happen. You're going to tell me who you were spending the weekend with, then I'm going to drive back to Wales. If you want a private room, you can make your own arrangements. Call your father. Isn't he Dr Fix-It?'

'Daddy's away.'

'Who were you with?'

'You're not going to fight?'

'With you? No, I'm done.'

'Not with me! With him. It wouldn't be fair. He's broken his shoulder.'

'Then I hope he thinks you're worth it. Name?'

227

'Fitzie.'

She whispered it.

Fitzie. George Fitzgerald, the supercilious Curly-Wurly eater I'd met at the CSA exam centre. What had he said? '*You're* married to Chloe Swift? Wow!' And what had Chloe said? 'He's just an old friend, Dan.' A bit gormless, she'd said. But her mother had liked him.

'Fitzgerald. I might have guessed. Well, he can pick you up, when you're discharged. Oh, no, he can't drive with a broken shoulder. Maybe Dee can do it. She's been a good friend, covering your tracks.'

'You never liked her.'

'Correct. That glamping weekend? Were you with him?'

No answer.

'Did you even go to the Mandala festival?'

'Yes.' She sounded outraged that I'd even asked.

'No wonder there wasn't room for me in your leaking yurt.'

She said she was sorry. For what? Getting caught out? She said she hadn't meant to hurt me. But, what? Whoops, shit happens?

She said, 'I wish you'd stop pacing and sit down.'

'No point. I'm leaving.'

'You only just got here.'

For a moment she looked truly stricken. Was I being too hard on her?

One of the other women was listening to our conversation.

'There doesn't seem any reason to stay. I don't quite understand why they're keeping you in. You seem fine.'

'Could you do something for me? Would you phone the clinic in the morning, tell them I won't be in? Please.'

'I will. And you'll let me know when you want to collect your stuff.'

'What do you mean?'

'Obviously you'll be moving out. No need to skulk around anymore. You can move in with Fitzgerald, all above board. Remind me, where does he live?'

'Here. Coventry.'

'Of course. Lovely. I thought his family owned half of Ireland.'

'I never said that.'

'Yes, you did. Well maybe they'll buy him a nice little practice somewhere. You can be married to a small-town GP. Oh, wait, you already tried that.'

'There's no need to be sarcastic.'

Maybe she was right. It just seemed the best weapon to hand.

A junior doctor came in.

She said, 'Dr Swift, we're going to move you up to Short Stay. You're on the list for a D&C in the morning. I've no idea what time they'll get to you, but you should be okay to go home later tomorrow.'

I wonder if she felt a change of atmosphere. She looked how I felt, poor blighter. Tired, going through the motions, desperate to rip off her scrubs and put her head on a pillow.

I said, 'Excuse me, why does my wife need a D&C?'

The houseman looked from me to Chloe and back to me. Chloe had her eyes closed. Even the loudmouth in the next bed had stopped talking and put down her phone. A pigeon tapped at the window. There was the distant sound of an ambulance siren.

Very quietly Chloe said, 'I had a miscarriage.'

The doctor said, 'I'm sorry, I thought…'

'Not your fault,' I said. 'I only just got here. I'm still catching up.'

'I'll leave you to talk,' she said, and fled.

I felt a twinge of sympathy for Chloe. She was busted. Confined to a hospital bed in an airless cubicle, gawped at by two strangers who looked like they just won front seats at the circus. Put well and truly on the spot and without her lover to protect her. I could see her deciding how to play it.

I said, 'Do you want to start?'

She said she'd been about to tell me.

'That you'd miscarried?'

'Yes.'

'But you hadn't told me you were pregnant. Which leads me to wonder. Whose baby was it?'

No answer.

'Does that mean you don't know? Or that you don't want to tell me?'

Silence.

'How far gone?'

She shrugged.

'You could save me the trouble of finding out.'

'Ten, eleven weeks.'

'So, not conceived while you were stuck at home with me. Therefore, potentially, Fitzgerald's or mine. There's no-one else in the frame, I presume? That'd be an interesting complication.'

Then she said, 'Look, it was a mistake. I was about to deal with it.'

'You mean you were going to have a termination?'

'Obviously.'

230

'Because you weren't sure who the father was? Or because it was a massive inconvenience to you?'

'Both. I'd told you I wasn't ready for babies.'

'And what did Fitzgerald say about it?'

'That it was up to me. Whatever I thought best.'

'Wait a minute. You had your period a few weeks ago.'

'Not really.'

'You pretended?'

'I needed time to think.'

'And you thought, this child might be Dan's but it might not, so I'll just get rid. Like a skin tag or a dodgy mole. Now you see it, now you don't.'

She said, 'I knew you'd be like this. It's a bit academic now anyway, don't you think? I've miscarried. I'm having a D&C. End of story.'

End of story, indeed.

Her final words were, 'Please don't forget to phone the clinic.'

I dashed to the car park, eyes down, collar turned up. I didn't want to run into Fitzgerald, see Fitzgerald, come within a country mile of Fitzgerald. Why? Like I was the culprit? No, because I was the humiliated muggins.

It was nearly ten o'clock when I got home. My eyes prickled with fatigue and I sat in the car for a while, too tired, too hollow to go into an empty house. My phone buzzed. It was Miriam Parry.

'Iestyn told us. What's the damage?'

'A few cuts and bruises, mild concussion, broken marriage. I'll be in tomorrow morning. Business as usual. I hear David's back in town.'

231

'Ah,' she said, 'the Colwyn Bay bush telegraph. That'd be Bethan. Yes, he's home, but he won't be working next week. He's going to ease back in, so you'll have Dylan Tew for another week or two. Did you really say, 'broken marriage'?'

'Yes. Beyond repair, I'm afraid.'

'Dan, dear,' she said, 'do you want to talk?'

I gave her the abridged version. I knew what she must be thinking. We all guessed, Dan boy. Wives don't usually keep buggering off to see their friends, Dan boy. You've been a prize sap, Dan boy.

But she said, 'What a shitty day you've had. Try to get some sleep.'

Then she said, 'Listen, David's got badminton tomorrow evening. Come and have a bite with me, have a natter, if you feel like it.'

'David plays badminton?'

'Code name for counselling.'

'Okay.'

'It'll only be cold cuts, mind.'

I went into our pointlessly large house, drank most of a bottle of red, ate every scrap of cheese in the fridge, went to bed, then remembered Monday was garbage day and ran down in my trackies and sock feet to drag the bins out. I woke early, with a hungover tongue and a snorer's sore throat. What was supposed to happen next? Chloe would come for her stuff. Not immediately, though. She wouldn't be feeling up to it for a while.

I wrote a few things down, to try to clear my head. Did I want to see her? No. Why? Because she might ask me to forgive her, to take her back and start over. And? People have been known to do just that.

I tried another tack. Without thinking about it too much, what was I feeling? Embarrassment. I'd been taken for a mug. Anything else? Anger, with myself for trying to play happy families and with Chloe for being so deceitful. Had she ever loved me? Possibly, in her provisional, child in a sweet shop way. All that time with me and she'd still kept George Fitzgerald's number. And before him there'd been the Lebanese guy who wore shoes with heels. Jamil. Had I loved her? Very much. Could I love her again? Definitely not.

Chapter 23

I chucked out Chloe's almond milk, zero-fat yogurt and zero-taste non-dairy spread. Then I phoned Mam.

'You're up early.'

'Did I wake you?'

'Fat chance. I'm like a blummin' guard dog these days, Dan. What it is, your Nan's taken to wandering. She can be halfway down the road in her nightie if we don't watch her. We've put a chain on the front door, so now it's the windows she keeps rattling. Good job they stick, eh?'

'Is she trying to go back to her old place?'

'It depends what you mean. She's forgotten the maisonette. It's the old house she talks about, where she lived when your grandad was alive.'

'The Aricept isn't helping?'

'I think she might be beyond the Aricept stage. Anyway, half the time she spits it out. What's wrong, Dan? I can tell there's something.'

'We're getting divorced.'

'Go on. I'm listening.'

You could tell Mam we were going to be hit by a giant asteroid, life on earth about to be wiped out, and she'd still say, 'go on. I'm listening.'

234

'Chloe's met someone else. Well, actually she's gone back to someone she was with before. I found out yesterday. I'm sorry.'

'What are you sorry for?'

'I feel like I've let everyone down. We've only been married just over a year.'

Mam said that was silly talk.

'No sense two people making each other miserable. You're young enough. Lovely handsome doctor like you, someone'll snap you up. You'll find the right one.'

'Will you tell people?'

'I won't be calling the Monmouth Beacon, if that's what you mean, in case you change your mind. But I'll tell your Da and your Aunty June.'

'I won't change my mind. There's something else. She was pregnant and she didn't know if it was mine or his. She was going to have an abortion, only she miscarried, with the shock of the accident, I suppose, and the whole story came out.'

'Oh Dan,' she said. 'Why didn't you phone me last night? What a horrible day you'd had.'

'I got drunk.'

'I'm not surprised. You deserved better than that.'

'Not that you're biased or anything.'

'I am biased. I make no bones about it. What do her people think about it?'

'I doubt they know. Laurence is away. It doesn't matter. I'm finished with the Swifts.'

She said she wished she was here, to give me a cwtch. As well she wasn't. I needed to dry my eyes, buck up and get to work, which I did, and the only reason I retrieved Eeyore from the bin before I left was that I'd decided not to be too mean

235

and bitter. From now on let Dr Curly-Wurly Fitzgerald sleep with a bloody stuffed donkey.

I sleep-walked through morning surgery. Three hours of niggling coughs, creaking joints and not so mysterious rashes. Iestyn put his head round the door.

'All right, then?'

'All right.'

'Wife okay?'

'Ex-wife, as of yesterday, but yes, okay.'

He scratched his beard. 'Oh dear,' he said.

'It's a long story.'

He withdrew his head, like a ginger mouse retreating into its hole.

Five minutes later, Dylan Tew came to look at me.

I said, 'Good morning. Have you come to inspect the damage?'

'Precisely,' he said. 'The walking wounded. You don't look too bad.'

'I'll survive. David's home, did you hear?'

'I did. They've not finished with me yet, though. Another week or two, Miriam thinks. Well, best foot forward. I'm always available for a half of Wild Horse, should the need arise.'

The word went round in no time. I was treated like the bereaved. Bethan not only made me coffee, she gave me two of her homemade flapjacks to have with it. I even got the kid glove treatment from Delyth. Did I want her to clear my afternoon list? Asked with mournful eyes. No, I damned well didn't. I wanted no time to think about myself. I wanted lots of patients, with mysterious symptoms. Bring it on.

The Underhills were exactly what I needed. Beverley and Dennis from Acocks Green, with Brummie accents you could slice with a knife. The kind of devoted couple who finish each other's sentences, but that day they were at loggerheads. Beverley said Dennis had had a funny turn over the weekend. Dennis said he'd had no such thing.

The diplomatic thing seemed to be to ask for Dennis's version first.

'Nothing to tell you,' he said. 'It were a normal weekend. Only, Saturday afternoon, she suddenly starts flapping, says I'm not acting right. Well, I'd just woke up. Nobody's a hundred percent when they've just woke up. Silly talk about getting an ambulance. I had to grab the phone off of her. And now we're here, wasting your time.'

According to Beverley, Dennis had had his usual afternoon nap, half an hour in an armchair, and when he woke he'd sounded drunk.

'I did not.'

'Allow me to know. You had terrible hiccups and you was talking like you was three sheets to the wind. And then you took a tumble.'

'Only because you'd left your bowling bag where you shouldn't have.'

Back and forth they went. It was good-natured, but each of them was adamant theirs was the right story.

I checked Dennis's blood pressure and did his ABCD2 score. How long did Beverley think the episode had lasted? Maybe five minutes. And then he'd seemed normal again?

'Normal as he ever is.'

They both laughed.

Had she noticed any weakness, say, in his hand or in the muscles of his face? Not that she could recall. He was scoring low on the stroke scale but not so low that I could ignore it.

I listened to his carotid arteries. There were no abnormal bruits. His retinas looked normal. Dennis's body wasn't giving

237

me any tell-tale clues. But, given his age, his slightly raised blood pressure and Beverley's description of what had she'd witnessed, there was a strong chance he'd suffered a TIA.

I said, 'Dennis, it sounds very much to me as though you had a tiny stroke. I'm going to send you through to the nurse. She'll take some blood. I want to check your cholesterols.'

'But we're taking them statins for cholesterol.'

'I know you are. I still want to see the numbers.'

Did he warrant a neurology referral? I thought so. If it had been a TIA it wouldn't show up on a scan, but a hospital appointment might make him take things more seriously.

He opened his mouth to object. Beverley took his hand.

He said, 'You're ganging up on me. Look at me. I'm as right as rain.'

'Let's keep it that way. If it wasn't a little stroke, good. If it was, it's a warning sign and not to be ignored. Next time you might not be so lucky.'

With some patients it takes a long time to wear down their resistance. Sometimes they start very bolshie, then they suddenly cave.

Dennis's eyes were teary.

'I don't know,' he said. 'Flipping old age. I hate it.'

Beverley fished out a pack of tissues.

She said, 'We're not old yet, Den. We're just slightly worn.'

I did the referral letter while they sat.

Dennis said, 'You're going to have egg on your face, Beverley Underhill, when they tell us there's nothing wrong with me.'

She said, 'I'll risk it. I don't want you carking on me when we've just spent good money on them tickets.'

They were going to see a Birmingham band they'd followed since 1963. The Yardleybeats.

'Long before your time, Doc,' says Dennis.

'Are they on at the big arena?'

'No, no. There's not that many of us fans left, the old stalwarts. They're doing a farewell tour, Coleshill, Walsall and Digbeth. Not the original line-up, of course. They'd all be in their seventies now. Baz Lea's gone.'

'Yes,' says Beverley, 'And Terry Pocock. He had a stroke. See what I mean, Den? If it can happen to Terry, it could happen to anybody.'

Dennis wasn't having it.

'Different case entirely,' he said. 'Terry Pocock abused his body. Keith Slack's still on drums. He's going strong. We're going to the Digbeth gig. It's in an old workshop, used to be a panel-beaters and now it's what they call a performance space. Marvellous what they can do these days.'

I said, 'I've no idea how long you'll have to wait for an appointment. Let me know if you don't hear anything. Beverley, if it happens again, call for an ambulance. Dennis, if your wife ever has a funny turn, do likewise. You have to look after each other.'

He said, 'What do you mean, *if* she ever has a funny turn. Life with her is nothing but.'

I called Miriam Parry's surgery to check if I was still invited.

'Of course,' she said. 'Come at seven. Don't bring anything. Just yourself.'

I didn't bother going home. I finished doing letters and tried to catch up on the *British Medical Journal* for half an hour. I couldn't tell you a single word I read.

Bethan and Delyth left, then Dylan Tew. Iestyn was the last.

'You'll lock up?'

'I will. I'm going to the Parrys. Miriam's offered to feed me.'

'You'll be seeing David?'

'I'm not sure. Have you spoken to him?'

'Barely. Two words and he put Miriam back on.'

'Nothing unusual, then. And I'm sure there'll be an element of embarrassment.'

Iestyn said, 'I'd invite you to ours to eat only it's a bit of a madhouse. Getting the children fed and settled, you know?'

I said, 'Don't worry, I'm not going to starve. I've always done most of the cooking anyway. I'm just going to see Miriam to talk it over, get it out of my head.'

He said, 'She's a good listener.'

Yes, I thought. And I wonder who's been a good listener for her?

Whatever impression Miriam had had of Chloe, however stupidly or wilfully blind she thought I'd been, she kept to herself. Their son Joe appeared a few times, raiding the fridge. Sixteen and a bottomless pit for snacks.

We unpicked the events of Sunday. Quite by chance, I'd caught Chloe having an affair. That had been her bad luck. If that dog hadn't run into the road. If Fitzgerald had been driving slower.

Miriam prodded a little. Had I truly never suspected? It had crossed my mind. But when Chloe was with me, we were fine. Mostly. Sex was good, I thought. We'd been slightly at odds about our plans for the future, but everyone said just be patient, give her time.

240

And then, while I'd still been winded from finding out about George Fitzgerald, a hefty kick in the balls. The baby, now lost, and the endless what ifs it was causing me.

I said, 'If they hadn't had that accident, Chloe probably wouldn't have miscarried. She said she was going to get an abortion. That could have been my child. Or she might have changed her mind at the last minute. Some women do. She might have decided to brazen it out and I could have spent years raising Fitzgerald's child. It would have come out, eventually. It'd grow up to look like peanut-head.'

'He looks like a peanut?'

'Peanut shell. His face has a waistline.'

Miriam made the observation that Chloe's miscarriage, sad as it was, had made things clearer for me. It was a double betrayal.

She said, 'I hope you won't leave us.'

'Why would I?'

'Unhappy memories.'

'But I don't have any, apart from yesterday. I like it here. Of course, I'll have to sell the house. Chloe'll want her share. What about wedding presents? We only got married last summer. Will we have to send them back?'

Miriam thought the Statute of Limitations specified one year.

'Don't rush into anything,' she said. 'Let the dust settle.'

'Your turn.'

'What?'

'You've had a shitty year too. How are you?'

'Coping, I think.'

'And David?'

'The detox was really tough. Like the worst gastric 'flu you can imagine, and then some. Becca tried to see him. I'd begged

241

her not to, but she went anyway. Wasted journey. They told her he was too agitated.'

'Did they give him anything to help?'

'No. He was offered Subutex, but he refused it. Typical.'

'And what's he like now?'

'Well, he's clean. That's a start. His moods are very labile. Crying one minute, snarling the next. I'm told it'll pass.'

'And he's seeing a counsellor.'

'Twice a week. He has to. That's the deal. It's not over though, Dan. Once an addict, always an addict. Going to work, knowing there's a drugs cupboard in the next room. Knowing he can self-prescribe. He could slip back any day.'

'How does that make you feel?'

'Anxious. It's like watching someone walking an endless high-wire.'

On Thursday evening Chloe phoned me.

She said, 'We should talk.'

'Okay.'

'I'm really, really sorry.'

'About what you've done or about getting found out?'

'Can't we be civilised?'

'I thought I had been. I haven't been round to Fitzgerald's and punched his lights out. Have you recovered? From everything?'

'Yes, thank you.'

'Back at work?'

'Next week. I thought I should come and see you.'

'You mean, to pick up your stuff? You don't need to see me to do that. You have keys.'

'No, I meant to talk things over. To see if we can patch things up.'

'Are you serious?'

She misinterpreted that.

'Of course I am,' she said. 'Darling, I really hope we can start over. I completely understand you're upset. I've been a bit of an idiot. Gone a bit haywire. You know, I think I'm still getting over Mummy's death. And then the whole Jen business with Daddy. I'm still kind of processing it.'

'So, you feel that you haven't been in your right mind?'

'Exactly. I mean, the whole Fitzie thing was nothing. Just a silly five minutes.'

'Does he know that?'

'What do you mean?'

'Does he know that you want to leave him and come back to me?'

'No, but if he did, he'd understand. You know, it wasn't anything heavy between us. He's more a friend than anything else.'

'The kind of friend who may or may not have made you pregnant.'

'I could kill that blabbermouth doctor. There was zero need for you to have known about that. I told you, I was going to fix it. And I just feel, if you and I went away somewhere, left Rhos and started over, we could be happy. We could go to couples thingummy. Counselling.'

I said, 'Here's what I think. You're deluded, Chloe. I don't know what planet you're on but starting over with me isn't an option. I could never trust you again. Maybe you were too young to settle down, although you weren't exactly a child bride. And as a matter of fact, I don't want to move away and start over. I like it here. So, I hope you haven't burned any bridges with your friend Fitzgerald, and I hope you'll be happy in your new life in Coventry.'

'I see,' she said.

And for once in her life, I think she did.

Chapter 24

Chloe said she'd come on Sunday morning to collect her things, if that was convenient. It was. I booked a table for lunch at the Pen-y-Bryn after church and invited David and Miriam to join me. That killed two birds. I could see David socially before he came back to work, get any awkwardness out of the way, and by the time I got home Chloe would be gone. I wouldn't have to witness her dismantling the hardware of our marriage.

Would she lay claim to the chocolate fondue fountain set regifted to us by some Orde-Sykes cousin who hadn't even bothered to remove the original gift card? I hoped so. Would she have taken the Love is Gentle, Love is Kind terracotta doodad of no obvious utility? She would certainly have been welcome to it.

We had the Sunday roast. David was tense when they first arrived, but he relaxed after a glass of wine. He said the only thing he remembered clearly about being detoxed was the diarrhoea.

'I was shitting for Wales,' he said. He got a stern look from two senior ladies at the next table, but it broke the tension at ours. There were moments of bluster, not like him at all, and moments of withdrawal, when he wasn't quite with us. We talked about their son, Joe, who was keen on a girl at school and had become a heavy user of hair products. We talked about Bethan's tumour that was responding well to treatment, and we talked about Dylan Tew.

'He's an excellent doctor,' David said. 'Odd, of course, but he has a sharp eye.'

'And a sharp tongue.'

'Yes. Dylan can empty a waiting room faster than anyone I know. Is he still buying those funny hats?'

'I've seen him wearing a couple of beauties. Unique to Colwyn Bay, I'd say. And I gather he never married. He doesn't strike me as gay though.'

Miriam said she thought Dylan's mother had seen off a few female contenders.

'And now,' she said, 'I suppose he's too dotty and set in his ways.'

I said, 'That'll probably be me twenty years from now.'

'I don't think so,' she said. 'I reckon there'll be a queue round the block for you.'

When I got back to Rhos, Chloe's car was outside the house, boot lid open, suitcases and black sacks inside. She was in the kitchen. It was the first time I'd seen her since our horrible goodbye in the hospital.

'Sorry,' she said. 'Running a bit behind. We'll be gone in ten minutes.'

'We?'

'Fitzie's upstairs getting the last few things.'

The fact that he was upstairs in our house, in *my* house annoyed me more than anything else about him: his slimy duplicity, his rich boy cockiness, the way he'd made a fool of me, I was managing to live with all of that. I just didn't want him ferreting in *my* bedroom. I didn't want him peeing on *my* lamp post.

'How's your head?'

'Fine.'

'What's the next step? Lawyers, I suppose. Please, let's keep it simple.'

'Yes,' she said, 'but I can't talk about that now. We need to get back.'

'Back to Coventry?'

'Don't say it like that.'

'Don't say what like what?'

'Coventry.'

'How did I say it?'

'Sarcastically.'

George Fitzgerald appeared. His busted shoulder was still strapped and there was a sleeping bag under his good arm, so I was spared the dilemma of whether to be noble and shake his hand or snub the bastard.

He said, 'Look what I found, Chlo. My old sleeping bag.'

I said, 'I believe that belongs to someone called Dunc. A friend of Dee's. But as things have turned out, perhaps not.'

Chloe turned scarlet.

'No,' says George F, 'I'm sure it's mine. It's smells vile though.'

I said, 'I can explain that. It's most likely sheep urine. I used it when I was at the lambing. While you were fucking my wife. A hot wash should fix it.'

What did Chloe see in him? Did he know she'd made a bid to come back to me? Would he have put up a fight or been quietly relieved? It was one thing to enjoy someone else's wife for the occasional weekend, but quite another to suddenly get outed and lumbered.

He didn't come back into the house. When I looked out of the window, he was in the front passenger seat, waiting for Chloe. She was pointlessly opening and closing kitchen cupboards. Was she reluctant to say goodbye? Even a tiny bit?

I said, 'We have two waffle irons, if you want to take one.'

Don't think so,' she said. 'So, I'll be off then.'

She was nearly at the door.

I said, 'Aren't you forgetting something?'

She looked at me and for one terrible moment I thought she might cry or try to hug me.

'What?'

'Your keys.'

She chucked them on the table.

'We'll talk, at some point, about the house, about money.'

'Yes.'

I stood on the step and watched her walk away. She'd almost reached the car when she turned.

'Forgot to say, Flo had a boy.'

'That's nice. All well?'

'Think so.'

'Does he have a name?'

'Theodore Henry. To be known as Ted.'

And then she was gone. I walked around the house to see what she'd taken. Not a lot. Her clothes, some bedding, her bathroom stuff. Eeyore. She'd left behind our wedding photo album. Eloquent. The rooms seemed echoey and I felt like a wrung-out rag.

I called the Packwoods that evening to congratulate them on the baby. Flo said she very much hoped we might still be friends, that they wouldn't be tarred by Chloe's behaviour.

I said, 'I hope so too, although it might be tricky. I think of you as family, but I can't trespass on Chloe's territory. Do you know George Fitzgerald?'

'Vaguely,' she said. 'He came to the Chummery a few times. Does he have an oddly shaped face?'

'Like a peanut shell. How's Ted?'

'He's a super-easy baby. One almost forgets one has him.'

'Who does he look like?'

'Henry, I suppose. Pink, and no hair. You will come and see us?'

'I'd like that.'

'You could bring that sweet old doctor friend.'

'Trevor.'

'Yes, Lils talks about him endlessly.'

'She should write him a letter. I can give you his address. He'd like that.'

'What a clever idea,' she said. 'You're terribly good with children. Vastly superior to their Aunt Chlo. But Dan, what will happen to your lovely house?'

'I'll suppose I'll have to sell.'

'How beastly.'

Flo could see the prospect of free seaside holidays going up in smoke.

'And you know, those Fitzgeralds have oodles of money. Chlo shouldn't be chasing you for funds and I shall tell her so.'

'Best if you don't. Let's leave it to the lawyers to sort out. Why don't you come and stay at half-term? I'm not going to be rushed into selling.'

'Truly? It wouldn't be uncomfortable for you? Reminders of Chlo and all that?'

I said, 'I think I'm past 'uncomfortable reminders' and you may as well come while I have all these beds. My next stop is likely to be a bachelor flat. Anyway, I'd like to meet Ted.'

Gradually the news about me and Chloe spread. I told the neighbours. They said they had wondered. I didn't bother telling Rob and Matt. Though they'd known Chloe, they were busy now with their own lives. They'd be less than interested in mine. Vaz was a different matter. To him marriage was a precious sacrament. He'd tell me I should take Chloe back and try again. I didn't call him.

I didn't call Trevor either, but not because he'd judge me. I knew he wouldn't, nor would he say, 'I told you so.' But I was tired of repeating the story, tired of feeling like a prize chump, tired of people telling me I'd get over it and find someone else. I became a bit of a machine. The first to arrive at the surgery every morning and the last to leave at night. At home I shuttled between just two rooms, the kitchen and the bedroom. I went to choir practice on Tuesdays. I changed my sheets on Saturdays. I cut the grass, raked the leaves that had started to fall, ate ice cream straight from the tub.

Dylan Tew recommended I get a cat. Miriam Parry thought anti-depressants would help. Mam said I should take a break, book a week somewhere sunny, maybe one of those singles holidays. I couldn't think of anything worse and anyway, I had a beach right outside my house. I just didn't feel like walking on it.

It was Thursday evening. I'd eaten, washed up my bowl, fork and spoon, ironed two shirts and flipped between channels without finding anything I wanted to watch. My phone rang. It was Trevor. At least, it was his number.

She said, 'This is Alice. Buxton.'

I felt sick.

'It's alright,' she said. 'He's not dead. Just in hospital again, with his chest.'

'Are you with him?'

'Yes. James is in Slovakia with his girlfriend, so they called me.'

'Is Trevor well enough to talk?'

'He's asleep at the moment. The thing is, he keeps having these setbacks and I can't come dashing to Birmingham every time. I've got a business to run.'

What did she expect me to do?

I said, 'I can visit him, at the weekend, if that would help.'

She said it wasn't really about people visiting him. It was about the future.

'How long will they keep him in?'

'Another day or two. He'd leave today if he could. You know what he's like? Telling the staff how to do their job. He wants to go home but he's not well enough to be on his own.'

Then she said, 'I wondered if you and your wife…'

'You mean, bring him here?'

'It'd just be for a few days. Maybe a week, while we sort something out for him.'

'When you say, 'sort something out' what do you have in mind?'

'I don't know. A nursing home, probably.'

I said, 'He'll never agree to that.'

'What am I supposed to do? James says he can't have him, and I can't take him to my place. We don't have room.'

'Have you discussed this with Trevor? If he's keen to go home, we could organise a nurse.'

Her tone changed. She was exasperated with me.

'So, you can't help.'

251

'I'll be happy to help, but I'm not going to bring him here against his will.'

'It won't be,' she said. 'He likes you. Anyway, he's getting to the stage where he can't always have what he wants. I'm busy, James is busy. We can't be at his beck and call.'

I offered to pick him up on Saturday morning.

'But only if he agrees to it. I won't be his jailer, Alice. If he wants to go home, you must let him.'

'If he goes home, he'll sit in that disgusting old armchair, phoning in bets and smoking himself to death.'

'Yes.'

An hour later the man himself phoned me.

'Is that the Talbot Hilton?' he wheezed. 'What's the availability of your penthouse suite?'

Chapter 25

When I arrived at Priory ward late on Saturday morning, Trevor was sitting with his coat on and a wheelie suitcase at the foot of his bed.

He said, 'Are you sure about this, Dan Talbot? I reckon my daughter has some nerve, dumping me on you.'

I said, 'Well it's that or stay here. You're not allowed to be home alone yet.'

'I know,' he said. 'I've got to be assessed. There's talk of assisted living. I've told them where to get off, but they'll still send somebody round. Let's get out of here before another box-ticker arrives with a clipboard.'

He'd shrunk in the few months since I'd seen him. I saw a difference in him. He said he saw a difference in me.

'You've put on weight.'

'True.'

'The contentment of married life?'

We'd stopped for a tea and a pee.

I said, 'I've got something to tell you. There is no contented married life. I'm getting divorced.'

He pushed his Bakewell tart away, half-eaten.

'Oh lad,' he said. 'Then turn round and take me back. The last thing you need is an old coffin-dodger under your roof.'

'No, I think you might be exactly what I need. I'll be glad of the company. It's a big house for one.'

'Yes,' he said, 'it is. Should I ask questions or just mind my own fucking business?'

'Ask away. There's not much to tell. Chloe picked up with an old boyfriend. She got in touch with him last year, when her mum died. I don't know when they started seeing each other again. I don't want to know.'

'And she's not just having a mad five minutes? It's serious?'

'It is for me. I think she's had a few second thoughts but too late as far as I'm concerned. So, she's gone, taken all her things. She never did settle in Rhos, and now I know why.'

'I'm very sorry for your troubles.'

'Want to hear something funny? She hated our new life. I'd become a boring GP, the scenery was over-rated, the shopping was pathetic. Guess where she is now?'

'Is this going to make me laugh?'

'Yes.'

'Hold on while I get my Ventolin puffer ready. Go on.'

'Coventry. And he's a trainee GP. He keeps failing his CSA.'

He did laugh. 'Coventry! That must give Cannock a run for its money in the Chav Stakes. Coventry, Cannock, Joke-on-Trent, they're all up there. Vying for shitty city of the year, just the West Midlands category, of course. Well, well.'

As we approached the Colwyn Bay Bypass I said, 'I can take you to Alice and Micky's if you'd rather. Speak now.'

'Very comical,' he said. 'Actually, I now see that Micky might have a role to play in my life after all. When all hope is gone, I'll move in with them and within a week she'll have killed me. Suicide by proxy. Not yet, though. There's life in me yet.

Let's swing by a supermarket. I need smokes and we both need a drink.'

I lit a fire. It was the first time I'd used the sitting room since Chloe left. I opened a bottle, cooked us bacon and eggs. Trevor phoned Helen Vincent.

'Helen, my love,' he said. 'This is your sleeping partner. I've escaped the jaws of Sandwell hospital and I'm recuperating at the seaside, doctor's orders, so I won't be in this week.'

The only other thing I heard him say was, 'No, Helen. I'll go when I'm good and ready. I still have my uses.'

I can sit in long silences with Trevor. Sometimes he appears to have nodded off but then he'll pick up the thread of an earlier conversation or make a random remark, such as, 'Alice is right, of course. The house is far too big for me. But I hate change, Dan. I've lived most of my life there.'

'Then stay put and accept a bit of help.'

'You mean like a total stranger in a tabard coming in every morning to hose me down?'

'Not quite. Anyway, you'd get to know them, then it wouldn't be a stranger.'

He said, 'You know, I never really thought about this stage. I was so sure I'd go before Mrs Buxton. Then she'd be the one who had to make a decision. Selfish of me. What's your Sunday routine?'

'Church. Then we could go for a drive, if you like. Get a pub lunch?'

'Whatever you fancy,' he said. 'Only I don't want to cramp your style.'

'I don't have a style.'

'Course you do. When you've put all this Chloe business behind you, you'll need to get out there and find a nice girl.'

255

Then he said, 'Somebody like that doctor lass you had a thing for.'

I acted dumb.

'Don't play the mystified innocent with me. You know who I mean. The one who showed us round the sheep farm.'

'Harry.'

'Yes, Harry. I knew she had a funny name. Is she still single?'

'She is, but there's that vet, Pete. I'm not sure what their relationship is. Was it really that obvious I liked her?'

He shrugged.

'Now I'm embarrassed.'

'Don't be. The ladies like a shy admirer. Or so I'm told.'

'Chloe used to say Harry had a crush on me. Perhaps she knew it was actually the other way round. Perhaps that's why she took up with George Fitzgerald.'

'Dan,' he said, 'from what you've told me, that ship had already sailed. Now, I'm going to step outside for two puffs of a coffin nail and then I'm for some kip. I haven't slept a wink in that hospital bed.'

For a week Trevor and I were the Odd Couple. I'd take him a cup of tea before I left for work in the morning. He'd be awake, propped up on a pile of pillows, trying to read the day's race cards on his tablet. It had been a gift from his son, James, to help him keep in touch, apparently. It didn't. He couldn't get the hang of it at all.

'Here,' he'd say. 'Pick a horse, any horse.'

When I got back in the evening, the fire was lit and the table was laid. Making dinner was my job. At home he'd been living on microwaveable ready meals. I thought he might like to rent a car, but he said he was content to walk from bench to bench along the seafront. One of the days he caught a bus into Llandudno.

'I had a pint and a ploughman's,' he said. 'I backed that no-hoper you picked out, second race at Uttoxeter, and it only went and won. If ever you tire of medicine, you could go on the telly as a tipster.'

Day by day his colour improved.

Alice didn't call me, so I called Alice.

She said, 'I suppose he's worn out his welcome.'

'Not at all. He's a very easy guest. But I know he'd like to get back to work, and he'd certainly like to go home.'

'Have you talked to him about the house? About downsizing.'

'It's not my job.'

'What if he gets another chest infection?'

'He will do. He might also develop heart failure. Why not wait and see how it plays out? I haven't known your father long, Alice, but I've seen him in action, with patients nearing the end of their lives. Keeping them comfortable, letting them decide what they wanted, that was his attitude. I'd like to think he'll get the same consideration.'

'How long can you keep him?'

'As long as wants to stay, but he's talking about leaving next week. He misses seeing patients.'

'It's ridiculous,' she said. 'Why can't he retire like a normal person. He's so contrary.'

'He's a good dad, though?'

'I'm not saying he's not. It's just…. Never mind.'

I'd have liked to repeat what Trevor once said to me, about their troubled relationship, about his fears for her, living with Micky's temper. 'The door's wide open any time she needs me,' he'd said. 'She's still my little girl.'

I didn't tell her, though. I suspected Alice knew all that perfectly well and if ever she had a sound reason to leave Wales it was now, to mend some fences and look after her dad.

Trevor wouldn't hear of me driving him back to Wombourne.

'Put me on a train,' he said, 'with a label round my neck.'

He said he was needed back at Weirdo Pants because Helen Vincent had booked some time off and he saw it as his job to hold the fort. It wasn't, but believing it made him feel useful.

He said, 'She's managed to get Clifford into respite care for two weeks. Well, that's the story. I have a feeling he might be travelling on a one-way ticket.'

Poor Helen. Cliff's stroke had clipped her wings as well as his. If only he'd reached hospital in time for thrombolysis. If only he hadn't been diddling a girl who was so freaked out by his stroke, she'd delayed calling for an ambulance. There were a lot of if-onlys.

Trevor left me on Monday morning. He said he felt as good as new.

'Sea air and good company,' he said. 'You can't beat it.'

'Come again, any time.'

'Thank you,' he said, 'but I'm very much hoping you soon won't have time for running a convalescent home. The next time I hear from you, I'd like you to tell me you've found a good woman.'

I said, 'Don't bank on it. I never did have a lot of confidence asking girls out and now I don't have any.'

'Dan,' he said, 'haven't you heard? Fortune favours the brave. Now bugger off. I can catch a train without a grownup supervising me.'

258

That was the morning I met another member of the Caddick family. Kezia, generally known as Kiz. She looked like her brother Leon, but with considerable breasts. Kiz said she had a rash.

'Where is it?'

'Under me tits.'

She started to strip off her top.

I said, 'Whoah. Keep your kit on till the nurse can come in to help me.'

Bethan was doing a vaccination so we had to wait. There was no file on Kiz that I could see. Was she registered with us?

'Don't know,' she said. 'Me brother comes here.'

'And do you live with Leon?'

'Sometimes.'

'Otherwise where?'

'Prestatyn.'

'So you're registered with a doctor there?'

'I think so.'

'Are you working?'

'Can't. I've got anxiety.'

'And are you taking anything for that?'

'They're like, capsules.'

'Lyrica?'

'Yeah.'

'Anything else?'

She thought.

'Not really. Just lorazzies.'

'You're taking lorazepam as well? Who's your doctor in Prestatyn?'

'I can't think of his name.'

With a brother who's a one-stop shop for pills I doubted she had much need of a GP.

259

'And when you're not visiting your brother, do you live alone in Prestatyn?'

'Depends. Sometimes I have the grandkids.'

Grandkids! I'd put Kezia at around forty but she had the kind of face I'd seen so often in Tipton, the women from the tower blocks on Brook Glen and Cherry Tree who could have been anything from thirty to fifty. Tired and pasty, with a 'don't mess with me' default expression.

Kezia was 36.

I said, 'You're very young to be a granny.'

'Not really,' she said. 'My Mum was fifteen when she had me. I was fifteen when I had Naomi and she was fifteen when she had Liberty. She's got three now. Lib, Duke and Ella. And see, I've only got two bedrooms. I'm waiting to get rehoused.'

'Doesn't your daughter have a place of her own?'

'She does, only he's there. Lee. She wants him out, only he won't go.'

'Lee's your son-in-law?'

'Yes. No. He's just Naomi's bloke. He's not their dad. Well, he might be Ella's. He says he is. He wants that test done. I don't know. Because the thing is, Naomi was still going with Django when she fell for Ella. It does my fucking head in sometimes.'

The tangled branches of the Caddick family tree. It was doing my head in too. Bethan joined us and Kiz hoisted her breasts so we could see the rash in the skin folds. The sweet smell of yeast mingled with the sharp smell of unwashed armpit.

Bethan said, 'Candidiasis?'

My thought exactly. We took a swab, to make sure.

I said, 'This is easily treated, but you'll need to play very close attention to personal hygiene.'

Kezia said, 'Say again?'

Bethan said, 'What Dr Dan means is, you need to keep yourself clean under your breasts. You're a big girl. You need to lift them up, wash with plenty of soap and water, then dry yourself properly. It must get like a Turkish bath under there. Why aren't you wearing a brassiere?'

'Don't like them.'

'You should get one, give yourself a bit of support. Carry on like this, they'll soon be knocking against your knees. And don't just get one. Get a few, so you can put a nice clean one on every morning.'

'Can I get a prescription?'

I said, 'I'm writing you up for a cream and a powder, both anti-fungal.'

'No,' she said, 'I mean for bras. Can I get a prescription for bras?'

There was something enviable about the Caddick view of the world. A gigantic warehouse of stuff and services that were free for the taking.

Trevor phoned me to say he'd got home safely.

He said, 'There was a letter waiting for me, from young Lily. She got two new bantams and she's named them Trevor and Buxton.'

'Flo said she often talks about you. You should drive down and see them. Go and inspect the new baby.'

'I couldn't do that. I hardly know them. I shall write back to Lily though, bless the child. I'll admit it to you because you won't laugh. That letter brought a tear to my eye. Mrs Buxton would have given anything to have a little granddaughter.'

I said, 'I might be speaking out of turn, but I think there's a vacancy for a surrogate grandad at Packwood Grange.

Henry's father's long dead and Laurence seems to be on a permanent honeymoon. In fact, he never paid them much attention even when Vinnie was alive. He tended to speak to them as though he was addressing a conference.'

'Well, perhaps I'll send something for the baby. Keep channels of communication open. What do you buy for babies these days? Bootees?'

'I don't think so.'

'No,' he said. I don't think so either. What a clueless old fart I've become.'

Chapter 26

Roy Savage's diagnosis was confirmed. He had non-Hodgkin's lymphoma. It's spread was limited, confined to his chest and neck, but it looked aggressive, so the treatment plan was for R-CHOP. He was about to start a few months of chemo, plus a targeted drug to knock out the cancerous cells in his lymph nodes. After that he'd have radiotherapy. He was very upbeat.

He said, 'The National Health. Ruddy marvellous. I haven't got one doctor, I've got a team. The chemo, it's like a cocktail. Three days in hospital, then I go home for two weeks, to rest up.'

'You'll need it. They've told you how you're likely to feel after the chemo?'

'Oh yes. I can handle it. And then, for the ray treatment, I'll have to wear this, like, mask, kind of a mould, to stop me moving about. Made to measure, mind. I tell you, it's ruddy marvellous.'

Bethan said, 'I see the flasher was in again.'

'He's got non-Hodgkin's.'

'Has he?' she said. 'Well, I wouldn't have wished that on him. Perhaps it'll stop him waving his chipolata at innocent ladies.'

Aggie Hughes's mother was coming from Poland. According to Iestyn, it'd be an extended visit, to help them with childcare. According to Aggie it'd be until they had a row and not a minute longer.

I said, 'Why don't you get a nanny?'

Aggie said, 'Iestyn doesn't want. He will like me to be stays at home mummy.'

'But you want to work more hours?'

'Of course. Else it is waste of my training.'

She had to drive to Manchester to collect her mother from the airport, so Harry Shepherd was coming over to do her Wednesday clinic. I hadn't seen her since the David drama. Did she know about me and Chloe? Obviously. Anyone slightly acquainted with me had heard, even the bread shop ladies. I could tell by the way they looked at me. Not that it mattered. I was over Harry. My crush was crushed. I felt over women in general, although people kept telling me that would change.

She came in to see me directly after my last patient had left.

'All right, then?'

'All right, then. I don't know quite how to start this conversation.'

'How about, you sit down?'

'No, I think I'll stand. I might need to make a quick exit.'

'You're making me nervous.'

'It must be contagious. So, I heard about your wife and everything. Miriam mentioned it.'

'It's not a secret.'

'No. I'm sorry. It must have been tough. Still is, probably. I'm making a dog's dinner of this. I was wondering how you fill your weekends, now you're single.'

264

'Same old, really. Go to Asda, push the hoover round, watch the rugby.'

'Okay.'

Ask her out, Dan, said the voice of reason. But no, on I droned.

'And this coming weekend, I was thinking of visiting a patient. She's been stuck in Glan Clwyd for weeks and she doesn't have any family.'

'That's nice. Well, you sound like you'll be busy.'

Finally, I mustered the courage.

'But if you were going to suggest something more exciting, I'm all ears.'

'Exciting? No. Different, let's say. I wondered if I could interest you in a bit more sheep husbandry.'

'Definitely.'

'You don't know what it is yet.'

Tell her you don't care what it is. Tell her you'll chuck your lonely, unvisited patient. Anything for a few hours with Harry Shepherd.

She said, 'We're getting the ewes ready for the tups. It's time for their wash and brush up.'

'Is that like one of those pre-wedding spa weekends brides go on?'

'Exactly. Lurve is in the air.'

'What would be my job?'

'It'll depend on your skill set. We worm them, check their udders, do their feet, dip them, clean their tails off.'

'Actually cut them off?'

'No, we just shear the fleece. Kind of give them a Brazilian. You interested?'

'Yes please. I can visit the Professor another time.'

265

'No, don't cancel that. You can do both. Who's this Professor?'

'Buddug Lloyd Humphreys. She used to teach at Bangor.'

'No!'

'Do you know her?'

'I know of her. She's famous. She taught Geth.'

'Your brother studied Medieval Welsh Literature?'

'Yes. Surprising, isn't it? I suppose you thought he was just a sheep-brain.'

I suppose I had. Gethin was the only son, destined to take over the farm. The most I'd have expected him to have done was a couple of years in agricultural college. But it turned out he was a scholar as well. He was a well-rounded man.

I told Harry the Professor's story. She'd been in ICU at Glan Clwyd. Her broken ribs were too crumbly to repair surgically so they'd had to compromise between stabilising her chest wall and keeping her properly ventilated. It had quite been on the cards that she'd get pneumonia and die, but she'd confounded them. Now there was another problem to solve. She was expecting to go home. The decision makers thought differently. They'd inspected her house and deemed it another accident waiting to happen. She was too frail, they said, too vulnerable for independent living.

'She's supposed to go into residential care. She refuses even to consider it.'

'And what do you think?'

'I hardly know her. She was more Iestyn's patient, so I've only met her once. She's a tough old bird, but she'd be safer in a care home.'

Harry said, 'Safer isn't everything though, is it?'

'I agree, but as a doctor I'm expected to stick to the script.'

'No, Dan. Do no harm isn't the same as remove all freedom and risk from somebody's life so they can live a bit longer and then die miserable. And there's no family at all?'

'She says not. And even if there was, she's such a difficult old cuss, I doubt anyone would have her. Remind me, why are you still standing?'

'Because I came in here to invite you out, and even though it wouldn't exactly be a date and even though you've said yes, I feel a bit of a twerp.'

'Don't. I'm really glad you asked me. So, this would be a non-date doing sheep Brazilians and pedicures?'

'Yes.'

'If I come, would I be allowed to take you on a proper date afterwards? Like, dinner? In a restaurant.'

'Only if you wash your hands thoroughly.'

I was still sitting, grinning at a pile of hospital letters, when she reappeared, bag over her shoulder, car keys in her hand.

'I was wondering,' she said. 'Would it be alright if Geth comes with us?'

'For dinner?'

'To visit the Professor, you lembo.'

'You mean, you'd come with me to the hospital?'

'I thought that's what we'd agreed. Sunday afternoon?'

'Of course. That'd be brilliant. Gethin can chat to her in Welsh. She hates speaking English.'

'Geth used to be like that. He was very militant when he was younger. A real take-no-prisoners Nasher. He did time.'

'Prison?'

'Six months in Usk, for attempted arson. He was with the Meibion Glyndwr. They used to burn down holiday cottages.'

'He seems such a quiet, gentle soul.'

'That's when he's around his sheep.'

267

'He must have a low opinion of me, though. A Welshman who can't speak Welsh.'

'He hasn't said.'

'Do you?'

'What, have a low opinion of you?'

'No. Do you speak Welsh?

'Adequately.'

'Should I learn?'

'I suppose that depends on whether you plan on staying.'

I drove up to Maes Glas on Friday evening. There was the best sunset ever as I crossed the River Conway. Harry was at the farm ahead of me. She said I could have one of the attic bedrooms. Mr Shepherd, a master of understatement, said there was a touch of damp in the attics so the couch in the little parlour might be better. Mrs Shepherd said I'd be sleeping in the bunkhouse across the yard. Bad enough, I'd been married when I pitched up for the lambing. Now I was something much more dangerous: a soon to be divorced man. I slept in the bunkhouse.

Actually, I didn't sleep. I tossed and turned, scratched imaginary itches, tried to identify worrying rustles in the straw down below, and then nodded off just before the cockerel started his dawn racket. Harry brought me a mug of strong tea. 'Breakfast in ten', she said.

Fly, the old sheepdog, escorted me to the house. Sausages, bacon, eggs still warm from the henhouse, mushrooms the size of a saucer, a mountain of toast and Mrs Shepherd's thick-cut marmalade.

Harry said, 'Tuck in. Don't be shy. This is the last you'll see of food till we've finished work.'

The first batch of ewes had already been drenched for liver fluke and worm and given a mineral bolus. It was what you might call pre-pre-natal care. Our tasks for the day were the three Ts: teeth, tits and toes. An old ewe with a broken mouth wouldn't graze well enough to grow a good lamb and a gimmer ewe with malformed udders wouldn't be kept for breeding. They'd be for the cull. A ewe with bad feet might be treatable.

Mrs Shepherd and Fly directed traffic. Harry worked with her dad. I assisted Gethin. I say 'assisted'. My contribution was to squib the foot rot spray as soon as he'd trimmed away any overgrown hoof. It was a one-finger, low-skill job. The way Gethin worked a ewe was something to behold. Mouth checked, teats checked, then he'd flip her over and start on her feet. Seventy, maybe eighty kilos of sheep, and he'd handle her like she weighed no more than a spaniel.

I said, 'I hear you studied under Professor Lloyd Humphreys.'

'I did,' he said. Clip, clip, scrape, scrape.

'She's been very ill. I dare say you'll see a big change in her, if you come to visit.'

'Bound to.'

We worked right through, apart from a pause for a glass of lemon barley water, to lay the dust.

The afternoon's task was tail shearing. I was teamed with Mrs Shepherd. My job was to hold the head and keep the ewe calm. A sheep's eye is a curious thing. The pupil is shaped like a letterbox.

'Next!' she'd say. 'Have you nodded off?'

She worked very fast.

I said, 'You seem like you've made a good recovery from your surgery.'

'My arm's still not right,' she said, 'but I'll live.'

She paused for a breather after we'd done fifty ewes, pushed her hair out of her eyes with her arm. This is what Harry will look like thirty years from now, I thought. I think I'm in love with your daughter, I didn't say.

'In my back pocket,' she said. 'There should be a couple of Milky Ways, if they haven't melted.'

I didn't feel I'd earned mine, but she insisted.

'Getting divorced then, is it?'

'Yes.'

'Not married long, I'd say.'

'Just over a year. She didn't like Wales. Turns out she didn't like me much either.'

'Well,' she said, 'there's sadness. No sense dragging it out, though. They used to tell you to stick with what you'd got, like it or lump it. I don't know if they were right. If a pair of shoes are paining you, it seems daft to keep wearing them.'

'My Nan used to cut holes in hers till the pain stopped.'

She laughed.

'Can't do that with a husband. You'd be had up for attempted murder. Right, let's crack on. I've got two episodes of *Hinterland* taped, soon as we're finished here. That's my Saturday treat.'

'Good, is it?'

'Oh yes. I've seen it before, mind. I know how it ends.'

'What about the dipping?'

'We'll do that tomorrow,' she said. 'These girls have been messed around enough for one day.'

I had a crazy, maybe kind of plan. In the morning, when Harry brought me my mug of tea, I'd pretend to be half asleep and in my fake grogginess I'd tell her how beautiful she was.

Could I pull it off? I wasn't sure how much of an actor I was. I'd had pretty good reviews when I played Innkeeper in the Year 2 Nativity at Croesonen but I suppose everyone's mother thinks they're the next Anthony Hopkins.

Harry didn't bring me any tea. The first I knew, Fly was yipping at me to wake up. It was gone eight o'clock and we were supposed to start the dipping at nine. I was late for breakfast. There was no bacon left, the toast was cold and in the chair where Harry should have been sitting was the last person I wanted to see. Pete. Pete, the handsome, single, saviour of precious pet dogs and cats and, no doubt, sheep-dipping expert.

He was friendly.

'Met you before, I think. Weren't you up at Easter, with your little girls?'

'Not mine. They were my nieces. Harry not up yet?'

'You're joking,' he said. 'There's no lying in on a farm. She's been charging around for hours.'

How did he know? When had he arrived? I'd turned in early, completely tuckered. Had he come late and slept over? Was he allowed to sleep in the house? Was he allowed to sleep in her bed? And now he'd arrived, what were the chances Harry would change her plans for the day? I'd have to visit Professor Buddug without her. I'd be spending the afternoon with a bad-tempered old lady and a monosyllabic, militant Welsh Nationalist. Great.

Pete put more water in the teapot and made fresh toast. He seemed quite at home. I heard voices in the yard. Harry had been up to the pastures with her dad and the working dogs, bringing the next batch of ewes down for their pre-tup. I watched her when she came in. I thought I'd know immediately by the body language what the score was between her and Pete.

271

Had they spent the night together? There was nothing to read. She poured herself a cup, warmed herself against the range, talked about how pretty the meadows looked with the mist not yet burned off. She was the most unselfconscious woman I'd ever met. I was just some smitten bloke. Maybe Pete was too.

My chance came after we'd run the first score of ewes through the trough. It was my turn with the broom, making sure they were properly immersed before they clambered out. They didn't like it. Harry said they'd like it even less if they got flystrike.

I said, 'About this afternoon. I realise you probably won't be able to come to the hospital now.'

'Why?'

'Now Pete's here.'

She said, 'But the reason Pete's here is so Geth and I can have the afternoon off.'

Then she said, 'Oh, I get it. You think Pete's my boyfriend.'

'Isn't he?'

'No,' she said. 'You numpty.'

We set off for Glan Clwyd straight after Sunday lunch. A three-car convoy. Gethin had put on a tie. *The* tie, according to Harry. He only owned one. He brought some Welsh books with him and Harry had picked a bunch of asters.

Like anyone who's spent time in ICU, Professor Lloyd Humphreys had lost weight. It made her look even craggier. She was dressed in day clothes, sitting beside her bed. She recognised Gethin the moment he spoke. Harry got a searching look, until Geth introduced her and she spoke in Welsh. I was apparently invisible. I went in search of information. When was she likely to be discharged? Was there a care plan?

The nurse said the professor's home situation had been assessed, as well as her ability to fend for herself. The social worker and occupational therapist had conferred and the bottom line was, they felt she needed 24 hour care.

'What if she doesn't agree to that?'

'She'll have to. It's for her own good.'

'She had a home help before her accident. Benilda. She was perfect for her. Can't they just increase Benilda's hours?'

She said I'd have to speak to a doctor if I wanted any more information. And what were the chances of that, on a Sunday afternoon? She paged the geriatrics reg and eventually a houseman appeared. He said Professor Lloyd Humphreys was blocking a bed.

'So, send her home.'

'We can't do that. She's At Risk. She'll be placed wherever there's a vacancy. She can always be moved to somewhere more suitable later on. You could talk to social services if you're not happy. Not today, though. Are you a grandson?'

I said, 'Did you know, she used to head a university department? Now she's got social workers telling her where she has to live.'

The houseman shrugged. 'We do the best we can,' he said. 'We really do.'

I found Harry glowering at a vending machine that had taken her money and failed to deliver.

'How's the visit going?'

'Swimmingly. I left them to it. She's impressive, isn't she? Even in carpet slippers. She's like a chunk of Snowdonia.'

When we got back to Professor Buddug's bay, she'd fallen asleep with Gethin reading to her. Chin on her chest. Geth wiped the drool off her chin and she didn't wake.

Harry said, 'Shall we tiptoe away?'

I'd never seen Gethin so animated. He said it had been a wonderful visit. Her mind was as sharp as ever. I was glad for him, but for myself, I wished I'd never come.

I said, 'You know they won't let her go home? I don't think she realises what's in store for her.'

'Oh,' says Geth, 'I think she does.'

He set off, driving back to Maes Glas.

Harry said she needed cake and the League of Friends cafeteria didn't have much left, so we settled for a Costa in Rhyl.

She said, 'You seem upset.'

'Not upset. Depressed. Why are we so crap at dealing with old age?'

'You think she'll be miserable in a care home?'

'Of course. She'll give up the ghost. Six months and she'll be dead.'

'She might not. She might grow to like it. I've seen it happen. High minds discovering they quite enjoy bingo and Stroke a Labrador. And if you've been living alone in a big old house, it can come as a relief, not having to worry about repairs and bills and what you're going to have for your tea.'

'That's one way of looking at it. I've got a friend who's heading in the same direction. He's still working but he's got COPD and since his wife died his kids are telling him he should sell his house and move into assisted living.'

'You're talking about Trevor?'

'You remember him? You've got a good memory.'

'Not really. I had lunch with him.'

'You did what?'

'He took me to lunch in the Queen Vic.'

'The old devil. He just turned up at the surgery and asked you?'

274

'No, he phoned ahead. He said he was staying with you and he'd love a chat. About your state of mind.'

'He did not.'

'He was worried on two counts. One was that you were turning into the sort of man who lives alone and arranges his kitchen spices in alphabetical order.'

'And?'

'Also, that you fancied me but the business with Chloe had knocked your confidence for six, so you'd probably never pluck up enough courage to ask me out.'

'He said that?'

'Was he wrong?'

'Partly. I don't keep my spices in alphabetical order.'

'That's a relief.'

'So, you invited me to the farm, to put me out of my misery?'

'Or to set the ball rolling. Don't be cross with Trevor. His intentions were good.'

'I know. I'm just feeling a bit pitied.'

'No need. I fancied you too. We'd have got round to it eventually. This is just a shortcut. So, you're still living in a house full of memories.'

'Not that many. We were hardly there together. I'll have to sell it. I just can't quite face it yet.'

'Probably best treated as a Band-Aid job. Rip it off fast and get the pain over and done with. Unless you think she might come back.'

'She won't.'

'If she asked you, would you give it another try?'

'No.'

'That was a decisive answer.'

'She's made it easy. I don't think I knew the half of what she got up to.'

'Where is she?'

'About to move to Solihull. Her new bloke just passed his CSA, and her father fixed him up with a job. It's what he does. Calls in favours from well-connected friends.'

'I'll bet he didn't fix you up with Parry and Hughes.'

'No, that was all my own work. I could have had that Solihull gig if I'd wanted it. Things might have turned out very differently. On the other hand, maybe not. I think the marriage was doomed anyway. But you don't need to hear about that.'

'S'okay,' she said. 'I have cake. I can listen.'

I told her the story. My chance encounter with George Fitzgerald at the exam centre. The completely avoidable death of Chloe's mother. Two random events that connected. And then my decision to move to Colwyn Bay whatever Chloe thought of it. That might have been the final straw, but I think the spark had already been rekindled under her thing with Fitzgerald by then. I prefer not to know.

Harry said, 'I only met her twice, at the Parrys, and I got the impression she was there under sufferance. Very beautiful, of course. Sorry. Wrong reading. I'll try that again. How about, it just goes to show, great looks aren't everything? Or maybe I'll shut up.'

'So, Trevor took you to lunch and asked you to take pity on me? How embarrassing. Like I had a neon sign over my head that said LOSER.'

'Not take pity. He wanted to suss out whether I had any interest in you. He's a doll, by the way.'

'Some people think so.'

'I told him that I liked you very much, but I thought it might be too soon for you. That you were still a bit fragile? Are you, Dan?'

'I don't think so. Wary, maybe. See, I thought you and Pete were an item. I'd kind of settled for admiring you from afar.'

She finished her cake.

'Let me tell you about Pete,' she said. 'I've known him all my life. His family are in Llanbedr. In fact, I think he witnessed me being potty-trained.'

'That might be hard to come back from.'

She hushed me.

'Let me finish. He has a very inflated opinion of himself, encouraged by his mother, and he's a victim of his own good looks. Women fall for him like skittles, he picks them up, puts them down, moves on. I'll be amazed if he ever commits to anyone. He's okay as a friend, and I'm always grateful when gives a hand at the farm, but I wouldn't have him if he was the last man in Wales. Got it?'

The car park of the White Rose Shopping Centre in Rhyl will always have a special place in my heart. It was where I stole my first kiss from Harry Shepherd. The second and third, she gave quite willingly.

Chapter 27

Fools rush in, and I certainly had with Chloe. Within a week of our first date she and Eeyore had moved in with me and within a month she'd learned to defuse any argument by wearing one of my rugby shirts and not much else. Harry and I agreed to take things slowly. On Sunday we kissed. On Wednesday lunchtime she phoned me.

Had I heard the news? Professor Lloyd Humphreys had gone AWOL from the hospital. It had been on the radio. She had apparently walked out of the hospital and taken nothing with her except for her handbag. Nearly 24 hours had passed without a sighting and her car was missing.

I said, 'That won't take her far. It's an old wreck. I'm amazed it even started. Have you talked to Gethin?'

'He's up on the maes, out of range. I'll catch him this evening.'

'Will you call me if you hear anything?'

'I probably won't need to. I bet it'll be on the news again.'

'Call me anyway?'

She said, 'Would that be in compliance with the Taking Things Slowly guidelines?'

As soon as Gethin heard the news he contacted the hospital. The story was, Professor Buddug had been informed by a social worker that there was a vacancy at the Plas Hyfryd residential unit and transport was being organised for later in the week. She'd appeared quite happy with the arrangement and they'd been relieved that she hadn't resisted what was, after all, for her own good. Later on, she'd said she was going downstairs to buy a newspaper and she wasn't missed until her afternoon cuppa was found, cold and untouched. A taxi driver remembered picking her up outside the hospital and taking her to Llanddulas but more than that he couldn't say because he was Bangladeshi and she'd spoken to him in Welsh. He'd dropped her off at her house at around three o'clock.

Harry said, 'What do you think?'

'She might just be making a point. You know? You can stick Plas Hyfryd where the sun don't shine.'

'But then what? Is she going to do a Thelma and Louise?'

'I doubt her car has enough throttle.'

That night her old Ford Capri was found in a pub car park at Nant Peris. It wasn't noticed till after closing time, so they said they'd start the search at first light. Harry had spoken to Gethin. She suspected he knew more than he was letting on.

'Do you think she told him what she was planning?'

'I wouldn't be surprised.'

'I wonder why Nant Peris.'

'Well, there's a lake, there are mountains. Plenty of options for a defiant exit.'

'You think she's dead?'

'This could be her second night out there. If she's on Glydr Fawr, it gets cold once the sun goes down.'

'They might never find her.'

279

'It depends how determined she was. They probably will. There'll be loads of hikers up there at the weekend.'

'Will Gethin join the search?'

'He says not. He says she was of sound mind and we must respect a person's wishes.'

It rained for two days and nights. I lay awake listening to it, wondering how long it takes to die of hypothermia. They say you just fall asleep. But how do they know?

On Saturday evening Harry and I met for dinner at the Italian. She was wearing a dress.

'Miriam's orders,' she said. 'I've been taken in hand.'

'Miriam knows about us?'

'Yes. Is it supposed to be a secret?'

'No. It just makes me a bit nervous. Like the eyes of Llandudno and Colwyn Bay are on me. Will Talbot screw up again?'

'The pressure must be unbearable. You could have worn a false moustache. Or I could.'

'You look lovely. You should wear a dress more often. Not that there's anything wrong with what you usually wear. I think I need a drink.'

'You're driving, right?'

'Yes.'

'Therefore, you can't cross the line between 'one glass of wine, officer' and 'ah, to hell with it.' Which is probably what you need, to loosen up.'

'Am I that bad?'

'Honestly? Maybe coming to a restaurant wasn't the best idea? You're worried about passing some kind of imaginary dating test. I'm worried about spilling food down Miriam's dress. Can I make a suggestion? Let's have a quick pasta and skip dessert? I have ice cream at my place.'

'So do I.'

'What flavour?'

'Flavours. Salted caramel, raspberry pavlova, mint choc chip. Possibly even vanilla.'

'You are an ice cream millionaire.'

That was how Harry came to spend the night at Pentraeth, although not in the marital bed. We tried out several locations and as I recall we woke up, appropriately enough, in the Trevor Buxton suite.

She said, 'This is a lovely house, but it feels like an off-season hotel. Why on earth did you buy something so big?'

'I hoped we were going to fill it with children.'

'Oh, Dan,' she said. 'If only you'd run it by me, or Miriam. Either of us could have told you Chloe wouldn't want more than one child. Preferably induced and by elective caesarean.'

'I thought she'd come round to the idea. Oh well. It'll be full to the rafters next weekend. Three girls and a baby boy. My sister-in-law and her family. I've invited them for one last visit before I sell.'

'Sister-in-law?'

'Chloe's sister, Flo.'

'Right. Don't worry, I'll make myself scarce.'

'No need. Flo's nothing like Chloe. You already met her husband. Henry, the chap who came up to see your rams.'

'Of course. Wellies and a three-piece suit.'

'Harris tweed, though. Henry always dresses like that. To not wear a waistcoat and tie would be his equivalent of walking around in Speedos.'

'I liked him. He admired Derek's testicles.'

'You have a ram called Derek?'

'Didn't you ever read the *Beano*?'

'Not for at least twenty years. Should I start again?'

'Too late. Derek's disappeared. In the *Beano*, I mean, not our Derek.

'Where's he gone?'

'No-one knows. Erased. I will stay out of sight though, next weekend. Best not to mix it, don't you think? It might annoy Chloe and to be honest, she terrifies me.'

'Why?'

'I don't know. Maybe it's the heels. They could be used as lethal weapons. And even though she's moved on, I'm not sure she'll be happy about you doing so.'

The Packwoods came minus Henry and Poppy. Henry had entered a promising young boar at the Berkshire County Show. Poppy had been invited to a friend's birthday sleepover.

Lily's first words were, 'Where is Trevor Buxton?'

'At his own house. I expect you'll see him some other time.'

'Aunt Chlo doesn't live here anymore either. Mummy told us and Poppa called her 'that bloody woman'. When can we go to the beach?'

'After you've chosen bedrooms and we've had lunch.'

Daisy said, 'Is there any bedroom we're not allowed?'

'Yes,' I said. 'Mine.'

Flo nursed Ted while I cooked fish fingers.

'What did you tell the girls about Chloe?'

'As little as possible. The story changes by the minute and I don't want to confuse them.'

'How does the story change? They're in Solihull, right?'

'*He's* in Solihull. Chloe's at the Chummery.'

282

'She left him?'

'She says it's a trial separation. She says he's become dull and predictable. I really don't understand her. Surely, that's why one settles down?'

'That didn't last long. Is she working?'

'She says she's looking for something. Well, she can't stay at the Chummery indefinitely. It's Daddy's home, after all. If he and Jen choose to spend time there, they won't want Chloe huffing around in a sulk.'

'Why doesn't she just rent a flat? Are you worried she'll ask to move in with you?'

'Not in the least. Farm smells, children, Henry. We're the last place she'd resort to. But I do wonder if she might approach you, about trying again.'

'She already did, weeks ago. I said no.'

'I see. I can't blame you. She has messed you around most awfully.'

And then I surprised myself by saying, 'As a matter of fact, Flo, I've moved on. I've met someone.'

'Golly,' she said. 'Isn't that super- fast?'

Daisy had come in without us noticing.

She said, 'What was super-fast?'

Flo said, 'The speed with which Dan has prepared lunch.'

Daisy said, 'That's a rather feeble fib. I'm having a top bunk and no-one else is allowed in my room.'

'What about Lily?'

'She's in Trevor Buxton's bed, arranging her books. I'm starving.'

Flo dished up lunch while I held Ted. He felt so light and floppy.

I said, 'Am I supposed to wind him or something?'

283

Daisy said, 'No, if you hang him over your arm or your shoulder and walk around, he winds himself. Wait till you see his nappies though. They are too disgusting.'

It was agreed we were each allowed to choose one thing to do during their stay. Daisy said Crazy Golf, no hesitation. Lily was still pondering.

Flo said, 'Ted wants to go on the Great Orme tram and so do I.'

I said, 'And I'd like to go to the Mountain Zoo to see the tigers.'

'I know,' says Lily. 'Let's go to the farm and see Derek.'

Flo mouthed, 'Who's Derek?'

'A Suffolk ram. Fancy your remembering his name, Lils.'

'I always remember names. There was a man called Pete and a nice lady called Harry. She showed Poppa how to check Derek's testinkles.'

Daisy said, 'You mean testicles, shrimp.'

The temptation was great. With Lily as my excuse I could take them up to Maes Glas for an hour. I'd get to see Harry, and Flo could meet her, without needing to know the full story. But then, even if Flo didn't pick up on the vibe, her girls would. They seemed not to miss a trick.

I said I'd think about it. I said Mr and Mrs Shepherd might be too busy for visitors.

Daisy said, 'Is Shepherd their actual, actual name?'

'Yes. Neat isn't it?'

'It's funny. Poppa could change his name to Henry Pigman.'

We were halfway round the Crazy Golf when Harry called me. Professor Buddug had been found.

'Sorry to interrupt your family time but I thought you'd want to know.'

'She's dead?'

'Of course.'

A climber had spotted a flash of white at the bottom of a gully by the Idwal Slabs and realised it was someone's hair. The mountain rescue team from Ogwen were on their way to retrieve the body.

'Is Gethin upset?'

'He's sad, but he feels she got one over on social services. Geth's not the sentimental type. He just hopes she died quickly.'

'I've been dithering about whether to call you.'

She said, 'I thought we'd moved well beyond dithering.'

'You remember the little girls who came up to the farm with Henry at Easter? Lily has asked to see the sheep again. I wondered about tomorrow? Would it be an imposition?'

'Not at all. Bring her.'

'The thing is, it would be all of us.'

'You mean, Chloe's sister?'

'Yes.'

'Does she know about us?'

'I told her you're a friend.'

'So, no snogging in front of her. Got it. I'll rein myself in. Just one thing. The tups are going great guns so it's probably a PG-rated scene up on the meadow. You might get some awkward questions.'

'Lily and Daisy live on a farm. They've seen their pigs mating, which I'm told can take quite a while.'

'I wouldn't know. With Derek and Eric it's all over very fast. Blink and you'd miss it.'

Flo quizzed me after the girls were in bed.

'You mentioned you'd met someone?'

'It's early days yet.'

'Well I should say it is, but still, good for you. Someone local, one imagines?'

'Yes. She's a doctor.'

'Chloe's been an utter fool.'

'Do you remember when Charlie was sentenced, and she threatened to cancel the wedding?'

'How could I forget? I've never seen Henry so angry. You know he'd secured her an excellent price for the hog roast. If she'd cancelled it would have put him in a very difficult position.'

'I wonder if I should have called her bluff. Now I look back, she had us on this ridiculously expensive, elaborate wedding merry-go-round.'

'Horrendous. The scenes we had over the girls' frocks.'

'I don't think she was anywhere near ready to settle down.'

'She was always a flibbertigibbet. I'm quite amazed she stuck at the doctoring. When we were children she was never contented with her own toys. She had to have whatever someone else was playing with. I was usually forced to give in to her, but as soon as she got what she wanted, she'd lose interest in it.'

'It seems she hasn't changed.'

'Henry and I feel very badly for you. And now if things work out, with your new friend, I suppose you'll fade from our lives.'

'Not necessarily. I mean, here you are, visiting. No awkwardness.'

'The thing is, we were thinking of asking you to be one of Ted's godparents.'

'That could be difficult.'

'Yes.'

'I mean, I'd be very honoured, but Chloe would be furious. She'd boycott the christening.'

'Yes.'

'Perhaps if you wait a while, until she's back with Fitzgerald, or happily paired off with someone else? She can't spend the rest of her life being cross with me.'

Ted stirred, ready for his next feed.

Flo said, 'I don't know. Chlo can hold a grudge longer than anyone else I know. And we were rather hoping to have Ted baptised before his voice breaks.'

Chapter 28

At Maes Glas the ewe lambs I'd seen born in April had been separated off from the rest of the flock. They were ready to breed but according to Harry, the rams tended to be less interested in them, so it was better if they didn't have to compete with the older ewes for attention. Nevertheless, Eric had been in among them and there were quite a few marked by the green crayon in his chest harness. It remained to be seen whether he'd been successful in impregnating them. They'd be scanned in January.

We went up to the higher pasture to find Gethin. He was watching Derek at work.

Daisy said, 'Look at that one, running away. She doesn't like him.'

Geth said, 'She's not in the mood. She might change her tune tomorrow.'

The news from Ogwen was that the weather had closed in and the attempt to reach Professor Buddug's body had been abandoned. She'd be spending at least one more night on the mountain.

I said, 'Did she tell you that was what she planned to do?'

'Probably wisest if I say nothing.'

'Someone will have to identify her.'

'I've told them I'll do it,' he said.

We drove back down to the farmyard and Mr Shepherd came out with a bag of Chewits for the girls. Mrs Shepherd stood on the doorstep with her arms folded. She gave me a smile and a nod. Did that mean she didn't know about me and Harry, or that she knew and didn't mind?

As we drove away Flo said, 'Look at these views. What a marvellous place to live. I could almost envy them. No children yet, though?'

'Who, Harry and Gethin? No, they're brother and sister.'

'Gosh, Dan, you might have said. One could so easily have put one's foot in it. She's awfully sweet.'

'She is.'

'I noticed the scar on her face. Was that from an argument with a sheep?'

'No, she was born with a cleft lip. It shows more when the weather's cold.'

'Rather lonely up there, one imagines, for a single woman.'

'She only visits, to help out. Her mother's not been well. Harry lives in Llanfairfechan. She's a GP in Llandudno.'

'Oh, I *see,*' she said. 'At least, I think I do.'

Daisy said, 'What do you think you see?'

'Nothing.'

'I know,' says Lily. 'But I'm not telling.'

Daisy called her a tiresome runt.

When I went to bed there was a Lily drawing left on my pillow. Two stick figures, one with lots of curly hair, and between them a big pink heart.

Two days passed before the weather cleared and they brought Professor Buddug's body down from Glydr Fawr. Gethin went to Bangor to identify it. Then it was transferred to

289

Mochdre, pending the coroner releasing it for cremation. There'd have to be an inquest, but it was surely clear that no-one had taken her up the mountain and thrown her into a gully. She'd seemed of perfectly sound mind when we'd seen her in the hospital, but she'd left no note. The fact was, we'd never know if she'd clambered up Glydr Fawr in a state of mental unbalance or with clear intent. I knew what I thought.

In her car they'd found an almost empty bottle of Snowdonia Dry Gin. At her house they found a will and a crowd of mice having a rave. The will bequeathed her entire library to her old university department and the crumbling, infested house to Benilda. But Benilda's whereabouts were unknown. The agency thought she'd gone back to the Philippines to visit her family. For the time being, there was nothing more to be done. Professor Buddug was kept in a refrigerated drawer and the mice partied on.

I was on my way to work, at a standstill in traffic, when someone rapped on my side window. Dennis Underhill. He and Beverley were walking to the station, heading to Birmingham to see The Yardleybeats. I asked him if they wanted a lift.

'No thanks,' he said. 'We're in a hurry.'

'Did your hospital appointment come through?'

'Next week.'

'Good. Enjoy the show. Give my regards to Brum.'

At the meddygfa David had called a meeting for lunchtime. Such a thing had never happened in living memory. There was only one thing on the agenda: measles. David had seen a confirmed case the previous week and two more were suspected in families registered with us. He was going out to see the children in their homes.

He said, 'I'm thinking seriously about telling antivaxxers to find a new GP.'

Iestyn said, 'Hang on, David. That's a bit extreme. The numbers aren't that bad.'

David said, 'But Iestyn, the number ought to be zero. You vaccinate your children.'

Iestyn said it had been Aggie's decision. He was ambivalent himself.

I said, 'But why? The autism connection has been completely discredited.'

'Still,' he said, 'it seems an unnatural thing to do to a small child.'

Bethan chipped in. She said, 'So is burying them. It's a shame my nan's not alive. You could have asked her. She lost two to measles.'

Iestyn held out against David's proposal to deregister parents who refused to vaccinate but he said he'd try to lay aside his personal reservations.

David said, 'Don't bother. Just send them to me or Dan. Or to Aggie, when she's in.'

Aggie was still very much a part-timer. I rarely saw her, but that week our paths crossed twice. The first time was over a couple I'd referred to her. Susan and Martyn Benbow. The Benbows wanted to discuss their failure to conceive. Susan was 38, Martyn was 33. They'd recently moved to the area from Oswestry, so we had nothing about them on our files.

How long had they been trying to get pregnant? Years, they said.

'Two years, or longer?'

More like ten, they said. Was Susan menstruating regularly? She seemed unsure.

'Do you have a period every month?'

'Not every month. Quite a lot though.'

Any miscarriages? Had Martyn had mumps since puberty? And had they had any investigations done? No, no, no. Nothing.

Susan said, 'We just pray on it, don't we, Martyn?'

She was overweight. She had some acne on her face and neck and a shadow of hair on her top lip. Was I looking at a case of polycystic ovaries?

There was something odd about them too. They listened intently when I spoke but avoided looking me in the face. Were they plain shy? Were they dreading probing questions about their sex life? I bottled asking them any.

I said, 'Dr Aggie Hughes is our fertility expert. Let me see if I can get you an appointment with her this week.'

They thought that was a great idea. Delyth shoe-horned them into Aggie's Wednesday clinic and I promptly forgot about them until Aggie bounced in to see me after surgery.

'Thank you for Benbows,' she said.

'Aren't they an odd pair? Ten years without her falling pregnant and they've never tried to find out why. Do you think she has PCOS?'

Aggie said, 'It could be. But not only. Listen, it is bit sad but very funny story.'

'Which you're going to tell me in strict confidence.

'Absolute. They didn't have sex.'

'No.'

'Yes.'

'You must have misunderstood.'

'Bull plop. I didn't misunderstand. I speak English good as yours. They didn't have sex. They thought just be in bed together and baby will come.'

'How is this even possible?'

'No-one told them.'

I said, 'Aggie, who needs telling? It's a very powerful urge.'

'They are very religious. They read Bible. In Bible it says, "he lay with her" or "he knew her".'

'But don't they read books, or watch films or talk to friends?'

'They don't have television. Perhaps they don't have friends. In bed only they hold hands and say prayers.'

'Did you explain what they need to do?'

'Oh yes. They were very surprised.'

'Pleasantly surprised?'

'Husband, yes. Susan not so much. When I did pelvic exam she was very anxious. She is virgin. She thinks it will hurt and she thinks is not hygienic because he uses his pee pee for wee wee.'

'Too much thinking.'

Aggie laughed.

'Well, that's one for your memoirs. And what about her fertility? What bloods are you doing?'

'DHEA, insulin, HbA1C, free testosterone, SHBG. For FSH and LH test we must wait for her period. She doesn't remember when it came before. I think she is bit slow. I think she is maybe not full tickets.'

'And did they dash out of your office to go home and try sex?'

'I told them go first in Boots shop and buy KY jelly. Dan, I don't think they will have baby but maybe they will enjoy to try.'

'Is that the strangest consultation you ever had?'

'No. When I was student in A&E we had man with Dove in his bottoms.'

'A dove?'

'Deodorant of Dove. He sat on it by mistakes.'

'At the practice where I trained, we had a girl who came in with a mobile phone in her vagina.'

'Mobile phone has corners.'

'Not hers. It was an old fliptop.'

The second time I saw Aggie that week she wasn't working. She came to the surgery specially to see me at the end of morning surgery.

'Danek!' she said. 'Is true about you and Harry?'

I said, 'It's supposed to be a secret. Kind of.'

'Why?'

'Because I didn't get my divorce yet.'

'So? We are modern peoples and is not your fault your wife was bitch.'

'How did you find out?'

'From Granny Gwenny.'

'And who told her?'

'Aunty Grace.'

'Harry's mum?'

'Yes. She told Granny Gwenny, "Dr Dan likes Harry very much. He comes even to help with sheeps." Granny Gwenny told her you are very nice doctor. You went to see Professor old lady because it was too far for Iestyn on bike.'

'I was just doing my job, Aggie. Does he have another driving test booked?'

'Yes. He will never pass test. He's very lovely man but is better he doesn't have licence. Don't change subject. You and Harry. We shall be family.'

'We've been on a few dates, that's all. And given my recent track record, I don't want people gossiping about us.'

'Is too late. If Granny Gwenny knows, everyone knows. One hundred eighty people live in village. Oh, Dan, this is such nice thing. Harry is best cousin of Iestyn.'

I called Harry.

I said, 'The cat's out of the bag. Your mum and your Aunty Gwenny have put two and two together.'

'Have they spooked you?'

'Not exactly, but I just had Aggie in here planning our future. Apparently, you're Iestyn's favourite cousin.'

'News to me. Dan, you sound on edge. Are you feeling like you're on a runaway train?'

'Aggie caught me off-guard, that's all.'

'We should talk.'

'Okay. My place or yours?'

'Mine. Yours still has a ghostly whiff of you-know-who.'

'You mean her perfume?'

'No. I think it's the Winnie the Pooh fridge magnets.'

Harry has a little cottage just back from the promenade. She'd made goulash and mashed potatoes.

She said, 'This all feels a bit formal. Do you want to go first?'

I tried to explain myself. That I didn't at all want to cool it with her, but I didn't even have my decree nisi yet and if we started parading around as a couple, her family would get the wrong impression of me. Easy come, easy go. A bed-hopper.

'Well,' she said, 'anyone who thinks that needs their head examined. You come across as shy and serious. That's the impression my family has of you. Also, I'm not a child, Dan. I'm 33. I have history. Do you want to hear it?'

295

'Not unless there's something big. Long criminal record. Abandoned children. Any stuffed animal that has to share your bed.'

'I have speeding points. When I was seven, I stole a Milky Bar. I'm not a virgin.'

'I know that.'

'Look,' she said, 'if you'd be more comfortable slowing down till your divorce is a done deal, I can live with that. I've waited long enough for Dr Right, so what's a few more months here or there?'

'Am I Dr Right?'

'I reckon so. The question is, am I?'

'Without a doubt. Do you know when I fell in love with you?'

'When I ruined my T shirt changing a tyre and Miriam lent me that gorgeous white dress?'

'No. When you asked me to carry your cake tin.'

'What cake tin?'

'It was the night we met. You arrived for dinner at the Parrys the same time we did, and you were trying to carry a bottle of wine, a cake tin and a duvet.'

'And?'

'You said "take the cake tin. The duvet's covered in dog hair."'

'And that was it?'

'I fancied you. You had mussed-up hair.'

'My hair is always mussed-up. Even when I was a junior houseman and I hadn't actually slept for days, I still looked like I just fell out of bed. But back up. What was the significance of the cake tin?'

'Homemade cake, dog hair. Things like that say a lot about a woman.'

296

'You're weird. And shocking. You were a married man.'

'And I wasn't looking for anyone. You just happened.'

'So, you thought I had a dog. You got that wrong. It was farm dog hair. And for all you knew I might have lobbed an M&S cake in the tin, intending to pass it off as my own work.'

'No, Harry. Basic powers of observation. The tin was warm.'

Once we'd unpicked my tangle of hopes and worries several things were clear. I loved Harry and I didn't care about public opinion. It was Chloe's reaction I was afraid of. I wanted a quick, clean divorce and from what I'd heard, she was very unsettled. If Flo was right and she was back living at the Chummery, did that mean she and Fitzgerald were finished, or was she putting him to some kind of test?

Harry said, 'You're here, she's miles away, wherever. There's no reason she should find out about me, not for the time being. And what if she does? She left you.'

'All true. So, we carry on regardless.'

'We carry on carrying on. Everyone at Maes Glas knows, Miriam knows. Have you told Trevor his gamble paid off?'

'No, but I will. And there's someone else I need to tell. My friend Vaz. He's a very devout Catholic. It's a conversation I've been dreading.'

'Go home, Dan,' she said. 'Call your Vaz friend, call your parents. Call everybody you'd like to tell, except anyone remotely connected to Chloe.'

'Too late, I'm afraid. Her sister twigged, after we'd been up to visit the farm. As soon as she realised you and Geth weren't a couple. Lily already had it figured.'

'Is Lily the eight-year-old?'

'The six-year-old. Terrifying, isn't it?'

Chapter 29

I sat down with my list. Mam was going to be the first person I told but an incoming call delayed me. Laurence Swift, my erstwhile father-in-law.

'Now,' he said, 'what can we do to sort out this rather ugly mess?'

No 'hello Dan, how are you?', no 'sorry my daughter has caused you all this grief.'

I said, 'Shouldn't you be having this conversation with Chloe? The ugly mess wasn't of my making. And what kind of sorting out do you have in mind? I already have a solicitor but maybe Chloe needs one.'

He said, 'The poor girl is terribly confused.'

I think Laurence was confident that one of his famous phone calls would repair the marriage. That I'd listen to his good counsel, Chloe would receive a personality transplant and we'd all live happily ever after.

Then he said, 'This Fitzgerald chap turns out to be not quite the thing. I pulled a few strings, got him a job in Solihull, and now there's talk of him bolting to Ireland. Extraordinary. Meanwhile Chlo's dug in at The Chummery, scarcely bothering to get dressed.'

So that was the problem. Laurence wanted his home back. He and Jen wanted to spend loved-up weekends there without Chloe slumming around in her onesie, resenting Jen's very existence.

I said, 'Laurence, the marriage is over. I'm sorry if that's causing you any inconvenience, but the best thing for Chloe would be to get back to work, and a proper job, not some half-baked private gig. I have to go. I have someone else trying to get through.'

I hoped it was Harry, with a good-night-I-love-you call. It wasn't.

Chloe said, 'You have to be kidding. That woman?'

I took a deep breath. She'd called to pick a fight and my best weapon was to be calmly polite.

I said, 'Can I help you with something?'

'Yes,' she said, 'you can tell me it's not true.'

'What?'

'About you and the ratty sweater woman.'

'Her name's Harry.'

'Whatever. Did you think I wouldn't find out? Did you think the she-brat wouldn't blab?'

That would have been Lily.

I said, 'It's not really any of your business, is it? You and I are finished.'

'Such a hypocrite. You condemned me because of a silly thing with Fitzie and all the while you were boffing Raggedy Ann.'

'I wasn't, Chloe. I was sitting at home, alone, wishing you were there and wondering why you weren't.'

'And what the hell do you think you're doing, inviting the Packwoods to stay? They're *my* family.'

'But they became part of my family, when I married you in good faith, and I've grown fond of them. They've asked me to be Ted's godfather, but I suppose you'd be uncomfortable with that.'

'Ha!' she said, 'that'll be Henry's idea. He'll stop at nothing to annoy me.'

'Why are you calling me? If it's about the house, I've told your solicitor, I'll put it on the market in the New Year.'

She said she didn't care about the house.

'You'll care about it when you don't have The Chummery to squat in.'

'I'm not squatting. It's my home.'

I said, 'No, it's your father's home. You're a grownup. If you're not going to live with Fitzgerald, you need to get a place of your own.'

That was all Jen's malicious doing, she said. Whispering to Laurence to throw his own daughter out on the street. The world according to Chloe. Jen and Henry and now me, conspiring against her.

She said, 'So are you really, seriously doing Raggedy Harry? What's that? An act of charity? Your good deed for the year?'

She was drunk.

I said, 'It makes me sad to hear you like this, but I'm not going to play games. I've moved on. Go to bed, Chloe. Sober up. Get your shit together.'

She left me in no mood for a conversation with Vaz, which was likely to include words like 'repentance' and 'forgiveness'. I emailed him instead. Vaz checks his emails about once a year so if I didn't hear back from him it wouldn't necessarily mean he was disappointed in me.

Da answered Mam's phone. He spoke very quietly.

He said, 'She's just now getting a bit of shut-eye. We've been having bad nights with your Nan.'

I heard Mam's voice immediately.

'I'm awake' she said. 'Is it our Dan?'

She came on.

I said, 'How did you know it was me?'

'Mother's instinct,' she said. 'And who else would it be? June never phones me after nine o'clock. Now, I haven't been in touch because I didn't want to interfere. Are you and Chloe patching things up?'

'No, we're getting divorced. It's already happening. Lawyers and everything. Mam, I want you to start looking at nursing homes for Nan. You can't carry on like this.'

'Is that why you've phoned? To nag me?'

'No, I phoned to tell you I've met someone.'

'See? Didn't I tell you you would.'

Then she started relaying everything between me and Da.

'Dan's got a girlfriend, Ed. She's a doctor. From a farming family, Ed. Sheep. Your Da says is it the place you mentioned before? Welsh Mules crossed with Texels?'

'Suffolks, not Texels. Her name's Angharad but everyone calls her Harry. I want you to meet her. I want you to come here for Christmas.'

Mam said she didn't see how they could, with Nan being the way she was. She'd started having night terrors. They were giving her Ativan, but she was still waking at around three o'clock, seeing things, crying out for help.

I said, 'See if you can get her into respite care for a few days. Worst comes to the worst, you can always bring her with you. Either way, I want you and Da to come. I want you to meet Harry. And you know I have to sell the house, so I don't know where I'll be this time next year.'

301

Mam said, 'What it is, Dan, those respite places get booked up. And then there's June to think of. She always comes to us on Christmas. If we go away, she'll be left on her own.'

'I thought she was Internet dating?'

'She is. She's not having much luck though. There was one, looked very nice. American army, quite high up, serving in Afghanistan. He was a widower.'

'And then he asked her for money.'

'Yes. How did you guess?'

'It's a common story. It's a scam.'

'Is it? He said his daughter had been taken ill and he needed to get back to America quickly, but his money was tied up because of some mistake the bank had made.'

'Please tell me she didn't send him money.'

'She was going to. Not that she's got much. I said "June, if he's got a sick kiddie, the army'll get him home." So, you've heard of this chap?'

'It's not one man, Mam. There are dozens of them. They sit at computers in Nigeria or Walthamstow or somewhere, preying on gullible women. Doesn't Aunty June ever read the papers?'

I called my brother. He listened while I told him what I needed him to do.

'Why me?' he said.

'Because we're family and it's time you did something.'

'Mam won't like me interfering.'

'Blame me. Feel free,'

'I don't know anything about those places. Expensive, aren't they?'

'They can be. But it depends on personal circumstances and all Nan's got is her old age pension. It's not like she's sitting on any assets. Anyway, we can chip in, if we have to.'

He said he didn't have money to throw around.

I said, 'Adam, do you ever think about getting old?'

'What do you mean?'

'You're single. Who's going to look after you when you get like Nan?'

'Won't happen,' he said. 'I'll top myself before.'

A lot of people say that.

I said, 'The trouble with the early exit plan is recognising when the time has come. You know? One minute you're in fairly good shape, enjoying life. The next thing you know somebody's spoon feeding you. Please, just make some calls, ask around. If you send me a list, I'll do the rest.'

My brother likes lists. When we were kids he had an exercise book full of them. Most Poisonous Snakes. Most Scary Rollercoasters. Breakfast Cereals of the World. Welsh Rugby, Most Yellow Cards. Welsh Rugby, Most Red Cards.

Within two days of our conversation he sent me a list of possible respite facilities. Mam was right. The prospects didn't look good. Christmas was a time when carers needed a break and care workers wanted time off with their own families.

Harry said, 'What about her GP? Is he on the case?'

'I assume so.'

'Don't assume. I've seen families absolutely on their knees and still not asking for help. It's the squeaking wheel that gets the oil, Dan.'

My family had been with the same practice for years. Todd, Little and Ellis. I remember what Sarah Little said to me when she heard I was going to medical school.

'You'll probably choose something glamorous like neurosurgery, but don't turn your nose up at general practice.'

They said Dr Little only worked part-time now, four afternoons. I didn't catch her until later in the week.

I said, 'I don't know if you'll remember me.'

'Eirwen Talbot's boy,' she said. 'Of course I do. Didn't you get a Lisfranc fracture, playing rugby?'

'That was my brother. I'm the one who went to med school.'

I told her the Nan story. Harry was right. Mam and Da hadn't asked for help.

'Leave it with me,' she said. 'No guarantees you'll get the dates you want but we'll find you something. But what are you doing up north? You should come home. This practice could certainly use a younger doctor. I'm getting tired, Dan. I'd like to spend more time gardening and less time looking at rashes.'

I said, 'I used to think I might come back, but my life's taken a different turn.'

'Married?'

And I was surprised to hear myself say, 'Next year, I hope.'

Susan and Martyn Benbow had become regulars at Aggie's clinic. They seemed to feel they should log their new-found sex life and report back to her. They hailed me from the waiting room as I was leaving for my afternoon off. They wanted to thank me for referring them to Dr Hughes.

I said, 'It sounded like the kind of thing she'd be able to advise on.'

'Oh yes,' says Martyn. 'She was very helpful. It's turned out very satisfactory. We're having tests.'

Susan said, 'And we've been having full sexual intercourse, every night. What a palaver.'

There were three other patients in the waiting room. They all grabbed magazines.

Martyn said, 'Dr Hughes says that might do the trick. We're still praying on it, mind. On getting a baby.'

Generally, I only saw Harry on weekends, but we'd speak most evenings. When I turned my phone back on after choir practice there were two missed calls from her. She had news about Professor Lloyd Humphreys. The body had been released for cremation and Gethin was going to attend.

'When is it?'

'Friday afternoon. It's short notice but it's not like there's anyone who'd want to be there. Maybe the university'll send someone. A token presence.'

'I can't go. I've got a full list. Maybe Iestyn could attend? She was his patient really.'

'I wouldn't worry. It won't be a proper funeral. Just a five-minute job, and Geth's willing to do it. He'll collect the ashes too, when they're ready. I think he's got a plan for them.'

'He's a good sort, your brother. Are you alright? You sound tired.'

'I've had some bad news. Mum's got a regional recurrence. She'd had a bit of chest pain, so they scanned her. It's in the lymph nodes under her sternum.'

'Shit. She didn't have radiation, after the mastectomy?'

'No. Her tumour was hormone-sensitive. She's been taking Letrozole.'

'So now what?'

'Radiation, and they might try a different aromatase inhibitor. I took my eye off the ball. I should have done a better job of monitoring her, but you know what she's like. She's so bloody independent. I'm not even sure she's talked to Dad about it.'

'Will you go up there for the weekend?'

305

'Not to stay. She'll say, "what's this, Cancer Watch?" I might just drive up and have a cuppa. Will you come with me?'

'If you want me to. If I won't be in the way.'

She said, 'Of course, I want you to. I'm worried about her, Dan. She's always been my big, strong mum. And now this. Anyway, if we're a couple, how could you be in the way? Are we a couple?'

'You know we are. Yesterday someone asked me if I was married yet. Do you know what I said?'

'Was, but now tunnelling out? Semi-detached? Watch this space?'

I said, 'Next year.'

'Really? Congratulations. Anyone I know?'

'I should have asked you first. It just slipped out.'

'Was that supposed to be some kind of proposal?'

'Pretty rubbish, wasn't it? Can we call it a dress rehearsal?'

'It depends what the actual performance is going to look like. It's only fair to warn you, I'd hate you to get down on one knee, with a ring in a box.'

'Damn. Back to the drawing board. Any other preferences I should know about?'

'Not before or after a candle-lit dinner. Not with a string quartet playing in the background.'

'Live or recorded?'

'Either. And no heart-shaped helium balloons. In fact, no heart-shaped anything.'

'Got it.'

Chapter 30

Mam said, 'I ought to be cross with you, going behind my back.'

'You got respite care?'

'Dr Little arranged it. I felt a proper fool when she phoned me. Not knowing anything about it. You shouldn't have bothered her, Dan.'

'I didn't. I just made a polite, 'concerned relative' call. Anyway, she was pleased to hear from me. She practically offered me a job.'

'Did she? That'd be nice. We'd have you on call.'

'You already have me on call. So, she got Nan in somewhere?'

'The Daffodils. It's out on the Pontypool Road. Seven days, only we have pick her up on the 27th, in the morning, so if we come to you for Christmas, we'll have to leave you on Boxing Day.'

'Okay. Do you want to come here? I won't be offended if you fly off somewhere to get a bit of sun with a u instead of son with an o.'

'Of course, we want to come. We want to meet this girl. Dr Little tells me you're getting married.'

'I might have given her the wrong impression.'

'So, you're not getting married? Well, how can you? You're not even divorced yet.'

'True. But when I am, I will. Don't worry, it won't be a big, fancy affair.'

'Good. Because I'm not buying another hat. The one I wore when you and Chloe got hitched? It's gone to the Marie Curie shop. Every time I opened the wardrobe the blummin' thing reminded me of what she's done to you.'

'She's done it to herself, Mam. She's split up from her new bloke. She's living back at the big house and she's miserable.'

'She wants you back.'

'But I'm no longer available. You'll like Harry. We'll take you up to the farm one of the days.'

'Lovely. Your Da's idea of a perfect Christmas. Course, first we've got to coax your Nan into the Daffodils.'

'Tell her it's a hotel. And don't drag it out. Take her in and leave.'

'I know. I am grateful, Dan.'

I said, 'It wasn't just me. Adam did some of the groundwork.'

This was stretching the facts, but I knew it'd make her happy. Her boys watching out for her. Getting along, working as a team.

'Did he?' she said. 'Bless him. See, he's not as bad as you make out.'

There had been five people at Professor Buddug's funeral: Gethin, three academics who had once worked with her, and Benilda who had arrived back from the Philippines to discover she'd become a woman of property. After the ceremony, Geth had driven her to Llanddulas to check on the house. He told Harry she'd been quite overwhelmed. It was a leaking, creaking,

308

infested wreck but it was more than Benilda could ever have dreamed of owning. Would she live in it? No, she was happy in her little flat in Abergele. She wanted to sell it and send the money to her family.

Harry and I went up to Maes Glas on Sunday afternoon. Mrs Shepherd was taking a nap.

Mr Shepherd said, 'Your mother's not so good. I'd say she's fearing the worst.'

Harry said, 'The treatment's going to take a lot more out of her than the operation did.'

'I know it.'

'She won't be able to work.'

'We'll see. She's a strong woman.'

'Even strong women are laid low by radiotherapy. I'm going to take some time off. You'll need help.'

'There's no need to do that,' he said, 'We can manage.'

Mrs Shepherd had been on the stair, listening.

'Manage what?' she said. 'You'd better not be talking about my kitchen. I'm not dead yet.'

We had tea and cake. When we were leaving, she took me to one side.

She said, 'Are you going to marry my girl?'

'As soon as I'm free. If she'll have me.'

'Don't take too long. I'd like to be around to see it. And make sure she gets those mammograms. I missed a couple. Too busy, see? She shouldn't need reminding, in her line of work, but you know what they say about the cobbler's children.'

'What do they say?'

'They're always the worst shod.'

Gethin's plan for the professor's ashes was to scatter them somewhere on the Glyders, to take her back to the place she'd chosen to die.

'The sooner we do it, the better,' he said, 'before we get snow.'

'We? You want me to come?'

'Harry says you can sing.'

'Sing what?'

'Do you know any Welsh hymns?'

'A few. Was she religious?'

'Not churchy. But I think a hymn would be nice. And Hen Wlad, of course.'

'Of course. How far up are you thinking of taking her?'

'You'll need proper boots.'

All week I practiced. I did it while showering, shaving and answering calls of Nature, until I had the words by heart. On Friday evening Gethin called Harry and said we'd better postpone. There was rain forecast for Saturday and the path up the mountain would be treacherous. Sunday dawned clear. We were to rendezvous at the Pen y Gwryd hotel at eleven and head up Glydr Fach.

At a quarter past, there was no sign of Gethin and he wasn't answering his phone. Harry said he quite often didn't. To Geth, a phone was just a tool, occasionally useful, but not required at all times. He could go for days without turning it on. He didn't wear a watch either. He claimed he always knew what time it was, as near as mattered.

He arrived just before twelve. There was someone in the pick-up with him. Benilda.

Harry said, 'You've been to Abergele? No wonder you're late.'

Geth said, 'Had to go up to Nant Clir too, to borrow Gwenny's boots for Benilda. Have you seen how tiny her feet are?'

Benilda, all 4 foot 10 of her, was in her Sunday best. Hat, gloves, handbag. A cat brooch on her coat lapel and Gwenny Hughes's walking boots padded out with two pairs of woolly socks.

We set off. The sun was bright but the wind was cold. Gethin was carrying a cardboard tube with the earthly remains of Buddug Lloyd Humphreys. Benilda walked beside him, doing her best to keep up, and every so often Geth would remember how much shorter her legs were and adjust his stride.

Harry said, 'Look at the pair of them. The long and the short of it. She's fitter than you'd expect. Fitter than I am, that's for sure.'

Fitter than me too. I spent my days sitting at a desk and my evenings lolling on a sofa. My 34-inch waist was a distant memory and my 36-inch trousers were getting snug.

We reached an easier stretch of open moorland and paused. To the north there was a small lake with a mountain rising behind it. That was Tryfan, according to Geth.

Benilda said, 'This is nice place. Let's put her here.'

Gethin had intended to go further but he deferred to Benilda. He took the lid off the tube.

'All right then, Dan,' he said. 'Ready when you are.'

He strode around, sprinkling the ashes, trying to stay upwind of them, while I sang *Gwahoddiad*. Mi glywaf dyner lais, I hear thy welcome voice, and Harry harmonised with me for the refrain, 'Arglwydd, dyma fi, ar dy alwad di,' Here I am, Lord, coming now to Thee. Geth said it was a good choice.

Benilda's hat blew away and we failed to catch it, but she didn't seem to mind. The sky had darkened over Tryfan so we sang one verse of Hen Wlad and made a hasty descent to sit in Harry's car and drink coffee from her thermos. Gethin told us about the Professor Buddug he'd known, twenty years ago. There had been a rumour she had a tattoo of a Welsh dragon, never verified. She'd had black hair, with just a streak of white at the front, and wore lots of big necklaces.

Harry said, 'Ooh, necklaces. Did you inherit them, Benilda? With the house?'

'No,' says Benilda. 'Mice has eaten all strings. I inherited drawer of beads. Tattoo was on her shoulder. I have seen. Not very big.'

Gethin remembered a scholar. Benilda remembered a fierce old lady who drank gin and liked Hello! magazine even though she didn't know who any of the people were in the photos.

Harry watched in her mirror as they walked back to Gethin's truck.

She said, 'Do you see what I see?'

Benilda and Gethin were holding hands.

Had Geth had girlfriends before? She thought he had, at university, but nothing serious, and then he'd come home to Maes Glas. There weren't a lot of dating opportunities when you lived at the end of a farm track.

'Did you think he'd ever marry?'

'I hoped he would. How old do you reckon Benilda is?'

'She could be thirty. She could be forty.'

'I'd say she's at least forty. Getting on a bit to incubate any grandchildren. Nice though. I like her.'

'You don't think Geth's after her inheritance?'

'You mean so he can add a derelict house to the derelict farm he's already got in his property portfolio? I wouldn't put it past him. All the man thinks about is money. You sang beautifully up there, Dan. You are such a catch.'

I said, 'So my mother keeps telling me.'

Three weeks had passed and I hadn't had a reply from Vaz. My fears hadn't been groundless after all. He'd have been appalled that I was getting divorced. I hadn't told him the full, sordid story but I knew what his views were. Marriage may not always be easy but it's forever.

Then one evening he called me.

'Dan,' he said, 'you will think very badly of me. We just got back from Kerala and I saw your message.'

He and Theresa had taken Margaret to meet her Indian grandparents.

I said, 'My news must have shocked you.'

'Yes,' he said. 'How can this have happened? You were so very happy on your wedding day.'

'Let's just say Chloe changed her mind.'

'Then perhaps she will change it again. Perhaps you must be patient with her.'

'I was. But you see, she found someone she preferred. Now she's not sure she even wants him. She's too immature to be married to anyone. And I know we're supposed to forgive those who trespass against us but frankly Vaz, I'm finding it hard.'

'Oh yes,' he said. 'It's easier to say than to do.'

'I'm so glad to hear from you. I was worried I'd lose your friendship.'

'Then you don't know me so well as you think,' he said. 'You are my very dear friend. I have something to tell you too. In April we will have another baby.'

Vaz may have been a slow starter but since he met Teresa there was no stopping him.

I didn't tell him about Harry. Time enough. It would have been ungracious to top his happy news with mine.

Mam was in a fluster about their visit. I was getting regular bulletins. She'd bought Nan new nighties for her little holiday at The Daffodils. Aunty June was going to spend Christmas with her daughter in Newport.

She said, 'So that's one thing less for us to worry about.'

I said, 'I wasn't worrying about it and neither should you. How many of your Christmas dinners has June eaten?'

'I haven't been counting.'

'And how often has she cooked one for you?'

'I wouldn't want her to. She's a terrible cook. Now, do I need to pack smart shoes?'

'Not really. I don't know. You mean 'going out' shoes?'

'Yes. In case we're going to meet your new lady friend.'

'You are going to meet her. She'll come here. You can meet her in your slippers. You're going to meet her family as well. You'll need wellies for that.'

The next evening it was the catering report.

'Now your Da's going to get you a nice rib of beef, properly hung, and a loin of pork. What about sausages?'

'They sell sausages here, Mam.'

'But are they as good as Powell's?'

'Tell you what, you bring some, I'll buy some and we'll have a blind taste test.'

'Am I being a fusspot?'

'The very idea.'

314

'I'll bring my bag of tricks. I don't suppose you've got yourself a cleaner yet.'

'Do not bring cleaning stuff. You're coming here to rest. Respite, remember?'

She said, 'We've never been away for Christmas before.'

Final call of the evening.

'What it is, I forgot to say, I'm making the cake tomorrow, but I'll ice it when I get there.'

I said, 'You don't need to. We can live without Christmas cake. Anyway, Harry's a great baker. She'll make something.'

Harry grabbed the phone from me.

She said, 'Hello Dan's Mum. There seems to be some misunderstanding. I've never made a Christmas cake in my life so please bring yours.'

'Well,' Mam whispered when I got my phone back, 'she sounds very nice.'

Harry said it wasn't a case of earning Brownie points.

'How many years has your Mam being making Christmas cakes?'

'Since time immemorial.'

'There you are then. Let her continue.'

'But it costs her a fortune, it's time-consuming and when it's done, everyone's too stuffed to eat it.'

'Doesn't matter. Those cakes are full of booze. They keep forever. My mum makes one as well.'

'We could have duelling Christmas cakes.'

'Except Mum might not feel up to doing it this year.'

'I'm sorry.'

'And that's my point, Dan. Imagine how hard it must be to let go of things you've always done, because you're feeling too crap or because someone in their great wisdom has decided they're not needed.'

'You're dead right.'

'Do you know something that's bugging Mum almost as much as the cancer coming back? She's not pickled any onions this year.'

'She pickles her own onions?'

'Onions, beetroot, red cabbage, eggs. She's an ace pickler.'

'What's the icing like on her Christmas cakes?'

'Jaw-breaker.'

'So's Mam's. Why do they do it?'

'Because they always have.'

Chapter 31

The Underhills were on my morning list, which reminded me, I hadn't yet had sight of a hospital report on Dennis.

Beverley walked in alone.

I said, 'No Dennis today?'

'You haven't heard, then,' she said, and her face crumpled.

The day I'd last seen them, on their way to the station, they'd caught the train to Birmingham, met up with old friends from Acocks Green and then gone to the Yardleybeats farewell gig in Digbeth. As they were leaving the venue Dennis had stumbled.

'He said, "I don't feel too clever. I'd better sit down for a minute", so we went back inside and a first-aider brought him a glass of water. He kept saying "what's going on, Bev?" and then he keeled right over.'

'A stroke?'

'Yes. They got him to hospital ever so quick. They said if it was a clot on the brain, he'd be in good time for some special treatment they do.'

'Thrombolysis.'

'That's it. So they done that, then they put him on a special ward and I thought he was looking a lot better. He couldn't speak properly but they said that might come back. Our Karen come up from Bromsgrove on the Sunday. She was always a daddy's girl. She got a little smile out of him. Then on the Monday morning he took another stroke. I'd only gone to get a cup of tea, couldn't have been more than quarter of an hour, and when I got back to the ward the curtains was pulled round him. They made me go and sit in a little room, then the doctor come and told me, you know… He was gone. They said he'd had a different kind of stroke. Not a clot. More like bleeding inside his brain.'

'It can happen. Thrombolysis is a gamble. Usually the benefits outweigh the risks. Dennis was unlucky. I'm so sorry.'

Beverley's not a small woman, but without her husband she seemed diminished.

'I can't get my head round it,' she said. 'I keep thinking it's a bad dream and he'll come back.'

What would Trevor Buxton do? He'd get out from behind his desk and sit, like a regular human being, with the distressed patient. He'd listen to their what-ifs. Refute their if-onlys. Let them share fond memories, or just weep. One of the many valuable things he taught me.

The funeral had been held in Birmingham. That was where all their friends were. The Yardleybeats had been informed and sent flowers. And now what? The daughter, Karen, wanted Bev to sell up in Colwyn Bay and move closer to her. I dispensed the conventional advice: don't rush into a decision; take time to grieve; be kind to yourself.

She said, 'I lie there at night and I think, when he had that funny turn, you know, weeks ago, I should have phoned the whatsit line, the 111. I could kick myself. But he was such a stubborn blighter.'

'From what I remember, that first episode was very brief. If you hadn't been with him, you might never have known it had happened. Who knows, there might have been others. The T in TIA stands for transient, and they are. My guess is, if you'd called 111 they'd have told you to see your GP as soon as possible, and you did.'

'My neighbour said I should be thankful he didn't linger. She said her brother was left like a vegetable. But I'd have looked after Den, don't matter what he'd have been like.'

'Had he enjoyed the Yardleybeats?'

'He had. Oh, it was a smashing night. We was on our feet, dancing in the aisles. Forty one years we'd been following them. Keith Slack's had a hair transplant. He's starting to show his age. Funny, isn't it? Inside I still feel about sixteen. Then I look in the mirror.'

Was she managing to sleep? Not really. Did she want a mild sedative, to help for a while? No, she found if she put two pillows beside her and pretended that they were Dennis, she'd eventually nod off. Should I have made his referral a more urgent one? Had I done the right thing by him? I truly thought I had. But during my lunch break I called Weirdo Pants anyway.

Mary answered. 'The Lindens.'

I said, 'Whatever happened to Tipton Road West Medical Centre?'

'Who's that?' she said.

'It's Dan Talbot. Remember me?'

'Dr Dan!' she said. 'Well I'll tell you no lie, I can't be bothered with that silly long name so when her Ladyship's not around I just say The Lindens. People still think of us as that, any road. How are you?'

'I'm very well. By any chance is Trevor in today?'

'He is. He's probably having forty winks, the poor old wreck. I wish you'd come back to us. You were the nicest trainee we ever had.'

'I heard you've got a nice lady trainee now.'

'Dr Bishan. She's alright. Very polite. Only I don't care for the food she brings in for her lunch, stinking the place out. She's been trying to get me to taste it but I dussen't. I've heard what those curries can do to you. I might end up powdering my nose all afternoon. Hold on and I'll tell Dr Trevor you'd like a word.'

'Dan Talbot,' he said. 'I haven't called you to see how you are because I thought you might tell me to mind my own business.'

'A bit late for that. Your Llandudno lunch date sends her warm regards.'

'Ah. You've found me out. Well, I thought, nothing ventured. And we did have a very nice lunch. So, did anything come of it?'

'Everything.'

'Is that all?'

'She's the one.'

'I thought she might be. Are you a free man yet?'

'Early next year, all being well. What are you doing for Christmas?'

'Hiding. I've had so many invitations. Pam Parker, the Boddys, Nurse Chris. Even our dear Helen. I mean, seriously? All the years we've known each other, I've never once set foot in her house and now she thinks I want to sit with her and poor old Cliff? Pull a cracker, wear a paper hat and try to stop them murdering each other. The very idea gives me indigestion. I don't know why people think it's so terrible to be on your own.'

'It's because it's your first year without Mrs Buxton. They'll forget about you next year.'

'Good. Because I shall manage perfectly well. Steak and oven chips for dinner, a bottle of Laphroaig and a boxed set of videos. Legends of Horse Racing. Did you know, your lovely in-laws invited me for Boxing Day? The Packwoods?'

'I didn't know. You should go. It's only an hour's drive from you.'

'I thanked them kindly, but I'll actually be going to Kempton Park with James and his bird. Anyway, as nice as the Packwoods are, it wouldn't have felt right. What if your Chloe had walked in?'

'She's not my Chloe anymore. Anyway, you'd have been safe. I hear she's going to Dubai for Christmas. Her brother's got a flat there. It's great that you'll be seeing James, though.'

'It will be. As long as I can remember what his girlfriend's name is. There have been so many of them, and they all look the same. Blonde and leggy, with cheekbones. So, did you just call to thank me for fixing your love life or was it to draw on my superior clinical knowledge?'

I told him about Dennis Underhill.

He said, 'You're not blaming yourself?'

'No. Well, ever so slightly.'

'You shouldn't. You followed the protocol, scored him on the ABCD2 and referred him to neurology. We can't keep them all alive, Dan, doesn't matter how thorough we are. And from what you've told me, he went out on a high. The Yardleybeats. Never heard of them.'

'His wife looked so lost. I wanted to give her a hug, but I thought I'd better not. Inappropriate, you know?'

'Don't get me started.'

'You would have, wouldn't you? Hugged her?'

'Yes lad, but I don't have a reputation to worry about. You've got your career stretching ahead of you. I'm dragging mine behind me. But for future reference, an older woman, recently bereaved, I think you'd get away with a consoling hand squeeze. Of course, now I'm a widower I might have to be more careful. There could be a few desperate women who misread the signals.'

'Not so desperate. You're a fine-looking mature man.'

'Oh yes, yes,' he said. 'But behind this rugged façade there are two very ropey lungs and a failing heart. By the way, the Bibby matriarch has gone to her reward, so that's one fragrant Tipton matron out of the running.'

'Kyle's mother?'

'The very same. She wasn't on our books, hadn't been for a long time, but cheerful news travels fast.'

'I met her once. That time Kyle collapsed in the street. His mum and his sister were both there and I couldn't be sure which was which.'

'They don't age well, the Bibby women. You wouldn't want to bump into one of them on a dark night.'

Neil Yorath was on my afternoon list. When I'd seen him previously, I'd prescribed a proton pump inhibitor for what he'd reported as heartburn and acid reflux. It had been six weeks. How was he? The same. Any difficulty swallowing? He didn't think so. Had he lost any weight? He wouldn't know. He never weighed himself. I hadn't weighed him either. Why hadn't I? Because I treat lots of patients for dyspepsia, I give them lansoprazole and they get better. Neil was a fit-looking 54. Maybe I'd seen him on a day when I was distracted by personal stuff. For whatever reason, I hadn't thought of him as a case I ought to monitor closely.

To give him another month on the medication and then review, or refer him right away?

It was when he pointed to my painting of the Brecon Beacons that I noticed his watch strap was loose.

'That's nice,' he said. 'I paint a bit myself. Acrylics. Neil's daubs, the wife calls them.'

He laughed.

I said, 'I'm going to refer you to Bangor, for a test. It's called endoscopy.'

'Is that the thing with the camera?'

'Yes.'

'It sounds horrible. Doesn't it make you gag?'

'They'll sedate you. It's an out-patient procedure but they'll keep you in for a couple of hours, to recover and most likely you won't remember anything about it.'

'Okay,' he said. 'Any particular reason you're sending me?'

Just erring on the side of caution, I told him. I didn't mention that he seemed to have lost weight.

Lilian Blacksmith could go to Bethan to get her blood pressure checked but she prefers to see me for a chat, and I humour her.

She said, 'I've done my Christmas shopping. They're all getting vouchers.'

I said, 'I haven't even started.'

'I believe you,' she said. 'You leave it up to us women. My husband never bought a present in his life. He was a lovely man, but he didn't have a clue.'

'Not even for your birthday?'

'No. I might get a card from him, if I was lucky. He used to say, 'Lil, if there's something you want, treat yourself. Only don't raid the gas money.'

'Your blood pressure's still a bit high for my liking.'

'It's your fault. I was reading about it in my magazine. It's called white coat syndrome.'

'I'm not wearing a white coat.'

'You know what I mean.'

'How do you feel? Headaches, dizzy spells?'

'Only when I look at you.'

'Any aches and pains?'

'Everywhere. Well I'm bound to at my age, aren't I? It's the getting going, first thing. I'm not so bad once I'm up and I've had a cup of tea. But sometimes I lie a-bed in the morning and I think, what's the point? I'm not needed any more. Surplus to requirement.'

'I'm sure your family don't think so.'

'They're not getting any younger. My boys are in their fifties. They've all lost their hair. I look at them these days and they're the dead spit of their dad. Have you got kiddies? I remember Bethan telling me you were spoken for.'

'No kids. Not yet. Are you still drinking Palomas?'

'How do you know about that?'

'You told me. You said you couldn't take statins because you were partial to a grapefruit juice cocktail every evening.'

'I still am. But I decided I'd got into a rut, so I've changed to Salty Dogs. Now that's a tasty drink. And I hope you're not going to tell me to stop drinking because I should hate to quarrel with you.'

I told her to enjoy her little pleasures.

'I intend to,' she said. 'That lady downstairs, the one who answers the phone, she's got a face that'd turn milk.'

'Delyth? She's alright. She might have the occasional off day.'

'More off days than any other kind, if you ask me. I like it when she goes on holiday and we get Dr Iestyn's mam. She's a friendly person. Well, it's lovely chatting to you, Dr Dan, and you're very easy on the eye, but I can't sit here all afternoon. I've got Zumba.'

My 3 o'clock was a no-show. I went to make myself a coffee and found David staring at the machine. Bethan sometimes delivers a cup to his desk, but she was out for the afternoon, having a hospital check-up.

He said, 'Miriam's keen to get one of these things. It looks like a flight deck.'

'Show you how it works?'

He stepped aside, and when I passed him his coffee he didn't scuttle back to his office. He seemed in the mood for a chat.

How was Becca?

'Doing an endodontics module. Loves it.'

Was Joe enjoying A levels?

'Hard to say. He only leaves his bedroom to go to school or to raid the fridge. Got five minutes?'

We went into his office. He has a Happy Families photo on his desk.

He said, 'It's coming up to a year since you joined us. How has it been?'

Where was this leading? A review of my performance, or had Miriam told him he should engage more?

I said, 'It's been good. Any complaints?'

'None at all,' he said. 'What I'm about to say is just between us, for now. I'm thinking of calling it a day.'

It came out of nowhere. I was stunned.

'You're very young to retire.'

'I'm 57. Not that young. It's because of my problem. My addiction.'

'Are you struggling?'

'Yes.'

'It might get easier.'

'We both know that's not true. I don't think I can be around drugs anymore.'

'So, what will happen to the practice?'

'I haven't decided. I own the building. I could sell, but I'd be happy to let it. If you and the Hugheses were interested.'

'You haven't talked to them?'

'Not yet. It'll depend on Aggie. Iestyn'll never make a decision.'

'He's not a partner?'

'No, salaried, same as you. Might you be interested?'

I said, 'David, this is my first year. I'm still a rookie, comparatively. I'm also mortgaged up to the eyeballs and paying for a divorce. I don't see any way I could buy in, and I'm not sure I'd want to. I like Iestyn and Aggie, but I wouldn't necessarily choose them as business partners.'

'I can see that.'

'I'll think about it. But if you've made your mind up you should talk to the Hugheses as soon as possible. For one thing, I need to discuss it with Harry and she and Iestyn are family. Anything so much as whispered at Maes Glas reaches Gwenny Hughes at Nant Clir within the hour.'

'So you and Harry are still…?'

'Very much so. David, are you sure about retiring? What will you do?'

'Don't know,' he said. 'My back's too fucked for golf. I might get a boat. Nothing ambitious. Just something to pootle around in.'

I called Harry.

I said, 'I've got choir practice, but I really need to see you tonight.'

'Great,' she said, 'because I need to see you too. Macaroni cheese at my place. Bring wine.'

Chapter 32

Harry said. 'There's something I need to tell you. When we did the full disclosure thing, there was something I didn't mention.'

'Go on.'

'It's about me and Christmas.'

'I know you enjoy it. I know you're looking forward to it.'

'It's a bit more than that, Dan. I tend to go Full Grotto.'

'Does that mean flashing fairy lights and one of those climbing Santas hanging from an upstairs windowsill?'

'Not quite, but you're not a million miles off beam.'

'It's your house.'

'Right. But what if it was your house?'

'You want to engrottify Pentraeth?'

'I could make it look lovely. You have high ceilings. We could have a super-duper tree.'

'We could. Seems a bit daft though, just for you, me and Mam and Da.'

'That's another thing. It'd be a great space for a party. It seems a pity to let it go to waste. You might never have another house like that.'

'Well, cheers. Ah yes, Dan Talbot owned a nice house once, for about five minutes. Are you saying you want to have a party?'

'I want *us* to have a party, as if we were a proper couple.'

'We are a proper couple.'

'With a big tree and plenty of food and you and your choir dudes singing carols.'

'I have no objection to a party, but I draw the line at climbing Santas.'

'Agreed. This is so exciting. Now there's something else I need to tell you.'

'You've already had two things. I think it's my turn. It's something far more serious than Christmas parties, and for the time being it must go no further than these four walls.'

'You're making me nervous.'

'Promise to keep a secret?'

'Cross my heart and hope to die, stick a needle in my eye.'

'David's giving up the practice.'

'No!'

'He told me today. But he's not talked to Iestyn and Aggie yet, so you absolutely mustn't say a word.'

'Lips sealed. Shit, Dan. Where does that leave you?'

'A good question. He's talking about selling the building, but he'd consider letting it. There might be a way for the practice to survive. Or not.'

'Why is he doing this? Does Miriam know?'

'She must do. You can't ask her.'

'It's ridiculous. What about money? Becca's still got three years at uni, then there'll be Joe to bankroll.'

'He said Joe doesn't seem interested in going to university. Apparently, he's going to become an Internet influencer and be a millionaire by the time he's twenty.'

'Yeah, right. What an idiot. This can't be the full story. Is David ill?'

'You could say. It's the addiction.'

'Do you think he's using again?'

'No, but I think he's terrified he'll slip. It must be tiring. Every morning you're facing another day of not giving in to temptation. If he deregisters, he's got a better chance of staying clean.'

'Even so. Aggie'll have a fit when she hears. Three little ones plus Iestyn the Ditherer, and now this. If you could buy the building, would you?'

'No. It's impractical, no matter how you reorganise the space. Some of the patients are half dead by the time they've climbed the stairs. Renting? I don't know. In the long run I don't think I'd want to tie myself to Iestyn and Aggie. Maybe David'll reconsider. Maybe he was just having a bad day. He said he might buy a boat.'

'A sure sign of insanity.'

'I moved here to put down roots and look what's happened. Marriage, gone. House, soon to be gone. And now my job's in question.'

'But you did meet me.'

'Which of course compensates for everything else. Okay, your turn. What was the other thing you wanted to tell me?'

'Guess.'

'You're going to moonlight as one of Santa's elves at the Bodnant Garden Centre.'

'Damn, you're good. But no. Guess again. It's good news.'

'They fixed that knocking sound your car's been making and it didn't cost an arm and a leg.'

'Gethin's getting married.'

'No! Benilda?'

'Isn't it wild?'

'But he's only known her a few weeks.'

'Yes, well, they're not children. I knew one day he'd fall like a ton of bricks. There's more to Geth than meets the eye.'

'What do your parents think about it?'

'They like her. What's not to like? She's a dear, and she's used to hard work. And they're glad he's getting on with it before the lambing.'

'It's happening that soon?'

'Christmas Eve. Llandudno Town Hall, eleven o'clock. They want us to be witnesses so you'll have to cut short your surgery.'

'And afterwards? To the pub?'

'Neither of them drinks. I said we'd treat them to lunch in Candles. It'll be just the four of us.'

'Surely your parents will come?'

'Mum's not up to it and apart from livestock sales, Dad goes nowhere without her. Anyway, if you start down that path the next thing you know you're feeding a multitude of friends and relations. Benilda won't have any of her family there so Geth said best to keep it simple.'

'Honeymoon?'

'They're having two nights in Aunt Gwenny's holiday cottage. Geth doesn't have a lot of cash to splash. But he's asked me to help him choose a ring.'

'Shouldn't Benilda do that?'

'I don't know. I've never been married.'

'Chloe told me exactly what ring she wanted.'

'No comment,' says Harry.

'Benilda and Gethin. Gosh. So, no more agency work for her. No more helping grumpy old ladies to get dressed. She'll be a lady of leisure.'

'No, Dan,' she said. 'She'll be a farmer's wife. Up at the crack. Losing sleep about money. And never again to wear a pair of elegant shoes.'

'Does she understand what she's letting herself in for?'

'She does. She's raring to go. Geth's teaching her to drive the pick-up.'

'She must need a booster seat.'

'Yes. They tried a beanbag footstool thing he found in the attic but then she couldn't reach the pedals. It's a work in progress. Tell you what though. She's a fast learner. I'll bet she gets her licence before Iestyn does.'

Harry ordained that our party should be the day after Mam and Da arrived. That way they'd get to meet all the people they'd heard me talk about. I wasn't sure it was a good idea. I ran it by Mam.

I said, 'I'm told we're having a party.'

'Lovely,' she said. 'I'll borrow one of June's sparkly tops.'

'You don't mind? You and Da don't really go to parties.'

She said, 'Only because we never get invited.'

In the course of the week there were several deliveries to the house. Cases of wine, an eight foot spruce, two smaller white, tinselly trees and a lot of Harry boxes that I was instructed not to open. One of them was labelled THREE KINGS, CAMELS, UGLY ANGEL, EXTRA TREE LIGHTS.

When I asked why we needed three trees she sighed and said, 'Leave it to one who understands these things.'

At the surgery it was clear that David hadn't talked to Iestyn and Aggie about his plans. Had he had a change of heart or was I still sitting on a secret? I began to feel impatient. Now

I'd recovered from the shock I found I was looking at the meddygfa through different eyes. The place was out-dated and inconvenient. It was the kind of surgery that I remembered as a kid. Just a doctor sitting in a room. Patients expect something better nowadays: nurse practitioners, wheelchair access, child-friendly waiting areas.

The shoe dropped late on Friday afternoon. Aggie arrived as I was seeing off my final patient.

She said, 'Danek, why we have meeting?'

I said, 'I didn't know we were.'

'David didn't tell you come to meeting?'

'No.'

I should have lied. Now I was in an awkward position. I thought the best thing was to make a quick exit, to be out of range when Aggie started throwing furniture and out of sight, just a voice on the phone, when she or Iestyn asked me, 'did you know?'

Bethan came in. She said, 'I don't want to worry you, but something's going on. David's sent Delyth home early and he's asked me to stay, for a meeting, if you please. Now Dr Aggie's arrived, wants to know what it's about. How come you've got your coat on?'

I said, 'I'm cold.'

'Oh yes?' she said. 'And I'm the Queen of the May. So, you're not staying for the meeting?'

I slipped in to see David. He was just sitting, computer turned off, nothing on his desk.

I said, 'Everyone's wondering why I'm not summoned to this meeting.'

He said, 'You already know what I'm going to say.'

'But David, don't you see how it looks? Aggie and Iestyn are going to be furious that I knew before they did, and rightly

332

so. They've invested far more of themselves in the practice than I have.'

He said he'd only confided in me on the spur of the moment. I'd happened to see him at the coffee machine. He'd happened to feel like talking.

I said, 'It won't do, David. Include me in the meeting. Just say you forgot to invite me. And when you make your announcement, I'll do my best to look as surprised as everyone else.'

'Okay.'

'And can I just ask, is Miriam okay with this decision?'

'Yes,' he said. 'She's as tired of it all as I am.'

In we all went. David said his piece. What little colour Iestyn had, drained from his face.

Aggie said, 'Is joke, yes?'

David, 'Of course it's not a joke. I thought I should tell you all now so you can think about it over the Christmas break and decide how you'd like to proceed.'

She said, 'How we can have Christmas break? This is end of world. Iestyn, say something. Dan, say something.'

I said, 'Have I got this right? You'd be willing to rent the building to us? Because none of us is in a position to buy it.'

He nodded.

'Plus, we'd need to take on another doctor. Financially, it'd be quite complicated. The alternative is to close the practice. Then we'd all have to find jobs elsewhere.'

Bethan started crying. Aggie got to her feet.

She said, 'David, you are horrid, crazy man. Why you do this at Christmas time? Iestyn, we go home now, give our childrens their dinner because soon they won't have no food.

Now soon we have to sleep in car and wash our hairs in public toilet.'

Iestyn said, 'Steady on, Ag. We'll work something out.'

She said something in Polish. Whatever its sentiment, it didn't sound like gracious acceptance of the situation.

Everyone left in silence. David looked at me as if to say, what's a man to do?

I thought we should cancel our party. Harry refused. She said if the Parrys and the Hugheses came, they could play nicely and anyway, our lives didn't revolve around them. Giles Tate was coming, with a date, Hilary Mostyn and Ebbe were coming, and Dylan Tew, plus we'd have some of her Needle Clean-Up team and my friends from the choir. In the event, Miriam said she'd come solo because David didn't want a scene with Aggie, and the Hugheses said they couldn't come after all because getting a babysitter was difficult so close to Christmas.

'See?' says Harry. 'You worry far too much.'

It was after dark when Mam and Da arrived. The house was in full party plumage and the only light was from the fire and Harry's decorations. Mam squealed when she walked in.

'Oh Dan,' she said. 'It's beautiful. Like something out of *Homes & Gardens*.'

Da looked around in wonderment.

He said, 'I'm glad you're paying the electricity bill and not me.'

Mam said, 'Where is she, then?'

But Harry had gone up to the farm for the evening. Her mum had just started radiotherapy.

I said, 'You'll meet her tomorrow. She's taking the afternoon off to prepare food.'

334

'I've brought my apron. Now be a good lad and help your Da carry the meat in from the car. We brought a few extra bits, for your freezer.'

A few extra bits. Everything bar the tail and the ears.

Mam was nervous about meeting Harry. She'd tried very hard to get along with Chloe, but I knew she'd never really relaxed around her. To Mam, the Swifts belonged to a superior tribe. They didn't, of course. Different, but not superior. In any event, Harry and Mam got off to a promising start because they agreed on two important points: that you can never have too many mince pies, and that I was the best thing since sliced bread.

Da and I left them nattering in the kitchen and went for a stroll along the seafront. He said coming away hadn't been easy. It wasn't him. It was Mam. She felt guilty. But then Nan had walked into The Daffodils as they were about to start a game of Bingo and she hadn't looked back.

'Now will you think of looking for a permanent place for her?'

'I suppose we could. Seems a pity, after we had the downstairs lav put in for her.'

'That's alright. It'll be there for you when your legs start giving you jip.'

Da said, 'I was sorry to hear about… you know?'

'Chloe?'

'Bit of a shock. Must have been.'

'I should have seen it coming. Harry's a very different type.'

'Oh yes.'

'Was Mam your first love?'

He didn't answer for a while. Then he said, 'See, there was a crowd of us. Teenagers. We'd go everywhere together, no pairing off. Not much, anyhow. But somehow I always knew I'd end up with Eirwen.'

'And did she always know she'd end up with you?'

He said, 'You'd have to ask her about that.'

Dylan Tew was the first to arrive and the last to leave. He was wearing an embroidered robe that looked like a dressing gown, and a velvet hat covered with glass beads. They were from Tajikstan, apparently. He'd bought them at an auction online.

He kissed Mam on the hand when I introduced them.

Mam whispered, 'He speaks very good English. Where's he from?'

'Hereford.'

Giles Tate is the junior at Miriam Parry's practice. He and I had barely exchanged more than two words, though I remembered him hitting on Chloe at the Parrys' wedding anniversary party. Or had it been Chloe hitting on him? With hindsight there were many things I might view differently.

He said, 'I've heard about David's plans. What do you think will happen?'

I told him I was trying not to think about it until after Christmas.

'Fair enough,' he said. 'Only I wondered if you'd heard about the new health centre, on the Conwy road. They just got planning permission. They'll be starting to build after the holidays.'

I knew nothing about it.

He said, 'Purpose-built, Dan. It'll have flexible space. Consulting rooms to rent, nurse practitioners, on-site pharmacy.'

His girlfriend said, 'On-site physio services too.'

Giles said, 'Claire's a physiotherapist, so she's interested. We both are. You and Harry should think about it. It's the future of primary care.'

'You'd leave Miriam's practice?'

He lowered his voice. He said, 'Look, if David retires, how long till Miriam decides to join him? Anyway, nothing lasts forever. I'm just saying.'

The house was buzzing. Some of the choir people knew some of the needle clean-up people. Dylan Tew knew everyone. That's what it's like around here.

Mam said, 'Don't look now, but there's two men over there got their arms around each other.'

'Hilary and Ebbe. They're a couple. Don't tell me you've never seen that before.'

Only in Cardiff, she said. And not that she minded. She'd rather see men having a cuddle than fighting.

'You and Harry getting along?'

'She's a lovely girl, Dan. Sensible, too. And of course your Da's chuffed to little mint balls, about going to see the farm and everything.'

'He was telling me that he knew you were the one for him, long before you got together.'

'Oh yes, that's the Authorised Version. The Gospel according to Ed Talbot. He conveniently forgets about taking Carys Pritchard to the pictures, and Valerie Griffiths. Back row of the Coliseum. But that's alright. He came to his senses in the end.'

'The old devil. Where is he?'

'In the kitchen, tidying up. What it is, he's not a great one for parties. He'll come out for the singing, mind.'

We'd had a discussion among the choir members and decided to go mainly secular. *White Christmas, Silver Bells, Rocking Around the Christmas Tree*, and then just one Welsh carol before we finished with *Have Yourself A Merry Little Christmas*. They left it to me to choose the carol, seeing as it was my party. I chose *Faban bach* and we sang it, close harmony, *Ar gyfer heddiw'r bore*. For this very morning, a little baby was born.

People had spread out all over the downstairs of the house but as soon as they heard singing, they came crowding back into the room. Someone turned down the lights. There was just the glow of the fire and the pinpoints of fairy-lights from the tree but I could make out Da, in the doorway, with his sleeves rolled up and a tea towel in his hand and Mam, beaming, in her glittery Aunty June top. She had her arm around my Harry. The three people I loved most in the world.

'Look,' someone said. 'It's started snowing.'

Also by Laurie Graham

DR DAN'S CASEBOOK
DR DAN, MARRIED MAN
THE FUTURE HOMEMAKERS OF AMERICA
THE EARLY BIRDS
PERFECT MERINGUES
ANYONE FOR SECONDS?
THE DRESS CIRCLE
THE TEN O'CLOCK HORSES
DOG DAYS, GLENN MILLER NIGHTS
THE UNFORTUNATES
MR STARLIGHT
AT SEA
LIFE ACCRDING TO LUBKA
THE IMPORTANCE OF BEING KENNEDY
GONE WITH THE WINDSORS
A HUMBLE COMPANION
THE LIAR'S DAUGHTER
THE GRAND DUCHESS OF NOWHERE
THE NIGHT IN QUESTION

For news of the next Dr Dan book and other projects,
go to http://lauriegraham.com

Printed in Great Britain
by Amazon

15735741R00196